I0736824

The Project

By

Adam Burnett

A HellBound Books Publishing LLC Book
Houston TX

Adam Burnett

A HellBound Books LLC Publication

Copyright © 2018 by HellBound Books Publishing LLC
All Rights Reserved

Cover and art design by Karla Cruz Ruelas - karla.cruz.ruelas@gmail.com
for
HellBound Books Publishing LLC

No part of this book may be reproduced, stored in a retrieval system, or transmitted by any means, electronic, mechanical, photocopying, recording or otherwise without written permission from the author This book is a work of fiction. Names, characters, places and incidents are entirely fictitious or are used fictitiously and any resemblance to actual persons, living or dead, events or locales is purely coincidental.

www.hellboundbookspublishing.com

Printed in the United States of America

Cover Art Created by

Karla Cruz Ruelas - karla.cruz.ruelas@gmail.com

Edited by

Angela G. Thornton

Adam Burnett

This is for Karla,

who lent me her laptop and closed the door

and made sure it stayed closed

till it was

all

laid

down

"Murder ought to be a more ceremonial occasion."

- Margaret Atwood, *Cat's Eye-*

J ohn Megolni took his eyes off the envelope and stared into his kitchen. It was dark. Glowing lines cut through the shadows like an electric blade.

The envelope lay lit on the counter. It was as a thing alive: John believed he could smell it.

This man, this breathing man with breath like a wounded bull, felt sick, worried, and the need to vomit came on him like an accident.

Jesus.

His eyes tried to focus on the dark points of the kitchen. He tried to see, but the shadows could only come so close.

He stared at the photos scattered pell-mell on the floor. Snippets of black-and-white at his feet. Dozens of 8x10's. His right leg weakened and his hand shot out to grip the counter. He tried to remember:

That last time...that last Goddamn Time: was it my hands...or The Hammer?

He couldn't remember. Magnificent lines like fine plumes of smoke jigged across his vision and he held the counter harder, held it like he was holding onto the last wisp of his sanity.

For the second time his stomach heaved, and this time there was no stopping it. Thick and viscous, it bubbled from his lips, soaked his shirt, landed with a *plop!* on the linoleum floor. Right from his guts, it felt like it *was* his guts, like someone had taken a fine blade and cut a smile into his belly, letting loose the churning things inside, the yellow-grey viscera, the worming reds, the bruised purples. He vomited until there was nothing left, and then he vomited some more.

A low moan came from somewhere deep within him, deeper than those roiling intestines and his tribal drum heart. Deeper than his toes that he couldn't feel touching the floor, deeper than that. Deeper than earth, rock, ash, and hell. It came from the deepest thing he knew: it came from his past.

The photographs were spilled across the floor like a cut deck of cards gone awry. Half of them were still in the envelope and there they would stay; John had seen enough.

I need to look at the return address, he thought, but the idea of moving, of actually reaching out and touching that…*thing* made his hands shake. A gaseous burp escaped his lips.

Satan is waitin'. Without warning, his face crumpled and hot tears stung his cheeks. How long since he had used that expression? How long since he had cried?

The envelope. His eyes sought it out, and he had to squint off the haze of cloud to see it properly: his name, his address, written in letters so uniform they could have been a typeface. No return. Then his gaze drifted and he realized that there were no stamps either. No postage. Whoever had sent this had brought it to his house.

My home, he thought, and it filled him with a fear so stark he felt his mind trip. *My home, with me in it, and Arabelle. Ara –*

As though his thoughts were so strong that she heard them calling through the floorboards, he heard the steps of his daughter above-the skipping steps that only eight-year-old girls possess-and he traced their movement across the ceiling above him, so distinct that he could almost *see* her brown curls bouncing, the half-peeled scab on her knee from last week when she tumbled off her scooter yet didn't cry. She was leaving her room and his eyes followed the sound, turning left in the hall, past the bathroom; she was heading for –

"Arabelle!" The word shot out his mouth on the slippery grease of vomit, turning it caustic, broken somehow, so that it sounded more like the death-croak of an asphyxiating lizard than the name of his only daughter.

She was nearing the stairs now and panic overcame him, more than panic, terror; it was stronger than the disgust he had felt at the photographs, stronger than the rush of forgotten memories: the fear of loss. An image came to him, of Arabelle skipping into the kitchen – his eyes stumbled over the counter and saw a jar of peanut butter sitting against the wall and his mind flashed: *You make her breakfast here! It's where she drinks her juice!* – and that was all it took. His throat cleared with a guttural roll, he spat, and then he was yelling, yelling for her to stay away, for God's sakes keep out, and he was moving too. Power had returned to his legs – not a lot but enough – and with long quick strides he shifted across the room towards the staircase and he was just in time – Arabelle was three quarters down the steps and he swept her up in his arms pressing her to his chest without a word, holding her tight. It was instinct, to want to hide her from the horrors of the world, to protect her, to see that she remained safe, it was a good thing that it was an instinct he possessed. Halfway up the stairs he threw a glance back, as though worried that the photographs were chasing him – later, in reflection, he would realize that they were doing exactly that – and saw that yes, a few of them had fallen all the way to the base of the stairs. He didn't know what those depicted exactly, but he had seen enough of the others to guess. The theme of the photos was consistent throughout, and it was one helluva horror show.

Of the ones he *had* seen, before his fingers fell loose like overcooked spaghetti and spilled them all over the floor, the running motif was clear. Silver glints of metal. Wide glowing eyes, some with terror, some with glee. Dark liquids were consistent throughout.

John knew that in old black and white movies, they used chocolate syrup in place of blood because in the absence of color no one could tell the difference, but John could. Color or monochrome, he knew what that liquid was. Whether in spilled blotches on the floor or flecked dots sprayed all over the walls, he knew. In one of the prints, the last one he'd seen before his mind and his grip said bye-bye, there was a mist of it so fine it created an outer-worldly, almost phosphorescent effect on the scene, making it seem surreal and staged.

John knew that it was neither. The blood was real. The body. And him, John: real. Now with thinner hair and a thicker face it might take a minute for someone else to make the connection, but for John, he knew the second he laid eyes on it. It was a younger him, but it was him, and he was staring directly at a camera he hadn't known was there, staring so intently John couldn't help but feel that his younger self was trying to warn him. Whoever had taken the photo had caught him – in more ways than one – just as he turned away from the business at hand – and that was what they had called it, wasn't it: *the business* – to throw a glance over his shoulder. His eyes looked sunken and serious, his face a grim mask of determination, his nostrils flared slightly with the strain of the work: *the business.*

But that face was one that had existed some twenty-one years ago and though the features might be similar, the thoughts and going-ons underneath were not. He was a different person, and as such, he had new business and that business was to make sure that his daughter never saw that old face. Never found out that it even existed.

Without any thought other than escape, John made it to the top of the stairs, Arabelle still pressed to his chest, and sprinted down the hall. His daughter tried to speak, but he was holding her so tightly the sounds came out muffled, soft; she could have been murmuring in her sleep, and this thought brought lovely panicked tears to his eyes. The bathroom. That was where he ended up. He supposed later that her own bedroom would have made more sense, but he chose the bathroom for its clean sterility, and before he knew what he was doing he was placing her into the tub, climbing in after her and slamming the curtains home. Then he was pulling her to the base of the tub, hugging her tighter than he had hugged his dying wife nearly half a decade ago, hugging her and crying and patting her hair as through trying to brush away the past itself.

--

Jack Barber was the kind of man who would stomp on the ground in the middle of an earthquake to try and get the earth to shut up. He drove an eighty thousand dollar car and still cut his own hair. He liked movies but not TV, loved classical music but hated opera, and believed that if a video game didn't have at least one decapitation per minute, it wasn't worth playing. Or in his case, designing. He was currently shaking his head.

"No, no." He pointed at the monitor with a ruler straight index finger. "I only want the blood to splatter on screen if it's from the player. And it's gotta move faster. Blood doesn't linger, it *flies. Splat!*" He slammed his hand on the table, palm down, producing a sharp crack. "And it's gotta stay, haze the screen a little. The more damage inflicted, the longer it stays…and-"

Pausing, he raised a fist to his forehead and flexed it several times, pumping the idea out of his brain the way a leech extracts blood from live flesh. He smiled.

"Replace a third of the first-aid kits with cleaning kits: Windex, squeegees, that sort of shit. Our hero can actually walk up to the screen and wipe it off, give us a clearer view."

The man to Jack's left smiled as he scribbled down notes. "Very meta," he mused, "do you think we sh-" but his question was cut off when the conference room door opened and a bright bush of red hair roughly the size of a Pontiac squeezed through. The eyes peering out from all that hair went to the boss like a baby to the teat.

"Jack, can I borrow you for a minute? There's something…" Her voice trailed off and Jack saw her face crumple slightly, like the skin of a balloon with a fast leak. "Something," she repeated, "that I think you should take a look at."

Jack threw a glance back at his crew. "Yeah, I think that's enough for today anyways gentlemen. Now look lively and remember: everything is about sex or money or both." He walked out of the room.

--

"What is it, Nancy?"

"You got some mail."

Jack turned and looked at her, trying to find her face under all that hair. "And?" As the fourth largest producer of action and RPG games in North America, Jack personally received at least fifty pieces of mail a day, half of which were DVDs of demos from would be designers looking for a job, the other half from mother's and clergymen denouncing him and his company as *purveyors of filth,* a hackneyed phrase that never failed to bring a smile to his lips.

"This one's moving." She stared at him, then quickly added: "I think."

"You think?"

Nancy nodded and her head jiggled like an overloaded palm tree caught in a stiff breeze.

Jack moved his gaze to her desk where there sat two large stacks of envelopes, most of them the unmistakable size of a DVD in its case. To the right, smack in the middle, was a slightly larger package, a slim box skinned in wrapping paper covered in…clowns? Jack took a step closer, and realized they weren't just clowns, they were clown *puppets*; there were strings coming out of their shoulders, their hands, and their feet. He looked back at Nancy with raised eyebrows.

"It was here when I came back from lunch. Sitting right where it is now." She pointed with a hooked finger to the other side of the box and Jack noted that she didn't step forward, didn't move closer to it, as though she didn't want to touch it, as though she were scared of it. "It's addressed to you right there," she said, indicating a neat label on the far side, "but there's no return address." She coughed. "And no postage."

Jack continued to stare at his secretary whose bushy red drapes-he had found out years ago-most certainly matched the carpet. They had slept together once and only once, on the eve that Jack's first video game – a first-person shooter about century-dead war veterans rising up from their graves to take up arms and once again save the world - sold its first million copies. They had slept together in a moment of triumphant joy and immediately afterwards decided that it would be the only time. Good secretaries, he rationed, were a lot harder to find than good lovers, though the red thatch between her legs had damn near leveled the playing field on that one, and when he told her exactly that he had been very pleased to discover that she took it as a compliment which led him to understand another of her qualities that he admired her for; she was as rational as any man he had ever met. From that day forward they were nothing but professional.

"Tell me."

Nancy shrugged. "Like I said, I came back from lunch and it was sitting there. I didn't think much of it, went to open it and then-" she threw the package a look usually reserved for rotten meat or bird shit on your hand – "the paper kind of…rustled. Moved, as if there was something in it." She paused, then added: "Alive."

Jack shrugged. "Well, there's only one way to find out," he told her, stepping forward and picking up the package with both hands. Nancy instinctively took a step back, the index and middle fingers of her right hand crossed. Jack noticed – Jack noticed everything – and threw her a curious glance; Nancy had never struck him as the superstitious type. He turned back to the package in his hand, shook it up and down several times, then watched it closely. For a full three seconds nothing happened, then the paper appeared to move, to press outwards. He frowned.

"You got an *Exacto X-Acto*?"

Nancy continued to stare at the package in her boss's hands, not moving, eyes narrowing.

"Nancy?"

She came back, unable to suppress a sudden shiver. For some reason she didn't want to be around when the package was opened.

"Uh, yeah. Top drawer. Next to the highlighters."

Jack moved with a fluidity usually associated with Russian ballet. The knife came out. Extended. Sliced. And the culprits immediately came forth.

Cockroaches, the biggest three Jack had ever seen, spilled onto Nancy's desk and for the first time in Nancy's five years as his secretary, she saw him waver. His face tightened, he dropped both box and blade, and pushed himself back three full paces; if there hadn't been a wall behind him he would have kept going.

The roaches were a deep golden red, the color of backlit wine, and each the size of a credit card. They immediately made for the edges of the desk, tapping rapid, insectile clicks on the smooth tabletop that pricked at Jack's ears and set the hairs on his arms dancing. Then they were over the side.

"Kill them," he commanded, and it took Nancy a second to realize that he was talking to her.

"Kill them," he repeated, this time the urgency in his voice – probably the only voice in this world that could have induced her to do what she did next – made her move.

With three quick steps she crushed the bugs out of existence, wincing with increasing disgust as the mandibles, abdomen, and legs were ground into skeleton flecked paste, with the last two still underneath her shoes, she stared up at her boss as though awaiting instruction what to do next.

He was still pressed against the wall, eyes wide and unable to shift from the path the roaches had taken.

"I'm – I'm sorry Nancy," he began, his voice cracking. "I – I don't do well with cockroaches." He swallowed and tilted his head to peer into the package; there was something else in there, but whatever it was, it didn't appear to be alive. When he spoke again his voice was grim and tight, the authority returned.

"Call security. Get them to check the cameras. And get a goddamn cleaner in here to take care of the floor." He finally relaxed enough to move away from the wall, but he made sure to not let his eyes drift down. The shell of the cockroaches were enough; he had no desire to see what they looked like turned inside out. A second later he made to leave, paused, then turned back.

"Don't forget to invoice the company for the shoes." His eyes went back to the package. "And whatever you do don't let anyone but security touch that thing." He pursed his lips. "In fact," he added, "don't even go near your desk."

He walked away a second later, beads of sweat bulging on his forehead like clear egg sacs ready to burst. He didn't look back.

--

The security cameras revealed nothing. Well, not *nothing* exactly, but they had clearly shown that whoever dropped off the package knew what he was doing. He had passed by exactly seven cameras, a hunched man with a strangely insectile gait – like a spider or a scorpion-on the way up to the thirteenth floor where the offices of *Deus Ex Machina Games* were housed, and in every one, in *every single shot*, he was looking away at the perfect angle so as to make his face completely unidentifiable. Splice all seven videos together, and you'd have a character sketch consisting of the back of a head and two ears. It was downright uncanny, not to mention creepy, to see the way the man avoided the eyes in the sky so planned, so precisely: it was no accident. No, this man was good. This man was an expert. This guy was goddamn Houdini, except his vanishing act consisted of him standing right in front of his audience yet completely invisible; he might as well have been the shadow of a ghost.

Other than the three roaches, the package contained a single DVD and nothing more. No anthrax. No severed finger or chewed off toe. Just three cucarachas and a flat circular piece of plastic with no label, no name, no markings. Jack examined the underside himself and guesstimated that the video on it was approximately twenty minutes in length. If it was a video. It could have been data for all he knew, but something in him told him no; place this sucker in a player and images would *move*. Now was the time.

He nodded at Nancy and it wasn't until she pressed at the tray that held the DVD, and the familiar click sounded, then the whirring, that Jack realized how nervous he was. He could feel his heart pressing at the insides of his ribs and his throat felt constricted, like he was breathing through one of those loop-de-loop *Crazy Straws* from the eighties . The video player popped up on screen, Nancy shifted the mouse and Jack watched as the pointer hovered over the play button. Nancy looked up with raised eyebrows.

"Jack?"

Jack stared at the screen for a moment longer, then nodded. "Satan is waitin'" he said, then frowned. He didn't know where he'd heard the expression before but it was familiar.

One click and the video began. Black for a few seconds and then white scratchy lines appeared horizontally, shimmying down the screen.

"Transferred from a VCR," one of the security guards said – there were two of them currently staring at the screen alongside Jack and Nancy-and Jack nodded. *What the fuck is this?* he thought, *and why to me? Why to –*

There came a flash of snow and then an image settled on the screen. It was unmoving and grainy – filmed in infrared, the scene was cast in an alien green hue – and depicted some kind of workroom, a basement perhaps, or maybe a garage. Something within Jack stirred, but he had no idea what it was or why; he began to analyze the scene the way he would one of his video games.

The camera was aimed perpendicular to the back wall, a table pressed against it, large and empty, and beside the table, a bucket and a mop or a broom. The floor was dirty, littered with chunks of things too misshapen to be identified, and there was a mess of something in the corner, some kind of dark fabric, or maybe a bag of garbage. Jack felt his skin begin to turn numb, and the flesh below followed suit; a great feeling of nothingness spread through his extremities, working its way up his arms and legs, intent on the core and Jack was convinced that if he were to roll up the sleeves of his two thousand dollar suit, he would actually see the color draining from his skin. And still he couldn't take his eyes off the screen, knowing that it was familiar but not knowing why.

Nancy was the first to speak, and she pointed as she did, to an object resting to the right of the screen, sitting beside what appeared to be an old box furnace.

"What *is* that thing? Looks like R2-D2 or something," and when Jack saw what Nancy was pointing at, and the dark line growing out of it like a thick tail, his eyes widened in recall and shock.

"It's a Shop-Vac," Jack said, and then all spittle evaporated from his mouth and throat, he felt his knees buckle; he grabbed the edge of the desk for support. This was worse than the cockroaches, oh so fucking worse. He would rather have eaten those goddamn insects than see this video, this simple static shot, would rather have gulped down a cockroach smoothie and done so with a great shit-eating grin on his face than have to see what he was seeing at this very moment.

"Grrn te ovvv," he croaked, gripping the desk harder. His entire body was numb now, and it took all his strength not to fall right over, to crash to the floor. He coughed, a great hawking bellow and tried again and thank God, thank *Christ* for small favors, it came out clearer this time.

"Turn if off."

No one had noticed Jack's struggles these last few seconds; all eyes were tight as lasers on the screen, waiting for something to happen. So far nothing had moved, but there was the hint that something was about to. There was an electric buzz, so faint and far off that it might have been the sound of the camera itself, but they all knew that something was coming; this was just that giant mother-fucking cloud leading up to the storm.

"Turn if off Nancy," Jack said, and she looked at him as if it were the first time he had spoken.

"Let's wait another minute and see if anything ha-"

As if on cue to Nancy's words, a figure stepped into frame. It came from the foreground so his face was hidden

- *how do you know it's a he Jack?-*

- because-

- because-

- because yoooou *know-*

and he walked directly into the background, a man of purpose. Jack watched, horrified, as the man reached the counter and began tooling around with something. *Only it's not a* counter, *is it Jack? Not exactly. It's a bench. A workbench. And what do we keep on a workbench? What indeed Jackie Boy, but none other than –*

"Turn it off now,"

"I just wanna see what-"

But Jack had seen enough and he lunged, a savage jungle leap, not at the mouse still cupped under Nancy's hand *(too slow too delicate)* but for the monitor itself, and he gripped its frame with his left hand while the other yanked desperately at the cable growing out of its back.

"Jesus Jack its-" but her words were lost on the man before her, like pebbles tossed into the eye of a tornado.

Jack's movements turned vicious now as his body wrestled with the cable but pull as he might, the cord refused to yield – in his frenzy he hadn't noticed the tiny screws on either side that held it firmly in place – but he saw them now, he narrowed in and his hands clamped on them like a crow at its carrion. They clawed in reckless form, scratching, trying to turn the tiny spindles and loosen their grip but no, the image played on and when Jack saw what was happening – he didn't have to look, not really, he already *knew* – he simply grabbed the monitor with both hands and brought it smashing to the floor where it shattered, sparked once, and died.

Jack stood above it, staring down at it the way a boxer might eye an opponent that had become personal, his chest heaving, blood scratched out of his fingers. He wouldn't notice until later, but he had completely ripped the nail off of the middle finger of his right hand; it hung on only by a thick cuticle and a small live wire of flesh.

No one said a word; they all stared wide eyed at this thing before them that had once been their boss, a man, but had morphed into something feral and unrecognizable before their eyes.

A second later, as Jack had known it would, the sharp sound of an electric drill, *pump-whirr pump-whirr pump-whirr,* blasted out of the computer speakers. He calmly reached over and clicked the speakers off. When he turned to the three people beside him, his face was empty, voided.

"Get out," he told them. He was staring at the place where the monitor had been; the space it had occupied now seemed huge and alive. They didn't protest. They didn't question: madness is not something you want answered. One by one they left the room, first the security guards, brows furrowed, then Nancy. She made it all the way to the door before she stopped, hesitating. One more look at her boss, and her one-time lover pressed her out the door.

Jack stood alone in the room, his legs as stable as water balloons as he stepped over to the chair and sat down. The DVD was still spinning in the computer but he couldn't hear it; at that point it was unlikely that he would have heard a trumpet blast mainlined directly into his ear canal. All he could think of, all he could hear, even if it was now only in his mind, was the whirring of that drill.

Guns are for pussies. That was what he had said, wasn't it? *Guns are for pussies. Drills are the way to go. More personal. They create a brilliant connection, almost sexual. Drills penetrate, first through the skin, drawing blood. Then flesh. Then bone. The hardest thing in the human body and a fifty-cent drill bit pierces it like piss through the snow. Once past the bone, well that was where the fun began, wasn't it? That was when the body really began to twitch, to get down with the dirty electric boogaloo.*

But I was just a kid, he thought, *just a punk kid who...and I haven't thought about it since...* He shrugged. He didn't know how long it had been, but *Christ, that was twenty-one years ago. Twenty-one years and fuck all, which in itself was some kind of yellowed miracle, but now...now.*

He remembered the DVD spinning in the tray and without conscious thought he ejected it, stared at it. Something occurred to him. *Maybe it's a fake. A recreation of the original event.* He chewed his lower lip, all the while shaking his head. *Possible, but unlikely. I mean*, physically, *it could be done. I could have done it if I wanted to, pretty much anything is possible with computers these days. Someone could have easily made a virtual reconstruction of the room. Filmed someone walking around in it, digitally altered to look like you. You've done it a thousand times yourself in your games, why shouldn't someone el –*

He cut himself off mid-thought. *It's real,* a voice in his head announced, and this time the other voice, *Denial*, stayed silent. Jack stared at the disc for another minute, his eyes full of hatred, rage, fear, and then he simply applied a little pressure and snapped the DVD in two.

A third voice in his head, one he didn't immediately recognize, piped in: *you think he didn't make copies? You think that was the only one? Ha!*

Who's 'he' the same voice retorted, who could 'he' possibly be? But he thought he knew. Could guess anyway.

They called me 'The Dustbuster'. Remember that? They called me 'The Dustbuster' cause I was always in charge of cleaning. Of taking out the trash. Of making sure no detail was ever overlooked, and I was good at it, wasn't I? Of course I was, we never got caught, did we?

Until now, the voice responded, and Jack finally recognized whom that voice belonged to; it was himself, only much younger. A teenager who felt he had the world at its feet and life by the sack.

You broke your number one rule, didn't you Jackie Boy? You always intended to go back and clean up those two final messes but somehow time rolled over time, things faded, and the thought of opening old wounds, and creating some fresh ones, didn't appeal to you anymore. You let it go. Let it recede.

You were sloppy, and now the mess has come back.

"I can't do it again," he said out loud to the empty room, "I'm a different person. I can't go back."

Then everything we've worked for is lost, said that voice again, and it hit him, really hit him. All the hours spent building something, creating. This office. This business. His home and his car. Respect and even a small touch of fame. Dignity. Stature. Power. That last one got him, snagged his consciousness, refused to let go. *But you've never felt power like you did back then, have you Jackie Boy? You have a hundred and fifty men working under you now and it's still only a fraction of the power you felt when you were seventeen and wielding an electric drill in a dirty workshop.*

"Okay," he said, "Okay." It made him sick to think it, to guess at what he was going to do, but he knew that it was unavoidable. And he nodded, his eyes wide and glossy, lost in a past he had forced himself to delete from his mind, the way he deleted bad code from one of his video games. "Okay," he said a third and final time.

He didn't realize it but he was crying.

--

The bell sounded and thirty-two seven-year-olds shot out of their seats like firecrackers out of their cardboard tubes, bounding for their book bags and baseball caps. Chairs were knocked over, papers scattered, a leftover sandwich was stepped on unnoticed, turning it into something biological and rank. One child, a little black kid named Arnold, ran up to Ms. Jarblonski, hugged her thighs tightly for three seconds, and then shot out of the room, a crazy grin on his face and a thick canine slobber on his right cheek.

"See you later Double J," he called over his shoulder, and though Jillian had scolded him before about calling his teacher by her initials, she couldn't help but laugh; the excitement of the last day of school was as infectious as the plethora of viruses these kids passed around to their classmates each and every day.

She bent down to pick up a forgotten book, saw that a rainbow of plastic markers had also been spilled across the floor, and began collecting them one by one, a lingering smile still tilling shallow wrinkles around her eyes, her mouth. By the time she had gathered them all the class was empty and silent as a tomb and though the whisper of a smile was still there, inside she was frowning; *we spend our youth running forward, always eager for the next step, never knowing until it's too late that each step we take brings us closer to the grave: the box.*

"Well, there's a cheery thought," she mused aloud and the *pop!* that came from the small of her back when she straightened up was like a little exclamation mark, emphasizing the point; dark the thought may have been, yes, but equally true, no doubt. Jillian shook her head, laughing as she heard the door to her classroom open, and looked up.

The woman standing in the doorway looked like she'd just had a fight with a small tank and lost.

"I don't know how you do it Jillian," the woman began. "They say patience is a virtue; you must be a living saint." She took three steps into the classroom and plunked herself down into the nearest seat, which was about five sizes and forty years too small for her. Her hair, usually slicked back and pulled tight into a perfect little croissant, was a wiry mess of blacks and electric greys; one thick clump hung down over her forehead, and scooped at her nose like a fish-hook. She sat there, staring up at Jillian with wide eyes, her chin propped on her two callused hands supported by two thick wrists.

Jillian laughed, a trilling sound both light and natural. "Believe me, I'm not always this way. I just find it impossible to get upset with kids, that's all."

The older woman smiled. "Well, your parents must have done something right."

Julian shrugged, the smile on her face fading. "My father was a factory worker, and my mother died when I was pretty young. I was raised mostly by my aunt, who was a cake decorator. Amazing stuff, really. She could make those really fine flowers, you know, thirty petals on each one, silver candy beads, all that crap. Draw pictures in icing one dab at a time, almost like…pointillism I guess. She'd spend hours on a cake, sometimes an hour or more on one little flower, to get it perfect. But with me and my brother-" she let out a short blast of air from her nose " – she'd smack us upside the head for tying our shoelaces too slow." She shrugged. "Priorities I guess." She looked around the classroom, surveying the damage. "And speaking of priorities, I should probably get to work on this disaster." There were papers everywhere. Marker caps and pencil shavings. Half-filled notebooks and forgotten finger paintings. Wads of gum so hard they would have to be chiseled off the undersides of the desks. She turned back to her colleague. "How's yours looking?"

"Like Hitler's bunker the day after. And speaking of little Germans-" and here she bore a feline smile that no man in recorded time had ever been capable of producing just so "-didn't I see one talking to you in the parking lot this morning...? Thought I might have caught a whiff of the intoxicating scent of summer romance in the air, no?"

Jillian blushed. "Hitler was Austrian, not German," she told the woman, who brushed the comment aside with a wave of her hand, "and Benedict is not little. At least I hope not." She winked at the woman, old enough to be her mother and then some, and felt a simple clutch of joy wring at her heart when she *whooped!* loudly at the joke.

"Jillian! You little devil you. You never told me-"

"And I still haven't," Jillian said, her voice equal parts humor and edge. The fact that it had taken the guy nearly a year just to introduce himself was something she found both depressing and excitingly adolescent.

"Are you going to see each other over the su-" the woman began, but Jillian had had enough of teenybopper gossip and cut her off.

"Curiosity killed the cat Margaret," she warned with a scolding finger, and then quickly changed the subject. "Now, I don't suppose you brought...?"

The older woman smiled, and five years slid off her face. "I thought you'd never ask." She stood up, moving with a surprising agility for a woman her age. Out the door she went, returning a minute later with an oversized purse. She closed the door behind her and made her way over to Jillian desk. From her bag she produced two Dixie cups and a bottle of French brandy, pear flavored. She poured them each a goody, handed one to Jillian, and raised her own glass in a toast.

"To the class of twenty-ten," she announced, and the cups crumpled slightly as they bumped. Both woman laughed, a winning sound, like the trumpet marking the end of a long and brutal war. They drank to their spoils, then she poured them each another. When the second drinks were gone, both women stood and the older woman spoke.

"Mine first, or yours?"

Jillian shrugged. "We're already here, might as well get started on this one." The older woman nodded in agreement.

"Probably better this way anyways; when you see what mine looks like, you'll turn tail and run."

"Ahh, I wouldn't leave you hanging like that."

"I know you wouldn't sweetie. I know."

And the two women began to clean.

--

By the time the work was done it was nearing five o'clock and Jillian was ready for bed. Her back ached, her fingernails were scraped and sore from trying to pick those last few stubborn chunks of gum out of the carpet, and her head was swimming a little; the sweet taste of pear still clung thickly to her throat, slightly cloying, she marveled what a beautiful day it was, the perfect day to be finishing school for the summer.

She made her way over to her humble little Honda Civic parked in the far corner – it was one of the few cars remaining in the lot of Derrryside Elementary-and almost dropped the box of paperwork she was carrying as she tried to fish her keys out of her purse. A minute later she had the key in the lock, about to turn it but not turning it, surprised to notice that the door was already unlocked; she could see the little knob poking over the edge of the window.

Strange, she thought, and bit her lip; she couldn't remember the last time that had happened. She was a little OCD about things like that, turning off lights, opening shower curtains *(never know who might be lurking behind them when you get up to throw a squirt in the toilet at three in the morning)* and *especially* locking doors.

Oh well, stranger things have hap –

She stopped, hand on handle, jaw slightly unhinged. She moved closer to the car, trying to peer through the glare of the late afternoon sun bouncing off the window. There was something on her seat, something she was *sure* hadn't been there before, and though the item itself looked simple and harmless, the fact that it wasn't hers made her distrustful, scared even.

It was a black audiotape in a clear case, and there was writing on the label but she couldn't read it from where she stood. She placed the box of papers on the roof of the car and opened the door, feeling cautious, wondering if the tape had appeared as a result of her unlocked door or vice versa.

"Maybe it's from Benedict," she heard Margaret's voice tease and again that schoolgirl giddiness fluttered in her chest. She pushed the thought away; high school hadn't exactly been a time of jubilation for her. Exhilaration yes, ecstasy for sure, but not of the variety she cared to remember. She shivered. No, not at all.

She reached in and scooped up the tape, wondering how long it had been since she'd held one in her hand.

Jesus, I can't even remember the last time I played a CD, *never mind a* tape. *It must have been –*

She stopped, her entire body chilled despite the generous warmth of the afternoon sun. There was writing on the tape. It was one word only, written in thick bold letters, letters so solid it were as though they were weighing the tape down, and she almost dropped it.

Jilly. Her name.

Only nobody calls you that Jillian. Not anymore. Not since-

She needed to sit down – she was afraid she was going to pass out and whack her head a good one on the hot concrete. A headline flashed in her brain: *Schoolmarm Splits Skull on Last Day of Class; Children Venerate Her Dislike of Homework!* She slid right into the driver's seat with her heart a rat-tat-tatting inside her chest and a noise inside her head like rusted metal being twisted into something alien and perverse. The tape – the tape –

She almost dropped it sliding in and now she looked down at it again, certain that she must have been mistaken before, that she'd misread it the first time, but the word was still there; blinking made no difference. *Jilly* it was and *Jilly* it was going to stay.

This has gotta be a joke, she thought. Maybe she'd mentioned her nickname to Margaret some time back, or Louise, or one of the other dozen cronies she ate lunch with every day, and they passed the info on to Benedict who thought it would be cute to –

No, no, no Jillian that's not it and you know it. Because Jilly is a name you never use. That you would never use. Jilly is a name so far back from your past that you stopped buying marmalade years ago because seeing the word 'jelly' on the label reminded you too much of it. Because it reminded you too much of...

She stared down at the tape, horrified at how one little inanimate object could throw her life into an absolute whirlwind in a few dry seconds.

Throw it away Jillian, just toss it right now. It doesn't matter what's on it, just get rid of it. But even before the thought could complete itself, Jillian knew she couldn't do that; the truth was like a shadow behind her: hidden but there, nonetheless. No, because it *did* matter what was on the tape. It mattered a lot, especially if it had to do with what she suspected it might. Jillian swallowed once, hard, the taste of the pear schnapps still thick in her throat, and she suddenly wished she still had the bottle. She coughed. *If this tape turns out to be related to what you think it is, you're gonna need something a lot more than some pear brandy to get you through it.*

"Enough," she said out loud, and it came out so desperate that it was almost a scream. "Don't jump to conclusions Jilly, don't go down-" and then she stopped, horrified at what she'd just called herself and stunned at how easily the name rolled off her tongue.

The tape, she thought, *listen to the tape and see what it is. But where the fuck am I going to find a tape de –*

Her eyes drifted over to the middle of the dashboard and she almost laughed; she would have in any other situation, but not this one, no no. Nothing funny about this one.

She'd bought the Civic used about five years ago from a lispy guy with the unlikely name of Porky, an ironic nickname she'd thought because the guy was skinny enough to serve as an extra from *Schindler's List.* He'd had long thinning hair, blonde and greasy, reminding her of a younger version of Riff Raff from *Rocky Horror* and an Aerosmith t-shirt that read "Tour of '79'".

The car ran fine, looked hardly used, and was well within her price range which, on a teacher's salary, was a pretty tight berth, and though she might have raised her eyebrows when she noticed the tape deck, *(it was after all 2005)*, Porky's asking price was so low it could have had a damn phonograph player and she still would have taken it. Still, she couldn't help asking about it as she counted out the cash a few minutes later into his creepily small and sweaty hands.

"Oh that?" he asked good-naturedly. He shrugged. "I installed it myself. Hard to get a car these days with a CD player, let alone a tape deck. But what can I say, I'm a sucker for the classics," only with his lisp it came out more like "I'm a thuckah for tha clathicth," and judging by his T-shirt, Jillian would have bet that he was.

Jillian didn't own any tapes – she'd thrown out all her cassettes, a vast collection of mostly eighties tunes spanning all the way from *A-Ha* right on down to *Yaz* about three lifetimes ago, so she didn't even know if the tape deck worked, but she figured there was no time like the present to find out.

She started her car and made to slide the tape in the slot; she got it halfway in before she stopped. It struck her how fast her heart was pounding and she felt out of breath; she closed her eyes and breathed, tried to steady the thump-thump-thump inside her. Once again she made a move to push the tape in, thought twice, and closed the car door; there was no one around, the parking lot was still empty, but one could never be too sure. Then she looked down at the tape once more, stared at it - her gaze was so intense 'glared' might be a better word - and took a deep breath.

"Satan is waitin'," she said, not registering that the last time she'd heard that expression had probably been around the time she was rockin' out to George Michael or Richard Marx.

The tape clicked home and for a few seconds: nothing. It wasn't going to work. In fact, she became certain that the deck was making a meal of the deep caramel cultured strip, chewing it into a wrangled mess that only a pencil could fix, but then she saw the knob on the left and realized the volume was turned down.

Static. That was all she heard at first so she turned it up louder, and then louder still. The static was blaring, all crackles and pops and hiss from a past that no longer existed, but she was convinced there was a sound behind it, something in the background she couldn't quite hear. She turned it up even louder – it was on full blast now – and leaned in to the speaker, ear cocked, face scrunched in concentration.

All of a sudden, it came. Sound trumpeted out of the speakers so loudly it rocked Jillian back in her seat: she let out a scream of surprise and her hand shot to lower the volume. Then she sat back, heart pounding twice as fast as it had been a second before the blast, and listened.

It took perhaps five seconds for her to realize what it was she was listening to, no more than ten. The sounds were liquid like, flowing, bending and melting together, though they certainly weren't music, at least not of the usual variety. Her eyes tightened, the right side of her lip pulled back in a *'huh?'* gesture and her head cocked in wonder. Was she listening to two people…*fucking?* She laughed out loud.

It was a joke. Oh, man it was a fucking joke, and she had fallen for it hook, line and sinker. Here she'd been worried it actually had something to do with her and it was just a shitty audio recording from what sounded like a second-rate porno; *is there such a thing as 'first-rate porno?* she wondered. She laughed. At first a slight chuckle and then a larger one. Then a full on guffaw. A few seconds later she was laughing so hard the sound of the tape was drowned out completely. She didn't know who could have left her the tape – certainly not someone from her work; she didn't know anyone there *that* well – but maybe Caroline, her best friend, had thought she'd needed cheering up and –

But what about the nickname, Jillian? What about 'Jilly'? You never told Caroline about that, did you? No, you never told anyone because –

The laughter disappeared as quick as it had come, but the sounds of magnetic sex still pumped through the speakers, tinny and thin. The woman was moaning with such intensity that Jillian had to assume it was put on (no porn star was likely to win an Oscar anytime soon but they were still *actors* after all) and then – Jillian leaned forward, listening harder – other moans came into the mix, deeper, baritone, and she realized it wasn't just a man and a woman involved, but *two* men.

Ménage a trois.

The phrase came to her like a perfume, drifting, but she quickly realized that it didn't fit with what she was hearing. That phrase suggested something sensual, loving, almost tender. What she was hearing was a threesome. Jangled fucking that was all flesh and thigh-slaps, slobber and teeth-marks. Arms and legs intertwined like some perverse version of a Hindu god, Brahma or Vishnu; she could envision tongues lapping at armpits, fingers probing at various holes, painful but welcome nonetheless.

Jillian's lips pulled back from her teeth like a growling dog; she had no recollection whatsoever as to what had seemed so funny a moment ago. Then the woman on the tape started talking, and gooseflesh blossomed along Jillian's arms and legs, spreading like ink poured into clear water.

I know that voice. I know it. I've heard it before, and those words. I've heard –

"We sure showed him now, didn't we guys?" the woman on the tape cooed, her moans intensifying. *"Oh yeah, we showed him gooooood."*

Oh Jesus, oh Jesus, oh Jesus, oh Jesus. She let out a gasp and her stomach didn't just do a backflip, it did a whole fucking Russian Olympic gymnast routine all over her gummy organs. She made for the door, missed the handle, and ended up vomiting the pear brandy all over the window. Finally, her hand managed the door and she half flung herself out, her body heaving as though her stomach was leading a coup against it and she could only hang there and watch, helpless and ragged.

It took several minutes to regain control, and by that time the noises coming from the tape were reaching a crescendo; moans and grunts poured through the speakers like some kind of pornographic orchestra, a symphony of sex. She didn't want to hear any more, *couldn't* hear anymore, she reached for the power button with a hand overcome by a palsy. She pawed at the knob once, twice – *turn it off,* her mind screamed, *end it end it!* – but not before one final thought crashed through her mind, straightening her spine and opening her bile coated mouth in a silent horror-struck scream.

That's you Jillian. That's you. Fucking and getting fucked. Filled out like a pig on a spit.

And right on the heels of this stabbing unwelcome revelation, came another, a memory as clear as a rural night sky: *There was so much blood...so much more than you thought there could be.*

Then the damning one, arcing and breaking like the moment of orgasm itself, finally achieved though unasked for:

And you liked it. You liked *it.*

She screamed, a high animal curl so sharp that it tore her throat and drew blood. Her hand flew to the clutch, her foot jammed on the gas, and the old Civic leaped forward like a jungle cat making for its prey, though it might be better said: like prey running from the leap. Because she *was* running, running from that one foe that can never be escaped no matter how fast your feet hit the pavement, despite the sparks coming from your shoes: the past. For years it had been behind her, and she had thought – erroneously she now realized – that that was where it would stay. But it had finally caught up to her, finally found her. That past was back, and it turned the blood in her veins into something both arctic and acidic.

Still not understanding that she couldn't outrun it, Jillian shot out of the parking lot of Derryside Elementary going a solid sixty miles per hour, oblivious to the fact that she was screaming at the top of her lungs as she drove and beating at the steering wheel as though it were on fire.

She forgot all about school. All about the summer vacation. She even forgot about the papers on the roof of her car as they blew away behind her like chunky exhaust fumes in a 2D world. If only she could forget it all.

1989

Jack Barber reckoned there were two kinds of people in high school; those who hated the place with a passion and couldn't wait to get the hell out of there, and assholes. He knew the former type existed because he was one of them but he never understood why the latter scuttled around the halls in such abundance. Everyone around him was so *obvious,* so window transparent, that sometimes he wasn't sure he could see them at all. They existed like quasi-phantoms in the peripheral points of his vision, floating by but never really there, haunting the halls the way their acne scars would haunt them into their adult life.

God this is boring, he thought. On the ground he spotted a metal pencil sharpener, picked it up, rolled it between his fingers and marveled at its construction. It seemed such a solid thing, well made, not flimsy plastic like most sharpeners, and he immediately went to work dismantling it, removing the screw, the blade, tracing the sleek lines of its design with a soft finger. He threw the screw over his shoulder without looking back while at the front of the class the teacher – he watched her for a second with a quiet disinterest-pushed shapeless words out of her mouth, words that meant nothing, malformed Styrofoam clumps that fluttered to the ground, useless, forgotten, dead. Jack turned back to the sharpener and placed the casing back on the floor where he'd found it; it was the blade that had his interest and he held it up to his eye, right up to it, marveling at its sharpness and wondering how many pencils this particular blade had dug into, had sheared. How many words had been produced thanks to the generosity of its cut?

He ran the corner of the blade along one of the veins on the back of his hand, wondering how hard he would have to press to draw blood, and how much of that red liquid would seep out. *Five to six liters in the human body*, he thought, and the image of all that blood, drained, made his heart flutter. *That's three big bottles of Coke*. It seemed like both a lot and a little at the same time.

His skin began to crawl, the fine hairs on his arm standing up like soldiers when the general walks in, and he knew that someone was watching him; he always knew when someone was watching him. He looked around, but nothing. Whoever it was had turned away just in time and Jack breathed out heavily; he didn't like the idea of someone watching him without permission. He continued to stare at the people beside him, willing them to reveal themselves, but they were all just ghosts. Ghosts at their papers. Ghosts in their books. One ghost was sleeping, dreaming her ghost dreams. Another held a shielding hand over his face while his finger went digging for ghost gold in his nose: subtle. His eyes drifted to the last desk at the back, in the corner opposite his own, and he stopped. There was a girl there, pale and plain. and she was staring at her own hand held out directly in front of her. She was rotating it back and forth, first staring at her palm, then at the back, then to the palm again. It took Jack a minute to realize that there was a spider on her hand crawling round and round her finger as she watched it. He watched her do this for perhaps two minutes – it was the most interesting thing he had seen all week – and then she really surprised him. She moved the spider right up to her own nose, a small button nose that seemed childish and out of place on her face, and stared down at the spider, and Jack tried to imagine how that nose looked from the spiders point of view – multiplied by eight, banking and cavernous. To the spider that face those eyes, that pearl of a mouth-tiny and slightly open-must be godlike. Staring into it must be like staring into the face of the Creator, the condemner, and the Angel of Light. To that little creature, the giant face that lords over it must be the world, the universe, and all that lies stuffed in the cracks between.

Now the spider was sitting on the plump cushion of her thumb and the girl stopped rotating her hand, drawing the spider still closer to her own all-encompassing face. For a second – a gleeful fucked up flash made Jack shift in his seat – he was convinced that she was going to stuff it in her mouth Renfield style, but no. Instead she moved her forefinger – to anyone who didn't know there was a spider on her thumb it would seem she was making that universal gesture of *this close* – but Jack knew better. He had twenty-twenty vision and he could see those fingers drawing together and the spider in between. He waited, waited for the spider to see what was coming – *you got eight eyes for Christ's sake, how can you not see it?* Jack's mind shot at the thing – but the next thing he knew, and it was the *last* things the spider ever knew, she had it clamped neatly between thumb and forefinger. Immediately the spider's legs turned to madness, straightening, bending, stabbing the air in a pathetic attempt to escape but it was got now, held by belly and back, for all the flailing in the world that spider wasn't going anywhere. The girl brought it closer still to her face – it was no more than two inches from her left eye-and ever so slowly began to squeeze.

A few seconds later there came a flinch, a tightening of her nose and nothing more, Jack realized that most likely the spider had bitten her. She didn't drop it though; her fingers never faltered, but continued on their press. Then came a small sound – everything around Jack was so ghostlike that he heard it clearly, even from across the room. It was almost as though the sound were in his head, like the crunch of brittle foodstuff between the molars, for he felt it as well as heard it.

Now that it was done, the girl leaned back in her chair, still staring at the mess, then she did a strange thing, even stranger than what she had just done. She rubbed the muck between her fingers, swirling it into an organic mixture of guts and gore, shell and ichor, until it was a brown-yellow paste. Bored, she simply reached over and wiped the mess on the wall, then turned back to the teacher at the front of the class, stared for a few seconds, and yawned.

Jack grinned - wide and angular the expression appeared to be ripped into his face - and turned away from the girl. Then he turned away from the classroom, and away from the world.

Still smiling, he concentrated on the desk in front of him and with the blade from the sharpener, began carving letters into its surface. Some time later, when the bell rang and the other students began exiting the class, he blew away the shavings and wiped it once with the back of his hand.

I don't like Mondays, was all it read, and he shrugged. It was as good a sentiment as any and when he stood up to leave, he knocked the razor to the ground without giving it a second thought.

--

Five days later that same pale-faced girl with dark eyes was barely through Side A of *The Queen is Dead* when the batteries of her Walkman started to crap out on her, the lyrics stretching like taffy, the notes melting like microwaved *Cheese Whiz.*

Ohhhhhhh mmmuuuthaaaaaa…….IIII caaaannn fffeeeeel….. thuuuuuuu sssssooooilllll fffaaaalliiinnnngg oooovvvuuuuhh mmmyyyyy hheeeeaaaaddd

She stopped the tape, cursed, and pursed her lips. "Well, there goes my plans for the night." She briefly wondered if there was a convenience store around here where she could grab some double A's but remembered that she had no money. She shrugged, thinking of a line from one of her favorite movies: *nothing to do when you're locked in a vacancy.* Thinking of Bender gave her a new idea. *You could five-finger discount a pack.* She clicked her tongue twice: definitely a possibility. *Let's see how you feel after you burn this bean.* She patted her left breast to make sure the joint was still there and then dug into her pocket for her lighter. Nothing there but lint and letdown. She tried her other pocket but the only thing she found there was the fact that she could fit two fingers through the hole in the bottom.

Well that's just fuckin' boss man. That blows my whole night. Jesus, I mean, I might be able to steal a pack o' batts but lighter, no way: they're right on the counter in front of the clerk. She sighed, biting her lip, thinking. Maybe if someone came by with a ciggie she could bum a light… *would have to be someone who looked* down *though. You can't exactly spark a doob in front of some sixty-year-old grand-pappy. If it's some teen, then they're probably gonna want some… besides this ain't exactly Grand Central Station around here. You've been sitting here twenty minutes and you haven't seen a soul, let alone a* smoking *soul. Although, I guess you could always…* Something about the last thought made her stop: *souls.*

She looked up across the street and saw her answer; it had been staring at her the whole time.

A church, large and looming, rose above her like a broken chunk of cliff, equally solid and ragged. With two great stained glass windows on either side of the front door, it looked like the massive face of a yawning jack-o'-lantern waiting to consume its parishioners: the effect completed by the fact that the lights behind the windows flicked and flittered, making the eyes seem alive and watchful.

"Candles," said the girl with the pale face, dark hair, and button nose, and then she was up and crossing the street, not bothering to check for oncoming traffic, her eyes transfixed by the portentously gloomy gothic visage before her. And then stepping inside a moment later, she gave a silent *fuck you* to Duracell; this would have been a great time to listen to *Cemetery Gates.*

--

Looking around, she shivered. It wasn't cold in the church – quite the opposite in fact; the candles threw a warm glow over everything – every time she set foot in one of these places *(which admittedly, was few)* she felt a dirtiness wash over her. She knew that such places were not made for her. She was a tourist: it was like being shown a sink and soap and then being told you weren't allowed to wash. You look down at your hands and for the first time realize how unclean they are; better to stay away from sinks and soaps altogether then.

She glanced down the row of seats. *Pews? Is that what they're called? That doesn't sound right, can't be right. 'Pew' is the sound a blaster makes in Star Wars: pew! pew! pew! Or what kids say when something stinks; they pinch their fingers over their noses and say p-ew.* She was surprised to see that the church was empty, relaxed a little, then saw the altar. Dark and looming, it sat there at the front of the church like a heavy rectangular beast, waiting. She could never think of 'altar' without also thinking of 'sacrifice'. Did they always go together? She didn't know too much about the Catholic religion but she was sure she'd read something about fathers sacrificing their sons to their God. Wasn't that why they cut off the end of little boys dicks: some kind of sacrifice to God or Jesus or the Holy Ghost of Christmas Past?

Whatever, she thought, *just get the hell out of here; this place gives me the creeps big time.* She stuck two fingers into her bra, fishing around for the joint, and had just found it when she heard a creak behind her. She whirled, the hairs on the back of her neck standing up, her stomach tightening as though anticipating a punch.

Nothing. Empty pews, *pew! pew! pew!,* and an empty altar.

She stuck the joint between her lips, then moved over to the candle closest to the door. She wasn't going to smoke it in here *(though that would be pretty bitchin',* she thought), she was just gonna spark it and book. She leaned in, the tip of the joint tickling the flame *(like the fingers of God and that guy – David? No:*

Michelangelo? No: Adam? in that gay painting in Venice or Rome), when all of a sudden a voice rose up from behind her, deep and penetrating, it rumbled over the pews and rolled like magma across the stone floor, pushing on her lungs, stopping up her throat.

> *Your own…personal…Jesus*
> *Someone to hear your prayers*
> *Someone who cares*
> *Your own… personal…Jesus*
> *Someone to hear your prayers*
> *Someone who's there…*

She almost screamed, and would have if the air hadn't been sucked right out of her. Her mouth opened, and the joint dropped though not completely; it clung to her bottom lip, held only by half-dried spittle. It looked like a finger pointing down.

Her eyes tore behind her, up, down, searching for the source of that sound; was it coming from the altar? From the stones themselves? No, she knew better. There was only one place those words could be coming from.

Her eyes sought out the shadows, the dark places that light couldn't penetrate, the hollows of existence that ate everything contained within, but she saw nothing.

Her throat had gone dry and she swallowed hard once.

"Who's there?" she managed to cough, not realizing that she was echoing the last words she had heard, her voice cracking.

The response came immediately. A thump, a thunk, then over the edge of the nearest pew she saw a sneakered foot kick up, a flailing arm all the way up to the elbow, and finally a head rising into view, and she sighed with relief.

It was a boy – *well, a guy, her mind countered; boys wore Ninja Turtle T-shirts and had no hair on their balls. This one, well, too young to be a man, that's for sure, but a pretty good chance he's got fur on his nads* and he looked more scared of her than she was of him.

"Whaa tha-" he croaked as he pulled off his earphones. He steadied himself. Squinted. From his point of view the candles were behind her so all he could make out was her silhouette and bewildered eyes.

"Who is that?"

"Who is *that?*"

"Oh, cool: echo," he told her and then, cupping his hands around his mouth, yelled at the top of his lungs "I wanna be an air force ranger!" When no echo came back, he shrugged. "Must be broken."

She smiled, scared but intrigued. "Are you juiced? Someone's gonna hear that and come running."

He shook his head, causing his brown hair to flop down over his eyes. "Nah, the priest here is chill. Half deaf too. Bit gimpy. Even if he did hear anything it'll take him an hour to get here." He pointed at the girl. "I've seen you before."

The girl narrowed her eyes. "And I've seen you. You a Mode fan?"

"You've read my file," he replied with raised eyebrows. "Well, looks like we've seen each other then." He sprang up and over the pew, sitting on the edge of the back, his legs dangling over the side. He was grinning back at her like an idiot with a secret. "Come over here a second. I can hardly see you."

She stepped forward, remembering the joint still dangling from her lips. She pulled it off with one quick tug but it was stuck to her lips and took some skin with it; blood seeped through the cut and she let it sit there, liking the way it felt, the way it absorbed the drifting heat from the candles around her.

He flicked a finger at the joint in her hand. "You always get laced by yourself?"

She took another step forward. "What about you? Do you always hang out by yourself in empty churches?"

Jack stared at her, lowering his head and looking her directly in the eyes. "You got a mirror?"

She shrugged. "Touché."

"I know why I'm here. What are you doing-"

"Why *are* you here?"

Now it was Jack's turn to shrug. "I don't know. Running from religion."

"And a church is the best place to hide?"

He laughed. "Well, this is the last place God would ever expect to find *me*, right?"

She snapped her fingers. "Now I know. Aren't you that guy who was staring at me a couple days ago in-" she pursed her lips and drew a breath in " – I wanna say *science class?*"

Jack nodded, his teeth glowing through the slightest of grins. "Yes. And I think you wanna say-" he copied her gesture, pursing his own lips and drawing a breath in " – history class."

She snapped her fingers again sharply. "That's the one. I always confuse the two. History class is the one with the middle aged teacher whose boobs orbit somewhere around her knees."

Jack laughed. "Right, right, and science class is the one with the roided-up middle-aged teacher who *is* a boob and whose brain orbits somewhere around his crotch."

"Right."

"Right."

They stared at each other, admiring the way the guttering of the prayer candles pulled and punched sometimes freakish, sometimes beautiful shadows across their opposite faces. Jack finally dropped his eyes.

"Are you gonna smoke that doobie or what?"

She glanced down, surprised to see it still clutched between her fingers. Her gaze drew an arc around the church and she shrugged. "Now that I'm in here, I'm not so sure. It's a little weird."

"Nothing like some Catholic guilt to stop you from doing something you didn't think was wrong in the first place, huh?"

She laughed out loud, revealing a set of small fine white teeth. In the darkness, and the lapping shadows of the candles, they looked sharp, bestial.

"Yeah, I guess you're right. You know what they say, 'Give a hoot, take a toot.'

"I think it was 'don't pollute.'

"Whatever."

"So?"

"So…yeah, sure. You wanna join?"

Jack grinned. "Does a nun wear hairy underpants?"

--

Twenty minutes and one joint later.

The two lay in the cemetery like corpses, pressed to the earth, unmoving. There were no stars in the sky but there was a full moon and an overhanging tree branch absent of leaves sliced through it, cutting the glowing ball into a series of tiny broken chunks.

"Man, I could go for some Joy Division right now," said the girl, dreamily. The candle they had pilfered from the church flickered beside her and the shadows it created cut a line right down her face like a Batman villain.

"Tears for Fears," said Jack.

"Till Tuesday."

"Eurythmics."

There was a pause as they each floated with their thoughts, their heads ballooning with unlimited string, their bodies each a puddle of blood and bones and melting flesh. And at the same time they both said:

"Duran Duran."

They rolled on their sides to look at each other, propping their heads up with a palm and bent elbow.

"What's your name anyway?" the girl asked, her eyes half open, her eyes half closed.

"Jack," he said, and the word came out like a blade, stabbing, and she liked it. "What about you?"

"Jillian," she said, and the word rolled out with a velvet texture that made his ball sac tighten.

Jack smiled. "Jack and Jill huh?" Then he corrected himself. "Jilly."

"Jilly? That's a new one."

He nodded, convinced. "Jilly Jill."

"I like that," she said.

"Me too," Jack replied, then he rolled back supine and stared up at the giant glowing eye popping out of the black sky.

"Do you feel like we're being watched?"

Jillian shrugged. "I always feel like I'm being watched. I got used to it."

Jack frowned and tried to peer into the darkness to his left, his right, but after staring directly at the moon for so long all he could see were weird arcs of light, transparent yellow stars; the darkness was too complete to pierce.

"I think we're being watched."

Jillian narrowed her eyes at him and gave him a playful smile. "Maybe it's the ghosts."

"Now *that* I like," Jack said, and the idea of ghosts made him relax. He lay back down and breathed deeply. The grass beneath him tickled the back of his neck, or maybe it was bugs, he thought. *Bugs.* Maybe the very bugs that had eaten at some of these corpses around them, beside them, beneath them. It registered in his mind that he had a hard-on but he didn't care. He was too happy, too contented to worry or mind. He closed his eyes and thought some more about the bodies and their ghosts, his smile deepening.

That was how Jack Barber passed into friendship with Jillian Jarblonski.

--

It was three weeks later that Jillian came to Jack and asked him his thoughts on Mr. Wolfe, one of the three husks of self-proclaimed 'educators' that purported to teach religion at their high school.

Jack shrugged. "I know that his first name is Rudy, a name which I always thought should never have been invented."

"Anything else?"

Jack was trying – most unsuccessfully-to French inhale the *Marlboro* he was smoking. Jillian shook her head.

"You look like a retard trying to give head when you do that."

"No, tell me what you really think." Jack rolled his eyes, but he was smiling. Jillian reached over and tugged on his left ear; with her other hand she took the cigarette from his lips and placed it to her own, sucking on it deeply.

"You gotta exhale from the gut, not from the chest; otherwise you push it out too fast. You gotta let it *drift*." Smoke cascaded from over her lips like a waterfall defying gravity; her nose sucked it right up.

"Looks like you're snorting jizz when you do that," Jack told her, and Jillian nearly gagged.

"Exactly." Jack told her, a mischievous grin cut into his face.

Jillian shrugged, palms raised. "What does that even mean?"

Jack waved her away as he took back the cigarette. "Nothing. Nothing. What were you asking about?" He went back to attempting the French inhale and Jillian realized that she'd been wrong previously; he looked more like a goldfish attempting to swim backwards.

"Mr. Wolfe. I asked you about Mr. Wolfe. *Ruuu-dee.*"

"Ah yeah, the pedo."

"The what?"

"The pedo. He's the only teacher on staff who uses the student washrooms." His face wrinkled in recall. "Always tries to talk to me while I'm takin' a leak. All the guys think he's a pedo. There was this one time I was in the can and this big guy, I don't know his name, but everyone calls him Erik the Viking cause he's got this big thatch of wavy red hair, was standing at the urinal when-"

A shrill voice cut through the crisp air and Jack and Jillian both looked over. It was a woman in her early sixties walking her dog and from the looks of her clothes, and the perfectly groomed canine, Jack would have bet that she spent more money on that dog than most parents spend on their kids.

"Mitzy!" she was exclaiming in a high thin voice – it cut through the air like a tin blade – *"Mitzy don't eat that! It could be poison!"*

Jack and Jillian turned to look at each other, their eyes wide, grins already growing on their faces. Back to the woman. She was making frantic waving gestures, trying to shoo the dog away from whatever treat it had found in the grass. Jack didn't know much about canines but he was sure she hadn't got this one from the local SPCA.

"Mitzy no! Poison! That could be poison! Bad dog Mitzy, bad dog!"

Jillian shook her head. "I thought they only came out at night. Freaks that is."

"Must have given her a day pass," Jack said, and they both laughed. Jack waved away the crazy who was still going on about poison and stomach pumps. "But what's all this about Mr. Wolfe anyway? You got a thing for the guy?"

Jack's words knocked the grin off Jillian's face quick as a backhanded slap. "No."

"Hey, I was just kidding, I -" He stopped, and for the first time since they'd arrived at the park he really noticed Jillian's face; her eyes were red and glossy and her cheeks held the high ruddy sheen of a drunk Englishman. Her head shook back and forth as though disagreeing with an invisible ghost.

"Hey, hey, what's happening? What's wrong?"

"Guys a fucking cocksucker."

"Well, I don't doubt that, but what does that have to do with you?"

Jillian shook her head, her lip a tight curlicue. "Forget about it. It's nothing."

Jack suddenly remembered the first time he'd noticed Jillian, with that spider pressed between thumb and forefinger, and it struck him that girls like this didn't get upset very easily; a drama queen she was not. So if she was upset, then she had reason to be upset. He looked her dead-on; there was no smile on his face now.

"Tell me."

Jillian nodded. "It was yesterday. In religion class. Wolfe was going on about some Adam and Eve bullshit, Garden of Eden, sin of temptation, all that juicy stuff. God made the world in six days and on the seventh day he rested. That last bit got me. I mean, why the hell would *God* need a rest. He's *God.* How could an eternal being, all knowing, all-powerful, possibly get *tired.* So I asked Wolfe if God had to sleep." She shook her head. "I know I was kind of baiting him, but at the same time, I was actually curious. I'd never thought about it before."

"Wolfe looked at me like I was a shit stain on his tighty-whities, so I went on. I said it stands to reason that any creature that requires rest after working hard would also require some form of sleep. Not to mention food for that matter. And if he did sleep, who looked after the universe while he was passed out? And did he dream? Imagine how fucked up the dreams of *God* would be."

Jack pursed his lips. "Maybe that's how he cooked *us* up." His smile was back.

"The fucker just folded his arms and stared at me like I was making fun of him or something, which I was, of course, but wasn't at the same time. I mean its *religion* class for Christ's sakes; I gotta get *some* entertainment out of it."

"Anyway, he got mad. Said I was being obtuse. That I was being sacrilegious and he wouldn't stand for it in his classroom. I said that if he wanted to talk about being obtuse, how 'bout we sit down and see how well the creationism theory stands up to evolution. He responded by saying that we were living in hedonistic times, and if you wanted proof of that just look at the waning attendance of churches these days. *I* responded that that probably had something to do with the survival of the species; all the religious nuts were dying out, and being replaced by human beings capable of rational thought. He said that was blasphemy, and I said it was impossible to blaspheme against something that never existed in the first place – why not speak reverently of the boogeyman while you're at it, just in case – and then he told me he'd heard quite a bit enough of me for one morning, and that if I didn't shut my mouth and start acting like a decent human being, he was going to yak yak yak. Well to be honest, I was glad to be done with it, because I knew that if we kept on with things I was really going to say something I'd regret like how could he be so unenlightened to promote a religion where the figurehead was the number one supporter of the immolation of children, where women were treated as chattel and daughters could be sold to the highest bidder as warm fuck-puppets." Jillian shook her head.

"I would have given my left nut to hear you say that."

"Well, I didn't. I kept my mouth shut. Don't rock the boat, you know. I was ready to let things go, I *did* let things go. And just as I was settling back into a nice little daydream involving Wolfe's wrinkled testicles and a rusty jigsaw, I catch out of the corner of my eye, Amanda Delwood, absolutely *glaring* at me, jaw pushed out so far I half expected her to stick a corn-cob pipe between her teeth and tell me she *yams what she yams.*"

Jack shook his head. "Amanda Delwood?"

Jillian nodded. "She's our age. Blonde bitch. Buttons her blouse up to eleven, and always has a giant fuckin' 't' hanging around her neck. Looks like her legs wouldn't part even if Moses himself were waving his arms."

Jack shook his head, pursed his lips. "No idea," he said, and Jillian inwardly smiled; she'd found herself a good man here, a real good man.

"Anyway, so I see her staring at me like she's just caught me fellating her dog, and I turn to her and say 'Can I help you with something?' and you know what she says to me? You know what she has the brass fucking balls to say?"

"I'm sorry, I still have the *fellating her dog* image in my head. Has anyone ever told you, you need to tone down your similes?"

"You want me to tell you this story of not?"

Jack raised his hands in acquiescence. "Go on, go on. What did she say?"

"She called me a *non-believer.*"

Jack mock fainted. "That *bitch!*"

Jillian aimed a cocked hand straight at Jack. "Make fun all you want, but that's a *horrible* thing to say to someone. Now, if she had called me a heathen, I would have smiled pleasant as punch and gone back to my woolgathering. A *bitch* even. Hell, she could have called me a smelly whore and it wouldn't have bothered me, but a *non-believer.* No. I'm sorry. Those are fighting words."

Jack drew his lips into a thin tight line. "I think you need to re-evaluate your criteria for-"

"I *be-lieeeeve* in plenty of things. The fucking audacity, the bold-faced *ignorance* of someone accusing me of being a non-believer, just because I don't happen to believe in the things that *she* does is the epitome of self-centeredness and the absolute absence of thought."

"So what did you do?"

Jillian deflated, her eyes drooped, and she shook her head a fraction. "I called her something back."

"What did you call her?"

Jillian mumbled under her breath.

"What was that? I couldn't hear you."

She mumbled something again and Jack raised his hands, shook his head.

"Nothing but pops and buzzers. Sounded like you said… *'humpstin?'*"

Jillian mumbled something a third time, louder now but still unclear.

"Enunciate Jillian, e-nun-ci-ate."

"Cunt stain, cunt stain. I called her a cunt stain!"

Jack's face opened like a time-lapsed flower blossom, his mouth a perfect 'O', his eyes threatening to pop. He stayed like this for perhaps five seconds, then he rocked back in his seat, his face too cloyed with mirth to even allow a laugh to escape; he pounded his fists on his thighs.

"Cunt stain: I love it!" Tears ran down his cheeks. "How did you come up with that-I've never heard it before." He wiped at his right cheek with the back of his hand. "Cunt stain!"

Jillian shook her head. "It wasn't exactly a high-brow comeback."

"Still, I think it was great. So succinct! So… *ripe!*"

"Well, it got me so *busted.* Wolfe heard me, kept me after class." She stared at the ground for a few seconds, then slammed her fist into the picnic table.

"Fuck!" She winced in pain, raised the hand to her face, and saw that she'd hit the table hard enough to draw blood. Jack's laughter dropped like a hat thrown at a wall.

"Jesus Jilly, calm down. It's not that big a deal – what did he give you, detention or something?"

She shook her head. There were tears streaming down her face that had nothing to do with her bleeding hand.

"Yeah, he gave me detention." She was staring. "*Private* detention." She said it the way someone might say they'd just stepped barefoot into a steaming pile of dog shit. Jack watched her, his mouth closed, his eyes unmoving.

"That *fucker*," she went on. "Thinks he can touch me, eh. Thinks he can… because…" Her face crumpled and her body lurched forward like a puppet whose strings had been snipped. Jack caught her, held her, and she spoke into his shoulder.

"He came up to me while I was doing some bullshit writing assignment he'd given me. I didn't realize he was so close until I heard his breath, this low wheezing sound, like an old man at an aspirator. Then I looked up and saw that he was standing right over me. He moved closer until his crotch was flush with the desk, then he kind of pressed himself closer. 'You're out of uniform,' he said, and at first I was so surprised at how he'd snuck up on me without hearing him that I was taken aback. I looked down and wondered what the hell he was talking about because I'm *in* my uniform. And I tell him so and he's like, 'But it's not quite up to code,' and he's staring down at me, and I'm suddenly aware of the fact that his crotch is less than a foot from my hand so I pulled it back, put it in my lap because…" Jillian's head was shaking, her eyes analyzing a dead patch of grass on the ground. Without warning her head rose, and she looked Jack dead in the eyes; to Jack it was like looking into two mirror image pools, both of which were being molested by rain.

"…because I'm not a whore," she finally said, the last word coming out *who-ur*. I don't sleep around, especially not for grades in a subject that means less than nothing." Jack, who hadn't so much as kissed Jillian yet, nodded.

"I believe you."

"I know you do," Jillian replied without missing a beat, and for that Jack kind of wished he *had* kissed her.

"So what happened?"

"So he's staring down at me with this look on his face like...like...I don't know. But no matter what it was that look itself should be illegal. There was nothing but *greed* and *take* in that look."

"What did he do?" Jack was no gossiper, he didn't care for the lowdown, the scoop or any other pathetic synonym you could come up for the common snoop. He just wanted to know what had happened to his friend so that he would know how to react. So that he could quantify his hate.

She shrugged. "He told me I was missing a button. I thought he meant that one of my buttons had popped off my shirt, but no. As soon as I looked down-" her lips pulled back in recall, her teeth bared in a half-snarl "- he leaned in. Said he would do it for me. I didn't know what was happening. For a second-I don't know why-I thought he was going to strangle me. Then he had his fingers on the buttons of my shirt, and he was pushing that little knob of plastic into the hole, and I sat there, unable to move, unable to speak, frozen with disbelief. And then just as he was finishing the last button – he'd done them right up to my chin – his hand dipped, and he cupped my tit."

Jack watched as Jillian's head tilted and she glanced down at the offending gland as though somehow *it* were to blame, and he knew that if he handed her a machete at that moment she would gladly hack it off with one swift swipe. But then he realized his mistake; he saw it in her eyes. She wasn't seeing her own breast, not at all; she was seeing the handprint that lay against it. Seeing the grease or the grime, like one of those black lights that reveals everything, that records all manner of touch and taint, and he wondered if she would ever be able to *un*see it.

"He didn't even try to hide the fact that he'd done it. There was no 'oops.' No 'sorry.' There was just the bony flesh of his hand on my left tit, gripping. And then you know what the bastard did? You know what he had the goddamn balls to do?" Her lip looked ready to crumble; it warbled with the show of a muscle spasm. "He fucking *squeezed.* Do you believe that? A touch wasn't enough; he had to fucking squeeze."

Her jaw gave way, betraying her as it dropped open and a great mess of spittle drooled out and distended from her face, creating a tiny pool of saliva on the dirtied surface of the picnic table and for a second she was linked, her face to the dirt by the fine gossamer threads of spit. She had no more words.

Jack stared at this girl in front of him, her bloodshot eyes in stark contrast to her pale skin, her black hair, and he thought that she had never looked more beautiful than she did right now. He took her hands in his.

"But you know what's really fucked up? It's not that he…*assaulted* me. I hate that word. Makes it sound like he bashed me over the skull with a fucking crowbar. No, what *really* bothers me is the reason. I mean, he's not the first guy in my life to try and take a squeeze at my tits, but it's the reason…the fucking reason he chose me to…*FUCK!*" she cried out, and the woman with her dog still a good fifty feet away shot a disparaging glance back, pulled tight on the dog's leash yanking it away as if the word itself was the poison she'd been talking about earlier.

"What's the reason?"

Jillian glared at Jack, her eyes cutting through the hair in front of her face.

"You know."

Jack shook his head. "No, I don't know. Tell me." He grabbed her wrist.

"I told you already."

If it were any other girl talking like this, Jack would have called it mind games and booked, but not with Jillian, no. If she was beating around the bush, then she had her reasons. He thought about it and after a few seconds it came to him. His mouth curled into a half snarl and he looked down; the answer was in his hands. His thumbs caressed the scars and she didn't flinch.

"You got it," she said, and now the tears were back and her jaw pressed out. "I saw him staring at them a couple of weeks ago. I thought he was looking over my shoulder to make sure that I was doing the assignment, but then I looked up and saw the direction of his gaze and I knew. I knew. He was so interested in the scars that he didn't realize I had stopped writing, that I was staring right up into his face. I watched as he turned his head to the side, ever so slightly, and licked his lips. Just once, tip of the tongue working at the bulge of flesh; it made me think of snail meat being wet by the rain."

Tears had formed two parallel lines on Jillian's pale face but if she noticed, if she knew they were there, she gave no indication. She talked in the voice of one reading a passage from a math theorem textbook.

"So he figured he'd got me. I mean, who's going to believe a basket case suicide, over a respected man of the teaching cloth. It's classic. The whole fucking scene is a goddamn cliché."

"But you're not. Jillian. You're not a cliché, *I* believe you."

"Whatever."

"You're a survivor, remember. We talked about it. Most people's bodies would have given up, deflated, left their souls in the lurch. Yours marched on, stood tall, kicked physics in the balls and ate logic for lunch. You are literally *living proof*."

Jillian sighed, exhaled. Wiped the tear tracks with her forearm. "I guess."

"You're stronger than you know Jillian. You just have to give yourself the chance to prove it."

"And I bet you're the guy to show me the way, huh?"

Jack smiled. "I'm the guy to try."

"Okay," Jillian said, "Okay." Jack's smile was infectious, and she sent one back.

"Bastard gave me real detention for all next week though. You believe the audacity of the motherfucker. Cops a feel and *then* gives me detention. That's gonna be exciting."

"At least you won't be alone."

"Yeah, sure, they'll be twenty other losers there too witless enough not to have gotten caught."

"Ahh, getting caught doesn't always have to do with a lack of intelligence. They call it 'dumb luck' for a reason you know. And there's good luck, and bad luck."

"Well if it wasn't for bad luck...you know how the saying goes."

"We found each other didn't we? I'd say that was pretty lucky."

"Agreed. Agreed."

"But when I said you wouldn't be lonely, I didn't mean you'd be hanging with strangers. I'll be there too."

Jillian started. "You? What did you do?"

Jack threw a careless shrug. "I'll think of something."

Across the park they heard that shrill voice rise up once again. "Mitzy, that was *poison!* You ate *poison!* Now I'll have to take you to the doctors to have your stomach pumped!"

Jack frowned. He could feel a headache coming on.

"But I don't think we can let this one slide Jillian," he said, trying to ignore the unwelcome throb that had begun pulsing in his head. "We can't let this bastard get away with this."

"I was hoping you would say that," Jillian replied as she curled her fingers over Jack's hands.

"Did you have something in mind?"

"Mitzy no, that's poison! You're eating poison!"

"I'll think of something." Her echo of Jack's sentiment from seconds ago was unintentional. Her face was blank, and pale, and unmoving.

Her fingers, round his, tightened.

2010

John's face was mathematically serious as he packed, weighing everything in his mind, the size, the volume; how much he could fit in the trunk of his car? He wasn't going to stick around and wait for more photographs to arrive, no; he was going to make like a librarian and *book*. At one point, passing Arabelle's room, he noticed the lines on the walls where he and his wife had scored pencil marks to record the growth of their daughter. It was one of many things he realized that he would have to leave behind. He reached out and touched them, ran his finger first from the highest mark *(just three weeks ago!)* to the bottom one, drawn the day Arabelle had managed to stand on her own for the very first time. His eyelids dropped while his thumb continued to caress the surface of the wall. It struck him that with his eyes closed he couldn't even tell that there was anything there as if the growth of his daughter was an illusion. After he left, whoever assumed the house would undoubtedly paint over those marks, and then they would be gone forever.

Images of the house flicked through his mind. His study where he worked and paid his bills. The corner of the backyard where he had planned on putting in a small above-ground swimming pool. The furnace that always gave three dry coughs to signal that it was kicking on. His workroom where he kept his tools. The screwdrivers, the drills.

The Hammer.

(The hammer, the hammer, oh God how many times had he held that hammer high, then brought it down?)

- an electric knife caked with black gore

(It was flesh.)

- Two moons of white lying on the table,

(They were eyelids John, they were someone's eyelids.)

Tears came then, burning his face, and the acid in his stomach churned harder, faster; he imagined it burning right through, eating at his guts, chewing through his flesh like an alien parasite, breaking him in two.

No, he demanded, *no. You have to keep it together. You have to keep your shit together. For Arabelle-*

A memory suddenly hit him, the night his wife told him that she was pregnant *(only she said 'We're pregnant," not "I", that was when you knew it was for real, that you two were in it together, forever).* John had asked what they were going to call it. Karen looked down, rubbed her still totally flat belly and said: "It's a girl, I'm sure it is, a girl, and if it is, I want to call her Arabelle," John laughed and asked her "Are you giving birth to a baby or to a freakin' Disney character?" Karen laughed even louder than John had and slapped him playfully on the chest and then they both hugged, and kissed, and then more...

A thought came to him that was somehow worse than all those delivered photographs combined because the things those photos depicted were past, they were done. But the thought was now. The thought was a fact.

You never paid for your crimes John. *You had nightmares for years afterwards, and sweated your way through a lot of bed sheets, but you never* really *paid for what you did.* His eyes drifted over again to the marks on the walls, the lines that marked the growth of his only child, conceived together and nourished in the womb of his dead wife.

But you will, he thought, *you will.*

His face crumpled then and his body slumped against the wall, pressing into it as though trying to pass right through it. He didn't move for a long, long time.

When he finally opened his eyes some minutes – *hours?!* – later the first thing he saw was a large wooden 't'. He blinked several times to clear his vision, then looked again. He sighed. It was a crucifix, and it hung silently just above Arabelle's bed. He didn't believe in religion – he didn't really believe in anything for that matter – but Karen had been raised Catholic and after her death he had never had the heart to take it down. Now, as he stared at it, something in his mind began to form, to take shape. He could feel it coming to him, inevitable, like a sneeze preparing to explode. And then it was there.

The 't'. The cross. Not the cross of the crucifixion, but the universal sign for pharmacy. John stared at it, reveling in the simplicity of the design and he felt himself calming. Breathing easy. *Two lines intersecting. Joining in the middle.*

You met them in a pharmacy that first time, remember? It was an ordinary day of you waiting calmly by the pharmacists counter until some old lady with glasses so thick she could look at a globe and see people waving came by and asked the pharmacist for help. And as soon as he stepped away from behind his counter you would be off, straight to the back, third shelf on your left, and then filling your pockets with Percocets and sneaking out again before the pharmacist even knew he'd been robbed. But things turned out a little different that day, didn't they? The store was unusually quiet – no grey haired grannies to be seen – and you were about to give up, to come back another day, when you overheard the couple in the next aisle talking about poisons and punishment and your interest was piqued and what a surprise – and great coincidence – when you stepped around the corner to put faces to their conspiring voices…and you recognized them. You didn't know their names but you'd seen them around. Once while taking night photos in the cemetery you found them stretched across some broken crumbling grave and you watched them for an hour or more, and though you couldn't hear them, only the soft occasional murmur of voiced thoughts, you liked them for the fact that they seemed so comfortable together, that they preferred to hang out in cemeteries instead of at the local roller-rink or record shop like your average cookie-cutter teenager. Then you saw them a second time, a week or so after, down at Ashburn Park, sitting on the grass on Homeless Hill, *so named because it was the local hotspot for junkies to spike their veins and bums to tipple their various poisons. She was blowing smoke rings, and he was punctuating them with a single poked finger right through the hole and then he tried to stick his entire arm through and the ring disappeared and they both laughed like the world was on fire. Something inside you shifted and it wasn't because she was beautiful, which she was, and he had a confident handsomeness to him you associated with professional dancers, which he did, but rather what existed* between *them, or more accurately, what* didn't *exist between them, namely: tension. They were totally open to each other, completely exposed and the feeling this created in you was not jealousy but rather a simple* want. *A void was revealed, just a glimpse of it, but a glimpse enough to let you know that it was there. Now here they were again, standing just feet away in a pharmacy and for the first time you saw how pitch black her hair really was – like a black hole in the shape of an inverted horseshoe – and the veins stood out on his bare arms like thick cables buried just below the surface of the earth. You didn't think about it, you didn't hesitate at all. Back then, when the thought of approaching a stranger, let alone two beautiful strangers, would have wrung a cold sweat from your skin and sent your heartbeat into overdrive, approaching these two seemed like the most natural thing in the world because this was fate – it was after all the third time, the charm! – and you walked right over to them and without pause asked –*

1989

"**N**ow when you talk about poisoning, are you talkin' about putting a turbo-booster on their shit cycle, or are you talkin' about something-" he dropped his voice to a low whisper " – more permanent?"

Jack's eye narrowed, screwed in on the guy standing before them. Tall and gaunt with dark greasy hair, he reminded Jack of a sideshow mechanic. He wasn't wearing overalls, but Jack felt that he ought to be. He gritted his teeth, not liking the fact that someone had been eavesdropping on their conversation and he was about to make a motion to Jillian when he saw that she was grinning. He took another glance at the guy, all the way from toe to top, and immediately assessed that he could take the kid in a fight. Jack never fought, not if he could help it, but it was always good to know.

"What's it to yah?"

John shrugged, the bones in his shoulders rising to give him a vulture like appearance and his eyes dropped to the bottle Jack was holding in his hand. They immediately flashed back to Jack.

"Nothing, nothing at all. But you should know that if you're planning on using *that* to make someone refund their lunch, it has a very discernible taste; put it in someone's drink and all it would take was a sip of it, a whiff even, to know that something was wrong. So assuming you wanted your little" – he coughed lightly – "surprise to *remain* a surprise, I would suggest putting that stuff back on the shelf."

Jack raised his palms. "What do you work here or something?"

John shook his head. "No, I've just always been fascinated with the idea that all these things here-" he reached over and tapped a few of the boxes of pills on the shelves, knocking several of them absently onto the floor in the process and apparently not caring a whit "-are all designed to help us, to heal us, *but*, take enough of them, or take them in the wrong combination and…"

"And you're strummin' a harp in heaven," finished Jillian.

"Or squeezing an accordion in hell," Jack added

John nodded, wagging a finger at Jack: "And Bingo was his name-o."

Jillian's eyes were moving from Jack to this new kid and back again. "So what would you suggest?"

John scratched at his upper lip on which there sprouted a few tiny shoots of blonde hair, thinking. He nodded.

"Well, assuming you don't want to kill anyone-" and here came the slightest of pauses that suggested he was assuming just the opposite " – and that you simply want to make them…suffer?"

"Go on." Jillian was grinning. She liked this guy already and she could tell that Jack was warming to him too.

"Well, there's a little ditty known as syrup of ipecac, also called Brazil Root. Got a sugary-sweet taste to it. Dump it in someone's Coke, and they probably wouldn't even notice. It's not gonna kill anybody – Karen Carpenter aside – but its gonna turn his insides out, that's for sure."

"That'll get him sick? Puking?" Jillian leaned forward, her hands bunched together tightly.

"The next best thing would be gagging him with a spoon." John shrugged. "But of course for *that* you'd have to get close to him. With this you can watch from a distance. Less splatter on your clothes that way. Not my style exactly, but hey, some say to*may*toe, some say to*mah*toe. Personally, I'd like to smell the bile. Just to know it was real."

Jack was watching this new guy carefully, one of his eyes screwed tighter than the other. At the guy's last crack, Jack finally smiled, nodding.

"Sometimes close is better." For the first time their eyes met, locked, and for a full ten seconds neither of them moved. Jillian stood off to the side, watching, believing that if she listened carefully and long enough she would actually hear the thoughts that were passing between them, like the hum of a live wire been brought low during an ice storm.

Jack finally nodded and for Jack to nod at a stranger, well, it was most people's equivalent to a hug.

"We'll just grab a bottle of that stuff and head out then," Jack said, reaching up to the shelf to pick up a box.

"Already taken care of," Johnny told him, and as he said so his hand passed over the left pocket of his jeans the way the shadow of a plane passes over a farmer's field.

This kid's got skills, Jack thought, and he smiled. They began making their way out of the pharmacy and Jack thought to himself, more deeply this time, *this kid's got skills.* He hadn't seen the bottle disappear and it had been right in front of his face. He suddenly wanted to say thanks, *needed* to say thanks. Jack wasn't a man who took on debts easily but he was overcome by a guttural requirement to acknowledge his new friend's help. And then his thought process doubled back and he realized he had used the word 'friend' and he wondered, *how could that be?* I just met him. But there was something there. Yes, there was something there. A snippet of the *Mode* floated by him:

Vows are spoken...to be broken
Feelings are intense...words are trivial
Pleasures remain...so does the pain
Words are meaningless...and forgettable
All I ever wanted
All I ever needed
Is here in my arms...

Without thinking, Jack looked down at his own arms. He saw the popping veins looking as excited and disconsolate as ever; they always seemed ready and more than willing to burst right out of his skin, like that marionette scene in *Elm Street 3*. There was a warmth on them and he saw that Jillian had placed her fingers in the crook of his right elbow. Not her hand – not all that – just the fingertips, they played on his skin like someone running their nail over the grooves of a vinyl record to create that *ziiiiiiip* sound. Without thinking, he reached up and patted this new kid on the shoulder, his hand staying there a few seconds longer than it had to because he wanted to really *feel* this guy, and for the kid to feel him. For the first time the three were linked, flesh to flesh to flesh.

Once outside they talked. John waited until they were a safe distance away from the pharmacy before he fished the bottle out of his pocket and handed it to Jillian. They smoked a cigarette together, then another, then another. Toward the end of the third one – what each of them sensed would be the last – John became quiet and didn't speak again until that last butt had been crushed by the heel of his shoe. All of a sudden he seemed shy and unsure. When he spoke, he looked neither of them in the eye.

"I got my old man's car tonight. You guys wouldn't want to go for a drive with me would you?"

He still couldn't look either of them in the eye and it occurred to him to question the world they lived in in which people felt ashamed about admitting – or providing direct evidence – that they liked another person. That they thought another person was rad.

For a minute no one said anything; it was too much like asking someone on a date and John braced himself for the inevitable *no.*

"It's got air conditioning," he added, and it wasn't until the words were out of his mouth that he realized it was probably the lamest thing anybody had ever said in the history of the civilized world.

The reaction was immediate. Jack laughed. He laughed loud and he laughed hard and right at the moment when John was on the cusp of mentally cutting himself for sounding like such a loser, he felt a strong arm around his shoulder gripping him, pulling him tight and Jack's warm breath pulsing into his ear. A glance to his right showed him that Jack also had Jillian gripped in a similar hug, and his head was thrown back so far it made John think of a can just opened, still hanging by a slice of tin.

"We're in," Jack told him, and he jiggled Jillian roughly but playfully in his arm; she squirmed, protested with a loud squeal, but was laughing all the while. "And don't worry about the air conditioning fellah – we'll keep the windows open." He was still laughing as they made their way over to the car, opened the doors, and found their way inside.

John paused in the driver's seat before starting the car. He was chewing on his lower lip. Finally he spoke.

"I don't know if you guys are interested but I kinda had this plan to-"

Jack cut him off with a raised palm. "We're following you kid. Surprise us."

And surprise them he did.

--

After nearly three hours of driving around, smoking cigarettes and listening to *Siouxsie and the Banshees* and a *Tears for Fears* album, Jack and Jillian were surprised when they finally got out of the car and walked up to the gate; there was a small sign denoting the name of the company, (*'Mendoza's Meats,'* was all it said in plain six-inch lettering) and a large sliding gate locked with a chain and a padlock. They turned when they heard Johnny slam the trunk and watched as he materialized out of the dark, the beam of his flashlight pointed upward. It perverted his face, elongated the shadows and deleted his nose altogether. His eyes were two deep puddles, his skin tawny as though jaundiced, his already thin face seemed stretched. He had a bag flung over his shoulder and a schoolboy's grin on his lips.

Jack motioned to the gate with his own flashlight, the one Johnny had given him when he got out of the car; "That things gotta be eight feet high. How are we gonna-" but Johnny silenced him with a raised palm. He spun the flashlight around in his hand and slid the barrel into his mouth. With his now free hands he fished around in his pockets and a second later came out with two tiny tools. Then he was at the lock.

"Hzzzrphhhh rrrsezzeee," he said in a half turn, nodding.

"Huh?"

Johnny removed the flashlight from his mouth, wiped away the saliva, and repeated. "Jacobson three-sixty." He laughed. "Why didn't they just lock it with a rubber band?"

Jillian and Jack glanced at each other; they shrugged, smiled, and turned back to this boy.

With the flashlight back in his mouth he dropped to his knees and began working on the lock with his tools. In less than two minutes there was a click and the length of chain fell limp as a piece of overcooked spaghetti. The wheels groaned as Johnny slid the gate open a couple of feet, affording just enough berth for the three to enter. Then he closed it back up, re-wrapped the chain through the fence and re-hooked the lock without actually clicking it home.

"In case someone comes by," he explained. He turned and motioned to the dark road ahead leading to the house of slaughter.

"Shall we?"

Jack was staring at his new companion. "Where'd you learn to do that?"

Johnny raised his shoulders as if to say he had no idea, as if the required skills for B & E were common knowledge, picked up in Home Ec. class, but then he explained.

"My family's from Hungary. I've been told that we're a curious lot, particularly when it comes to science and how things work." He pursed his lips. "I don't know how true that is, but I've worked in a hardware store since I was ten. Electrical stuff. Plumbing. Paints. I don't know, tools always made sense to me." His eyes shifted between Jack and Jillian. It was hard to tell in the darkness without actually sticking the flashlight directly in his face, but Jack had a strong feeling that Johnny was blushing, and that made Jack like him even more.

"Renaissance man huh?"

"I'm just interested in how things work."

Jillian coughed. "And speaking of how things work, why the hell would they put this building so far away from the road? It looks like it's about a quarter of a kilometer up the way here."

Both men turned to look at her; her hair was so black it disappeared in the night, turning her face into a floating mask, a specter in the dark. She wasn't really expecting an answer but Johnny gave her one.

"It's a psychological thing. People driving by hear the sounds of screaming animals, braying of bovine, the snorting of swine, and they're reminded of the fact that those burgers they so fancifully fry come from actual living creatures. It seeps into their consciousness the way I'm sure the black blood of those creatures has invaded every crack and crevice of the building itself. It's a structure of death, like the gas showers of Auschwitz, the incineration plants of Treblinka, and it gives birth to guilt. And when given the choice between guilt and ignorance, people will choose ignorance every time. The world is so much less cruel and death-dealing when eyes are closed."

Jillian was watching him carefully. "And which do you prefer?"

"My eyes are wide open," he said, matter-of-factly. "Death is life and vice versa, one is a beginning and one an end. The only difference really is that one happens first and the other follows. If we had to die *before* being born then people's views on death would be a whole lot different."

"I take it you're not a religious fellow."

Johnny shook his head. "I take my hat off when I walk into a church, but I don't kneel for anyone. Like I said, my eyes are wide open."

Suddenly his face distorted, crumpled in on itself in disgust; he smelled something, and it wasn't a fistful of daisies. A second later Jillian's and Jack's did the same thing. Jillian actually gagged.

"And that's the other reason they keep these damn things so far from the street." He shook his head. "They stink worse than fresh shit."

Jillian shook her head. "I don't know if I can go any closer." The stench was so thick her eyes were beginning to water. The gourd was rising in her throat like a ball in a toilet tank.

"You'll get used to it," Johnny said.

And then he was moving forward, adjusting the strap of his camera bag as he went.

--

A little five-fingered prestidigitation by Johnny and they were inside the factory. He winked at them. "You sure you guys wanna do this? This ain't the teacup ride at Disneyland."

Jillian faked concern: "You mean we won't get any cotton candy at the end? Heavens to Betsy, *nooo!*"

Jack pouted. "And I wanted to get my picture taken with *Great Mouse Detective.* Can we at least ride The Matterhorn?" He crossed his arms in an exaggerated expression of defiance.

Johnny showed his teeth. "No, you most certainly can not. Actually, it's more like The Haunted Mansion. Well, if The Haunted Mansion happened to be dunked in five-thousand gallons of fishing chum and pumped full of dead animal farts. But-" he raised his arms and shoulders " – c'est la vie!"

Jillian laughed. She couldn't remember when she'd had such a good time, she really couldn't. *Ironic,* she thought, *that being in a house of death should make me feel so alive.*

And actually, her mind went on as she followed the sway of Jack's flashlight down into the corners, up into the rafters, and zigzagging across the walls, *it really* does *feel like it's haunted. I mean, when you think of all the death, the absolute* tide *of murder that occurred here...well, it would be a little nuts if there weren't a few unhappy souls floating around these corridors. Animals or not, when you still a half million or so beating hearts a year, and bleed out how many million gallons of blood, well that's gotta leave a trace of something behind, and I ain't talkin hard to scrub stains. I'm talkin'* presence. *A wraith of butchery. A full —*

"Moooooo!"

Jillian laughed and screamed at the same time, slapping at Jack on the shoulders, on the chest, on his arms.

"Asshole," she told him, but she was shaking her head and her nose was pinched in a vain attempt to hold back a smile.

"Sorry love, couldn't help it, you looked so utterly daydreamy there for a second, I had to break the spell."

Jillian rolled her eyes, then looked around, concerned. "Where'd Johnny go?"

"Turn on the lights. Somewhere over there," he said, indicating with his flashlight the general direction to the left.

"Funny, for a guy who said he's never been here before he knows a lot about this place."

"That's because I never said I'd never been here before." The voice came from Jillian's right, was spoken directly in her ear, and made her jump a full foot and a half forward.

"Stop *doing* that!" she shouted, a throaty laugh giving a push to the reprimand. She pointed an accusing finger at him. "And you did so." She turned to Jack. "Jack, am I right?"

Jack's eyes narrowed. "Sorry, I left my stenographer at home. I'll have to take his word."

"I *saaaaid,* that I'd never been here *with* someone before. Meaning, you guys were the first. But as it so happens, I know all about this place."

Jillian's shuffling fingers were caught in the beam of the flashlight. "Details please."

"My uncle Mikey worked here for years, my dad's brother. Me and him were close, he told me everything there is to know about this place."

"Everything?"

"Everything."

"Such as?"

Johnny held out three taut fingers in front of Jillian's face. "Three. Two. One." He raised a gunned hand high above his head and pointed at the ceiling which exploded in a blaze of thousand-watt incandescent light. Jillian and Jack both recoiled, shielding themselves with bent elbows.

"Such as the fact that the lights take exactly one minute twenty-one seconds to warm up." He took off his camera bag, fished around inside it, and brought out an old Nikon 35mm. No longer needing his flashlight, he dropped it into the bag; Jack followed suit and threw his in too.

"Just leave these by the door for safekeeping," Johnny said as he kicked the bag aside. Then he took a step forward, swung the camera strap over his neck, and raised his hands up like a preacher at an Alabamy tent revival.

"Lay-deeees and gennamen – let there be light!"

Jillian whooped. Jack let out a *yip! yip! yip!*

Johnny stomped on the spot. "Now ladies and gents, cannae gettah *wooooahhh carcass?*"

"Woooooahhhh *carcass!!*"

"I can't hear yah." He slapped his hands together three times, flesh on flesh, and each one was the crack of a bullwhip.

"Now cannae gettah *bathed in blooood?*"

"*Bathed in bloooood!!*" Jack and Jillian's voices rose in revelry, coming back to them in echo.

"Now one more time, can I get a, '*This is ma*-aye *body, and this is ma*-aye *blooooood!*

Once more they followed suit, repeating the proclamation, their voices rising drunk and free in the vast private space that was now theirs, theirs and no one else's, Jillian's voice high and wild, Jack's low and throttled with the unmistakable power of youth.

"*This is ma*-ayyye *body, and this is ma*-ayyyyeee *blooooood!!*" Jillian let loose a piercing *yayayayayayayayaya!!* scream; high-pitched and unyielding.

For a moment they paused, glancing at one another the way satisfied participants in an orgy might regard their recent partners after all orgasms had been pumped out, all coital contractions quelled.

Johnny stood in the middle of them both, a smile a mile wide on his face, his eyes the bright whites of an asylum resident high on his pleasure. He held out his hands; it didn't occur to him that he'd known these two less than four hours. He'd seen them. He'd heard them.

They were the best friends he'd ever had.

He held out his hands, and they each took one; he turned from one to the other.

"Now, who wants a front row seat to stare death right between the eyes?"

It was a perfect question, perfect in its honesty and lack of taint. There were no pretenses, and that was a rare enough thing in this world to render it divine.

They skipped to the next room like wild Indians heading home from a massacre both vicious and victorious.

--

The first room they came to was so sterile it seemed a parody. About a thousand white coats lined end to end, one row on top of the other.

"What is this, Jesus' walk-in closet?" Jack asked, but Johnny shook his head, gesturing to the opposite wall.

"Look at the helmets."

Jack and Jillian did; there were rows and rows of white hard-hats, and a single row of yellow.

"The yellow ones are for the supervisors. The rest: the peons," Johnny explained. "You guys might want to grab one of those jackets. It's gonna be a cold one." He went over and took the first coat off the rack, slid into it. It hung large on his skinny frame but it didn't look out of place. Jack and Jillian put on their own coats.

"And now for the main attraction," Johnny announced, gesturing to a lone door awaiting them opposite the one they had entered by.

"I feel like Alice going down the rabbit hole," Jillian told Jack as they moved forward.

"Well remember to feed your head," Jack returned, opening the door and waving her through.

Johnny was right behind them.

--

Kids entering candy stores couldn't have had more obvious expressions on their faces. From the moment they stepped into the room, their jaws dropped, their eyes widened and their gait slowed. The temperature plunged a good twenty degrees, cold enough to render their breath into something visual; puffs of cloud burst out of their mouths and floated across the room. And the room was glorious.

Metal and flesh; those were seemingly the only two elements that comprised the world that was this vast *chamber*. Bodies hung one after the other like some great closet of death. The animals were so perfectly sliced and with such precision that the rib bones looked like giant zippers opened wide to reveal the mutilated genitals of some alien form.

Jack did a quick calculation. "There are over four hundred corpses in here," he announced. "That's like ten tons of pork. Jesus Christ."

Johnny nodded. "Jesus Christ is right. Imagine this business if the Jews and Muslims ate pork too."

Jack moved closer to Jillian, who was caressing one of the carcasses lovingly.

"What strange hunks of flesh they are," she told him when she realized that he was beside her. "Look at the colors. I mean the pink and the reds are obvious, but the blacks too. Greys the color of angry rolling clouds. And look at these blues, right here. So deep. Solid."

Jack touched it with her, their hands rubbing the flesh in unison.

"I see what you mean. These aren't the colors you usually associate with food. I mean the color itself makes it look like something not fit for consumption. Looks more like something you'd discover in an abandoned field with a splintered baseball bat beside it."

If Jillian heard him, she gave no indication. She was still lost in her dream.

"No," she said, her voice soft and trance-like. "This is the color the ocean would be if you were drowning in it." Jack looked at her when she said that and he didn't know if it scared him or satisfied him to see how deeply involved she was with the flesh. At that moment he wished he had his own camera, to record these two beauties together, woman and beast, life and death. He turned to Johnny who, seemingly reading Jack's mind, was fiddling the focus ring on his camera.

"You got color film in that camera?"

Johnny shook his head. "I only shoot black and white."

"Gods and Monsters." It came out of Jillian's mouth in a dreamy jetsam.

Both boys turned to look at Jillian.

"What was that?"

"They look like monsters now, skinless, hairless, all sinew and bone. But one can imagine that when they were alive, before man came along and murdered them, they were gods. Veritable gods. And we kill them to eat them, we destroy these gods for food. Human carnivores: the accepted social disease…"

"I think they're the most beautiful things I've ever seen," Johnny said, as he aimed his camera at the row of dead beasts, focused, and clicked the shutter home. "And I love the fact that now, even in death…" he tapped the camera with a single nail "they'll live forever in film."

The next room they entered solved the mystery as to where all the pigskin had gone. Great coats of skin, like rinds of some old eaten fruit, hung in sheets one after the other. The color was strange, a yellow-rosy hue like drying snot, and all along the seams there was writing, actual writing that looked like it had been scribed with lipstick. Indecipherable foreign symbols that solidified the fact that these once living things, were now just products in the great Ford assembly line of Food America.

Beyond these hanging skins were a vast series of what looked to be wooden gymnastic horses, lined row after row like dominoes, and draped over each horse, were more pigskins laid flat. With all insides removed- but all the legs, faces and heads still intact – it looked as though each pig had been stepped flat

"Look's like Leatherface's porn stash," Jack said just as Johnny was about to snap another pic, and Johnny laughed so hard he accidentally triggered the shutter and had to take another one.

Moving along, the trio came to a room that contained the largest, most complicated series of conveyor belts, roller wheels, and pulley systems any of them had ever seen.

Jillian marveled. "It looks like a life-size version of *Mousetrap,* only about a thousand and one times more complicated," she said.

Johnny nodded. "This is the internal room, so named because it's where all the *parts* come to get sorted out."

"The *parts?*" Jillian asked, stepping forward.

"Yeah, you know, the gizzards, the lungs, the hoofs, the eyeballs, the anal cavities, that kind of stuff."

Jack laughed. "I hope they don't mix any of those up."

Johnny shrugged. "No big deal if they do. Half of it ends up in the same place anyways."

"And where might that be?" Jillian looked concerned but Johnny only laughed and began walking forward in an exaggerated goose step. Then with one hand cupped around his mouth he advertised:

"Getchur hawt *daaaawgs!* Getchur hawt *daaaawgs!* Getchur nothin' but lips-and-assholes-beaks-and-belly-button-private parts-of-horses hawt *daaaawgs. "*

Jillian shook her head. "Grody."

"You asked."

The next room was very similar to the first; cow carcasses hung as the pig corpses had from hooks as thick as a human neck, exposed spines rolled up and down the torsos like miniature roller coasters. The floors were surprisingly clean, no traces of blood and not a buzzing fly to be found.

"Imagine the dinner party you could have with this meat," Jack mused, amazed by the sheer quantity of it all.

"In this fucked up place?" Jillian asked, "yeah, right. I can see the invitations now: *You are cordially invited to dinner and the end of the world.* Please bring your own kill-bib, and only those with bone saws will be able to partake in dessert."

Jack was laughing. "True, true. And I suspect the cold might be a bit of a turn off as well."

"The cold keeps the bugs away," Johnny explained. "Not too many bugs fancy sub-zero temperatures. And the floors are cleaned more rigorously than most guys clean their dicks. Blood stains easily, even concrete see, so it's gotta be taken care of before it's allowed to set in."

"Where do they get killed?" Both men turned to look at Jillian. Johnny's fears that Jillian might be a little squeamish had long ago been assuaged, but he was surprised to find how consistently impressed he was with her; her curiosity knew no bounds.

"Right through that there door," he said, and without warning held up his camera and took a snap of her just as she turned to look. She was so intrigued by the door that she didn't hear the click of the shutter as it spiraled its way home.

They moved on to the strangest room yet.

--

The room was a massive box. If Jack had to guess he would have said it was a perfect cube; the roof seemed as high as the walls did wide. In one corner lay a great pile of bones; long and curved, they looked impossibly huge.

"What, are they killing fuckin' mastodons in this place?" Jack asked in surprise. "Looks like Fred Flintstone's been chowin' down in here."

"I think that there is your answer," Johnny told him, motioning to the lone carcass inhabiting the room. He took a step back and snapped a picture.

It was some kind of bovine, possibly a cow, more likely a bull judging by its enormity, which was roughly the size of a small Buick. None of them had ever seen an animal so big before and Jack wondered out loud if they weren't creating a new breed of animal in this plant. His lip curled in both disgust and wonder as he examined it more closely.

Its throat was slashed, its skin removed, and the head-still intact – was held only by a strip of flesh the size of a child's thigh. The head hung pendulously, so large and heavy it appeared that all it would take would be one sharp tug and the sheer weight of it would separate body from cranium.

Where its eyes should have been were only two dead sockets and underneath the body was a perfectly round puddle of black blood, fully congealed, so that it resembled jelly rather than liquid.

"Weird," Jillian whispered as she walked around it once, twice, three times. She held her hand out as she did so as though about to touch it, but she never completed the gesture with actual contact. "For some reason this one doesn't look like the others. Something is off…" She turned to the guys. "You know what I'm talking about? Do you see it?"

"See it as much as I feel it," Johnny said. He was nodding, and so was Jack.

"It's because it's alone. And the eyes. The gouged out eyes make it look more like some kind of sacrifice rather than something being prepped for sale in the market. There's something ritualistic about this one." Jack turned to Johnny. "Your uncle ever tell you about this room?"

Johnny, who was moving in as near as he could to get a close-up shot of the monster's upside-down face, shook his head. "In all my travels with Mikey he never mentioned anything like this. I got no idea. But goddamn is it creepy without the eyes. It's like they didn't want it to see what it was they were doing to it. Didn't want it to see their secrets." He snapped three shots in quick succession. "I wonder what it feels like." He motioned to the empty eye sockets. "In there I mean."

"Stick your fingers in and find out." That was Jillian, and there was no challenge in her voice. This was no double dog dare; it was presented more like an offer of opportunity.

Johnny stared at Jillian for a second, reading her, trying to determine if she was goading him or not. A second later his face relaxed, and he swung the camera strap from over his head, placed the camera on the floor away from the pancake of blood.

"Okay," he told the two, twiddling the fingers on both his hands the way a concert pianist might warm up before a show. He stepped forward with no hesitation and both Jack and Jillian moved in to get a better look.

Johnny stood there a moment, glancing first from Jack to Jillian, his face utterly impassive, eyes unblinking. He moved in closer to the hanging corpse, his own eyes drawn to where the animal's should have been.

There was no hesitation. No pregnant pause. He simply moved his hands forward and inserted three fingers from each of his hands into the eye sockets of the beast. His face was so unresponsive at first that he could have been plugging up the holes of a bowling ball. And then he let out his breath and his face relaxed and his eyes drooped ever so slightly; he looked like a man who'd just experienced a small but lovely orgasm.

"What does it feel like?" It was Jack who asked, but the words had been on the tip of Jillian's tongue as well. They were both watching Johnny's face, his hands, the connection between him and the animal, with a shameless curiosity.

"Words can't describe," Johnny said, his lips barely moving, his fingers playing gently on the inside of the prodigious skull. With a nod of his chin he motioned them to join him.

The two moved as though in a dream, their feet soft on the ground. They came to Johnny as though pulled by an invisible string-the twine of fate perhaps – and they slowed not a whit until they were flanking his body.

Jillian got to him first, she looked him directly in the eye before she joined his fingers in the skull. She marveled at how comfortable she felt in front of him, as comfortable as she felt with Jack actually, though she had spent nearly every day in the past three weeks by his side. A thirsty desire to kiss him came over her but it passed quickly and for that she was glad; nothing like that had ever happened between her and Jack and she didn't want to give either of them the wrong impression.

Then Jack was there too and his fingers slid into the left cavity to join with Johnny's and then they were all there, three persons, twelve fingers, diving into the depths of this gargantuan beast who had forfeited its life…for this.

Their fingers probed, sometimes sliding over each other's, sometimes only exploring the aperture itself.

Jillian's jaw trembled. Her eyelids fluttered as someone experiencing a seizure in their sleep.

Jack's fingers flexed and loosened, flexed and loosened. A part of him wished he could tear that thing's head off completely, and grasping it firm, thrust it over his own head like Atlas finally redeemed.

Johnny stood there melting slightly, wilting like wax in heat, overcome by the simple joy of proximity, of closeness on a level he had never previously encountered. He felt, as the sunbather feels the sun, the simple joy of living. Life licked at the pores of his skin.

"I feel…" he began, and the sentiment hung in the air like a firecracker shot into the sky, waiting for the moment of burst.

But it never came.

Never had the chance to.

Without the slightest warning whatsoever, all light around the three disappeared.

The room, and these three teenage somethings, their fingers still deep within the head of this bestial creature, was suddenly plunged into a darkness, black as pitch.

2010

Jack waited until he got home to open the envelopes. The entire drive back he kept glancing at them and at several points – stopped at a red light waiting for a line of schoolchildren to clear the crosswalk – he stared so hard he half expected them to burst into flames. His thoughts were so intense he believed he could squint lasers, and he kept hearing the sounds from that video, the DVD delivered to his office: the whirring of the air drill, *pump-whirr pump-whirr pump-whirr*, seeing the shop-vac in the corner, what Nancy had said resembled R2-D2. He couldn't escape the tactile memory of lunging for the computer monitor, scratching at the cables like a man buried alive would scratch at the lid of his coffin. *I've got the absent fingernail to prove it,* he thought, fanning out the fingers of his right hand, palm down, like a woman admiring her new manicure. His hands curled round the steering wheel of his car and squeezed until the flesh turned white. Another glance at the envelopes. He didn't know whether he wanted to rip them open or rip them to shreds. He settled for quiet self-loathing.

It had taken less than a week for the first private investigator to deliver the whereabouts of Jillian Jarblonski. He'd gotten the call that morning telling him to come in to pick up the details and less than an hour later, the phone rang a second time and it was the other investigator – *Goldsmith* or *Goldsmound* or something like that, Jack had already forgotten-telling him the same thing. Two hours later he had the envelopes in his hand and though they couldn't have been more than half a centimeter thick, he had never felt a heavier set of papers in his life.

Of course he had tried to find them himself first. Last week he'd driven nearly two hours north to hit up a dingy little internet café; it was a pain in the ass but there was no way he was going to use his own computer, or any in his city for that matter, to start a digital search for two people that he had such delicate plans for. No, digital searches leave digital trails, trillions of little ones and zeroes that never go away, that hang on out there in cyberspace just waiting for the right person to come along and decode. Jack may not remember all the things the three of them had done back in that year of eighty-nine – that year was to him like a chapter torn out of a book– but he did remember his motto. The creed that superseded all other desires, all other forms of want: *Leave no trail.* But apparently Johnny Megolni and Jillian Jarblonski had also remembered the rule because his search had come up as empty as a whore's heart.

He immediately knew what he had to do. Jack Barber was a competent man, a smart man, but he knew when to admit that he was out of his element. A visit to a private investigator was what he needed, and visit a private investigator he did – two actually, one to find each of his old friends: there was no way he was going to get one guy to search for both, no no no, too many connections there, giving away too much information for sure. *Why not just send a note of confession to the police printed on company stationary while you're at it? Any private investigator worth his pit stains would read the papers and make the connections:*

"Hey, what a coincidence? Why just three weeks ago that Jack Barber came into my office looking for a Johnny Megolni and Jillian Jarblonski and here they are, both missing. Hmmm, maybe I should report this to the police – seems they might be interested in something like that. Oh, nah, never mind. Probably an uncanny coincidence. And oh, my head's getting cold, think I'll just stick it back up my ass and warm it up a bit, huh.

No, two investigators had been the way to go, and seemingly it had worked. He had proof of that sitting on the passenger seat beside him. Two envelopes, one for each of the best friends he had ever known. He hadn't looked inside them yet, but he knew. He *knew* that they contained the information he needed.

He felt like he was going to throw up.

Sitting in front of his building, listening to his car engine *click click* as it cooled, he stared at those envelopes that sat like some unwelcome passenger on the seat beside him. His fingers refused to make the move, to reach out and touch them; it would be too much like making contact with a corpse. Eventually he shook his head and, feeling the gourd rise in his throat ever so slightly, curled his hands around them and lifted. No, they weren't as heavy as the bodies he imagined them to be, but they were pretty damn heavy, and he had to take a minute to steady his breath before he was able to get out of his car and make his way inside.

Once there, he dropped them on the coffee table – he imagined them smashing right through the glass table top like a fumbled bowling ball - but they barely made a sound. He poured himself a drink - fuck that two fingers shit, it was a damn near full pint of Johnny Walker Black - and sat down on the sofa.

The envelopes were identical, yellow manila, eleven by thirteen, of about the same thickness. One contained the information about Johnny Megolni and the other, Jillian Jarblonski, but he didn't know which was which.

That could help you decide, he thought. *Whichever one you open first, could be the one you...* His mind wouldn't let him finish the thought but he knew, deep down, he knew that final damning verb. His mind wouldn't let him think it, but he knew it started with a capital 'K' nonetheless.

He shook his head. *Simple chance won't work here. It has to be like the old days. I have to be methodical. Logical. And above all I must not get caught. So who's first then?*

He scowled. *You're just putting off the inevitable Jack. You're just* – but even this reflection was another stage of procrastination. He cursed, drank, then reached over and grabbed the envelopes, both of them, and tore the ends off with an almost savage distaste. Their contents dropped to the table, and he shuffled through them quickly. The words meant nothing to him: he tossed all writing aside, all typed printouts. What he was looking for was –

He stopped, his breath gone. Thrusting his face out of a speeding car window couldn't have done it faster. There was no air to breathe, no oxygen to –

Jillian. Johnny. Both of them, in separate pictures, but both of them nonetheless. They were older of course, time spotted, but it was them, no doubt about it. Jillian's hair was lighter and her face had lost the roundness of youth, but the eyes were the same: deep and cutting and fully aware and Jack reached out and rubbed her right cheek with his thumb as though trying to rub away the wrinkles that cut into her face like words carved into a wooden desk.

Johnny looked more solid, his baby face gone completely – *no more* kid *Johnny, I guess,* thought Jack – but his eyes were brighter than Jack remembered, more alive, and this actually made him seem younger.

With shaking hands Jack raised the glass of whiskey to his lips and took a sip; his jaw was trembling too, and he spilled some liquid, which leaked down his chin, leaving a cold streak. There was a dizziness on him that had nothing to do with the booze.

"My old friends," he said, and when a tightness rose up in his throat, he coughed it away as one clears out a wad of acidic phlegm. His back straightened. He cracked his knuckles.

For an entire three minutes there were no discernible thoughts in his head. He just continued to stare at the photos, his eyes roaming back and forth between the two. Finally he spoke aloud.

"So which one? Who's first?"

Kid Johnny. The answer came to him in an instant, crisp and blazingly clear and he questioned: *Why him? Why Johnny?*

Jack sipped his drink, thought better, and took a thirsty man's gulp. He barely felt it slide down his gullet before the answer came to him.

Because he's the one most likely. He was the one who knew about cameras. True, it was photographs in the beginning, but video would be the next logical step. And it was Johnny who usually picked the locations; he could have set it up beforehand. He had the means and *the method.* Jack shook his head, took another swig of whiskey. Something didn't sit right. *Johnny was your friend. He cared about you; he proved that. Remember the night in the basement, with the roaches?* His thoughts shifted: *so Jillian then. But is she any more likely? Do you really think she'd blackmail* you?

Jack mentally wagged a finger at himself. *Don't let ego – that inflated leech-get in the way of your judgment Jack. She was seventeen; how many men do you think she's had since? She may not have been technical savvy like Kid Johnny, but she was brutal when she wanted to be, when she needed to be. Remember that first time with the old man? The way she used her fingernails...and that time with the cross? How she used it like an icepick to...* Jack shuddered, both disgusted and amazed at how adept the mind was at erasing things it didn't want to remember. *Only it never fully formats the old hard drive, does it Jack? They seem like they're gone they don't appear when you do a scan of the old memories, but they're there nonetheless, aren't they? You just gotta know how to read the code. How to dig in deep to see what's buried underneath. We buried a lot, didn't we? And not just memories...*

He let loose a shudder, so complete that his entire body shook and he spilled a good slosh of whiskey onto the face of Jillian's photograph. In the dim light of his apartment it had the dark and odious tint of fresh blood.

Yeah, we buried a lot alright, and it wasn't no animal. It was human, and it was alive, and we killed it. That *was how it began.*

That first night when we buried bone.

And flesh.

Jack stared down at the photographs; the whirlwind of time was upon him and he found his eyes opening and closing, opening and closing in a series of pathetic squints, not because he was trying to blink away what he was seeing, but because for the moment he couldn't see anything at all. His brain had been thrown against a brick wall. All conscious thought was deleted. He stared without seeing, eyes open and blank. It was like looking into the ultra-bright flash of a camera that kept popping again, and again, and again, and-

1989

- again and I'm going to wear my flash out pretty quick."

Johnny's voice was wet, but it cracked as he spoke. He hadn't lost his shit down the drain just yet, but life had its hand on the flush valve.

Jack's words came out cool as vapor off a frosted beer glass when he asked: "Johnny, what just happened?" He was wiping his hands, still wet from their exploration of the eye-socket, on the inner thigh of his jeans. Even in his concern he felt something sexual, rubbing cold ichor from the tips of his fingers onto the cloth that covered his crotch. He felt a stirring there that he didn't immediately dismiss.

Johnny had already fired off three shots of his camera – one for each living heart beating within the room – in vain attempt to discern what had happened, why the lights had suddenly gone dead. One lit up Jillian's face-a snapshot tilted up and to the left at an angle that suggested not fear exactly – that was too simple an emotion-but a perverse mix of terror and ecstasy, equally entwined as entrails on a spit. The second shot had shown him the pile of bones in the corner, curved and dry yet specked with small patches of clinging flesh – tissue that simply refused to let go – and Johnny understood that only decay would show it its true path. And finally, the head of the beast itself, whose vacant eyes were all the more deadened in contrast to the electric glare of the Nikon 35mm.

"Johnny?" Jillian's voice was barely a whisper but in the darkness, it sounded louder than Gods'.

"I. Don't. Know." Johnny's own words were tight, heavy with thought. He jumped on the only explanation his mind could come up with.

"The lights were on a timer to turn on. Maybe they go off after a certain amount of time."

"Or maybe there's someone in the building with us." Jillian was thinking about what they had been doing a moment ago when the lights went off and if at that moment she heard the sound of mooing she truly believed she would lose her mind.

"Let's just find our way out of here," Jack said. Problem: solution. That was the Jack Barber way. "You got your flashlight Johnny?"

"I put it in my camera bag…"

"Which you left at the entrance," Jack finished. He didn't blame Johnny in the least. It was himself that he cursed for being so stupid, for not thinking ahead.

"Okay, okay, let's not panic. For now let's assume like Johnny said; the lights were on a timer. All we gotta do is make our way back. Easy-peasy, jap-an-easy, huh?"

Jillian shook her head, remembered that neither of the guys could see her, and continued shaking it anyway. "Except it's not so easy. It's black as Satan's asshole in here. I don't even know where the door is."

"Okay, okay, no worries, no worries. The low battery light is on on my flash but I should be good for another half-dozen flashes or so before they die completely. That gives us roughly one flash per room. All we have to do is remember where the door is in each room and move together. Agreed?"

Jillian nodded, again remembered the darkness, and said "Agreed."

Jack coughed. "Well, it's better than standing around here with our dicks in our hands."

Johnny laughed. "You've got your dick in your hand?"

"Don't you?"

"I do now." He was giggling.

Jillian couldn't help but laugh too. "You guys are disgusting."

"No, what's really disgusting is that I was about to suggest that you hold both our hands Jillian." Even in the dark she could hear the smile on Jack's lips.

"You. Wish."

"Okay, let's do this. Does anyone know which way the first door is?"

"I think I do," said Johnny. He had got a glimpse of it in that last flash of the camera. "I'll hum. Just follow the sound."

He hummed. They followed. And eventually, they made their way out of the great square room full of dead meat.

--

About half an hour and half a dozen flashes later, they found themselves searching through Johnny's camera bag for the two flashlights they'd left there. Johnny took his and went back to the room where he'd first found the controls for the lights. As far as he could tell nothing had changed; the light switches all seemed to be in the same position and nothing in the room had moved. Same old half-eaten bag of Cheetos on the desk beside an ashtray brimming with Pall Mall butts – all stained with cheese powder of course – and a Playboy with a woman done up to resemble Jessica Rabbit on the cover, corners also stained with Cheeto powder, and, inexplicably, a bowling ball case that contained nothing but a pair of binoculars.

For a second he considered swiping the Playboy but thought better of it; its absence might be noticed and raise an alarm, and who knew when he and his new friends might want to come back here in the future for a little late night hi-jinx? Besides, did he really want this girl Jillian thinking he was some maxi perv-o who couldn't get a real girl so had to rely instead on soft-core skin mags? He shrugged it off.

When he came back a minute later, he was stumped.

"Everything looks the same. Musta been on a timer like I thought."

Jack shrugged. "Weird. At any rate, I'd say it's time we got the fuck outta dodge. As much as I like this place, I have to admit that it gives me the creeps. Too many dead eyes around. Too many things that could be watching."

Johnny punched him playfully on the shoulder. "Don't you know the dead don't see, man. And they certainly don't tell no tales."

It was an old adage they would come to prove first-hand in less than an hour's time, on a long and lonely road where they would come to kill an even lonelier man.

The first.

--

Driving around afterwards with nowhere to go and even less to be, Jack riding shotgun, and Jillian in the back, talking rat-a-tat fast, enthusiastic. Strung out on the natural high only bored teenagers can experience after an abnormal and macabre adventure in flesh. Johnny nodded more than spoke, smiled more than laughed. He was having a good time too – he'd never thought he would enjoy going on his photo shoots with other people but now realized that it was nice; companionship rooted him in reality, made the things that happened to him more concrete, definite.

The road wound before them, the curves as random as boiling spaghetti, and Johnny liked the way the headlights of the car only illuminated so far ahead. It made the immediate future seem unknown and unknowable. On all sides there were trees, great reaching monsters that didn't just grasp at the black sky but nearly blotted it out completely; they rose and curved, cloistering the road so that all light was shut out save that from the headlights of Johnny's car, and perfuming the tunnel in a rich bank of oxygen and musk.

Johnny liked the focus of it, the ever changing yet always constant destination, and every time he blinked it was like seeing a new snapshot, a photograph wholly absent of color save the single solid yellow line perfectly dividing the scene down the middle. The darkness drew him forward for he never knew what was waiting just around the bend, or what lay in the unrevealed places hidden in the vignette of the world. Despite this, Johnny felt in control; the steering wheel was his, the gas pedal too. The car was an extension of his body and he used it to usher two human beings he barely knew around this mortal coil and for that he felt alive, needed, and strangely: beautiful. If either one of his passengers had asked him point blank what the greatest moment of his life was, he would have answered without pause: *this one.*

But in his joy – not *ecstasy,* no not that, though that would come soon enough - there was something that bothered him more than he cared to admit. It nagged at him like a torn cuticle, and it had to do with back there, in the slaughterhouse: the lights. It had been his suggestion that they had been on a timer, but only he had seen the switches themselves and there was nothing to indicate that they would go off after a certain period of time. His uncle had told him about the time it took for them to warm up, but why would they shut off like that after…what, thirty-five minutes or so? If it had been an hour spot on then it would have made more sense, but thirty-five, forty minutes? It didn't add up, and that wasn't all. When they'd got back to the car he couldn't be sure, and he didn't want to freak his new friends out or make them think he was a paranoid pussy, but getting into the driver's seat his eyes happened on the ground just outside the door, and right there, right where his foot would go were he getting *out* of the car – *we don't get in*to *a car the same way we get out of one, remember Johnny* – was the tip end of a discarded cigarette butt. It wasn't his; it was a Pall Mall. *Who the fuck smokes Pall Malls but world-frightened pensioners and welfare cases,* he wondered. *But more importantly: why does it look so fresh?* He tried to imagine his leg lifting out of the car, his left foot pressing down on the earth, and couldn't get around the fact that his foot should have pressed directly on the butt. *So why does it look so untouched?*

He'd shaken his head; *it's a matter of millimeters,* he scoffed, there's no way he could know exactly where his foot would have dropped. Better to push it away. Better to think it nothing and let it become nothing. And he had, but… He brought himself back to the moment.

" – lights went out, I swear I thought I was gonna turn my keks into a Mars Bar factory."

"Nice image Jackie Boy." Jillian was laughing, a deep throaty grit usually reserved for decaying lounge singers or evil cartoon step-mothers, that laughter sent a shiver down Johnny's back that was nicer than any touch he'd ever received. She went on. "It's not too late you know, Johnny here-" Jillian reached up from the back seat and patted him on the shoulder "-could take another snap of it. Would be a great end to his little photo essay."

Johnny joined in. "Oh yeah, for sure. Would make perfect sense, could call the whole thing *From Slaughter to Shit: The Beautiful Journey of* Meat! "

"Yeah, hey, why not?" asked Jack. "See the incredibly detailed process of how animal flesh goes from barnyard to burger to your own briefs in petrified black and white." He turned and grinned at Jillian. "Sounds like an award winner to me. Pulitzer prize winning shit." He raised his eyebrows. "Literally."

Jillian was shaking her head as though trying to buck the image from her mind. "Ugh, gag me with a fuckin' spoon man, you're gonna make me wretch."

"Says the girl who just had her fingers stuck in the corpse head of a half ton carcass of decaying skin."

Jillian waved a defensive finger at Jack. "Death doesn't bother me; *shit* I can do without."

"One and the same sweetheart, one and the same," retorted Jack.

Jillian waved him off the way one tries to waft away a bad smell. "Next topic, next topic."

Jack rolled his eyes at her but he was grinning. "What do you propose, princess?"

Jillian shrugged. "I don't know. Johnny? It's your car, what do you want to talk about?"

Without warning, tears welled up in Johnny's eyes. He couldn't have put into words how grateful he was for Jillian asking that question, for caring about what *he* wanted. It was not something he was used to and for a moment his chest tightened as he tried his best to fill it with air. He swallowed but-*he couldn't believe it! –* he didn't care if they saw it or not; they weren't the kind of people who would judge him. If there was laughter it would be with all three; there would be no pointed fingers with these people.

"I don't know." He glanced behind at his savior. "I guess I was wondering-"

THUNK!

THUMP!

THUMP!

The car jolted, lifted slightly on one side as though experiencing a speed bump, and then continued to roll on as normal as you please. Johnny's hands gripped the steering wheel, his eyes popped like sudden headlights, and a dry gasp ripped at his throat.

The only sound was the hum of the engine and the roll of the tires as they turned. The night became infinitely darker, colder, yet conversely more alive; a great moment was upon them.

Jack spoke first, his voice piano-wire tight. "Christ on a cross, what was that?" He had turned in his seat, trying to peer out the rear window but it was so dark he might as well have been trying to see with the hole of his ass. He turned to Jillian. "Did you see anything?"

Her head shook back and forth, her lips so tight there was no division, as though she possessed just one almighty lip. He turned to Johnny.

"You?"

Johnny mirrored Jillian's gesture. "I was looking back. At her." He shrugged.

"Stop the car."

Johnny didn't question, didn't hesitate, and it was interesting to Jack to note that he didn't slam on the brakes either. Johnny slowed, his foot never jamming, until the trees no longer blurred and the road halted its curve.

"It was probably a raccoon or something. Maybe a rabbit."

Johnny looked at Jack directly. "It sounded bigger than that, more substantial."

"Maybe a deer," Jillian interjected. Her tone was helpful and for that Johnny was impressed. There was no panic in this girl's voice. It calmed him, rooted him. He didn't hesitate with his next suggestion.

"Let's take a look at the car first. It could have been a bag of garbage for all we know. People throw bags of trash out their windows all the time." Three sets of eyes moved from one face to another, reading, gauging, then all at once three doors opened.

Standing in front of the car it was hard to see the car itself; the headlights lit up the three teens but not much else.

Jackie shrugged. "Jilly, you got a mirror or something?"

With her head tilted down she had to raise her eyebrows in order to see him. "A mirror?"

"Yeah, yeah, a mirror. Like a compact or something. You got one?"

She flashed her palms. "Who am I, Gloria Estefan? I haven't looked at myself in a mirror in three days, what the fuck would I be doing with a compact?"

"I don't know." Jack turned to Johnny and wrinkled his lips in a half Elvis/half Johnny Rotten stance as if to say: '*women: pffft.*'

Johnny smiled. It might have been his *dad's* Buick, who he gave less than a shit about, but they were clearly in this together and that was all that mattered to him.

"I got those flashlights. In my bag."

Jack nodded. *Flashlights will do.*

A second later Johnny was back with the flashlights. He handed one to Jack and kept the other for himself.

"On the count of three?"

Johnny nodded. "On the count of three."

Jack: "One."

Johnny. "Two."

Jillian raised her arms over her head: "Oh will you two just do it already, turn on the juice."

Both beams honed in on Jillian's face, so bright she had to shield her eye with a bent elbow.

"You want us to turn on the juice?"

"Oh-oh, is that what you want?"

"Oh, Johnny, I think Jilly Jill here wants us to *turn on the juice.* Whatcha think?"

"Yeah, yeah, I definitely got that impression too. It was something in her turn of phrase. The urgency in her voice that suggested some kind of... some kind of... *Je ne sais quoi...* desire, perhaps."

"Yeah, yeah I sensed that too. I really think she wants us to-"

"Oh bag your faces will you! Just shine them on the car would you."

Jack laughed. "Take a chill pill Jill," he told her, but when she turned to him – her pale face glowing perfectly in the stark blaze of the halogen lights, her eyes looking as yellow and hungry as Pac-Man in motion – he saw that she was really worried, and he acquiesced. A slight rotation of his hand and the state of the car was theirs.

Blood. It was obvious from the get-go. If one didn't know the situation, they might have assumed it to be something darker, oil or tar perhaps, but there was no escaping that *THUNK! THUD! THUD!* that told them otherwise. They'd hit something, no doubt. The only question now was what it was.

Johnny was right, the sound had been too strong, too heavy to be a rabbit or rodent. And judging from how high the blood went – not splattered exactly but smeared – suggested that it wasn't just a weighty thing, but a tall one.

Jack nodded. "I think you might have been right Jilly Jill. A deer. It had to have been a deer." He moved in closer. "There might be some evidence. Maybe some fur or–"

Jack's lean in suddenly turned into a recoil.

"Shit," was all he said but when Johnny shone the flashlight on Jack's face, he could see that all blood had been drained from his flesh; he was as one of those animals he had just photographed. The face was empty. Voided.

"What is it? What?!"

Jack only pointed and repeated the sentiment: "Shit."

Jillian and Johnny moved together in unison, neither of them having any idea what to expect. When they saw it they both turned to each other, eyes wide, mouths slack.

Mixed in with the blood, just inches above the half rusted fender, was a torn piece of cloth, a corner from a shirt or a sweater.

"We hit a person," Johnny said, and even in his fear he was glad that no one corrected him by saying *you.*

"We have to go back," said Jillian, "Maybe they're still alive."

Johnny was nodding, already starting to move in the direction they had come. "Yeah, yeah, we might be able-"

"No." Jack's voice was as final as the closing of a prison door and it made Johnny falter, Jillian too.

"But Jack, we gotta see if-"

Jack raised his hands and cut Johnny off again. "We'll go. We'll go and see." His voice was eerily calm, his eyes unfaltering. "But first turn off the engine of your car. And kill the headlights."

"But it would be faster to drive back. We could-"

Another wave from Jack. "We can't be seen. If another car comes by, we can't be seen." His face was cast down and the light from Johnny's car threw his eye sockets and lower lip into shadow. "Just in case," he said finally, and Johnny and Jillian understood. Johnny glanced at Jillian, she nodded once and that was all it took to set Johnny in motion. Less than a minute later the three of them were walking along, side by side, toward the place where they'd hit whatever the hell it was they had hit. They didn't speak as they went, walking through the night that was as calm and quiet as an occupied tomb.

They walked, their flashlights swaying back and forth sweeping the road, the ditches, the edges of forest on either side. They walked for what seemed like half an hour though it was probably more like three minutes, five at most, and just when they were about to give up, to shrug their shoulders and declare this one of life's great unsolved mysteries, they heard a noise. A small whimpering sound at first: a babel of pain and suffering.

A scratching/dragging sound that conjured images of grain and earth. Thick bubbling, like boiling tar. And until that point they figured there was still hope. It could have been a deer. The piece of cloth on the car could have been there already; it wasn't impossible. But all that changed when the next, final damning sound reached their ears, causing all three to stop and inhale sharply.

Words. They cut through the night and stabbed directly into the heart of each of the three, and though the air that night was warm, almost hot, they each felt a chill that froze the contents of their stomachs. A second later they saw it, their flashlight beams honing in on it like sharks to torn flesh and leaking blood.

Jillian let out a little gasp, more of surprise than fear.

Jack said nothing, only walked toward it with that Jack Barber stride, confident, powerful, ready.

For some reason Johnny thought of the animal corpses from less than an hour ago. The flesh. The meat. The possessive scent of death. Only this one was fresher. Freshest of them all because it was still alive. Johnny didn't know why – he couldn't even see *where* the man was injured, never mind how badly – but he had a feeling the poor bastard wouldn't be breathing for much longer. This was the end, and Johnny was going to bear witness to it, the thought of that excited him in a way that a thousand animal corpses never could. Never would.

By the time he reached the body he was practically running.

--

To say the man was injured was like saying Hitler probably wouldn't have been a very good play date. All over his body there were tears and seared flesh that pushed out blood so untouched it looked alive. Their flashlights caught it, lit it, turned it into something brilliant and neon erotic and all over his face there were more cuts and digs, bits of gravel and grit that contrasted perfectly with the pure whiteness of his sweat soaked skin. It was amazing, Johnny thought, to witness this thing in front of him, this thing that was surely dying, and to note that he had never seen anything that looked more alive in all his life. For a second, he had an itch to go back to the car and fetch his camera but he pushed the desire away; this was a once in a lifetime opportunity: better to live in the absolute moment. He wanted to be there waiting with his mouth open, close enough to inhale the man's last dying breath. He wanted to *taste* it.

"He's not wearing any shoes." Jillian was staring at the man's feet with an impossible-to-interpret look on her face. "Why would he be walking out here in the middle of nowhere with no shoes?" She turned to Jack, brow furrowed.

"Because he *was* wearing shoes when he was walking," Jack responded. He focused the beam of his flashlight on the man's feet, then slowly drew the blade of light along the road; about twenty feet away it caught a pair of sneakers sitting on the asphalt, side by side, as though waiting at a doorway for their master to sidle in.

"Jesus. Do you think we pulled him that far? Or did he drag himself?"

The beam returned to the man, lighting up his right arm. The elbow of his jean jacket was torn right through and a knob of bone poked out of the hole; it was so white it looked like it had been soaked in bleach.

"I think his dragging days are over," said Jack. His eyes narrowed as he knelt down beside the man, who was now shivering. He had a mane of white hair – he looked like a dog who had never once known a home, or a bed, or a friend – and a short stubbly beard peppered black and white. His nostrils were currently fanning in and out like something you might find running the streets of Pamplona; his eyes were rolled back so far in his head he could have been a sock puppet with Ping-Pong ball eyes.

"Hey old timer. I said *hey* old timer." When the man didn't respond, Jack turned and looked at his companions. He shrugged, then turned back.

"I said *hey* old timer! Can you hear me down there? You still with us?"

Jillian watched fascinated as Jack reached over and lightly slapped the man several times on his stubbly cheek. A sound escaped from Johnny's lips that was either a gasp of surprise or a pant of laughter but she was too fascinated by Jack and the man to turn around and confirm which.

A groan rose from his lips, so guttural it sounded like one of those great stone wheel contraptions slowly rolling to crush grain and corn into powder. Jack raised his hands above his head, back straightening.

"It lives! By god it *lives!*" He turned to Jillian and Johnny.

"Thoughts here anyone? How you think we should proceed."

"Well Jesus Jack, we gotta get him to a hospital. He's royally fucked up."

Jack sighed, his face deflating slightly. "I was afraid you'd say that."

"Well, what else did you have in mind? I mean, *Jesus,* look at him." Only Jillian couldn't help but notice that Jack *was* looking at him and didn't seem at all bothered by what he saw.

Finally, he shrugged. "Okay then, let's pick him up. We'll carry him to the car."

"Wouldn't it be easier to go get the car and come back for him? It's kind of a long walk to carry him all the way."

Jack nodded. "Right. Right you are Jilly, right you are. So, how 'bout me and Johnny here head back, grab the vehicle and you stay with him and keep him company?"

"Why do I have to stay? I don't wanna stay."

"Don't worry, we'll leave you a flashlight."

"Sit on it and rotate Jack, that's not the point. Why leave *me* here alone?"

"Well, not that I really wanted to say something in front of Johnny here," he turned his back to Jillian and winked at Johnny – "but I'm not so sure we can trust our newfound friend here. Who's to say he won't split on us the second he gets behind the wheel? No, no, I think it would be better if I went with him, to make sure, yah know."

Jillian looked down at the man and tried to decide what scared her more about him; the fact that he was dying or the fact that he was old. She would never grow old, of that she was certain.

"Oh fuck it, let's just try to carry him."

"Right again Jilly, right again." Jack threw another wink at Johnny who didn't quite know what to make of it but liked it, nonetheless. Excitement spread in him like spilled ink on wrinkled parchment, filling in the cracks, dripping and sloshing along the crevices; his body alive with both black ice and blue heat. *Something is going to happen.* His breath caught in his throat and he repeated the sentiment: *something is going to happen.*

"Okay me and Johnny will grab his arms; Jilly you take the legs. Be careful not to get blood all over your clothes."

The three bent down, flanking the man from all sides. Then their hands dug in, scooping, but they barely had him off the ground when the screams began.

They were not the type of screams they had expected.

Eyes bugged, mouth gaping wide enough to cram a child's foot into, the man was suddenly fully awake, and he was not happy.

"You sons a bitches – you killed me! You murdering sons a bitches – you goddamn killed me!" The three teens shifted in surprise and his tone shifted also, from anger to pain. "*Awwwwwwrghhh.*" His head thrashed back and forth like a rabid dog, his teeth clamped open and shut – they sounded like the end of a metal cane rapping on fine China – as he tried to bite the hands that helped him.

"I'll kill you. I'll kill youse all. First you hit me, then you try to lay hands on me, then you steal my wallet to boot. You goddamn sons an' daughters a whores-"

Once again he tried to move his arm, and they watched as the bone popped out even further at the elbow, stretching the flesh like saran pulled too tight. Another scream exploded, and he writhed but still they held their grip, each looking to the other, unsure of what to do. The man was moving around so much it was like trying to hold on to a live wind and then without warning he let out a tight ripping fart. Jillian, who was close to the point of exit, instinctively let loose her grip on the man's legs; his lower half fell to the ground with a dumb thud. Gravity then pulled the rest of him down where he lay on the pavement, cursing and scratching at the ground with his one good hand. Jack raised his hands and motioned to the man, palms held upward.

"You see this? You *see* this? You try to help a guy and he *shits* all over you."

Johnny was waving his hand back and forth in front of his nose. "Literally in this case I think. Jillian, you sure that was just a fart?"

Jillian shrugged, inched as close as she dared, and sniffed; her face imploded.

"Oh gag me with a spoon man. I really think he *shit* himself. What the hell are we gonna do now guys?"

Jack leaned down and stared the guy in the face. He had calmed down a little – at least he was no longer screaming – but his breath was still coming in torn strips. A bubble of snot repeatedly inflated and deflated from out his nose.

"We're just trying to *help* you man. Now, if we pick you up again are you going to-"

A cough from his throat and a solid yellow-green mass shot from the man's mouth, landing *splat!* on Jack's left cheek, just below his eye.

"You can take-" his words came in ragged gasps " – your *help-*" more hitching breaths – "and shove it up your queer boy *ass, JACK!*"

Jack's eyes closed; he reached up with one hand and wiped the spit away. He did it slowly, calmly, and there was an almost erotic texture to the whole scene. When he opened his eyes a second later, he looked surprised. "How did he know my name?"

"Jesus Jack, let it go. The guys delusional." She pushed Jack aside, bent down to try to straighten the guy out a little. "He probably doesn't-"

"Cold sweetie?"

The voice sounded so strange, so calm and soft, that for a second she wasn't sure where it was coming from.

"What are-"

"Cause from where I'm laying, those nipples look like they could sharpen skates."

Jillian had just enough time to realize that it was *him* that was talking, this old dying bastard below her, before his one good arm slid up and under her shirt and grabbed her right tit. Her mouth dropped open, too shocked to make a sound; he wasn't just copping a feel. He wasn't going for a cheap thrill. For a second, it felt like he was trying to rip the damned thing clean off.

Jillian screamed, a yowl of pain and distress and her body instinctively bucked back, away from her assailant but he had a grip so tight on her breast that she actually dragged him with her a little and the bruises that formed minutes later would stay with her for nearly a week.

"You fucking *pig*," she thrust at him, and when he still didn't let go she pounded, hitting him exactly where she knew it would hurt most, namely in the wounds that were already there. Finally, his grip released and Jillian fell back on her ass, *hard*, so hard she rocked right back and cracked her head a good one on the pavement. For a second, Johnny made to move, to help her, but Jack waved him back with the slightest of hand gestures.

Rubbing the back of her head roughly with one hand and her breast with the other, Jillian rose. She stared down at this thing before her, no longer a man to be pitied, but something wholly different. Without any mental reference to what he had done to Jack just seconds ago, she spat on him, an explosion of saliva and hate that splattered across his torso, his crotch, his face. If there were any justice, she would have spit acid, and the things it touched would have burned out of existence.

"What is it?" She shook her head and her dark hair whipped slick lines of negation across her face. "With guys." Both fists clenched, her teeth as tight as diamonds. "Who think." She tilted her head back now, looking up at neither the stars nor the ghost trees nor anything physically around them. "That they can just grab. My. *Tits*. Whenever the hell they feel like it?" She leaned down, leaned right down and got in his face, the way a shrew might scold a baby in its crib. "You got an answer for that?" She paused for a second, a brief moment where silence hung in the air like a perfect fly ball ready and willing to knock out the sun.

"Do you?!" Her voice was hysterics, her arms two hurricanes orbiting somewhere above and beyond her ears. And then it was like the power dropped. The raw power of nature, the wind and torrent of water and earth, ash, rock and flesh, fell like a stone, to land square and intact in the heels of her feet. It charged her up, then she charged.

She was a good three kicks in-stomps! cracks! digs!-before either Jack or Johnny realized what she was doing. Her feet simply flailed on the face, the hands, the ribs, hitting home to the man on the road already nine-tenths dead.

Jack watched – eyes wide and mouth slightly curved-and to him it was like watching a dying flower, a flower drooped, withered and sun starved, suddenly bloom and shoot tall above all others. A second later he was by her side, and his kicks beat such similar time to hers it were as though they were dancing. The dance was a waltz, and the waltz was as no other waltz in life or death had ever been.

Johnny joined in too, and though at first it was kicks, sharp little caustic jabs, it was his hands that did the job in. *Any man can walk around*, he thought, *any man can use his feet, but it is something of stature to use one's hands. Toes can take you places, but fingers, only fingers can do this:* he inhaled as his fingers found the throat, that charming gasping throat, and his own head dropped back, his chest swelled like a Roman gladiator as his fingers found the flesh, the loose flesh, and under his fingers, that flesh pulled tight.

The three became one, not just in spirit and purpose, but physically as well; their flailing arms blended, their feet melted into the others, their torsos meshed. They were possessed with purpose that purpose was pure and simple – at that moment any one of them would have attested it in front of God Almighty Himself – *just.* It was for the purpose of release, of unleashing all anger, distress and hatred that had been heaped on the three of them since birth. Too many years they had all stewed in the putrid juices of sin and loneliness, that only the unloved and unlovable know too well, and this was their opportunity to rinse it all away. This was their baptism: a raw Bacchanalian orgy that blessed them in blood. And blood there was: on their clothes, in their hair, in their mouths. Pieces of flesh flew, ragged and still quivering, stuck under their fingernails and specked their faces. More bone came exposed. An eyelid was torn clear from the face. Shattered teeth were pressed into the mouth, the cheeks, the throat. The man became a body, and the body became a lump and soon it was nothing more than an unrecognizable mess of pulp and weight, glistening with a thick coat of red-hot ichor.

Finally, they slowed. Their feet grew still. The fingers no longer clenched. Their jaws loosened enough to let air in. They breathed. They calmed. And then stopped.

All good things must come to an end.

There they all stood, silent around this no longer living man, and none of them – they were human after all, remember always, they were human – had the slightest idea regarding what to say. None of them had been here before. None of them had a touchstone.

Finally, the newest, the quietest of the three spoke. He didn't cough before he said it. He asked no one's permission for the floor. He required no conch. He simply opened his mouth and his truth fell out.

"I wanna do that again."

And the silence that answered was neither damning nor dissuading.

--

After it was done, and they had calmed down enough to get their heads together, Jillian suggested that they get the hell out of there lickety-split. Jack shook his head.

"We have to clean this up. We can't leave him here."

Johnny nodded. "He's right. Come first light someone is gonna see this and when they do the cops'll come lookin'."

Jillian was skeptical. "How? What are we going to do with him? Or what's left of him?"

Jack stared down at this lump of torn clothes, bone, and cooling flesh. He was weighing the thing in his mind the way a butcher might weigh a handful of ground beef on a scale.

"What you always do with bodies," Jack said matter-of-factly. "We bury him." His lips were tight; he could see it all in his mind. "We carry him fifty feet into the woods, we find some sticks, rocks, whatever, and we dig a hole. Drop him in and cover him up."

"And that's it?"

Jack shrugged. "It's a modern convention that murder is a complicated thing. People die everyday by the simplest means necessary. Guy stands on a stepstool to change a light bulb, slips, hits his head in just the right spot-" he reached over and pressed his forefinger to Jillian's left temple " – and bang, lights out."

"So to speak," said Johnny.

Jack was serious. "Yeah, so to speak. People die every day, there's no reason to make it something more than it is. We take him in there," – with a nod of his chin he indicated the dark forest in front of them – "and we put him in the ground. The earth takes him back, and he becomes food for the wiggly things."

Jillian still seemed unsure. "Sticks and rocks eh?" She was biting on her lower lip which-she had no idea-was splattered with the man's death blood. Logic finally made the decision for her: "What other choice do we have?" She turned to Johnny.

"You okay with that?"

"Totally. And I can do you guys one better on the sticks and rocks thing." He motioned once with his hand. "Follow me," he said, walking back in the direction of the car. Jillian turned to Jack expectantly to see what he would do, then glanced down at the body on the pavement but after a few paces Johnny turned around, a grin on his face. "Don't worry about him," he said, waving at the dead thing on the road, "he's not going anywhere." A minute later, they were headed toward the car in a half-jog-half-run.

--

"Do you always keep this kind of shit in your trunk?" Jack asked, gliding the beam of the flashlight over the various items in the back bowels of the vehicle. Besides the one piece of camera equipment he could see, a tripod, there was also a mini sledge-hammer, a spade, a red gallon gasoline tank, a tackle box, and a hammer.

For a second, Jack considered reaching out and opening the box but then thought better of it. It wasn't that he was afraid he might offend his host, but rather that when someone opened his trunk to show you his secrets, it was usually best not to take them all in at once. The same thing was true, Jack reckoned, with people's hearts.

Johnny shook his head. "Standard emergency stuff."

Jack looked from the gasoline can to Johnny's face. "That thing full?"

Johnny didn't so much as pause. "Yep."

"Pretty dangerous driving around in a car with a couple gallons of gas in your trunk."

Johnny shrugged. "Says the guy who just helped me shit kick a guy to an early grave."

Jack returned the gesture. It was an answer he liked so much he considered shaking Johnny's hand. Instead, he rested one hand on his shoulder and, with his free one, gestured to the tools in the trunk. "Let's get this shit together. We've already been pressing our luck being out in the open like this. Every minute gone by makes it more likely that some car's gonna come racing by to light up our guilt-ridden faces."

Johnny nodded. "You're right I-"

"I don't feel guilty." They both turned to Jillian, their flashlights centering on her face at exactly the same moment and she had just enough time to wonder why *she* didn't get to carry a flashlight; *must be a phallic thing,* she thought, *and handing one over now would be like voluntary castration to them.*

"You don't?" Johnny's face was curious, Jack's held a hint of knowing admiration.

"No," returned Jillian, "I don't." Her legs were spread apart, her arms crossed over her chest; Jack had the feeling that had an eighteen-wheeler come barreling into her back at that moment, the driver would take a header through the windshield and the transport itself would be sold for scrap the next morning.

"Hitting him was an accident, wasn't it? We didn't mean to do it. But him grabbing my tit like that, like I was some goddamn public property. Like I was some kind of whore who owed him a cop of my mammary glands because we happened to hit him with a car. What the hell was he doing out here in the middle of nowhere, in the middle of the night anyway? I guaran-fuckin-*tee* you he was up to no good. So, I say good riddance. I say *fuck him*. Christ, I wish he was still alive just so I could kill him all over again." Without realizing it, she reached up and rubbed the violated breast. She spat on the ground. "Now, let's put this fucker in the ground where he belongs already. I get to throw the first handful of rotted dirt over the old bastard's corpse. Hopefully it'll be full of worms and the feast can start early."

Both men stared at her. Jack, who knew her well, only smiled, while it occurred to Johnny that this was the most she had said since they had met. He found himself falling a bit in love with her. Not a lot, but enough. He looked at Jack.

"What about you Jack? Do you feel guilty?"

Jack's lips twisted in consideration. "Guy had to have been what? Sixty-five? Seventy? And violating our dear friend here like that," – he made a bowing gesture toward Jillian that was both chivalrous and comical, yet in no way disrespectful – "who exists at but the tender age of seventeen." Jack shook his head decidedly. "Nope. The man was a pedo for Christ's sakes. Molesting someone fifty-years-plus your junior? This says: Guilty. Just sentence: already carried out."

Johnny laughed, he actually *laughed*, and it felt good, the way laughter should. It wasn't forced, and it wasn't short; it crowded on his insides and pushed itself out so hard and fast that it actually hurt his belly, that made him laugh all the more.

Jack turned to Jillian. "I think we know this guy's stance on the matter. Now, what say we stop waxin' philosophical here before a car comes by and we end up in deeper shit than an incompetent plumber?"

She nodded and together they grabbed the tools they needed. They were about to start walking when Jack thought of something.

"Hey Johnny, you got some paper? A pen?"

"Yeah, in the glove box."

Jack ran over to the passenger side, climbed in. Thirty seconds later, he emerged. They watched as he placed a single sheet of paper under the windshield wiper directly in front of the driver's seat. Johnny, curious by nature, walked over and trained the beam of his light on it. He looked over at Jack.

"Nice."

Jillian too was curious. "What's it say?"

"It says: "Out of gas – walking ahead – please stop for a ride if you see me."

Jack shrugged. "People get suspicious if they see an abandoned car. Might call the police. But if they see the note, they'll keep driving, thinking that maybe they'll be able to help someone out, but when they don't…"

Johnny took it up: "They'll assume that someone already picked the driver up and no worries. Problem solved. They'll continue on their way and-"

"And said car disappears from their conscience," finished Jillian. "You've got a mind, Jack."

Jack snapped a finger. "Leave no trail," he said, "that's all. Now, shall we?" He gestured off into the darkness like an usher showing one to their seat at a theatre show.

Together they ran back into the night, back to the body, their tools held tight in their hands like knights with their weapons of metal and wood.

--

With fingers sore and blistered, they collected various bits of deadwood to lay across the grave. Then they scattered half-rotted leaves to complete the tale. It was hard to be certain in the forced light of their flashlights, but after surveying the job for several minutes after they were done, Jack nodded, satisfied. It probably wouldn't hold up under the scrutiny of a cop who was actively *looking* for a grave, but to anyone who might happen to be hiking by…well, he was pretty certain that the old bastard would stay sleeping undisturbed in the ground for some time. Give it a few weeks, a month or two, and things would be right back to normal on this little plot of land. "Smoking time," Jack said, and they all lit up.

Sitting around, puffing away, a great sense of calm came over the three of them that had little to do with the smoke in their lungs.

"It's like we have our fingers in that skull again," Johnny said out of nowhere, but both Jack and Jillian knew exactly what he was referring to. It *was* like that feeling hours previous when they molested that corpse with their fingers, only this was more. More real somehow, because this time together they had changed something. There was now one less person on the planet because of them.

They marveled. Think of all the food they had saved. Oxygen that would no longer be wasted in his lungs. Piss and shit that *he* would never excrete. Pension money he would more than likely drink away. *Poison* he would put into the world. In many senses they had done the planet a favor, and now, smoking their cigarettes and reveling in their joined thoughts, they couldn't help but feel an organic sense of accomplishment. They weren't heroes by any stretch – even Jack wasn't egomaniac enough to think *that* – but there was no denying that they had done *right*. That they had done *good*. But there was one more problem to contend with, and not even Jack had an answer for it, so he proposed the question to the others.

"What about the blood on the road? Or the blood on us for that matter? What if someone sees it tomorrow in the light of day and gets to wondering?"

"Then they'll probably assume it was some road kill that, only half dead, went squirming its way back into the forest."

Jillian tried too: "Yeah, think about it. Even when we hit it – *'it!' How quickly the man had become a simple nondescript 'it!'*-we assumed it was an animal. A deer right? So why should anybody else think otherwise?"

Jack said nothing. There was too much at stake to answer with a knee-jerk response. He thought. He thought some more. And finally it came to him. Despite all the digging and the groaning of his back, he sat up straight. They had turned off their flashlights long ago so the only light was the moon itself and the intermittent flaring of their cigarettes as they inhaled, but even in the semi-darkness his smile was apparent.

"The gasoline," he said. "No one would question a black mark on the pavement. They'd assume it was just something that fucked-up mother nature had wrought upon the road. Go on their gay way."

Johnny nodded; he liked the way this guy worked. Jillian, well she was already a disciple.

"Sounds good to me. I guess that means another trip back to the car then?'

"Better safe than sorry," Jack said. "But don't worry about it. I'll go." He made to stand, and it happened so fast, so ultra-fucking simultaneous, that later, neither Johnny nor Jillian could agree as to which happened first – it seemed impossible that they occurred at the *exact* same fraction of a second – but a bolt of lightning flashed across the sky, lighting the world up as if the world's biggest camera flash had exploded. A second later a bullwhip of thunder cracked the night.

The rain came. Not misty forgiving rain. Not drops that simply flew and splattered, but rain that drilled it's way to the ground as though answering a call home. Rain demanded by gravity to draw to its will. Great globs of it pummeled into the earth and the three of them stood, raised their arms, and took this as a sign that what they had done was right in the all seeing eye of the world. The blood on the road would disappear, never to be seen again. Their tracks would be covered. The fresh grave would be pounded mercilessly by an aquatic force that would make all ground around it equal; it would seem as untouched earth. Perhaps not even the natives had set foot upon it.

It was perfect. It was providence. It was somehow fucking biblical. Born in blood – the calf – and now baptized, and all sin was washed away. Or at least all evidence of it.

Jack raised himself off of the rock he'd been sitting on. A pea sized drop of rain hit the end of his cigarette and it sizzled as though in pain; he didn't care. He stood, held his arms aloft, and reared his head up at the sky. He breathed. And then without thinking what he was doing he quickly removed his clothes.

They were dirty, soaked with mire and blood, but as he raised them to the sky and felt the rain soaking through, he knew they would be cleansed. Johnny followed suit, and then Jillian, stripping off their false skin until the three of them stood stark naked and soaked, holding their soiled clothes up to the sky as though an offering to some primitive godhead, unable to see but knowing that the accumulated blood was running off them in rivulets, disappearing into the earth the same way that old man had disappeared some short time ago.

The scene to the world appeared only in vignettes, when, every twenty-one seconds or so, another brilliant flash of lightning exploded in the sky, rendering them visible once more, bringing them to life again and again. The scenes were this:

Jack, wringing his shirt as though it were his own heart, ridding it of all cancer and pain.

Jillian, her mouth agape in a silent scream, her hair so black it negated space, waving the manufactured cloth of her t-shirt as though trying to fan flames ever larger than the world itself, while cold punches of rain threw down upon her face. Turning her nipples stark and wooden hard, and drawing wet lines round the blonde hairs surrounding the soft curve of her belly-button.

And Johnny: Kid Johnny. Simply stood there statue still, his face upward, his eyes death closed. His mouth open as wide as it could be, lips furled to present to the world his roaring gums, as though sucking the soul of the universe through his gritted teeth, loving every fucking split-second of the whole ordeal.

--

They held hands as they walked back to the car, naked as babes, with Jillian in the middle, Johnny on the left, and Jack on the right. There was no sense putting their clothes back on; they were soaking wet, and it was a warm night. Together they cut a track right down the center of the road. They weren't worried about cars; they would be able to spot any car that came by a lot sooner than those in the car would spot them. Their eyes were wide open.

By the time they got back to the car the rain had tapered off to an ethereal mist and the interior lights from the car turned the bulbous drops of rain on their skin into tiny pinpoints of glow. Some drops were bigger than others. Some so small they were barely there, needing only a swift breeze to evaporate them into nothingness. But those that remained turned the surface of their flesh into a mini-cosmos, constellations both bright and dim, and for a moment it seemed as though the world was not just theirs, but that they *were* the world.

Johnny fished a couple towels out of the trunk – rags really but they did the trick – and nobody looked at the other while they dried their naked bodies, though neither did they look away. They were just about to climb into the car when Jack looked at Jillian, a watermelon-sized slice of a grin on his face.

"Did you say *'a cop of my mammary glans'* before?" A laugh exploded direct from his belly. "Man, you really listen to too much *Smiths* sweetie." He patted her on the head and there was nothing condescending in the gesture; his hand was as soft as a goodnight kiss on the forehead.

Jillian closed her eyes as she drew the towel tighter around her body.

And then he was opening the door for her, tucking her into the car and shutting it tight behind her, smiling all the while. A moment later, and John had slid into the driver's seat, started the car, and pulled back onto the road with the engine rumbling comfortably beneath their bodies. It had a lackadaisical purr that lulled some weariness out of their muscles, loosened the flesh off their bones. Jillian felt like she could have fallen right asleep. Jack believed he could have watched her. And Johnny, Johnny was content just to be the driver, to take these people where they wanted to go. Rolling on with nothing but the sound of the motor amongst them, Johnny felt he could have driven forever. But no.

When they had driven some miles – that whole area with the body, the burial, the impromptu shower, existed in some momentary bubble forever receding further and further behind them – Jack turned to his driver.

"Now tell me why you *really* have all those tools in your trunk."

Jillian, in the back and half asleep, didn't open her eyes, but surely her ears twitched.

Johnny stared straight ahead, his face impassive. His hands were curled around the steering wheel at exactly ten and two, and they didn't move in the slightest. It didn't take him long to decide; after what he and these other two had been through in the last few hours, he knew there was no reason to hold anything back. Besides, it was hard to hide anything when you were buck-fuckin' naked.

"The slaughterhouse," he said, and for a minute that was all he *planned* on saying, as though that were enough, as if that summed it all up. It dawned on him that as close as he felt to these two J's in his car, they couldn't read his mind, so he went on.

"My uncle told me that they usually get their shipments of fresh animals on Saturday mornings. They're kept in the holding pens for the entire day, examined, sorted, whatever. On Sunday begins the slaughter."

Jack nodded, his suspicion hardening into fact.

Johnny turned in his seat to look first at Jillian, then Jack. When he spoke there was no shame in his voice, nothing held back. "I wanted to see them – to see them die. To see what they looked like slightly *before* the bludgeoning. And when they did die – when they were *murdered"* – to Jillian it sounded like he said the word in slow motion. It curled into her bowels and set her heart to a double beat; she instinctively reached up and rubbed her bruised right breast-"I wanted to be the one who held the sledge-hammer."

"And photograph it as well." Jack rolled down the window and lit a cigarette. A breeze swirled within the car that touched each of them one at a time. "Tripod. Camera. Sledge-hammer." He looked directly at Johnny. "Is that it?"

Johnny shook his head. He had been honest this far; why stop now?

"Hammer: yes. Sledge: no." Without adjusting his hands on the wheel he craned his head to look directly at Jack. "I told you before, back at the pharmacy: I like to smell the bile. I want to see the grey matter up close. To see it wriggle on the end of a cold metal tool." He extended his right hand over to Jack, fingers split in a 'V' and Jack instinctively handed him the lit cigarette. Johnny inhaled deeply on it, exhaled, while from the back of the car Jillian watched them both, trying to decide which of these men were more fascinating than the other. And then it struck her that they *were* men; if not before, then surely they were now. After all, they had been through tonight, surely they had earned *that* distinction.

She leaned back in her seat, her arms no longer covering her bare breasts but at her side. Her head pressed back against the cushion of the seat. Her mind drifted, too many thoughts to name, too many emotions to conclude. But somewhere in all that something a question surfaced, bubbled, and popped. *If they've just become men, what does that make me now? What does that make* me?

2010

Jillian had never asked Jack directly, but that didn't stop him from coming up with an answer; what that that made her, in Jack's mind, was an instigator. Three days had passed since opening the envelopes that contained the details of Jillian Jarblonski and John Megolni's current lives, since then not a waking minute hadn't been spent thinking about the two of them, or all three of them, together on that first night.

Who knows how things might have gone that night if Jillian hadn't begun kicking. Beating. *Clawing*. Who knows what might never have happened afterwards, if she hadn't knocked over that first domino, by driving her foot into the squishy parts of the poor bastard they had accidentally hit? If she had started things once, who was to say that she hadn't started things a second time?

Jack had all the details on her and Johnny and pouring over them again and again he had now come to the conclusion that she was the candidate most likely. Johnny had been married and he had a kid. Jack still couldn't believe that: back then Johnny might as well have had 'Virgin' tattooed on his forehead it was so obvious, and that suggested stability. That suggested normalcy. Nine to five with a mortgage, a station-wagon in the driveway and a fire-engine red tricycle on the lawn. As fucked up as Johnny had been back then, it seemed pretty obvious – assuming his sources were correct – that Johnny was now living the straight life. He couldn't be the one.

Jillian on the other hand... Single. Never married. Shitty teaching job with shitty teachers pay. Drove a ten-year-old Civic. He sighed. She was a woman simply hanging out in the waiting room of life, and it didn't appear that anyone was going to call her name any time soon.

So she'd decided to make her own appointment.

Of course, Jack considered the possibility that he was wrong. It *could* be Johnny. It *could* be a third party. But how unlikely? How unlikely indeed. No, if it wasn't Johnny then it had be Jillian; it *had* to be. And if he was wrong, well, he couldn't help but think that in a way he would be helping her out by putting her out of her misery. Of ending the monotony that her life had become. She'd become a Smiths' song: *Teacher Lost Something (It Was Her Life),* or *Should Have Suicided When I Had the Chance,* he believed that if she were still seventeen and could see herself now, she would agree.

Twenty-one years. That was how long it had been since Jack Barber had had murder on his mind. Twenty-one years since he'd slipped on those gloves. Now he didn't know whether it scared him or impressed him at how easily those gloves slid right back over his fingers, like putting on a second skin. *Kill or be killed,* he thought, *and since I have zero intention of giving it up, that brings me here...*

Sitting on the rooftop of the twenty-eighth floor of the *Casa Rosada,* Jack marveled at the absolute ease with which one was able to gather information these days, if only they had a computer, the know-how, and ten little digits with which to do the typing.

After coming to the conclusion that Jillian was the one most likely, Jack made another trip out of town to hit up a run-down internet café, there he spent the afternoon deep in research. Now that he knew where Jillian was, the information came easy and in less than two hours he had all the details he could need about the three closest buildings to Jillian's apartment. The first was a waste of time: an ice-cream shop that was three months behind on its rent – it was a single story and therefore useless for his purpose. The second was more promising: a smallish office building, eighteen stories, located three hundred meters from Jillian's. Unfortunately, it was located on the opposite side, Jillian's apartment faced east, the office building was on the north-west side, so that ruled that out. Actually, Jack was kind of relieved at that one; with office buildings always came security guards and cameras the fewer eyes that saw him, human or electronic, the better. And so that only left option three, which, like that proverbial bowl of porridge, turned out to be *just right.*

It was an apartment building less than a quarter of a kilometer away, twenty-eight stories, and most importantly, *it was modern.* No concierge. No keys. Every door in the place used numbered passcodes. Hacking into that database wasn't easy – it took him nearly a full hour – but Jack always enjoyed a good challenge and he was smiling most of the time while doing it. It made him think of Johnny, all those years ago, picking the lock of that gate leading up to the slaughterhouse, an action that he was in more ways than one, now repeating. Jack had been genuinely impressed with Johnny's dexterity with his tools – *what a skill!* – and remembered thinking what a great team they all made back then. Johnny could break into things physically, Jack electronically, and Jillian – well, he guessed at that time she was the emotion behind it all. The reason the two guys were trying to get into things in the first place. The Freudian interpretation of this wasn't lost on Jack and he smiled in spite of himself. It made what he was about to do harder, but still, all the more necessary.

He went out and bought a fake moustache, a large flat portfolio case and a baseball cap: that last one felt so alien on his head he cringed when he put it on; the only thing that every touched his hair was shampoo or delicate feminine fingers, but together the three things made him look exactly as he wanted, namely, like someone else. He waited until it was dark and then off he went.

Of course he couldn't take his own car – *leave no trail!*-so he opted for public transport, getting off nearly a full kilometer from the building just in case, and from there he went on foot.

The passcodes worked like a dream, first to gain access to the lobby (he took a cue from the man in the security video from his own office building and moved slowly, purposefully, and always avoided the glowing eyes in the sky) and then he took the stairs: elevators had cameras these days and he didn't want to push his luck. He used the final code to enter the open air of the roof. Stepping out into the night air he barely suppressed a shiver, and this made him frown. It wasn't particularly cold outside, actually it was quite warm, and he knew that the shiver came from inside him, as though his body were chilling itself, hardening his blood and his heart in preparation for what he was about to do. His teeth hurt, and he realized that he was clenching his jaw but when he told himself to relax, he did. A minute later and the large portfolio case was open, its contents arranged like a picnic spread. He went to work.

It took him no more than fifteen minutes to get everything in place and when everything was ready, the tip of his rifle stuck out no more over the lip of the *Casa Rosada* roof than a replaced cork sticks out the hole of a wine bottle; he lined the sights with absolute confidence.

After the success of Jack's second game, *Art of Bullets,* in which players were not only required to shoot their targets dead, but actually gained higher scores by hitting certain points directly (one boss, a Columbian cartel drug-lord named *Jesus,* could be killed with a single bullet to the head, but the player only got full points if they first managed to shoot him once through each palm, once through each foot, and *then* the final damning shot through the forehead) gun makers were busting down his door to get him to feature their products in his next game. The end result being that Jack had scored so many free shooting lessons he was now capable of blasting a zit off a sexless teenager's nose - generally his target video game audience - at five-hundred meters. With the setup he had now – an army grade M24 Sniper Weapons System with a fixed-power scope-he could probably pop that same kid's whitehead without him noticing the *squirt!* He knew all about distance, wind resistance, trajectory, and he had worked everything out to a T, and so it was with the utmost confidence that he loaded the gun and lined up his sights, aimed directly at a floor to ceiling window exactly two-hundred and thirty-seven meters away. He checked, rechecked, and then re-rechecked his calculations again. There could be no mistake. He wanted to do this in one shot and one shot only. All he needed now was for Jillian to open her drapes and this waking nightmare would be over.

--

While Jack, always a man to make things happen, was readying his sight, Jillian had opted for a more passive route. Maurice Ravel's *Bolero* played in the background-she had it on repeat and it was on its fifth loop, climbing in tune to the throbbing of blood passing through her temples. She lay in the bath, naked and motionless, with water right up to her neck and a three-quarter empty wine glass the size of a fishbowl balanced on the lip. Beside it sat a urine-yellow bottle of pills, and beside that, a tiny razor that glinted in the candlelight like a hard sun. Capsules and cuts that was her plan, dull the pain and then bleed it out. Like the man Michael once crooned *if you're gonna do it, do it right*. And she intended to. She had no choice.

The water was hot, almost scalding. She didn't care if she burned her skin – she would welcome the pain actually – but the truth was that she barely felt it. She liked the fact that she couldn't tell where the sweat from her pores ended and her tears began. She could almost imagine that the entire tub was filled with the offspring of her weeping. The progeny of her pain. She smiled without smiling.

"That should have been a Smiths' song," she whispered to herself, her voice hoarse from the tears, the wine and the steam; she could still feel that rough spot in her throat from when she'd ripped it open while screaming at the car stereo. She closed her eyes.

One week had passed since she'd found the tape on the passenger's seat of her car and since then she'd had time – nothing but, really – to think about what it meant.

Her eyes drifted over to the candle. It was hazy and perfect in the steam of the bathroom and she wondered if the flame could actually feel the moisture in the air, thick and pressing. Did the fire feel pain? Did it feel constantly assaulted by the surrounding humidity ? After nearly an hour of burning, it was three quarters down to the nub; wax ran over its side and formed strange musings on the casement of her tub. *Would it ever give up?*

Her eyes moved to the razor on her left. The pills. If the candle went out, and she still hadn't done it, she knew she never would. Her breath was so shallow she wasn't sure she was breathing at all and with half-closed eyes her gaze drifted lower still. Her wrist. The left one that hung limply from over her knee. She brought it closer to her face while her right hand rose from the water, pulsing steam off the flesh as it moved. Thumb caressed the scar on her wrist. Memory caressed some recess of her brain she hadn't visited in years.

It hadn't been a real suicide attempt; if that were the case she would have done it plain and simple, no fucking around with razors in the rain: she would have taken a swan dive off a goddamn bridge right into the path of a twelve-ton Mack truck, but like so many other over-thinking and under-loved girls aged fifteen, she hadn't known it at the time. At the time it was nothing but real. At the time, it was the best thing she could think of to do, but like a sad number of things up to that point in Jillian's life, it had ended in failure.

Awakening hours later she had wondered briefly if she were dead. Her head pounded something fierce and she felt about as put together as a cracker long soaking in a bowl of tepid soup. But then she saw the blood, a pathetic puddle soaked into the comforter of her bed, she would later tell her father that it was menstrual, a word that she knew would shut him up faster than a blow to the chops, and she understood that somehow she had lived. At the time she didn't know why – providence, fate, and accident were all equally likely, she figured – but it was, and ironically so, Jack who explained her non-fatal mistake to her months later: the fact that she had used horizontal cuts instead of vertical ones. *Blood clots quicker than you might think*, he had explained with the tone of one who had not only studied such things, but actually invented them, *and the body wants to survive, even if you don't.*

She liked that idea, and somehow it made up for the fact that she had fucked up what was intended to be her final grim gesture to a world too cruel to care, too ugly to inhabit. Her body was tough, even if her mind was weak, and she loved her body for that. She reveled in it. She discovered it the way one might discover masturbation – surprised and intrigued at being both the toucher and the touched. Through the foundation of her body, her mind became strong, and together they turned power, but even with power there existed shame. Perhaps because this newfound power stemmed from something weak and contemptible, she kept it hidden. It was like inheriting the physical characteristics of a parent that you despised.

Jillian carried those scars around with her for a long time afterwards, for a long time she tried to hide them, under bracelets and make-up, sarcasm and smiles held for a fraction too long to be real. Over time they faded, blended into her skin as just another part of her and weeks would go by before she noticed them, remembered them, reflected on them. Weeks turned to months, and months to years, then one day she'd be buying groceries and reach for her debit card; her sleeve would pull back and she'd see one of the scars, really *see* it, and she'd think, *oh yeah. That was me, I remember that. How wonderfully strange that the person who did that was me, and now not me. How I've passed on. How much better I've become.*

Her memories of that time with Jack Barber and Johnny Megolni were like those scars, only not like them too in that she bore no physical mark on her body to indicate what they'd been through. As Jack had been fond of saying back then, *leave no trail*, and they hadn't, not on her anyway. Mental refuse, sure, but over time that could be cleaned up. Scrubbed and white-washed until there was nothing but the vaguest of stains left, and then only visible if you got down on your hands and knees and *squinted.* But Jillian never did that, oh no. She stood tall. She looked up. Walked straight and never glanced behind her. She couldn't do that anymore. Not when someone was tapping her on the shoulder and whispering her name.

Someone out there knew.

The sounds from the tape came back to her, the jangling discordant sounds of real sex, the screams, moans, the pandemonium of uninhibited fuck; even in the heat of the bath water, she shivered.

Someone out there *knew.*

Not for the first time, she wondered if it could be Jack or Johnny; perhaps they were playing a cruel, torturous joke. She vetoed the idea; they may have been sadistic at times, but never towards her. No, she was their girl, their Jilly Jill, and they had never been anything but protective of her.

They loved you. She closed her eyes to the thought. Closed her eyes to everything, wishing she could lay here forever, breathe in deep and-

Bang! Bang! Bang! Jillian started, yanked out of her reverie. All of a sudden there was banging all around her and the thrust of someone yelling; it swooped down on her: *the tape! Someone was playing the tape!*

Jillian sat up straight in the tub, her arm knocking the giant glass of wine; it fell to the tiled floor with a delicious crash, sending shards of glass scattering like ice chips. The wine splattered, red and deep, standing out in stark contrast to the virgin white tiles of the bathroom floor.

It's happening again, she thought, *I'm there,* seeing the scene through eyes gazing into the past. It was the workroom all over again. No, no: the snow. That night in the snow when the blood froze on her face, cracked her lips, turned her hair to dark crunchy icicles.

More banging, more screams. Someone was in her apartment! Someone was playing the tape!

Without thinking, Jillian put her fingers to her mouth, stuffed them in to stifle the scream she could feel building there, deep down within her. *How did they get in? How did they know? Not important. Protect yourself. Kill them if you have to, but don't let them get to you.* Her eyes tore around the room, saw what she needed, and her fingers grabbed for the razor, knocking over the bottle of pills in the process, sending them scattering to mingle with the wine and the broken glass; they immediately started to dissolve, like tiny snowmen in a great puddle of blood. No matter. She focused on the razor, held it tight between thumb and forefinger, her eyes darting, desperate to see into the mad shadows set to dance by the flickering of the candle flame.

"Who's there?" she called, and she was surprised - *amazed* was more like it - to find that her voice was solid, forceful. She was holding the razor so tightly it was cutting into her own flesh but she didn't care; as pathetic a weapon as it was, it was all she had, and it made her feel less vulnerable, like *she* was in control.

She rose from the tub, not bothering with a towel, not caring about shame or hiding from whoever it was on the other side of the bathroom door. Steam billowed off her in thick waves of pulsing heat. When she climbed out of the tub, careful not to step on any glass, the light of the candle cut through sections of the fog in bursting rays, curling around her silhouette.

She moved with the agility of an aged gymnast, a little slow maybe, but confident, solid. Ready to pounce at any moment, she held the little straight razor between her breasts and belly-button, concentrating on the space in front of her. Guesstimating the height of her would be tormentor, her elbow stiffened with tension as it readied to spring out and slice at the jugular of whoever was standing on the other side of the door.

In a flash came three movements so fluid that they seemed as one. With her free hand Jillian yanked open the door. Then she sidestepped. Then came a twist of her wrist, ready – more than ready, oh so much more – to fillet whatever flesh it found…but there was none. All that greeted her on the other side of the door was the nearing crescendo cascade of that dead Frenchman's masterwork, and she stood there framed in the doorway, soaking wet and alive, feeling, despite the three-quarters bottle of wine she'd consumed, as aware and awake as she'd been in over twenty years.

Her breath was heavy, her mind raced. The trumpets were blaring now, the violins sang, the bassoons blew and the bass drum pounded its steady thump, so core to the piece and this scene that she wondered if it were not her own heart that was producing the throb. Her face contorted; *what happened to the yelling? The banging? Who turned off the tape?*

Then she heard it again, only this time she knew it wasn't coming from her own apartment. There was yelling, that was for sure, and there was banging, but the origin of the sounds was below her, from *down there.* She stared at the floor of her apartment, wide-eyed and confused, half expecting the ground to open up and a red-horned man-goat come clip-clopping up a molten grey staircase, but there was only dull carpet. She cocked her head in confusion as she made her way over to the stereo; with a flick of her wrist she cut the volume off completely and that was when it hit her.

" – oddamn music for the last hour and a half now turn it the fuck down before I call the goddamn cops!" This outburst was immediately punctuated by three solid and evenly spaced thumps, presumably from a broom or the handle of a plunger, that resounded in her toes.

Silence then. She let out a breath she hadn't known she was holding and her eyes slowly scanned the room once more, still not fully trusting her solitude.

"It's about goddamn time!" she heard her neighbor half mutter, half shout, and she rolled her eyes. This was a guy who had been trying for three years in a row – unsuccessfully thank God-to campaign the condo board into banning babies in the building. As Jillian recalled, the crux of his proposal had hinged on the 'generous' stipulation that expectant mothers were to be given a six months eviction notice, a full four more than what was required by law. For a moment, she considered walking over and turning the stereo back on, even turn it up a notch or two, but didn't think she had the emotional energy to deal with another onslaught. Instead, she stepped across the room – the hand holding the razor had finally relaxed, but she held it still – and opened the drapes that cut her off from the rest of the world.

The building she lived in had forty-two floors and she was on the twenty-first, right smack in the middle, the meat in a great working class mile-high, and that was fine with her. It was one of the tallest buildings in the area so that even from the twenty-first floor it commanded an impressive view. The city glowed below her. Dinky cars moved about their tracks, filing on and off the highway at a speed that seemed unrealistically slow; it was a wonder they ever got anywhere at all. The lake to her left – so large it was impossible to see the other side-was a black void; it could have been the edge or the end of the world.

Jillian stood there, drapes wide, legs spread, arms akimbo, as naked as a babe just slid out with the afterbirth riding tandem. It touched on her with a surreal lightness that minutes ago she had been contemplating ending her life, had gone so far as to prepare the pills and ready the razor. She glanced behind her at the bathroom door across the way, and could see from where she stood the candle's hypnotic flicker, the dark blotches that could have been oil, could have been blood – but which she knew to be wine and imagination – puddled around the floor. She nodded. It was a room from her past, and already it was passed. In a few minutes, she would grab a rag from the hall closet and go sop up the mess, being mindful of the glass, careful of the cut. She knew she would do these things naked, would put on no clothes until everything was taken care of, all mess cleaned and placed in the proper receptacle. Things new to this world required no clothes for they had nothing to conceal. The idea was foreign to them: it existed not.

"Life," she said out loud, and the empty room did not eat it up. Instead the word stayed there, solid as the table lamp, concrete as the walls that surrounded her.

"Life," she repeated, and breathed. She'd tried to give it away once, to bleed it out, and her body fought back. She'd almost tried again tonight, but this time it was her mind that wouldn't allow her to let go; it wanted to hold on too much. She considered what this meant.

I won't run from it, she thought, and the words came out from her mind like a queen's address to a subject who had forgotten their place. It was not a wish. Not a desire. It was a command, and the idea of it, the fucking *bold-faced idea* of it, wowed her.

I've forgotten how much I love it: Life. Dealing with little shits in the classroom all day has...

She dropped the thought. She dropped the razor blade too, but she didn't notice that. It fell to the carpet with an unimportant *flof.* Then she reached up, pressed her hands to the cold glass, to the world in front of her, and she liked the feeling so much she pressed her body too. Her breasts and her stomach, and the face of her thighs, all of it, mashed against the full-length window as though she were trying to seduce it, trying to bring forth from its coldness something warm, something *there.*

Her pubic hair, still wet, pressed a moist triangle into the glass. Her breath fogged the window, and she loved it. It proved that she was still alive. She marveled that she could affect things.

She pressed her body harder, threatening to break the glass. Daring the window to crack and send her spiraling twenty-one stories down to concrete and death.

The concrete didn't stand a chance.

I'd forgotten all those things I did when I was stupid and cold but now I'm wise. And hot. And alive. A feeling overcame her like a faint. She pressed harder still against the glass, her feet digging into the carpet, her toes curling in a mad ecstasy of defiance and push. Her fingers were splayed so wide the muscles pulled and without considering what she was doing, she opened her mouth, inhaled deeply and extended her tongue; she licked at the glass, a long and pulling stroke.

I'm alive, she thought again: *I'm alive.*

Her flesh was flat against the window-pane; were it possible, she would fuck it.

This time, I won't run from it.

The young face of Jack Barber flashed in her mind. Beside that face: Johnny Megolni. She pushed harder still and she swore she felt the glass give a little, move.

I wonder what they look like now.

And without realizing what she was doing, her hands curled into fists.

--

Jack Barber had been a murderer once, plain and simple, and here he was, about to test the old adage that people never truly change. For nearly three hours he'd been sitting on this rooftop waiting for some sort of sign that Jillian was home, that he wasn't wasting his time, and now he'd finally got it, though it didn't come from where he'd expected it too; it came from Jillian's neighbor.

There was a stop-watch beside Jack's knee and every two minutes it let out a tiny beep, signaling that it was time to take another look. Up the binoculars went and his eyes scanned, first Jillian's apartment – curtains still closed – then all the surrounding apartments, above, below, left and right. He'd done this nearly two-hundred times since he'd arrived but now it finally paid off.

Directly below Jillian's place lived a man who couldn't sit still, or sit at all for that matter. He paced back and forth in his apartment arranging and rearranging things as though the Queen herself were coming over for tea and crumpets. He smoothed the cushions of his couch. He rearranged the boxes of cereal and crackers in his cupboards. Then he removed all the crisper drawers from his refrigerator and scrubbed the tracks below with a toothbrush. Jack shook his head but at least it was some form of entertainment: classic OCD. Jack raised one eyebrow and considering downing this man too, put him out of his misery. And then all a sudden, all that watching came to a head, when the man went to the hall closet and pulled out a broom.

Who sweeps their apartment at almost twelve o'clock at night? Jack asked himself, rolling his eyes, but then the man did something wholly unexpected. It wasn't cleaning that was on his mind, oh no. Instead, he took the broom up in two tight hands and began poking the handle of it into the roof of his apartment, banging. And yelling by the looks of his snarling mouth. Jack sat up and leaned forward.

Up to this point, Jack didn't even know if Jillian was home, hell, she could have been out of the country for all he knew, but no one, including OCD crazies, would bang a broom on the roof of their apartment unless something was going on upstairs, surely. Unless maybe someone was stomping around. Or shouting. Or playing music too loud.

Jack smiled. *What do you want to bet the singer has got huge hair?*

His eyes narrowed in on Jillian's apartment window, willing the damned curtains to open, to rustle, anything to let him know that all of this wasn't a colossal waste of his time, that she actually was home. Was it his imagination or did it now seem like there was a bit of light seeping out from behind those curtains? Like maybe she had turned on a light in a room at the back of the apartment… Was that a shape moving behind them, a shadow…?

Below her apartment, the man appeared to relax a little. He waved his hand once at the ceiling in a dismissing gesture, then he was returning his broom to the closet. He went back to fluffing the pillows on his couch for the third time and Jack tilted his wrist ever so slightly and Jillian's window came back into view, only this time…

Yes! Houston, we have movement! Jack's heartbeat doubled as he watched a hand trace the edge of the curtain, feel around and then yank the thing wide open. Jack didn't hesitate. He waited not one second; this could be his only chance. The binoculars fell to the floor of the roof with a dull thud, and Jack moved smooth as smoke to position himself at the ready of the sniper gun. He leaned in, grabbed the trigger, closed one eye and focused the other, his breath held steady in his throat.

It was her.

He saw *her*.

The face was the same as the one in the photograph, yet different. The photo was black and white; the real Jillian existed in live Technicolor, her midnight black hair he couldn't believe he had somehow forgotten about - *they don't make* vampires *with hair that dark,* he remembered thinking about her three or four lifetimes ago - and her cheeks were a blushing red that suggested she'd been shouting, exercising, or sweating, or perhaps all three. Jack blinked one, twice, and had to swallow hard. It was Jillian Jarblonski alright, and she was buck-fuckin-naked.

A hot breath escaped Jack's mouth and he had to swallow again. A sweat broke out on his forehead and he didn't know if it was a result of his gun or his groin. After twenty-one years it was his first sight of a girl he had once loved and here she was, naked as a jaybird and… His eyes widened in disbelief: *what the hell was she* doing?

At first she just stood in front of the window, taking in the view, but now she was actually pressing herself against it. Through the sight of the gun-at four-hundred times magnification-he could see plumes of steam fogging the glass around the edges of her flesh. He could see her skin pressing into the windowpane, her forearms, her lips, her breasts, forcing themselves against the glass as though…

Jesus, she looks like she's trying to fuck *the thing.* He shook his head, readjusted the sight ever so slightly, and looked again. Her rich thatch of pubic hair was as dark as the hair on her head and Jack couldn't help but smile in spite of himself.

Once an eighties girl, always an eighties girl, he thought, then frowned.

Guns are for pussies, he thought suddenly, a flash of his teenage philosophy when knives had seemed exquisite and the peen of a hammer a work of art. *The power of destruction,* he thought. The ability to destroy something that can never be made again. That was what he had told Johnny and Jillian way back in the day when they had first set about their business: *guns are for pussies.* Yet here he was, twenty-one years on, about to murder someone in the most cowardly way he could fathom.

What the fuck happened to me? he wondered. He was sweating so much now that his finger felt slippery on the trigger. He didn't know if he could do it. He eyed that bush of hair between Jillian's thighs and felt his breathing grow shallow. His head swam slightly. *When I said guns were for pussies, that was* not *what I meant.*

He swore through gritted teeth. *Now is the time Jack: Now. Or never.* His finger played over the trigger, sliding over it in a perversely sensual design, as though caressing the curve of...

All of a sudden, Jillian jerked out of view; Jack shook his head in disbelief. One second she was there, then the next, gone. But he hadn't even seen her move. He'd had her narrowed in his sights when –

He shook his head when he realized what had happened. The sight had moved of its own accord, but: impossible. It was on a tripod and the tripod –

Jack glanced down and saw the problem immediately. His heart was beating so fast that throwing up seemed inevitable, but his hands went back to the sight and readjusted it quickly, expertly.

The window was empty.

The curtains were still open, but the window was empty. Jillian Jarblonski was gone.

Jack fell back on his own ass, hitting it a little harder than he'd intended, and let out a bellowing sigh. Then he rolled over on his side, pressed his face into the rough gravel of the roof, and closed his eyes. He began to laugh, unable to help it. He didn't know where it came from exactly, perhaps from relief that he hadn't actually done it, that he wouldn't have to worry about the potential consequences of committing murder at age thirty-eight. Perhaps it was out of the joy of proof that he really was a different person than he had been all those years ago, no longer a murderer but a man capable of compassion, of reason, of care.

Or maybe it was due to his imagination's conjuring of the image of Jillian's face, were he ever to tell her how close she had come to being murdered with a bullet square between the eyes. And saved only by the grace of the erection still jutting full at attention from between his legs.

150

1989

Waking up the next morning after Mendoza's Meats and the old man on the road, the only thing to prove that any of it had actually happened was a pile of damp clothes on Jillian's floor, and a claw-shaped bruise on her right tit. The day after that the clothes were dry, and any fear or remorse she might have felt about what they had done was dissipating as surely as those water molecules had. A few days later she awoke to discover those dark, mold-cultured bruises on her breast were barely discernible; she had to rotate her body this way and that several times in front of the mirror to see that they were still there. And after her morning shower they didn't seem to be there at all as though she had simply washed away the final remnants with soap and H2O. It was much the same way with her conscience on her way to meet Jack and Johnny at the cemetery.

It was the first time they'd seen each other since that night at the slaughterhouse. It both amazed and delighted her to discover that they looked exactly as they had before; there was no trace of murder in their eyes, no footnotes of guilt written in the lines of their faces. Jack was laying on the ground chewing on a long piece of yellowed grass sprouting from his lips. Johnny was stepping around the cemetery and snapping photo after photo of the tombstones.

"So," he began, adjusting the focus ring on his camera as he framed the shot, "when are we gonna add one of our own to this here macabre collection?"

Jillian smiled; she hadn't expected them to get right into it, but was glad that it was Johnny who brought it up. It would make what was on her mind so much easier to express.

Jack turned to Jillian, reached out and gave her neck a warm squeeze. "I have a feeling Jilly here has something to say about that." He pursed his lips at her. "Am I right?"

Jillian suddenly felt very nervous; her heartbeat trebled in her chest as she glanced around the room. "You think it's safe to talk about here?" she asked, her voice hushed and tight.

"Safe as any place I reckon," said Jack, "after all, dead men tell no tales." He grinned. "I think it's okay Jilly. Now what did you have in mind."

"Well, it's about Mr. Wolfe. She was watching Jack intently, trying to gauge his reaction.

Johnny felt a little left out. "Who's Mr. Wolfe?"

Jack returned Jillian's gaze; their eyes were locked, but when he spoke he spoke to Johnny.

"He's the religion teacher at our school."

"The guy's a douche bag with wings," Jillian cut in, then shut up. Jack went on.

"A lot of people think he's a pedo and a pervert and while I'm not so sure about the first, Jillian has irrefutable proof of the latter." He bowed his head slightly to Jillian. "Can I tell him?" She nodded.

"He felt her up about a month ago. Then, the fucker had the brass balls to give her detention. When we met you that day in the pharmacy that's who we were buying that shit for."

"The syrup of ipecac? Is that what you're planning to-"

An image of the old man on the road grabbing her breast flashed in her mind and without warning, a fury erupted in Jillian. "Fuck that syrup of ipecac shit. It seemed like a good idea at the time but now that I've-" She paused here, searching for the right words, and Jack nearly filled them in for her, but kept silent. *Now that you've tasted murder,* he thought, *and realized that it wasn't as bitter as you thought it would be. That it was in fact quite sweet. And oh so addictive...*

"Now that I've thought about it," she went on, "I've realized that throwing up isn't good enough for that piece of shit. Throwing up might actually do him some good, like an enema for the soul. No, I really want to make him suffer. And to make sure that what he did to me..."

"He won't ever be able to do to anyone else again." Johnny nodded and Jack read the expression on his face well, thinking: *it's a sentiment, a desire, that he himself has known first hand. But who did Johnny want to stop? And stop from doing* what?

"What is it with my tits that makes guys think they can...cop a squeeze. I mean, first Mr. Wolfe with the left one. Then that old fuck with the right."

Jack raised his eyebrows. "Let's hope nobody ever goes for your snatch; we'll have to build a concentration camp."

"Funny guy."

Johnny took a deep breath; the thought of Jillian's breasts, her pussy, and all these dead bodies surrounding made him hot. He had to swallow while his fingers plucked at his shirt, fanning it.

"So what *did* you have in mind?" he asked, and though his voice cracked as he spoke, neither of them appeared to notice.

"I have a few ideas. But whatever happens, I want him to suffer. I'd appreciate any suggestions."

Jack and Johnny watched her, her face as impassive as a judge, and in a way, that made sense. She was the judge, jury and executioner.

"Whatever it is, we can't be stupid about it. We don't rush it. Nothing rash, like the other night." Jack eyed them both, boring his eyes into them, making them understand how serious he was. His words that followed were so heavy they could actually see the capitalization. *"And We Leave. No. Trail. Agreed?"*

Johnny nodded once. "Agreed." Jillian too.

"I want you guys to swear it. Swear to me now that above all things, we leave no trail."

"What are we swearing on?" That was Johnny, and his face looked dead serious: fitting considering their location.

Jillian glanced around. Frowned, wondering. Suddenly, it came to her: *what did she cherish above all things?* Answer: *The Mode.*

"I've got it," she said, her voice low and solemn. "We swear on the lives of Gahan and Gore, Fletcher and Wilder." She held out her hand, palm up. Johnny reached out and placed his over hers; a second later and Jack's noticeably larger hand gripped them both.

They gave no shake. No letting of blood was necessary to seal the deal: skin on skin on skin was enough for all of them. They nodded.

"Leave no trail," they whispered, each nodding once, and a chill came over them all that had nothing to do with the weather.

Without thinking about what she was doing, Jillian placed her arms around the waists of these two boys – *men*, she reminded herself, her hands tightened their grip – and began leading them out of the cemetery. She felt just fine. Sometimes, as they passed stone after stone, her head lulled to one side and she found it resting on the shoulder of Jack, and at others, on the shoulder of Johnny, by the time they made their way out to the street and into the living world she couldn't remember which shoulder belonged to who, and that felt just fine with Jillian as well.

2010

Jillian Jarblonski awoke the morning after her near suicide attempt with a nagging headache and battery acid excitement in her veins. She considered taking a couple Excedrin for the hangover but dismissed the idea; she had work to do, and she wanted to be fully aware for it. Besides, the headache actually made her feel better. It reminded her of the fact that she was alive, and she intended to stay that way.

In the year or two after the three of them had vowed to stop seeing each other, to stop doing what it was they had been doing - *and what they had done, they had done well* - Jillian wondered, on a number of occasions, whether Jackie Boy and Kid Johnny had actually stopped as well. She'd always assumed they had, but now realized that her only basis for that assumption was because *she* had stopped; she now saw the fallacy of such logic. It was like believing your partner would never cheat on you because *you* would never cheat on *them*, a conjecture so naïve it was almost laughable.

Only *not* laughable because it was so damned obtuse. And so, she searched.

Not as computer illiterate as Johnny yet not nearly as tech-savvy as Jack to use a proxy, change her IP address, *and* go out of town, she knew that computers were the way to go; she did her searching at the local library and although she came up with a number of unsolved murder cases that had occurred in the last twenty-one years, there were none that she could directly connect to her former mates of mayhem.

For starters, she didn't know where they lived; they could be anywhere. Hell, they could have both died ten minutes after she last saw them, and she would have no way of knowing. It dawned on her that she was going about all this backwards. Forget about the crimes: focus on the criminals.

She nodded once, her fingers moving over the keys, and they hovered there for a few seconds, unsure. Johnny first, or Jackie? She weighed the odds, decided that Jack, always the careful one - *leave no trail, remember?* – was much less likely to have any internet presence and went with Johnny. She typed in his name, made to press 'enter', and stopped.

What if I find him? What if his face pops up like in one of those joke emails that tells you to stare at the picture for one whole minute and without warning after thirty seconds a screaming demon flashes on the screen and scares the living shit out of you? She shook her head. She'd already done more thinking about the past in the last few days than she had in ten years, she couldn't imagine what seeing an actual photograph might bring back.

Coffins were made to be closed, she thought, *and to stay closed; that's why there's no handle on the inside.*

Her index finger hovered, her eyes narrowing on the button below it and she marveled at how important that key suddenly was. *Return.* That was what it said in clear white letters.

Return.

She knew that if she pressed it, that was what she would do: Return. To the past. To a cave of memories that she had decades ago placed a mental string of dynamite sticks around and blew to kingdom come. To strange times of her youth when causes and effects were unequaled. Where parallel lines zigzagged, and things that seemed brilliant and larger than the exploding cosmos were right on the money.

For years afterwards, she had hated herself – like the adulterer just climaxed – and contemplated turning herself in seventeen times a day. The thrill of youth was absent and settling upon her was the lead heavy weight of consequence and guilt. And for a time, she simply *was*. She existed as something empty and directionless, a balloon pushed round by whatever breeze came its way.

But she *was* regretful.

She *was* repentant.

And from that last moment the three of them were together, that rapturous moment conceived out of black nihilistic conviction, and delivered in shiny freshets of deep cardinal blood, Jillian herself had been reborn. She had become *good*.

Like the ex-smoker who remembers the doctor pointing to that dark spot in the X-ray of his chest.

Like the ex-drinker who recalls trading the last of his dignity for one last shot.

The ex-prostitute who stands over a snoring, slobbering John and swears *never again,* and means it.

She rejected it. And when she threw that life away, she made sure it stayed away.

But now: *Return.* The key waited beneath her finger like a cigarette just dropped off the rolling line. A smoky shot of an eighteen-year-old scotch. That gulping desire to feel wanted again. To feel whole. To imbibe in that which once made you real: Alive. *Return.*

It made the smallest of clicks as her fingers forced it down.

--

Nothing.

Nothing even remotely connected to the boy she'd once known. Jillian relaxed in her chair and glanced around at the other patrons of the library. Her heart was beating fast in her chest and it came to her that she'd half expected a swat team to come crashing through the windows, guns drawn, twenty-one-year-old warrant spiked on the end of some black weapon of metal and powder.

Only nothing. To her left a woman sat reading a thick green novel by Danielle Steel. On her right were two Asian girls sitting across from each other, both thumbing their cellphones. An elderly man with thinning grey hair and a bushy white moustache that reminded her of Mark Twain sat half-slumped near the window, a fallen book at the foot of his chair. Some guy contemplating a newspaper.

Where's the bolt of lightning? she thought, and almost managed a smile. But no, no smile for Jillian today. There was still one name on the list and she had the feeling that she'd saved the worst for last. She glanced round once more – already she was expecting the sleeping old man to have torn off his mask, to be approaching her with an upheld badge and a sneer of contempt on his face – but everything was as it had been.

Using a single index finger, she typed: J-a-c-k B-a-r-b-e-r.

She tried to swallow and found she couldn't, felt that if her heart beat any louder a librarian was going to come round and tell her to *shushhhh.* Her finger hit home.

Jack Barber.
Jack Barber.
Jack Barber.
Jack Barber.
Jack Barber.
Jack Barber.
Jack Barber.
Jack Barber.
Jack Barber.
Jack Barber.

His name appeared ten times, in every slot on the search page, highlighted, each one like little footnotes pointing huge throbbing fingers at the things they had done together.

It wasn't just his name. It was:

His photo.

His face.

Him.

Jack-Fucking-Barber.

Still alive, and the apparent head of some software company in the city, less than two hours away.

Jillian blinked, again and again, feeling dizzy.

Somewhere around her - behind her, above her, inside her: she couldn't tell which – someone coughed. One of the Asian girls giggled a million miles from nowhere. The rustle of a newspaper thundered as though the pages were being stuffed directly into her ears. The rough snort of a snore tore through all of it and Jillian's eyes went back to the screen:

Jack Barber.

He looked older of course, deeper somehow, thicker but not overweight. More like the things he'd seen over these past twenty-one years, the things he'd done, had become a part of him, solidified him. It scared the holy shit out of her to realize that Jack Barber was as real as he'd ever been, more real in fact. He was out there somewhere in this world, living, working, doing whatever it was that he had been doing ever since that gloriously fucked up night in the blanketing snow, when they'd suffered the final act and did what they'd always planned to do. Here he was, right in front of her on the computer screen, so real that she felt certain that if she reached out and touched the cold glass of the monitor, she would be able to feel the heat from his cheek, scratch the stubble, run her thumb across his lips and tell him –

"Handsome devil that one eh."

The words came to her so softly, so quietly, she believed they had formed in her own head. Funny that because the voice didn't sound like Jack had sounded exactly, but the way he might sound were he to have aged say twenty-one years and…

Her head shot around, her eyes zigzagging in her skull like the marbles in one of those *Labyrinth* games from when she was a kid. The woman was still engrossed in her book, the Asians: their cellphones. The old man was still dead to the world asleep, only now there was a great dollop of drool hanging off his chin like a bungee jumper waiting to be hauled back up. The man with the newspaper was gone but his chair was still there, empty save the newspaper he had left behind.

Then the voice came to her again, this time from directly behind her.

"There's more to life than books you know, though not much more." From behind her she saw a hand extend, a wrist, a forearm, and then a finger pointed directly at the face on the computer screen.

"Oh you handsome devil," she finished without thinking. It was a lyric to one of her favorite songs, though one she hadn't heard in years. She closed her eyes, refusing to turn around, knowing that if she did, the past was going to up and kick her square in the cunt.

"Jack," she managed to whisper, her voice cracking horribly on the *k*. It made her realize that she'd been waiting twenty-one years to say that name. To say it to *him*.

She didn't see the man behind her nod his head, but she felt it. She didn't have to turn around; Jack was the only man she'd ever known who could make her *feel* his actions, and Jillian felt them all. And then something totally unexpected, unexpected yet wonderful happened. Jillian knew that she should be scared. This was too much of a coincidence to imagine that Jack had found her by accident. So it was him that had sent her the tape, and now he was coming to collect whatever the hell it was that he planned on collecting. He was here to get what he wanted because that was what Jack Barber always did, no exceptions. He: Got. What. He. Wanted.

What happened was this: she felt safe. Filled aware with the fact that Jack Barber had not come to hurt her at all. That he was, as always, on her side.

It didn't occur to her until later, much later, that perhaps that was also what Jack Barber had intended all along.

She turned around to face him.

--

Two hours, four Mai Tais *(hers)* and six neat Johnny Walker Double Blacks *(his)* later, both parties were convinced. Convinced and exhausted, not to mention a little drunk. It had been a hell of an emotional reunion; talking in hushed tones about murders you'd committed some two decades ago has a way of wearing people out. But still, Jillian couldn't help but ask.

"I only got an audio tape Jack. I'm sure you remember that I'm curious by nature. What *exactly* was on your DVD?" Actually the curious part was only half true; Jillian wanted to confirm that it wasn't a video recording of the audio *she'd* received. In other words, some kind of low grade porn snuff film. Just the thought made her feel nauseous, and she promised herself that her last Mai Tai would remain exactly that; it was too easy for her to imagine that video ending up on the internet somehow...

"To be honest, I didn't watch the full thing. Only saw about thirty seconds of it, forty-five at most. Got so freaked out I practically threw the monitor across the room." He held up his hand displaying his one mangled finger. "Ripped a nail off."

"Well, you never were exactly one for subtlety."

Jack laughed. "Have you *seen* the video games I produce?" Jack shrugged, and watching him, a part of Jillian ,probably the part that was currently marinating in light rum and triple sec, felt sad, and nostalgic, and somewhat bitter, that she had been missing him make that shrug these past twenty-one years.

"No, I haven't. At least I don't think I have. I just found out what you've been up to about fifteen seconds before you snuck up behind me and scared the sacred shit out of me."

"Well, my last brainchild involved a protagonist whose weapon of choice was the ripped off limbs of the people he was trying to kill. Jack shrugged, raising his open palms in a *what can you do gesture* and Jillian couldn't help but laugh.

"So the boy I once loved grew up to be a boy who makes video games, is that what you're telling me?"

Jack stopped swirling his glass of whiskey.

"You were in love with me?"

Jillian eyed him. "I said I loved you. That and 'in love' are two different things."

Jack nodded. "Right you are Jilly Jill, right you are," and he made to take another sip of his whiskey.

Without warning, her hand shot out to cup the rim of his glass, shielding it; her face was corpse pale. "Don't call me that Jack. Not now. Not ever again."

Jack stared down at her hand, noting the lines that hadn't been there the last time he'd held them. The veins. The sporadic liver spots. He tried to think back to all the women he had ever been with in the interim, who had touched his hair or his hands or his face, and tried to think of one who came close to having hands like the ones inches from his mouth. But all he could think of were two opposing digits, a finger and a thumb, slowly crushing the life out of an arachnid twenty-one years ago in a high school class that meant less than nothing… and the fascinated eyes that hovered and watched above, taking it all in.

"Okay," he said, "okay," and Jillian relaxed. Jack did too, though it took a few minutes for his heart beat to return to normal: *those hands. Jesus how had I forgotten about those hands?* He looked her direct in the eyes.

"So what was on the tape that you found?"

Jillian froze. *The thoughts going through my head are the only privacy that I have left,* she thought, *but if he keeps looking at me like that, I won't even have that.* She considered lying, covering up. Recounting some other scene, perhaps with that teacher – *what was his name? what was his name?* – but she couldn't. Not because she couldn't think of it – *Rudy something or other. Rudy Wolfe. That was it. Rudy Wolfe the tit-pinching pervert masquerading as a disciple of the son of God. More like a son of a bitch he was. How did you manage to forget about the time he stood over you like some kind of* – Her mind stopped, pulled the plug. She wasn't prepared to go there. *Wouldn't* go there. She had never been anything but honest with Jack when they'd been together and she had never, not once in all her dealings with him, had any reason to think otherwise about him. And so she told him.

"Sounds of sex," she said, and the words weren't fully out of her mouth before she found herself reneging on her previous promise that she would cut out the booze before things got out of control. Her mouth was desert dry.

"Oh," said Jack. "Oh." He nodded the smallest of nods, so subtle it could have been a tick.

"And what about the DVD?" Jillian would have rather died right then than go into the sounds in more detail.

"It was the workshop. Electric drill and all."

Jack watched as the color, alcohol infused, slowly drained from Jillian's face, like an hourglass bleeding sand. When she picked up her drink her glass was shaking, so he reached over and cupped his own hands over hers, steadied them. He glanced around the bar before he spoke again.

"That was a long time ago Jillian. I can honestly say I've forgotten most of it."

"But someone else hasn't. Someone else remembers it all with a *vengeance.*"

"Not to mention a *video.*"

Jillian closed her eyes and her head dropped into her palms. She began rubbing her temples so hard it looked as though she were trying to grind the memories out her head. When she looked up again a minute later her lower lip was trembling.

"I know it wasn't you Jack. I know that, now. Before, well I wasn't so sure, but now that you're here, I can't remember how I thought that in the first place."

"Ditto."

"So..." She didn't want to say it. Saying it would make it real. In the end it didn't matter; Jack said it for her.

"So that only leaves one." Jack looked directly at her. "Kid Johnny."

"Oh, Jesus." All bones left her then, and she half fell, half slumped onto the table, dropping her face into her crossed arms. *"Jesus Jesus Jesus,"* she whispered again and again and just when she thought she was going to fall apart completely, to melt into a mass of gelatin flesh and slippery blood, she remembered her vow from the previous night that she wouldn't run from it. The bones in her body regrew. The muscles stitched themselves back to her core. She sat up, swearing that she wouldn't crumble again. She wasn't Christ; she needed no third fall. When she spoke, she spoke quickly.

"It has to be. I mean, even when I thought there was the possibility that it was you, I still thought him the one most likely. He was so into cameras. Recording everything. Documenting." Jillian felt her head swimming – she hadn't thought of Johnny's camera in a dozen years at least – but she got on top of the wave and held it down, got it under control. "Man, we were fucked up back then." She looked at Jack as if to ask how that had happened, how had they seemingly turned out so normal.

Jack shrugged. "That we were. But let's be honest Jilly J-" He stopped, shook his head. "Jillian. Johnny always was the most fucked up of the three of us. The loner. Remember how we met him – he was trying to rob a pharmacy. And the slaughterhouse. The pictures. His obsession with recording the process of death on film." Jack's voice once again dropped and when he spoke he used one hand to hide half of his mouth. "His hammer."

Jillian blessed herself. She actually reached up and made the sign of the cross – forehead stomach, shoulder shoulder, kiss on the mouth - just as she had been taught before she hit puberty and discovered logic.

"No more Jack. No more of the past, please." She looked at him with eyes pleading. "I feel like my head is going to explode. It's too much, too much and it's too fast. All of it coming back like this, and after twenty-one years. The flood. I feel like I'm drowning. That it's going to wash all over me and…and…" Her breathing hitched, drew in a great gulping gasp, and she began to cough. Jack reached over and patted her on the back, nodding all the while.

When she was finally okay, he nodded. "Ok, no more. I promise. But we have to figure this shit out."

Jillian smoothed out her face, wiped her nose and the sides of her mouth. "I don't get how he could have done it. I mean he would have had to know ahead of time where we-"

"He did. Don't you remember, he always *did*. In fact, it was always *his* idea where to…yah know." Jack raised a thumb and ticked it off with his other index finger. "The slaughterhouse. That was where it all started right. And the drive. I mean, I get that that was an accident" – *until* you *started murdering the poor bastard,* Jack thought – "but the old church. He ticked off another finger. "The funhouse." Another digit went down. "Those were all his ideas and he knew about all of them *beforehand.* You remember when I asked him that time, how he knew about all those places, you remember what he said? Something like: *these kinda places are easy to find when you've got your own car and no friends.*"

"We were his first."

"Huh?" Jack shook his head; he'd been thinking about something, a memory, and trying to decide if it was real or not, and therefor worth mentioning.

"We were the first friends he ever had. You remember that?"

Jack shrugged. "So why would he do this to us now? We had some good times back then and-" Jacks face reddened. "I mean, together, we had some good times. In spite of the other stuff… you know."

Jillian was watching him closely. She couldn't remember if she had ever seen Jack Barber blush before and the sight of it made her grin. He was right too, she had to admit. That year she was seventeen, in spite of all the fucked things they'd done, was one of the best years of her life. Her mind refused to voice its darker assertion – it stayed lingering on the sidelines of consciousness: *perhaps* because *of all the fucked up things we did.*

"Don't worry Jack, I know what you mean." Something came back to her all of a sudden and it made her smile deepen. "Jackie Boy. We used to call you Jackie Boy."

But the look on his face wiped that smile clean away

"I haven't been a boy for a long time Jillian. And that name was a husk of my former self that I have long since shed."

Jillian understood of course. Hadn't she just told him that she was no longer Jilly Jill? He was looking her dead in the eyes.

"Have you considered the possibility that there's a fourth party in this? Someone we don't know about?"

Jillian hated the way it sounded in her mind, too gangster-y, but she said it anyway. "You mean a loose end?"

Jack shrugged; *it's possible.* But then he shook his head. "But unlikely."

"Why?"

"Johnny was a *photographer.* He lived for that shit. You remember that time when he got that hamm-" Jack stopped, remembering that Jillian didn't seem to have a stomach for this type of stuff anymore. "Don't you find it a bit of a coincidence that someone sent me a *video* of us...*doing stuff,* and one of the guys we were with at the time happened to have a major hard-on for all things film?"

"I don't know. Photos and film are two different things."

"Moving pictures, Jillian, that's all they are. How hard do you really think it would be to make the transition? How hard do you think it would have been for him to get his hands on a video camera, take it to the place where he knew we were going to be and hide it...fuck, wherever. Under some drop-cloths. Through a hole in the wall. *Anywhere.* Do you really think it would have been all that difficult for him to sneak off for a second or two and hit a record button. To transfer the audio from the tape. Come on, easy-peasy-"

"Jap-an-easy," Jillian finished. She remembered that little ditty from way back when but she couldn't remember who it was that had been fond of saying it.

"The question is: why now? Why twenty-one years later? I just. Don't. Get it."

Jillian's face dropped, as serious as a mortician's. "Maybe he misses us."

Jack placed his hands together to cover his nose and mouth, so that his fingertips were resting in the divots where his eyebrows began.

"Fuck."

"What? *What?!*"

Jack shook his head, repulsed by the thought, but knowing that it was important.

"There's something I forgot to tell you. When I got the DVD. Someone delivered it to my office, I told you that right. But not by post. Someone was there; they physically dropped it off. And when I opened it..." Jack's face curled into a grimace of disgust. He didn't blink for fear of letting the image scuttle back into his mind's eye.

"Cockroaches. When I opened the envelope there were three cockroaches. The biggest fuckers I've ever seen in my life. Huge. Unnatural. They were like...like..."

Jillian waited on his final word, waited with bated breath like an accused waits for the jury's final verdict.

"Monsters," Jack finally finished, then he fell silent as he looked down, staring into his glass of whiskey before him.

Jillian shuddered. She couldn't help it. It shook her like a full-body heave. Her face met Jack's.

"Together," Jillian said, "three monsters together. In one place."

Jack swayed a little as he picked up his glass of whiskey.

"Not yet," he said, and downed it in one final swig.

--

Jack and Jillian left the bar. For a long time they walked, not talking. Every once in a while one of them would glance at the other and they would nod once or twice, but they never smiled. They were both deep in thought, and these were the types of thoughts that did not encourage mirth. Eventually they came across a park that turned out not to be a park at all but rather a very tiny graveyard attached to an even tinier church, a monastery, and Jack motioned to Jillian and she bowed her head and into the cemetery they went.

There was a lone bench made of wood, the color of old tea, on which they sat and their eyes roamed from stone to stone and it quickly became clear that every body in that yard was that of a woman, all sisters, all nuns.

"So," Jack finally said, after they had sat there long enough for the approaching night to touch a slight but present coldness upon them both.

"So."

"Any thoughts?"

Jillian blew a puff of cool air up her face, raising her bangs up ever so slightly before they settled back down across her forehead.

"About a million."

"Any we can use?"

"We?"

"Yeah, we. Unless you wanna go this thing alone?"

Jillian shook her head quickly. No. She didn't want that.

"So?"

The idea was in Jillian's head, or at least the basis of it, but it was malformed and that scared her; she didn't like to think what it could turn into if allowed to solidify completely. Finally she gave up trying to fight it and spit it out.

"Well, we have to confront him. We have to do something. We can't sit here and wait for-" Jillian stopped, cut herself off. *Futile* she told herself, though she didn't know if she was referring to the thoughts in her head, or the possibility of getting out of this mess unscathed.

"Agreed," he said. "But the question is: how? You know he'll deny everything."

"Whether he's innocent or guilty."

Jack nodded. "And therein lies the rub. So we gotta do it in such a way that we catch him off guard. So that if he's innocent, we *know* he's innocent."

"And if he's guilty? If it was Kid Johnny that sent us all that shit…what then?"

Jack had an answer for that, or at least he thought he did, but it wasn't the one he gave to Jillian now.

"Then we cross that bridge when we get to it."

"How? I mean, how do we approach him?"

Jack shrugged. "The same way I approached you: with my hands empty, and as a friend."

"His guard will be up. He'll be outnumbered and he'll think something's amiss. He may have been crazy, but he was also crazy smart."

"That's why you'll have to go alone."

Jillian stared at Jack. For a second he seemed to be very far away from her, as though standing at the other end of some bare and lonely field, and not only that, he seemed not to be a person; she couldn't tell exactly what he was, but she knew that it wasn't human. When she blinked a moment later, the feeling was gone.

"Why me?"

Jack met her gaze, and kept it. "Don't you know?"

Something in Jillian deflated a little. She knew, and there was no point pretending she didn't. Not with Jack, not now, not ever.

"Do you think that's fair? I don't really like the idea of toying with his emotions."

"Like the way he's been toying with ours?"

"We don't know that."

"No, we don't, which is exactly why we have to do it this way."

"Okay, so what? How do we do it?"

"Simple. You call him up and ask him to meet you."

"Just like that?"

"Just like that."

"And what if he says no?"

Jack stared at Jillian and his eyes cut into her like a filleting knife into the belly of a squirming pink fish. She nodded; even at seventeen and without a firm grasp on her own emotions, Jillian Jarblonski had known from day one how Johnny felt about her. A woman's mind is a helluva filing cabinet, and she never forgot it either. She sighed, acquiesced.

"You're right; he won't." She rubbed her eyes. The alcohol was wearing off, and it was making her tired. She wondered if Johnny had managed to retain that awkward adolescent charm the way Jack had managed to keep up his hard good looks and the edge in his voice, she had to suppress a smile. It had been a long time since she'd met a man as adoring as Johnny. Benedict was a nice guy after all but...*but he never committed murder for you, did he Jillian? He never grabbed a man by the hair and pushed him face first into a bucket of –*

Jillian's body let loose some kind of movement that was half shiver, half shudder. She felt her toes curl within her shoes.

"So where do I tell him to meet me?"

Jack was prepared for this question. *The tough sell,* he thought, *but the most important of all. It can't be somewhere public. If it is Johnny behind all this, he won't reveal himself in a public place. He might show up, act all prim and proper – with a wife and kid he's got the act down to a T – but the cat will undoubtedly stay drawn up tight in that ol' proverbial bag. And besides, public would be bad for them all; twenty-one years ago we vowed never to be seen together again, and I still have reasons for wanting to keep that promise. If there is a fourth party – someone else that we haven't even considered – then I don't want any more fodder for their camera. I want no more proof of any connection. So you need to get the two of them together privately. But somewhere you can hide, and observe. I'm ninety-nine percent sure that Jillian has nothing to do with all this, but I need that final one percent. And until then, I keep both of them in my sights. Figuratively and literally.*

"The funhouse," Jack said, and then waited for her to explode. He gave her five seconds. It took less than two.

"No fucking way are you out of your goddamn mind!" She couldn't have jumped up faster if he'd told her that the bench she was sitting on was covered in wet paint. She stood over him, arms waving, hands swinging close enough to his face to throw a breeze on it.

"Why not?"

"Well, for starters it's a super public place. They'll be a million kids running around. Parents. Security guards. I thought we wanted to keep this on the lowdown. To keep this between ourselves."

Jack nodded in assent at each thing she said, preparing his rebuttal. When she was done, he raised a single flat palm in her direction.

"All good points. All sound. Except for several very important facts."

"Which are?" Jillian couldn't have sounded more skeptical if he had told her that the sun was a giant Gobstopper and the moon was made of government cheese.

"Well, for starters it closed down two years ago. Sold to some developers who wanted to turn it into some huge condo property. Retirement community, something like that."

"So it's gone then." The relief in her voice was as obvious as blood in the snow.

Jack shook his head. "The deal went belly up less than two months after everything was signed and sealed. A lot of missing money. Rumors of mob connections gone sour and something about a strip-club that burned down under mysterious circumstances. And then the guy who brokered the whole thing was found in a two-bit hotel room…with a pool cue stuck far enough down his throat to tear a hole right through his stomach and into his intestines. Of course this wasn't announced in any official capacity, but according to some people in the know, he'd had some kind of acid – battery I think – funneled into an opposing orifice. Ate him up from the inside out."

Jillian stared at him wide eyed. "Christ on a cross," she whispered. "How do you know all this?"

Jack was interested to note – one might have even said amused – that Jillian didn't seem at all put off by the gruesomeness of the scene he'd just described but in response to her question he simply held up both his hands and wiggled his fingers.

"The internet has many a locked secrets sweets and in these babies, there happens to be a key to any one of them. But that's beside the point. The park has sat pretty much untouched these last few years. No one wants to go near it because of…well, because of the associations with all that happened."

"But why there? There must be a hundred other places we could pick that have less… personal connections." She began the question in earnest but realized she knew Jack's answer before it was fully out of her mouth. She saved him the trouble. "It's *because* of our history that you think it's better. Johnny will be unable to resist."

Jack nodded. "You got it Pontiac. But there's another reason too, and this is the most important. There are a million places that I can hide. Places higher up where I can see everything. Believe it or not your old pal Jack has become somewhat of a sharpshooter with a sniper rifle and I'll be there ahead of time, waiting, watching, making sure he doesn't try anything."

"And if he does?"

"It's an abandoned park. No one around for a good kilometer. No one to hear the shot, and even if someone does, plenty of time for us to get the H out of D before they show up. It's the most secluded place I can possible think of."

Jillian stared at Jack, watching his face for something – she didn't know what, but she knew that she would recognize it the moment she saw it – but she saw nothing. Only that hard intelligence and razor tight jawline that she had always admired. *He's never let me down before,* she thought, *never once. And he's probably the only man alive who I can say* that *about.* She gave him a single nod. Then she cracked a smile.

"Jack Barber, a sharpshooter. I never thought I would see the day. Weren't you the one who always said guns were for pussies?"

For a fraction of a second Jack's mind did a frantic somersault – *I almost blasted a quarter-sized hole about two-and-a-half feet above yours less than twenty-four hours ago,* he thought, but he never missed a beat. Instead, he mirrored her smile perfectly. "People change," he said.

"That's true," she said, nodding, "people do change."

Jack stared at this woman beside him as the cool air of the cemetery picked up her hair and sent it whipping around her ears; it made Jack think of a jockey whipping his horse, not to make it go faster, but out of anger and spite and malice. He shook the image away and shivered. It was three days shy of the first day of summer but it felt colder, as though there should be orange and red leaves scattered over the graves and children readying themselves and their costumes for all hallows eve.

"You're using me as bait." She didn't look at him when she said it, she didn't have to. The look she was giving him flowed out of her the way a block of ice sends out cold plumes from all sides.

Without warning Jack placed a hand on her shoulder and she flinched, not because the hand was offensive on her body, but for the opposite reason. *Oh Christ, she was seventeen again.* She was sitting on a picnic table in a park feeling helpless and lost and there was some rich bitch woman screaming about her dog *Princess* or *Misty* and how it had been poisoned and Jack – he was seventeen too though he seemed so much older, so much more together – had his arm on her shoulder, just as he did now and she found it hard to breathe and for a few blizzard seconds she didn't know if it was her in the *past* or her in the *present* who was confused, or both, both of her selves lost in the moment of time, 1989 or 2010, what was the difference? To her wonder/horror, as though Jack, Jack now who had gained a few pounds (but it suited him) and who had a few greying wisps of hair winging their way out of his temples, it were as though he were reading her thoughts because he was reaching over and taking her hands, her *wrists,* in his hands. And caressing his thumbs over the veins that joined her palms to her arms, she was so fucking confused, so drunk on self-hate and as-of-late returned confidence, that she couldn't help close her eyes and let it wash all over her, like a perfume, or a wave of heat, or a soft searching tongue on her sex.

"They're almost gone," Jack said, and when she opened her eyes, she saw that he was staring down at her wrists, staring at the tiny raised slits that had once seemed so prominent and now... well, it was like he said; they were almost gone.

"Still there though. If you know where to look."

He didn't take his thumbs off her wrist and she thanked God for that. He was the only man who had ever touched her there, and it was something more than sex; it was life. It was *her* life. She thought about how close she had come to repeating history just last night. The razor was still sitting somewhere on the carpet of her living room where she had dropped it while in her trance.

"So are you," he said, and all his previous words came back to her from that fall of 1989. How he had instilled in her so much worth. He never turned her into a survivor; he simply made her realize that she herself *was* a survivor. She remembered where she was now, in the year 2010: in a graveyard, surrounded by the decayed bodies of generations of women who had given their lives to God. Who had lived and died in the habit – so to speak – of sacrificing all for the good of the One. She then thought of that dog, *Misty* or *Princess* and she wondered – *Mitzy! It was* Mitzy *I remember now!* – if that crazy woman's irrational fear had come true. *Had* Mitzy been poisoned? Did that dog actually die? The question brought her full circle, and she stated her original point.

"I may be a survivor, but you're still using me as bait Jack." And this time she looked at him directly.

He never flinched. In fact he didn't so much as blink. What he did was match her eye for eye, and God help her, when he finally spoke, she believed him.

"It worked the last time didn't it."

It wasn't a question, it was a fact, and she couldn't help but nod. Out of nowhere the wind picked up, drawing a howl across the scene. Then it too died, like everything else in this space.

Bait. In her mind she spat the word, as though trying to get a hair off the end of her tongue. But Jack was right, it *had* worked the last time, hadn't it? Worked all too well in fact. And she remembered their trap.

1989

Jillian would have felt more comfortable stepping out from behind the screen *naked* than she did wearing her school uniform – the embroidered blouse and the pleated kilt only served to remind her how much she fucking hated that bastard Wolfe and what he'd done to her - but thankfully she found a serene comfort in the fact that this was a step in the staircase that would lead up to the gallows from which said Cocksucker would hang. And it didn't hurt that it was one of her new found best friends that was behind the camera, clicking away and making adjustments as needed.

"You know they don't have to be perfect, right?" asked Jillian, a playful smirk on her face. "They're not going to *Tiger Beat* after all."

Johnny shrugged. "I never do anything half-assed if I can help it."

Jack, who was sitting on an overturned milk crate at the back of Johnny's basement, watching them both and smoking a cigarette, coughed. "So long as you remember that you can't keep them. *Any* of them. Not even the negatives."

"Oh, I'll keep the negatives all right." Johnny reached up and tapped a single index finger on his temple. "I'll keep them right here."

"Perv," shot Jillian, but she smiled as she said it and Johnny once again clicked the shutter button.

"Gotcha."

Jillian did a little dance across the room, playing it up for the camera and it made Jack a little sick to watch; he had never seen Jillian acting like this before, being all coy, flirty. Common. *Man she must really want to get this guy bad,* he thought, and any respect he had misplaced for her quickly returned. She was a real engine that one, and she put the *revv* in revenge. He shook his head.

"No, no, gotta move back Jilly Jill. From that angle you can see the exposed wiring and the corner of the screen. No good."

Johnny nodded, amazed at how easily Jack kept his cool. Johnny was getting a little hot under the collar watching this girl prance around in front of him, *for him*, but it was Jack who was making sure everything was in line. When Jack had said before *'Leave No Trail'*, he hadn't been kidding. Originally, he had wanted them to take the shots in a forest so that there could be no trace back to them – a public space and all – and the only way Johnny could convince him that his basement would do just fine was by bringing them both down here and showing them how nondescript the back wall really was. A vast sheet of drywall with not so much as a single visible nail. No way the photos could ever be matched to this location, so long as Jillian stayed within the frame.

"He's right," Johnny said. "I think I got a bit of those green wires in the last shot. Move a little to the right again." Johnny checked, nodded. "That's better." He blew off a few more shots, then stood up straight. "I think that's enough of those ones. Do you want to…"

It was a miracle his voice didn't crack as he said it because he knew, as Jillian and Jack surely did, what he was about to ask. They were doing a *series* of photos after all, and that was the end of the first. And in the second… He swallowed while he waited for Jillian's reaction, certain that she would deny him. Chicken out and re-neg. Instead what she did was shrug and begin unbuttoning her blouse.

She got right down to the second last button before she stopped. Johnny deflated a little; he knew it.

"You guys really think this is necessary? I mean, don't you think the slutty poses *with* clothes will be enough?"

It was Jack who answered her, and Johnny thanked God; if he had tried to open his mouth at that moment all that would have likely come out was a frog's croak and a quarter cup of drool.

"We need a guarantee Jillian. The pictures will entice him, no doubt. Tweak his curiosity for sure. But if that's all it is, he might smell a rat; take it to be some kind of trap. But, if you show a little skin…"

Jillian nodded. "He'll know it's for real."

"Damn skippy. And let's be honest, once he sees the tits you got he'll be as horny as a toad. Moth to the flame, yah know."

Jillian shrugged. "Well, you got me there – they are some fine ass tits. *Just One of the Guys* quality."

Jack laughed. "I am aware."

Jillian made to unbutton the second to last one and stopped. "I think you guys just wanna get another look at my bodacious ta-tas."

"Would it make you more comfortable if we took off *our* clothes?" Jack asked through a joker's grin. The second the words were out of his mouth Johnny broke into a cold sweat; it had been one thing that night when they'd all been high on the kill, covered in blood and needing a cleanse, but if Jillian asked them to strip here, now, in his own basement where he had surely jerked off a hundred times at least…it would be too…well, he didn't think he could do it. He didn't even know how he was going to take any pictures he was trembling so much.

Jillian stood there, her eyes moving back and forth from one to the next as though sizing up the possibility. "Wellllll," she began, and then let loose one great whooping laugh. "Nah, just kidding." She shrugged. "What's the big deal about showing two boobs-" she glanced down her shirt, then looked up and pointed at Jack and Johnny " – to two even *bigger* boobs." She giggled then, and Johnny felt like he was being given a gentle massage up and down the column of his spine.

"Make with the nipples already," shot Jack, dropping his cigarette butt into the empty can of Coke at his feet, "I got a bone in my pocket that I wanna burn and I ain't getting' any higher watching you two."

Jillian shook her head, still laughing. "I bet you got a bone in your pocket Jack Barber. And if you don't now, well…" And without further ado she reached down and unbuttoned those last two buttons, opened her shirt and let it all hang out. Johnny almost dropped the camera – he would have if the strap hadn't been curled around his neck – and it took him a few seconds to recover; he was glad Jack was behind him and couldn't see how red his face had become all the sudden.

Jillian saw the fumble and the redness rising, and took it as a compliment. Then she arched out her back so that her breasts stood out firm, placed her hands on her hips, and pouted ever so slightly.

"Now tell me Kelly LeBrock's got anything on these bad boys."

--

Johnny met up with Jack and Jillian the next afternoon in Ashburn Park, his camera still hanging around his neck. The park was populated with the usual winos, dopeheads and glossy-eyed whatevers. Someone had brought a boom-box which was currently blasting out a tinny version of Richard Marx's *Right Here Waiting*. Then it was The Bangles with *Eternal Flame*, Madonna's *Like a Prayer*, which then segued into *A Little Respect* by Erasure and finally Fine Young Cannibals' *She Drives Me Crazy*.

It was a great day to be alive.

He told them that he had developed the pictures and they had turned out great. He told them that the ones that had some link to his house, the ones with the wires, and one that had somehow gotten his own hand in the shot, he had burned. What he didn't tell them was that he had masturbated to the nudie shots seven times in the last twelve hours and that his dick felt so raw he might have gone at it with a cheese grater. He handed Jillian a manila envelope containing all the eight by tens, which she opened – though not before giving a quick glance around to make sure no one would be able to see – and began flipping through them like cards in a deck.

"It's so rad that you can do this on your own man. What a cool skill."

Johnny shrugged. "Well, it's all my dad's equipment, and he doesn't really use it much anymore.

All I do is buy the film and the photo paper, and the chemicals."

"And load the camera, set the camera and monitor the lighting and take the pictures. Mix the chemicals and develop the film, and time it just right then fix it good and proper on the paper itself." She was shaking her head and laughing. "Don't be so modest Johnny; you should be proud."

Johnny turned a shade of red almost as deep as when he'd actually taken the pics. He wanted desperately to change the subject.

"So what now? What's the next step?"

Jack, who had glanced over and watched as Jillian thumbed through the pictures, stood up and stretched. Then he turned to Johnny.

"Tonight we make a little home delivery to ol' Mr. Dicklicker himself. Johnny we're gonna need you to make the actual drop off. Dirty perv already knows me and Jillian so we can't risk being seen. We'll do it late though, really late, so it should be no problem. Easy-peasy, Jap-an-easy. And then we wait."

Johnny nodded. He had no problem with any of that, but he did have one question.

"How'd you get his address?"

Jillian and Jack both laughed, but it was Jillian that answered. "The same way the sneaky bastard misses school four days a week and still manages to pass; he's had access to the school files since his first day of grade nine."

Johnny nodded, impressed. "Nice one."

Jack raised his shoulders and held out his palms as if to announce "what can I say?" Then he pursed his lips. *"Before* grade nine actually. I wanted to make sure I had a good timetable first year and that all my teachers were the ones with the biggest tits."

"Pig."

Jack raised his eyebrows and arched his back, breathing in. Then he took another obvious glance at the photos still sitting in Jillian's lap.

"What can I say, I love tits."

"And *that's* why you're a pig."

"If that's what I am, then so be it. The crow doesn't hate itself for feasting on carrion, and the shark doesn't self-loathe at the clouds of blood it spills into the ocean. I am what I am and that's all there is to it. Gimme five pounds of fat with a nipple on it and I'm all in. Now," he looked over at Johnny, "I think the real question is: what are we gonna do? But before we answer that, I must first ask *you* a question: did you think of a place where we can go?"

Johnny nodded. "I did. It took me about two hours of sifting through old photos"-and here Johnny neglected to tell them that during his search he had to stop at least three times to go rub out another one in front of Jillian's snaps-"but I *knew* there was somewhere that would fit and lo and behold, I finally found it." He turned to Jillian. "There's a pic of it in the bunch I gave you. It should be on the bottom."

Jillian quickly shuffled through to the last picture – she was almost there anyway – and drew out the photo in question. They all stared at it.

The thing looked like something M.C. Escher might have drawn were he trying to illustrate a church in the mind of Stephen King. It was a straight rectangle, four times as long as it was wide, and it caved in the middle as though tired, like a donkey that has seen too many winters and not enough love. The steeple stood right at the front and it rose up high and pointed, curving in like the business end of a calligraphy pen. The roof was missing most of its shingles, and in these spaces the color was so black it were as though one was looking through the photograph itself into a chipped void. Any windows it might have once had, had long been smashed and even the trees were barren and stark, and stood like bars around it as though trying to keep it locked up tight, or, perhaps, to keep the rest of the world from getting in. The grass, where there was any, was dry and stiff, the non-color of old corn husks, giving the idea that it would scrape your skin, give it a paper-cut slice, if you happened to walk within two feet of it.

"It's perfect," said Jack, and he slapped Johnny on the back. Jillian was nodding too, and she turned to Johnny and smiled.

"Thank you Johnny," she told him, and she meant it. It was one of the nicest, most thoughtful gifts anyone had ever given her: a place to murder a man who was not fit to cast a living breath.

She imagined the man inside this church, caught like a rat in a trap, squirming and crying, pleading for his life. He wouldn't be so interested in her tits then, would he? The scars on her wrists would be no get-out-of-jail-free card, would they? Without thinking of what she was doing, she spat on the ground and when she saw the saliva fly from her mouth, she wished that it were blood. His blood. *That old hypocritical cocksucker.* She slowly slid the photographs back into the envelope.

"Where is it?"

"Not too far, 'bout an hours drive. You know where highway twenty-one turns into the Back Harlow Road?"

Jack nodded. "Vaguely. Never been there myself."

"It's totally deserted. No one around for miles. Used to be a mining town I think. Mine dried up, people cleared out. I've been out there a few times to take some pics. Houses with beds still made. Rusted cans of food on the shelves of the corner store. Chalk so old it would turn to dust if you so much as looked at it, sitting on the ledge in a classroom that hasn't seen any learning in over forty years. No one around to bother us. It's a total ghost town."

"How'djoo you find it?"

Johnny gave a shrug only a teenager could produce. "Places like this are easy to find when you've got a car and no friends."

Jillian smiled at him. "You've got us now." Jack winked at him and Jillian let loose a shudder as a score of gooseflesh blossomed on her arms. "I'm stoked," she announced. "But what about…-" she glanced around to make sure no one was in earshot " – afterwards. What are we gonna do with…it?"

Johnny was watching her face carefully – he loved the way her bottom lip curled, revealing tiny pearl-like teeth when she said the word 'it' – and he nodded at her.

"I have a few ideas. In the basement of the elementary school there was a boiler room. And this massive furnace as big as a king-sized bed. We could lay it to rest there."

Jillian liked the idea. "Send him off Pentecost style. Cloven flames and all that fairytale bullshit." She turned to Jack. "What do you think Jackie Boy?"

Jack nodded in assent. "Fire leaves no trace; the ultimate eradicator."

"But we don't burn him till we've bled him dry. I want that fucker to suffer." Her voice was cold as clay and both boys turned to look at the girl between them. Jack was thinking of that day in the park when he had held her wrists and consoled her and with that in mind, he said:

"Don't worry Jilly Jill, we will." He frowned. "What about his car?"

Johnny shrugged. "There's a quarry a half a click from the church." He made a diving motion with his hand: *"Kerrrr-plunk!"*

"Perfect," Jillian said, 'it's perfect."

Jack nodded his assent. "Flame licks flesh, water eats waste." Jack and Jillian's eyes melded their gazes together. "Agreed: perfect."

Johnny watched the two of them carefully, holding *his* photographs and drawing closer and closer together-though neither of them moved so much as an inch-and he wondered if one day *he* would ever feel that closeness. He hoped.

"Let's get out of here," Jillian suddenly told the others, and she stood up and began walking down the hill that led to the edge of the park. Jack and Johnny followed suit and watching her move, they both had the same thought: that she moved like a ghost. Floated like a ghost. Left no trace behind her, like a ghost. They were almost at the bottom of the hill when Jack turned to Johnny.

"By the way Johnny, Jillian was right. They're some great photos; you got a real talent."

Once again Johnny blushed, but this time he didn't bother trying to hide it; he had a feeling that Jack would have resented it if he did. There could be no secrets between them he realized, and in his mind he moved a little closer to them.

When they got in his car, Jillian sat in the passenger seat and placed the envelope filled with her own naked pictures on the dashboard.

Jack told them which way to go.

--

A few days later and everything had gone to a tee-like that giant one growing from the top of the church they were now in-right up until the moment when Rudy Wolfe opened his mouth, his lower lip torn and bleeding and turned the color of cold offal, and began calling for Jesus.

That was when the shit hit the fan.

Less than twenty-four hours earlier, they had parked Johnny's father's car as far down the street from Mr. Wolfe's house as they could, while still maintaining visibility on it. They didn't have to wait long before the living room lights went out and then they waited a little longer, just in case. After that Johnny was down the street like a Halloween cat, slinking and nearly invisible with the large manila envelope in his hand, sealed with Mr. Wolfe's name scrawled across the front. Inside the envelope were a dozen of the most enticing photos, and a letter explaining to Mr. Wolfe how attracted to him Jillian really was. How she thought about him every day, and how she had planned the whole *unbuttoned* incident in hopes of getting his attention. How she hoped with these new pictures she might captivate him a little more, and how as she knew that any meeting between them in public would be viewed with the utmost scrutiny, she knew a place... The letter ended with a promise that whatever pictures he brought along with him to the suggested church, she would re-enact for him in the flesh.

"That's to make sure he doesn't leave the goddamn pictures at home when he comes to meet you," Jack had explained. *"Wouldn't that be a bitch – we go all out of our way to do this in private, and then we end up getting caught because the old pedo left the pictures lying on his coffee table beside a box of Kleenex and a knuckled tub of Vaseline."*

Three sharp knocks on the door and Johnny disappeared into the bushes across the street, waiting and watching, his grin the only thing visible when a minute later the door opened and a man – perfectly matching the description Jack and Jillian had given him – stepped out and picked up the envelope with a look of queer curiosity. Wolfe took the envelope inside and turned on the living room light; it stayed on for the next fifteen minutes or so then abruptly went off. Of course, Johnny had no way of really knowing, but he was certain that the guy had rubbed one out while looking through the photos.

You and me both, thought Johnny, feeling himself once again growing hard, and deciding that enough was enough as he headed back to meet his friends waiting down the street.

The next day it was an open-window cruise down highway twenty-one with the stereo blaring the likes of Bon Jovi, Roxette and Tears for Fears. When they finally turned down the Back Harlow Road, Jack reached over and turned off the stereo; music had no business in a place like this. Hell, *life* had no business in a place like this but they pressed on, forcing the car down a gravel road so overcome with brush and branches it was like driving back in time, into the Old Testament.

"It looks like what Morrissey, Sylvia Plath, and Wes Craven might come up with if they put their heads together and decided to make an amusement park…with no amusement," said Jillian when they finally got out of the car and surveyed the once town.

Johnny hadn't been lying, and neither had his photographs; it was a ghost town in its purest form. It stretched wide and open, like one giant tomb, silent as a stone and half as welcoming. No tumbleweeds blew by, but the fact that you could see grass growing from the roofs of nearly every building around made it clear that though real estate might be dirt cheap here, this was no place to start a family. To end a life maybe, but that would come later when the line between day and dusk began to melt together.

They saw exactly three cars the entire time they were there and all three of them were missing their tires. Not to mention the windows, the bumpers, the hubcaps, the gas tank cap and pretty much all the guts from inside as well. The upholstery of one was completely torn with gouges so long and deep it looked like it had been raped by the horn of a rhinoceros while another had had all upholstery removed completely; in its place, pressed into a series of divots that looked both black and grotesquely organic, were the skeletons of what appeared to be three baby kittens, only two of which still possessed a skull.

It was a town born with murder in mind.

They wandered around for about an hour, entering buildings as they pleased, urinating wherever they wanted. There was an electricity in the air as that before a storm and the clouds pressed grey against a sky that was less than blue, as though God Himself had lowered the saturation over this single plot of dying land.

Jack felt every breath he took trickling down his throat as though imbibing the sweetest of liquors.

Johnny's fingers danced in the air while the rest of his body stood still, as though playing some invisible piano.

Jillian was wet in a way that had nothing to do with her menstrual flow but everything to do with blood.

All three of them were hungry.

It was twenty to five when the sound of the motor reached them and Jack nodded. He had expected the guy would come early; men were as eager for sex as children were for Christmas. Waiting was never an option.

They heard the car coming long before they could see it – it was so quiet out here if one closed their eyes tight enough they could actually hear the grass grow, the paint peel, the worms rot and the dirt take their place – and when they did, the three began to move. There was no great rush; everything was already in place – all weapons both metal and flesh were at the ready – and they moved toward the church like devout parishioners lulled by the tolling of a Sunday bell.

Johnny held his hammer at his side, its handle so warm, it were as though it were an obscene growth from out his palm.

Jack held an electric drill, battery powered and firm; he believed things electrical were both the lock on life, and the keyhole to death.

And for Jillian, who had the deepest emotional investment in all of this, it was the knife: she knew a certain truth and would not let it go. With a knife you can do it fast or you can do it slow. It can be used to end a life, the jugular the heart the temple straight into the throat, tearing esophagus and windpipe, or to begin pain: the eyeball the earlobes tongue fingers belly sliced kneecap nostrils one and two, or right to the testicles, like a plastic sword into the olives in a dry martini. A knife creates a connection, as primal and red-fucking-ravishing as the act of sex between man and virgin woman. First night. Sliding in, destroying flesh, making sure that the whole body is never whole again. *Holed* maybe, but never whole.

Together the three of them walked, close but never touching, and that electricity in the air intensified till one could almost hear that dry charged crackle threatening to explode, to ignite. To burn.

But not yet. Not quite yet.

The hum of the motor drew nearer. More color leaked out of the sky. And the three reached their destination – the old church – with plenty of time to spare. They readied themselves by climbing into the shadows of the holy house and waiting.

--

Rudy Wolfe's mind was a torrent of conflicting thoughts and convictions as he climbed out of his car and into the afternoon sun – it was unseasonably hot for October but that was fine with him-to survey all that was around him. The air was coated in a heavy silence, broken sporadically by the low droning buzz of some insect got too near, and the grass surrounding him stood perfectly still; it was as though he had stepped into some eighteenth-century painting and, in a way, he had. The town had been founded in the late seventeen hundreds and the ultimate master painter – God – had sure put together a masterpiece with this one.

For perhaps the thirtieth time since receiving the package late last night, Rudy wondered why Jillian Jarblonski had chosen *this* place to meet him, but in all honesty, he didn't mind. It was out of the way. It was hidden. And most of all, it was *safe.* No way would anyone see them here together, and even if they did, no one would recognize him. But just to be on the safe side he had stopped about ten kilometers from the dead town, next to a little stream that ran beside the Back Harlow Road, mixed up a handful of mud and smeared it all over his license plates so that even if someone did recognize him, or his car, there would be no way to prove it. He was, as far as he was concerned, anonymous.

The road leading up to the church that Jillian had specified was too overgrown with brush to get close to by car, so he had parked about a hundred meters away and as he walked down the path, long stems of grass – some blades were wide as his thumb – pressed him on, coaxing him, pushing him toward the House of God. Only once did he stop when he heard a strange creaking sound, the sound of old timber and rusted metal twisting together, but he continued along again when he figured it to be just the swaying of an old barn door or the mild cry of some abandoned house settling.

"Jil-i-aaar," he called, a boys grin on his face, a man's hard-on in his pants, as he moved closer and closer to the church. His breath was so shallow he felt dizzy, his excitement as obvious as the sweat on his brow and back. The girl was already here, he knew that, for he had draped – much in the way a priest drapes the cloth which he has used to clean out the chalice after the ceremony of the Eucharist - over his left forearm a number of pieces of the girls' clothing. The first piece he had found soon after turning off the Back Harlow Road; it was hanging from the corner of a faded-and in several places, bullet eaten – sign proclaiming the name of this little village. It was too faded to read but Rudy was not concerned; he recognized the insignia on the sweater the second he saw it – how could he not, he saw about twelve dozen just like it every day at school – and he knew that she was here. His heart did a double skip, and he glanced down at the passenger seat beside him where sat the small stack of black and white photos she had left him. A wash of saliva entered his mouth, and he pressed on. A minute later, dripping from an overhanging branch in the middle of the road, he found a second garment – a blouse-and this time when he got out of his car to pluck it down, he smelled it, and the scent emanating from the cloth was so sweet and ripe, that he had to take a step back and steady himself on the hood of his car. It was her alright, he had been breathing her in for nearly two months, he would recognize that scent anywhere. This time when he got back in the driver's seat he had to adjust his trousers to accommodate the bulge in his pants.

The next item was her kilt, and at this one he felt a little sad for he had very much looked forward to seeing her in it, to bending her over, pinching a single pleat and then peeling it slowly upward to reveal that tiny gate that would lead to carnal heaven. It joined the growing pile of clothes folded over his arm.

Making the hour-long jaunt to this place Rudy had more than once allowed that naysayer – Skepticism – to rear its head and taunt his ego, but as he collected the fourth item – her bra, still warm to the touch – and finally, her panties, any sort of rationale or distrust that he might have had swimming around in him was drowned completely. Sure he was nearly three times her age but in that he had an advantage, for he understood how emotions could rule those less wise and learned in the ways of the world. His mind went back to the countless times in class that he had caught Jillian staring at him with what appeared to be a glare of contempt, but his wisdom had taught him that with women – especially *teenage* women – it wasn't uncommon to confuse lust and disdain, or in the very least, to cross those wires until they became pretty much the same. Hatred suggested passion, and passion, whether born of lust or loathe, could readily be turned into the other if the second party was aware, conscious, and brave enough to do so.

With her panties in his hand, Rudy Wolfe stopped; he was close enough to the church to know that this was the last item he would find, and he took time to relish it. He raised it once to his nose, pressed it tight to his nostrils, and inhaled its perfume much in the same way a sommelier might appreciate a long sought after Beaujolais. With the item of dress pressed to his face he appeared ready to stuff it whole into his mouth, and indeed his tongue shot out, quivering yet steady, and gave a quick nip to the lightly stained crotch of the cloth. The taste was exquisite, unheard of, incomparable, and he almost dropped the collection of photographs that he held pinched in his right armpit. He was lucky he didn't; bending down was not an option at this point for he had achieved an erection that would have put his seventeen-year-old self to shame, and what's more, Rudy feared what any friction might do to his sex. Right now he was a hair trigger waiting to go off.

He hurried now, his forty-eight-year-old heart beating like an introductory drumroll, and in less than a minute he was at the church door. Without thinking about what he was doing-term it Catholic reflex or Pavlovian response-he very quickly mindful not to drop the clothes or photographs-reached up and blessed himself. He was about to sin; he knew that, but like all practicing Catholics, he knew that absolution was just a confessional box away and even if it was to be a thousand *Our Fathers*, what he was about to experience on the other side of this door would make it worth it. A quick glance at those panties draped over his left forearm told him so.

He swallowed hard and readied himself. Straightened his back. Reminded himself to breathe. And then just as he made to open the door, trying his best not to drop his collection of teenage goodies, he happened a glance to the east. The sun was already setting, casting a primordial glow married with all variations of red, orange and gold upon the land. The world shimmered in the heat of the light, like leaked gas, and in that shimmer Rudy thought he saw a man, standing tall and mute – impossibly tall, two meters at least-some three hundred feet away, but then he blinked and the illusion was gone and when he blinked again, forgotten.

Without thinking of what he was doing he reached up and pulled the gold cross he always wore around his neck from out the collar of his shirt. He placed it to his lips and bestowed upon it a single kiss.

Then he pushed at the door and stepped inside.

--

He awoke about an hour later to the sound of soft singing. High pitched and choir-like, it rang in his ears:

"Let's have a black celebration
black celebration
tonight...
To celebrate the fact
That we've seen the back
of another black day...

The words abruptly stopped.

"I think he's awake," came a voice, and Rudy Wolfe's mind, already dulled by a thick and steady ache coming from the back of his skull, tried to place it. It was young, surely, but deep and masculine, suggesting that the owner had several years ago passed through those awkward gates of puberty. Rudy's vision was spotty, and he blinked several times in an attempt to clear it; then it came to him that it wasn't his vision that was spotty but the place he was in. It was dark, rife with shadows, the ceiling was peppered with holes that looked punched, and cracks that looked torn. He tried to turn his head to one side but couldn't; something was holding him in place that he couldn't see. Then a moan rose up from somewhere around him and it took Rudy almost a full minute to realize that it was drifting from his own mouth. The pain in his head was becoming sharper by the second.

"Oh, he's definitely awake." It was a female voice this time, and one that was familiar.

Why am I here? How did I get here? What was I doing right bef-

Understanding came to Rudy as he placed the voice: Jillian. It was the girl, Jillian Jarblonski, whom he was supposed to meet here.

"What tha…" he began, but the words were mumbled; his tongue seemed overlarge in his throat as though someone had stuck a great hypodermic into its base and blasted a giant air bubble right into this lolling wedge of meat. He tried again to move his head, and that's when it struck him that his head was stuck – glued it seemed – right to the floor, or table, or whatever it was that he was lying on. He gritted his teeth, held his breath, and tried again, and this time the pain flared so bright across his vision that he came very close to passing out. His eyes fluttered, and he felt hot tears drip down either side of his face.

"I wouldn't do that again if I were you." Back to a male voice but not the same as the first one. This one was deeper, more authoritative. "We cracked you a pretty good one on the back of the head. Opened your coconut up enough to see the bone of your skull. It's congealed now. Any movement on your part and you're not just gonna leave a bit of blood and hair on that there stone; you're gonna leave *flesh.* I'm talkin' *pieces* of you."

"What the heck is going on here?" Rudy hated how low and pathetic his voice sounded, how it cracked as he spoke, but he couldn't help it; a fear was upon him such as he had never known. Not the fear of God. No, he'd been familiar with that since his childhood when Father Intintola gave him twenty-one lashes on his bare behind with a thrice-folded cincture, for stealing communion wafers from the tabernacle. The priest thought Rudy had stolen them simply because he was hungry; little did he know that the boy did it because he thought it would bring him closer to God. By a strange coincidence it did; Rudy, unable to sit for the next week, found himself kneeling whenever his legs got too tired to stand and by simple force of habit, always managed a short prayer whenever he did.

No, this may be the house of God but God was not here now. The devil was in this place-Rudy Wolfe could smell him-and he felt his testicles rise up to his body as though his lower half had been plunged into ice. The Devil. Old Screwtape himself, living and breathing right in his very presence. He could feel him all around, swirling in the rank heat of this church, taunting, gloating, rejoicing. But Rudy had survived the lashings of Father Intintola all those years ago, *and* the beating he had received immediately afterward when his blood father found out what he'd done. That time it was no slippery cincture that seared his skin, but good old-fashioned flesh and bone meets flesh and bone; he would survive this. He felt an anger welling up inside him and it helped to quell the pain a little. There was no way these damned kids were going to get the best of Rudy Wolfe, not while he still had breath in his body and Belief in his Soul. He was about to open his mouth to let these punks know exactly that, when something pierced his side, opening up his mind to what *real* pain was.

Twenty-one lashes? Hell, it could have been a thousand and one lashes all those years ago and it wouldn't have come close. This was pain *beyond* pain. This was white-hot lightning ripping apart his veins from the inside out. This was brain circuitry overload, one-point-twenty-one gigawatts mainlined from toe to temple and his body rose from off the table like Frankenstein's monster. The congealed spot of blood on the back of his head made an awful tearing sound as it parted ways with the stone surface he'd been lying on. He rolled once, twice, as though the pain in his side were fire and this was the way to put it out, but all he succeeded in doing was rolling himself right off the table and dropping – as fast and hard as a cinder block – to the floor below. For a second he withered, spasmed, the pain too great to think about anything other than greatness, and then somehow managed to get himself under control. Whatever it was that had been stuck in his side was gone now and slowly, far, far, far too slowly for Rudy Wolfe, the pain began to diminish and his breathing returned to him, his vision cleared slightly, he was again afforded the possibility of thought.

He rolled over on his back and opened his eyes. He could see now what it was he'd been lying on before: a stone table, waist high, as solid as the faith of a true believer. And carved into its side were three symbols: a single cross in the middle and two fish turned inward. *An altar,* he thought. *The place where mere bread and wine became the body and blood of Christ.* This thought gave Rudy comfort and his breathing slowed. But then he remembered *Genesis 22:6: "Abraham took the wood of the burnt offering and placed it on Isaac his son, and he took in his hand the fire and the knife,"* and it suddenly seemed to him that he could smell smoke, smoke in his nostrils, in his heart, and in his head. It struck him that an altar was not just a place for praying, for rejoicing, for taking in the holy spirit and making it one with the flesh, but also a place for sacrifices. And a place where living things were delicately placed to die.

But God would not forsake him, would not leave him like Jesus' disciples did in the garden of Gethsemane. Rudy Wolfe believed that with all his heart and soul, and he acted accordingly. He may have been a sinner – and surely this was a punishment for his transgressions – but his God forgave. His God was merciful. His God was Just.

And so, mustering all the fight that he could, all the energy contained within his battered and bleeding body – he drew energy from that building rage within him- Rudy Wolfe breathed once, as deep as the wound at his side would allow, and bellowed the name of the only thing that could save him. He called it loud and he called it true, his voice was powerful enough to send the roosting crows on the roof winging off into the deepening sunset. To stir the bats that hung in the dark places, cause them to batter their heads around in surprise at their rude awakening. And to send a single stark chill down each of the spines of the three teens present.

"Jeeeeeeeeesuuuuuuuuuuuusss!" he cried, his voice was so loud the very air around his mouth, and the meat around his throat, seemed to ripple with the reverb.

The church fell silent.

Rudy's body lay still.

Jack, Jillian and Johnny could only hear the strong breathing in their own throats as they each took a single step back from this man lying on the floor in front of them. Their eyes moved from one to the other, silently asking what it was they should do next.

It didn't matter their questions.

It didn't matter their thoughts.

And none of them – not a one of the three – had any idea whatsoever that *Jesus* was about to answer. He wouldn't answer with a blessing or a reflection. Nor a coded story that spoke of *forgive thy neighbor*. This Jesus answered with the gnashing of teeth, a bloodthirsty growl, nails readied for ripping. And when he came, he came running.

--

All any of them saw was a shadow.

It didn't just enter the church, it flew in, a dark mass like a thick gas capable of moving at lightning speeds. None of them knew what it was, what to make of it, until they heard the guttural growl emanating from its belly, saw the whips of drool swinging round its mouth, and heard the harsh scraping of keratin on the floor, so dry they half expected to see sparks flying from under its belly. It paused for only a second, took all in – it's Master lying on the floor, that battery smell of blood, the sweat: nervous, excited, raw and sexual – and then it moved as only an animal can move: instinctive, primordial, flawless.

"Get those fuckers Jesus," was what Rudy Wolfe screamed, and get them Jesus did.

Why it went for Johnny none of them knew, though all could have ventured a guess. He was smaller than Jack, less menacing, and the smell on him was one of sexual excitement rather than rage or dominance. Even though Jillian held the knife that reeked of its Master's blood-as well as the lingering scent of her own menstrual flow, which was coppery and sharp and somehow *stiff* – it ignored her completely. Teeth barred, the whiskers around its mouth excited and erect, it launched itself at the thigh of Johnny Megolni and bit down, hard. If it hadn't been for Johnny's erection all the dog would have managed was to poke a couple of holes in a perfectly good pair of jeans, but Johnny was excited in more ways than one and a single tooth managed to pierce the flesh of his penis, drawing blood from the wound and an inhuman howl from his lips.

At age seventeen, it was the closest Johnny had ever come to a blow-job.

Without pause he dropped to the floor and wrestled with the dog, one hand trying to pry it off of his crotch by tugging at the collar around its neck – the dog tag that hung there was in the shape of a cross – while his other hand groped blindly around the floor for the hammer he had dropped when the dog burst through the window frame.

Rudy Wolfe, meanwhile, was using this distraction to plan his escape. He quickly sized up the scene. The girl and the other guy were too engrossed in what was happening to their buddy to notice that his eyes were once again open, that he was now fully aware, and though he probably could have stood up and ran for the exit, he wouldn't leave his dog like that. And besides, he could see the knife in the girl's hand – that *slut* – and he decided right then and there that he had come here today to stick something in her and stick something in her he would. His fear was gone, replaced with a fury as white hot as the flames of the seventh plague of Egypt.

When he moved, he moved fast – what he lacked in the vigor of youth he made up for in pure adrenaline and rage - kicking his leg out hard, perfectly aimed to the back of her knees. She dropped to the dirty floor beside him like Goliath felled by the stone, the knife in her hand let loose and sent skittering ten feet to the right. Rudy was after it in an instant and he was so focused on it that the cut in his side became nothing more than a stitch, a cramp to be ignored and dealt with later; when the knife was his he whirled, certain that she would be up already and right after him but to his pleasant surprise he saw that she still lay on the ground, rubbing her head, trying her best to sit up. Her black hair was in her eyes and in the ever-increasing darkness of the church it cut lines of negation into her face, as though slices of her no longer existed. It gave Rudy Wolfe an idea.

Back he strode to her, the knife held low at his side, and as he walked he stole a glance over to the other two; what he saw only increased his confidence. The skinnier boy – the one who'd had the hammer before – was still writhing on the floor trying to detach the dog from his crotch and it flashed in Rudy's mind: *if the kid wasn't Catholic before, he'll be well on his way after this. A circumcision by Jesus himself, can you beat that?* And then on the heels of that thought: *Pretty good chance that kid won't be beating* anything *for some time: Ha!* The other guy was also preoccupied, trying his damndest to pry Jesus off but he could barely get close the dog was so riled up, ripping his head back and forth like a madman trying to bite his way out of a straightjacket. So it was just him and the girl, and that was fine with Rudy. Just *fiiiine*.

The first thing he did when he reached her was to grab her by the hair and yank it, hard. He would have much preferred to be yanking her hair for completely different reasons but there was something equally satisfying about this type of intimacy. Rudy had never much been one for violence, but now that he was a part of it he took to it like a great white takes to its first taste of blood.

Rudy Wolfe was suddenly alive and feeling glorious.

"You. Little. *Bitch!*" he spat at her, pulling her into him and wrapping one arm around her waist. The other hand still held the knife and he brought it up to her throat, pressing it to the flesh but not yet drawing red. Something tickled her collarbone; glancing down she saw that it was his cross, that damned gold cross he always wore around his neck, and it was rubbing against her skin. She shivered, and the man tightened his grip, his mouth so close to Jillian's face that when he spoke she could feel hot spittle explode into the cavity of her ear. She could smell his breath too, hot and rank, and it pushed the odor of raw onions and burnt chicken down her throat. For a second she started to gag, her gourd rising, but Mr. Wolfe pressed the blade tighter to her throat and she somehow managed to get it under control.

"I came here to fuck and fuck I'm going to. So I'm either going to stick you with my dick…or this here knife." His pudgy fingers reached up and roughly caressed her face, squeezing her cheeks together so that her lips pursed out in a grotesque mimic of a swimming fish and then the hand dropped, fell below her neck where it found her breast. He placed a hand over it, cupping it – beneath that hand Jillian's heart beat galloped, and if there'd been any hole in her body the blood would have come boiling out of it-and for a second his eyes dropped to look down her shirt, but immediately they were up again.

"Not so fast there."

It took Jillian a second to realize that her teacher wasn't talking to *her* anymore but to Jack who stood on the other side of the room, staring at them both with nothing but his drill in his hand. His hair was a mess, his chest was heaving, but the look on his face said he was far from tired. And even further from giving up. He looked like a man who was ready-and more than willing-to murder the world.

Johnny still lay on the floor, panting, but he had finally managed to get the dog off him, which now stood about five feet away, shaking. There was a deep crimson stain growing around Johnny's crotch.

"You damned kids," he finally said, and the hand covering Jillian's right breast tightened, squeezing the flesh, twisting the nipple. Jillian bit back a cry; she didn't want to give the bastard the satisfaction. The muscles in Jack's arm tightened, and he made to step forward but Rudy stopped him with a sharp shake of the head.

"One more step and I'll slice this girl an entirely *new* slit. Though one," and here he smiled, a shit-eating grin if ever there was one, "that I don't think you'll be as interested in playing with." He shook his head. "You think you can mess with a man of God. *Here?* In *His* house. Oh no, no, no . Don't do that. Don't even *think* you can do that. This is a home game. I'm on my turf. And I've got Jesus on my side." And as if to prove it, his eyes darted down to his dog, nodded at it, and whistled while giving a sharp *come over here* snap with his head.

The dog didn't move and two by two, everyone's eyes drifted over to where it stood. First Rudy's. Then Jillian's. Johnny's next. Only Jack's never strayed; his eyes were locked on the forehead of Rudy Wolfe and the terrified girl who was shaking below it.

"*Jesus!* I said come here." The dog stared up at him, clearly torn. It wanted to move. It *needed* to go when it's Master called, but…"

A single step was all it managed before it collapsed to the ground, its body convulsing, rising once, twice, no third time. One small whimper, then the body fell silent, twitching slightly but making no sound. It was only then that Rudy saw the puddle of blood slowly leaking from some unseen wound on the dog's body.

"What the-" started Rudy before emotion got the best of him. Jesus had been his dog – and a loyal one at that – nearly sixteen years. Hell, that dog was almost as old as these kids and they'd done something to it, killed it somehow. And like that he decided that he wasn't just going to kill the girl, he was going to murder all three of these heathens. He was going to take them apart piece by piece until they all looked like something that should be hanging in the window of a Chinese butchers come New Years Eve.

"What did you do to my dog?" The man's voice was cold, but it suddenly lit with rage: *WHAT DID YOU DO TO MY DOG?!"* he bellowed, and Jillian flinched under his grip.

"Nothing as remotely cruel as what I'm going to do to you," Jack said, narrowing his eyes at the man. "Let's just say I introduced Jesus' mind to a little science." Jack smiled, raised the drill and gave it three sharp blasts. For a second Rudy looked like he was going to cry, but then his face stiffened. He could mourn for the dog later; right now he had some blood to let.

"Just for that, I'm gonna do your little slut girlfriend first, and make you watch." Rudy's mouth was so close to Jillian's ear now that she could feel his teeth scraping her earlobe as his jaw hinged up and down; the stubble on his face ground into her cheek like fifty-grit sandpaper. Still, she didn't give up. Wouldn't give up.

"Jack?" she asked, knowing that somehow he would help her. That he would have the answer.

Jack stared back at her, his eyes pinned to hers, and it struck her that if this was the way she was going to die, here and now in a grimy neglected church, having the sight of Jack Barber's eyes as her last, then there were worse ways to go. But no such thing. As always was the case, Jack Barber came through.

"It's no use Jillian, we can't beat him. *I* can't beat him." He raised his hands in defeat. "He's got us through and through. He's a man of the *cross*… he *sees* everything." Jack stood there staring, his eyes drilling into her own and then for a second, so fast that surely only Jillian noticed, his gaze darted down to her neck, then back again. It was enough: she understood.

Jillian sighed. "You're absolutely right Jack. Mr. Wolfe, he's absolutely right. You've got us between a rock and a hard place. And you obviously have the-"

Jillian's hand shot up so quickly Jack didn't see it move, and he had been waiting for it. Later, when it was all over, he smiled to himself – *that's my girl*, he thought – glad that she was on his team. But whether he saw the initial movement or not, he saw the outcome.

Her hand shot up, grabbed the cross dangling over her shoulder, and with a magician's flick, stabbed the pointed business end of it directly into Rudy Wolfe's utterly surprised face. The first jab was a miss – it struck him on the forehead – the next as well – this time it grazed his cheek – but no more than a second had passed before she was going for a third and this time it struck home, a bull's-eye pop right into the center of his left eyeball.

The knife dropped, his grip on the girl relaxed completely and his hands flew up, his body convulsing, his brain a mushroom cloud of flaming pain and atomic rage.

Jillian didn't miss a beat; they had lost their advantage once; she wasn't about to let that happen again. In a flash she was back in front of the man, and this time it was *her* that gripped *his* hair and with strength she hadn't known she possessed she tugged back on his locks, forcing his face to the sky. Once again her hand shot out, gripped the cross around his neck this time when she tugged on it, it came clean off his neck. For a second she held it up to her face, staring at it, fascinated by the run of gore clinging to its base, and then she drew it back like an archer readying their bow.

"You came here for some fucking, Mr. Wolfe," she told him, fury emanating out of her like a coat of flames, "Well now you're about to get *fucked.*"

She slammed the cross home and this time she required no three tries. It found its mark, his seeing right eye, and there was a barely audible *pop!* as the little white globe burst – Jack thought back to the first day he'd laid eyes on Jillian and the spider she'd crushed without flinching – and then the man was really thrashing about, both his hands covering his once eyes, his body rallying against time and space, smashing, banging, cursing his life and these kids and a God that had forsaken him. For about thirty seconds, the three teens watched as this man writhed all around the church, bumping into pews, cracking his head on one of the decaying walls, then finally tripping over his own dead dog, falling head first to the ground and smacking his forehead a good one on the concrete floor. There he lay, still conscious and curled into the fetal position, whimpering with a voice so high it could have been the dog itself making the noises, if the dog itself wasn't dead.

Jillian moved toward him with no great haste; the man was hers now. No more women would he bother, no more feels would he cop. She licked her lips as she approached him and began walking circles around him, her legs bent at the knees and curled at the hips, so that she looked like a great spider circling its web, its prey. She was smiling.

"Kind of ironic, isn't it? I mean, what is it all those T.V. evangelists are always shouting about? Or their stupid converts? *I see I see!* Well, Mr. *Wolfe,* can *you* see? Can you see now that you brought *yourself* here? That it was *your* decision, not ours, that led to this. We didn't kill you Mr. Wolfe." She looked up through one of the many holes in the roof; from where she stood she could only see a chunk of sky. "At least not yet: you killed yourself." She shook her head then kicked him once, twice, not hard, just hard enough to remind him that she was there. That she was the one in control.

"I don't want to start any blasphemous rumors Mr. Wolfe, but I think that God's got a sick sense of humor. And when *you* die, you can expect – nay, you can bet your goddamn *soul* on it – to find us laughing…" She kicked him once more, but this time it was merely a tap with the side of her foot and when he recoiled in fear, unable to see what was coming and always expecting the worst, she actually did laugh a little. She turned to Jack and Johnny.

"I've had enough of this piece of shit, gentleman. You boys want at him?"

Johnny was now on his feet; in one hand he held his crotch, which he was gently massaging, testing for damage. It seemed okay. In the other hand he held his hammer.

He grinned.

Jack still held his drill, which he revved several times, mostly for effect. It made him feel good to see Rudy Wolfe cower at the sound. He walked towards the man on the floor.

Jillian meanwhile had retreated to a corner of the church. There was a lone pew - *pew-pew-pew* she thought crazily - and couldn't help but smile as she sat down on it and lit herself a cigarette. She watched her boys go to work through a haze of darkness and smoke, amidst the strange and perfect shafts of muted gold light.

It went on for some time.

She didn't blink once.

2010

Jillian stood in the center of the grounds below the fifty-foot statue of Paul Bunyan – he was so tall she could comfortably stand between his legs-with her hands in her pockets and her lower lip in her mouth. Every once in a while she would remove her hands and absently rub the scars on the opposing wrists; she had no idea she was doing it and would have called *bullshit!* if someone had told her so, but she was. And whether she knew she was doing it or not, it brought her comfort. Lord knew she needed it now.

She thought about the phone conversation she'd had less than twenty-four hours ago, placed from a phone booth as per Jack's suggestion, with a number he'd provided. She'd kept it short, and she'd kept it simple, also as per Jack's suggestion, and when she finally hung up, she felt such relief that hot tears sprang to her eyes and drew even hotter streaks down the curves of her cheeks, one, she thought, for each of her lost friends. Johnny hadn't sounded surprised when she told him who she was why she was calling. Why should he have; he'd been waiting for her call for the last several days – either hers or Jack's-from the moment he realized that packing up his and Arabelle's things and heading down south was no way to solve the problem before him. He'd tried that once before and knew it wouldn't work.

"I had a feeling you'd call," he said, and his voice was so calm it was chilling.

"I need to see you," she told him, trying to hide the waver in her voice.

'Okay."

"I don't want to get into it over the phone, but do you know what this is about?"

"I have a pretty good idea."

"So you'll meet me then?"

There was no pause. "I'll meet you."

"Thank you."

"You're welcome."

He's still in love with me, she thought randomly, and then bit her lip hard, whether to stifle a smile or a scream she didn't know.

"Where do you want to meet?"

This was the part she was dreading; she hoped he didn't react the way *she* had reacted.

"In the old place, from the last time." She didn't have to say what the last time was; she was pretty certain that for her, Jack and Johnny, *The Last Time* was a phrase that was thought about in capital letters, and always referred to the same thing, now and forever.

There came a long pause and then, finally: "I don't want to go inside."

She sighed as sweet relief flooded over her.

"Neither do I. How about in front? By the friend of the blue ox." She shook her head as soon as the words were out of her mouth – it all sounded so hammy, these code words, like something out of a bad *Hercule Poirot*

TV adaptation – but she never took the receiver away from her ear.

"Okay."

"Okay. How about at noon?"

"Too early. I have to-" and here Johnny paused again. He'd been about to say 'find a sitter for my daughter' but he thought better of it. "Do some stuff in the morning," he went on. "Can we make it around six instead?"

"Six is fine." The words sounded alien in her head; she couldn't believe she was doing this, couldn't believe she was setting up a meeting with Johnny Megolni

"Okay then."

"Okay." She glanced at her watch. Jack had suggested keeping the conversation short, less than ninety seconds, but that mark had already come and gone. Out of nowhere Jillian was overcome by the need to pee; she pushed it away.

"One last thing."

Jillian winced. "What's that?"

"Have you talked to him yet?"

That got her and for a second, Jillian was so caught off guard that she almost asked "Who, Jack? Or whoever is sending us this shit?" but it struck her that either way her answer had to be the same.

"No." It came out normal, nonchalant, but in Jillian's mind it was iciest syllable she had ever uttered. It was the first time she'd ever lied to her friend.

Another pause. *Had he noticed? If he was the one who sent them the stuff, then there was a pretty good chance he was still keeping tabs on them, in which case he would know she'd lied. Would that put her in his bad books? Would she wake up in the middle of the night to see a hammer heading for –*

"Me neither. Tomorrow then?" His voice sounded totally calm, honest.

"Tomorrow."

And after they hung up that word echoed in her mind for hours, cast shadows in her thoughts and robbed her completely of anything remotely resembling sleep. Until tomorrow was no longer tomorrow, but now. Now.

For about the hundredth time since she'd arrived she surveyed her surroundings, and with every sweep of her eyes, what she saw made her shiver.

Trash cans lay overturned. Signs once brightly painted, exclamatory in fire-engine reds and electric yellows, were now faded to the color of long dead roses and weak piss. The rides that she could see – the *Tilt-a-Whirl* and the *Moonwalk* – looked like abandoned auto-wrecks in a scrapyard. Most of the machines had been plundered for metal and wiring; bones picked clean by financial vultures. Off in the distance, she could see the parks lone roller-coaster, its climatic drop standing out from the horizon like the spine of some once great dinosaur that had neglected to feed these last twenty-one years. There came a glint off the top of it and that brought her comfort; it was Jack as promised. She couldn't see him but he could see her, and he'd promised her that anytime she looked in his direction he would flash a mirror at her. Three times already she had looked, not wanting to stare in case Johnny happened to be watching, each time Jack had responded, causing her heart to skip a beat with the knowledge that there was a gun pointed exactly in her direction. And knowing that all it would take would be the twitch of Jack's index finger to send a human to his death.

She looked away. Scanned the park again, searching for anything moving, for a ghost to step out of her past and greet her, but there was nothing. Finally, her gaze fell on the statue above her and she almost jumped. Its paint was chipped in places, revealing sore-like blots of dark rust; on his blue overalls it was weird, on his face it looked downright creepy, and made her think of a junkie who had made far too many trips to his dealer and far too few to his doctor. But it was the axe that he held in his overly large hands that really freaked her out; it made her think of Johnny, and his hammer, and the things he had done with it.

Jillian stepped out from under the statue, not wanting to be near it, to have it over her. That face. Those legs. That axe. She shook her head, throwing another glance at her watch; Johnny was late and that wasn't like him. She thought this and then almost laughed. *What do you know about Kid Johnny these days Jillian? I mean the guys not even a kid anymore. Hell, Jack said something about Johnny actually having a kid. Now that's a scary thought.* She tried to imagine what the spawn of Johnny might look like but all her mind could conjure was a head-shake inducing image of that *Chucky* doll from the *Child's Play* movies. She scolded herself. *People change, Jillian. You've changed. Jack's changed, I think. Why not Johnny too? Maybe when we made that vow all those years ago, on that last morning with the sun racing to its rise as the eighties let loose its death rattle, maybe the old us really did die too. Maybe, we didn't just kill a man that night but a part of ourselves as well. And out of his death came a rebirth. A conception of –*

Jillian felt a pressure on her left shoulder, a tap, tap tapping that was so soft, so gentle, it could have been the past itself, finally catching up to her. Or Death come to collect her once and for all, perhaps a little pissed at how many times she'd managed to slip through His piano key fingers. Then she came back to herself, here and now standing under this stupid statue on an even stupider mission that had all been Jack's plan and she realized that it wasn't just her imagination playing with her senses, but that someone was actually tapping on her shoulder, someone real and as physical as herself.

"Oh Jesus!" she gasped, her legs suddenly about as stable as those jelly-bracelets she used to wear all the way up to her elbows when she was twelve years old and she would have fallen, would have crashed right to the ground if that same hand that was a tap, tap tapping hadn't shot out and grabbed her armpit, held her, steadied her, and hoisted her up.

She turned around and the surprise she'd felt at being snuck up on trebled, for she couldn't believe the face she saw before her, grinning and waiting for her to speak.

"You're late," was all she managed, still trying to get her breathing under control; it was coming in short hitching gasps.

Kid Johnny – no longer a kid and so much more handsome than she remembered him to be – stood before her, pressed into her actually for he was still half supporting her with his hand hooked under her armpit. Their faces were inches from each other's, so close that Jillian could smell his breath-hot and sweet it sent a tickle of dancing hairs across the nape of her neck – and she had just enough time to wonder about the state of her own breath before she was solidly standing on her own two feet and Johnny was stepping back, giving her some space. He reached up then, peeled away the cuff of his sleeve, and glanced at his watch.

"You're right," he said, tapping the watch with his index finger. "About twenty-one years late by my reckon." And as it had been with her and Jack's reunion, she felt seventeen again, a girl too cynical for her age but also more full of life, full of dreams. *Why did I ever let this guy walk out of my life?* she asked herself, and then she remembered where they were. And what they had done here all those years ago, high on drugs and death, when that feeling of invincibility had come crashing down around them, leaving them with nothing but a cold emptiness and the metallic taste of lingering blood in their mouths.

Jillian felt dizzy. Too many ghosts to contend with in too little time; her brain couldn't keep up.

"I need to sit down," she managed to breathe, when Johnny once again put out his arm to steady her she waved him away. She couldn't stand that touch again; it was too electric. Too much of a mainline straight to the past. And walking over to the nearest bench she happened to throw a glance to her far right – later she would swear her eyes were drawn to the place like a compass needle drawn to the north – and there it was, as it had been those twenty-one years previous: the funhouse. The sign was still there, proclaiming *Laff in the Dark,* only now it was barely legible, the paint faded and peeled. Beneath the words was a giant clown face carved out of wood, the paint either faded or chipped away to give the impression that it was baring its teeth in a snarl rather than a smile. The doors were boarded. Any lights that had once lit it up were now either broken or removed and the structure itself tilted to one side, leaning as though tired or sick. *Leperous,* she thought, *falling to pieces the way a leper drops parts of itself, one chunk at a time.* And just before she was finally able to turn her eyes away, to overcome that magnetic pull, it came to her: *the last time we touched, all three of us, was in that building. Right in its heart. We were young and stupid and had no idea the consequences of what our actions might bring, but we were alive. Oh so alive, and when we breathed, we breathed as one. We were covered in blood and we were naked and we did more than just touch that night. We –*

Her knees buckled just as they reached the bench and she sat down, hard. The jolt brought her back to reality, to the present. A second later, Johnny sat down beside her and when he adjusted himself she realized with a quick horror that he had a bag slung around his shoulder, a bag that looked big enough to hold a hammer and little else. She tensed. He saw it, paused, and moved slightly away, giving her more space. She sighed, nodded, and her face relaxed. Still, she had to ask.

"What's in the bag Johnny?"

He smiled at her – no malice, no signs of long-desired revenge – just good old friendship as they had once known some twenty-one years ago. She relaxed a little bit more.

"Actually I prefer plain old 'John' these days if you don't mind," and he winked at her. "But to answer your question: photographs."

"Oh," she said, and then it dawned on her what he probably meant and she repeated the sentiment, this time in a much deeper drawl. It had a sound like air seeping from an old tire.

He nodded once; his face grim.

"What are they of?" It was the last thing she wanted to know, really, but the question couldn't be avoided.

"The past."

"Oh *Jesus,*" Jillian said, and reached up and pulled down on her face, stretching the bags under her eyes even further.

"They were delivered to my house. Not mailed, but dropped off by hand in my mailbox. Do you know anything about it?"

Jillian's stomach churned, but she managed a shrug. "I got a tape. Audio. Someone left it in my car. They were…" she thought about how to word it without actually saying it all. "…familiar sounds," she finally finished and then nodded, hoping that would suffice.

"I see. Any idea who left it?"

She stared at him. She couldn't believe how handsome he'd become, more handsome even than Jack. He looked ten years younger than either of them. His face was smooth, barely so much as a wrinkle, and his eyes shone with a brightness that she didn't remember him possessing all those years ago. *He looks like a man whose face should be suspended above a tuxedo,* she thought, and her mouth went dry and she had to cough before answering.

"No. Do you?"

"I've done nothing but think about it for the last few weeks. Well, that and…" but his voice trailed off, and he didn't finish the sentiment. "Well, I've come to two conclusions."

"Which are?"

"That it wasn't you that sent them, and it wasn't Jackie Boy."

"What makes you so sure?"

Johnny shrugged. "Because you didn't know an aperture from an asshole, and neither did Jackie Boy."

"Jack. He prefers Jack these days."

"I thought you said you hadn't seen him?"

The color drained from Jillian's face as she realized her mistake.

"I-" she began, but Johnny cut her off with a shake of his head.

"I'm not mad. Hurt maybe, but not mad."

"It was nothing personal Johnny, I-" she caught herself, backtracked. "*John.* Sorry. We just thought…"

She shook her head profusely. "Oh *Christ,* I don't know *what* we thought. I've been so fucking confused these last few weeks I don't know if I'm coming or going. But I swear, we never really thought that…I mean, that *you*…"

He raised both his hands to her, palms outward. "All's fair in love and war," he told her, and then folded his hands and stared at her pleasantly. "But you did think it, right?"

She shrugged. "I'm sorry. It was just that…well, I got an audio-tape, Jack got a video. We put two and two together and…well, you seemed like the one most likely."

Confusion washed over John's face like the shadow of a racing cloud. "Forgive me, but maybe I'm missing the connection. *Why?"*

Jillian sighed, trying to remember what Jack had said when she'd pointed out the exact same leap of logic. It came to her.

"Moving pictures. That's all videos are, moving pictures."

John's hands tried to find his pockets; it made him uncomfortable to think that Jillian could believe this about him.

"Well what about you guys?"

"What about us?"

"Well, it was your idea all those years ago to bait your gym teacher with those nudie shots. By your own logic, if we're basing the present solely on the past, then it stands to reason that you might employ the same tactic."

"It was my religion teacher actually." She dismissed it with a nod. "So, we're at an impasse then?"

John shook his head. "No."

"No?"

"No. I already told you, I know it wasn't you or Jack. What's more, I know that it *couldn't* have been you or Jack. And what's *more,* I can prove that it wasn't me either."

"You can *prove* it?"

"Beyond a shadow of a doubt."

Jillian stared at him, trying to remember if Jack had said anything about John having a wife. She knew he'd mentioned a child, but what about a woman...? She shook her head. *More important things at hand here Jill. Just cause you haven't gotten laid in...*her mind did a quick calculation, but the number was too depressing, so she quickly covered it up with speech.

"That's not necessary John. Honestly, that's not necessary at all. We just had to be...cautious."

"I understand. So did I. But can you speak for Jack? Do you think he'd say the same thing if he were here? Let's be honest, Jack was always the sharp one of the group. Jack never missed a beat. Do you think he'd be so quick to let me off the hook if he were standing here right now?"

Jillian sighed. She felt tired. She couldn't remember the last time she'd felt so tired. Maybe after her suicide attempt when she was fifteen years old. Maybe right before it. Maybe never at all.

"I don't know. I honestly don't know." She looked at Johnny – she didn't give a damn if he wanted to be called John now, he would always be Kid Johnny to her – and like that the answer came to her. She stood up. Walked a few feet towards the center of the clearing, shooting a disparaging glance at the Paul Bunyan statue as she did.

"Why don't we ask him?" she said, and then she was waving her arms.

--

They watched him make his way slowly down the side of the tracks, carefully, so tiny he seemed another member of a flea circus; they almost had to squint to make sure that he was really there. Jillian turned to Johnny.

"About him. I hope you understand John, it was nothing personal. We had to be sure. We just had to be sure."

For a long time John didn't say anything, only continued to watch Jack make his slow descent while his teeth moved, searching for an elusive tear of skin on his lower lip.

Finally he nodded. "I'm not surprised. I know he was always on the lookout for you Jillian, that he'd do anything for you. But why was he way the hell up there?"

Jillian was tired of all this deceitful bullshit; she opted for putting all cards on the table. "He's got a gun. A sniper rifle. If you had tried anything…" She turned to look at Johnny, her face tight and grim, ashamed. She was shocked to see that he was smiling.

"A gun! Ha! You're pullin' my dick! Jackie Boy toting a rifle?!" He slapped his knee. "Wasn't he the one who always said guns were for pussies?"

"He also said that yuppies oughta pay taxes by bending over and letting the poor fuck *them* up the ass once a year, but now he drives an eighty-thousand dollar car…with a bottle of hand cream in the glove box."

Johnny could barely contain himself he was laughing so hard. "Oh, man that's rich. I mean, he's rich, obviously, and that's great but…" His laughter was so fierce now he was snorting, unable to catch a proper breath. "Is that true about the hand cream?"

Jillian shrugged. "No. I don't know, probably. But it's true about the car. It's an Audi A8 in cornflower blue."

Johnny laughed even harder, so hard that he doubled over and had to hang on to Jillian for support. "Oh, my God stop. Stop! You're killing me. I mean, you're talking about a guy who used to light his matches off his teeth."

"Well, he probably still does; only now he can't feel it cause they're all capped in solid fuckin' gold."

Johnny threw his head back, his mouth open so wide he looked poised to eat the world, and let out such a bellow it actually hurt his insides; his temple throbbed in response and he knew that if he laughed any harder, he was going to give himself a headache. Jillian was right there beside him, letting loose a cackle she hadn't heard in years, staggering around like one of those drunks they used to see in Ashburn park every first of the month when the welfare checks came out. Drained, they both managed to drag the other back over to the bench where they plonked their asses down, rag doll style, and tried to shake the grins off their faces. They were both laughing so hard they had tears streaming right down to their chins, and they had just managed to get themselves under control when a shadow fell across their line of sight, then stopped; it cut a perfect line between the two of them sitting on the bench.

"What's so funny?" Jack asked, his eyes roving from one of his old friends to the other and then back again. The gun was back in the portfolio case, his binoculars too. His jaw looked like it belonged on a wooden Christmas toy designed to crack nuts.

Jillian and Johnny both looked up at him at the same time, Jillian's left hand and Johnny's right shielding the sun from their eyes so they could clearly see their friend.

For about ten seconds no one moved until finally Johnny spoke, shattering the silence like a hammer to thin glass.

"Cornflower blue," was all he could manage, and then he and Jillian were back to the giggles, leaving Jack standing there with a curious look his face, shaking his head and smiling all the while.

--

The three sat and talked for an hour or more. They started with no small talk; they dove right in and the topics ranged from music to work, family to sex. Where had they been these last twenty-one years, how had they been living? Had they heard any good albums lately, did they still smoke pot? Had Jack or John experienced any homosexual experimentation over the years? Had Jillian finally got up the nerve to go clamming? What was their poison these days? Red wine for Jillian, Black Label for Jack, and Johnny hadn't had anything stronger than orange juice with a shot of grenadine in well over a decade. Did they follow politics, sports, art or the space race? What were their passions, what were their indifferences? No questions were left unanswered, no topic taboo, unless it concerned anything that had occurred on or before that final night on New Years Eve some twenty-one years previous when a decade died, accompanied by the razor sharp screams of a man who would not live to see the sunrise.

Eventually the horizon hazed, the sky bloomed with a deep rose red hue, and the rolling smiles on their lips disappeared, sinking into mirthless plains. They had avoided the real conversation long enough, and it was time to get to it. Finally, when the conversation lulled so deeply that there was a full minute when no one spoke,

Jillian took it upon herself to get things going in the direction she knew they had to move.

"John says he's certain there was a fourth party involved. That he can prove not only that it wasn't him that took the pictures, but that it wasn't either of us as well."

Jack stared first at Jillian, then at John. "Is that so?"

John nodded. "T'is." He took a deep breath, then exhaled into his protruding lower lip; it blew the hair out of his eyes, if only for a second.

"Care to enlighten us then?"

John didn't immediately reply, but continued to sit, staring, as still as a photograph. Finally, he reached for his bag.

"These pictures aren't pretty, and not for the weak of heart. In fact-" his eyes dropped so low one might have thought they were closed completely " – if you look carefully in one of them you can actually *see* a heart. Still in the cavity." He shook his head slowly back and forth: sad. "Not beating." He handed the envelope over to Jack and Jillian, then turned away; he had seen enough the first time.

Jack removed the stack of photos from the envelope. Jillian let loose the tiniest of gasps when she saw what was printed on the surface of the first, but she didn't turn away. Jack did nothing more than blink. He flipped to the next one.

"Oh Christ," Jillian whispered and though she wanted to close her eyes, she didn't; this, she felt, was her penance. Seeing the horrible things they had done, reliving them through the eyes of a different person. And there she was, young, confident, so sure of her purpose. And there was Jack, thinner, more svelte, but looking solid as a bull. And Johnny too, skinny and with longer hair, he looked wiry and electric at the same time.

The photos were grainy, sometimes with a little motion blur, but there was no denying who these people were. It was them, all three of them, plain and pure.

"Now the first thing that I noticed was that all three of us are in the photos together. Right there that tells us that it couldn't have been any one of us that was taking them."

"What about timers?" That was Jack, and he looked directly at Johnny when he asked.

"That was my first question too, and one that got me. Any decent camera nowadays – even as far back as '89 – would have had a built-in timer, usually five or ten seconds wait – and that would explain how one of us could have taken a picture without actually being beside the camera at the time of the click, but there's over fifty photos here, which means that person would have had to been repeatedly walking back and forth between the camera and the..." he paused here, searching for the right word. "...scene," he finally continued, a frown breaking over his face. "And then it struck me. *Fifty pictures. Fifty!*"

"That's at least two rolls of film." Jack again.

"Exactly. So, whoever was taking these would have had to stop in the middle of it all, wind out the old roll, remove it, and insert a fresh roll, all without the other two of us noticing. Still, not impossible."

"Maybe impossible considered all of us were covered in blood."

Both men turned to look at Jillian but she didn't return their gaze; she was starting too intently at the photographs Jack held in his lap. She appeared transfixed by them, hypnotized. Finally she looked up. "Am I right?"

Johnny nodded. "You're right. Film is very sensitive. It has to be kept clean of dust and dirt, never mind-"

"The innards and DNA of a dying man." Again both men turned to look at Jillian. Jack was overcome by the urge to wrap his arm around her; Johnny felt a faint urge to vomit.

"Yeah, that too. But even with all that, it is still *possible*. I mean triggers also exist that can set off a camera from fifty feet away. However..."

"We finally come to 'however'," Jack said. "I have a feeling this is what I want to hear."

"It is." Johnny motioned with a come here gesture. "Hand me the photos."

Jack did.

Johnny took the photos in his lap, winced when he saw the top one, and quickly began flipping through them; it only took him a few seconds to find what he was looking for. He held them up to Jack and Jillian side by side.

"Notice anything strange about these two?"

Jack shrugged. "Aside from the fact that they depict us in the throes of committing about two-dozen felonies, not rea-" Jack's mouth snapped shut. He moved closer to the photos, squinting. Then, he looked directly at Johnny. "Good eye son, good eye."

Jillian didn't get it. "I don't see it. What? What is it?"

Jack pointed. "Look at the first pic. Look where it's focused. You can clearly see the tools on the wall there. Christ, it's so clear you can even read the name on the Shop-Vac." His hand glided over to the second photo. "Check out that one."

Jillian saw it immediately. The background was no longer in focus; you could barely *see* the tools let alone tell what they were. Now it was the foreground that was crisp and clear.

Jack whistled. "Someone was changing the depth of field with every picture taken." He looked first at Johnny, then at Jillian. "Someone was in the room with us the entire time."

1989

Christmas, like old and age and death, comes whether one likes it or not. And Christmas had come yet again.

The three of them sat, lounging in a booth in an empty *Dunkin Donuts,* talking and drinking coffee, or sometimes sitting unspeaking, listening to the insectile buzz of the fluorescent light directly above them, or the faint drone of Christmas carols on the tinny speakers located somewhere near the rear of the coffee shop. Jack had his back to the wall with Jillian's back pressed to his chest; he ran his fingers absently through her hair while Johnny, in turn, was folded into Jillian, and she toyed with *his* hair. If they had been any more comfortable they would have fallen asleep.

It had been over two months since Jillian's date with Rudy Wolfe, and the rumors about his disappearance were finally beginning to subside. Still, since Johnny didn't go to their high school, Jack and Jillian thought it only fair to let him in on the gossip.

"The most common one is that he joined a monastery."

Jillian snorted when Jack said that. "Well, he certainly saw the light of the cross. At least until he didn't."

Jack patted her on the head affectionately. The murder had been so long ago, that it now seemed like something they had seen in a movie, or read about in a dime store novel.

"Anywaaaaays, there are a few theories as to why he joined the cloth, the most prominent being as a way to conceal his latent homosexuality."

Johnny laughed, "Good luck with that one; surrounding yourself by a bunch of pent up men who haven't seen a woman in God knows how long, yeah that's the way to cure yourself of the cocksucker blues. What were the other theories?"

"Oh the usual, you know. The whole pedo thing came back of course. Tales of Wolfe having a taste for little boys."

Johnny said nothing.

"Don't forget about the sex change?"

"What's that now?" Johnny cocked his head to one side, curious.

"Yeah, that's my favorite. Word around the hallway is that ol' Rudy was really a sheep in wolf's clothing, so to speak, and that he was finally realizing his dream of getting the old *snip snip* and fully transforming into his true self." She laughed. "How do people come up with this shit?"

Johnny turned to look at her and when he spoke his voice was very low. "Well, they're not that far off are they, really? I mean he did get the old *snip snip* in the end."

"He got a lot more than that," returned Jack, his eyes watching the clerk who was slumped in a booth near the front of the shop. The guy – only a year or two older than they were – appeared to be sleeping, but every once in a while his hand would lift and he'd take another puff off his cigarette. He hadn't even opened his eyes when he lit the thing. Still, Jack felt uncomfortable talking about such things when anyone else was around.

"Hey Jilly Jill, get anything good for Christmas?"

Jillian shrugged. "My brother got me Depeche Mode 101. That was about it. The rest was all….you know, the usual crap."

"Isn't that a compilation album? Don't you already have all their stuff?"

Jillian shrugged. "What can I say: I just can't get enough, I just can't get enough," and they all laughed. "What about you? Any good scores?"

Jack exhaled a great puff of smoke, and watched as it exploded against the buzzing lights above them, mushroom clouding its way into oblivion.

"Nothing worth mentioning. What about you Johnny?"

Johnny didn't say anything for a second, then he laughed. "Oh yeah, it was a regular Holly Jolly Christmas around my house this year; I got a carton of cigarettes. My old man grabbed me and said, 'Eh, smoke up Johnny!'"

Jack and Jillian had both seen *The Breakfast Club* enough times to get the reference, and they smiled; Jack hugged Jillian tighter and Jillian, in turn, tightened her grip on Johnny.

"We have a present for you Johnny?"

Johnny sat up slowly and turned to look at his friends. "You do?"

Jillian's lips curled back, revealing an army of tiny perfect teeth. "We sure do. Don't we Jackie Boy?"

Jack nodded. His teeth were also showing, but they weren't the little pearls that Jillian's were; his teeth were big, thick, and looked strong enough to leave their mark on a steel bar.

"Indeed, we do." Without warning, he wrapped his arms around Jillian's waist and lifted her up, then slid his leg underneath. Now they were all facing the same direction, toward the large window that looked out onto the empty parking lot. Depending on how they focused their eyes they could see either the complete darkness in front of them, or themselves.

"What is it?" Johnny's heart was beating fast. He couldn't remember the last time he'd gotten a real Christmas present, if ever, but somehow he knew that this would be a *real* Christmas present.

"You wanna tell him, or you want me to Jilly Jill?"

Jillian, crushed in between these two boys but as comfortable as a dandelion spore in a gentle breeze, licked her lips.

"I wanna tell him," she said, and her face grew crafty. She turned to face Johnny.

"It's your turn now Johnny," she told him as she stared directly at him, her face coy, her eyes overlarge.

Johnny stared back and swallowed. He was pretty sure he knew what she meant but at the same time he couldn't believe it. As much as he loved these two people beside him, he'd always felt somewhat unsure... as though he were just a tourist in this whole affair, and eventually he'd be asked to leave. But what Jillian was saying now, what she was proffering...well it was like being given a lifetime membership to the club. Hell, it was better than that. He was going to be a partner...a *partner*, and he would have as much a say in things as either of them. When he spoke his voice was a whisper, though whether because he was afraid the clerk might hear or because his words were hoarse with emotion, was not clear.

"Are you saying…?"

Jack reached out and clasped Johnny's hand. "That's exactly what we're saying. It's your turn."

"And I get to…to choose?"

"Of course. That's the whole point."

Johnny grinned, his lower lip trembling slightly. It was the nicest present anyone had ever given him.

"Well, Merry Christmas to me then," he announced, snuggling in closer to their bodies. And in his mind his decision was already made.

--

Johnny came to them three days later and told them that he had decided.

Jack was impressed. "That was fast."

Johnny shrugged; he wondered what Jack would have said if he told him that he'd known less than ten seconds after hearing the offer.

Jillian rubbed her hands together, trying to warm them; there were six inches of snow on the ground, and it was colder than a nun's cooch. "So who is it? Who's the lucky guy?"

Johnny was playing with his zippo, flicking it on then passing his hand over top, seeing how close he could get his palm before pulling away. He flicked it closed.

"Oh you're gonna love this. A real P.O.S., with capitals, you know what I mean? Works in a porn theatre, lives his life in an alcoholic haze. Easy target I should think, and very well deserving."

"What's his damage?"

Johnny *pffffffff*'d out of his mouth. "The easier question would be *what isn't?* Let me put it this way; this is the kinda guy who cuts his toenails on the bus and clears his sinuses by pressing a thumb to his right nostril, and dropping out a dollop of snot the size of a ripe blueberry on the sidewalk for all to admire. About as human as a Cabbage Patch Doll with its head ripped off. I mean, this guy's so disgusting, so fucking putrid, its known in the neighborhood that if you ever leave your cat or dog out overnight, good fuckin' luck; this guy'll chloroform the shit out of it, and turn it into his own personal fuck-puppet. I mean, if half the stories are true then he's got more crabs than Captain Highliner, and his dick probably looks like a prop from *Dawn of the Dead.*"

Jack's eyebrows narrowed and a grin opened up like a split melon. "And, how exactly did you come to be acquainted with this globby bottle of cheap stinking chip oil?"

Johnny tapped the pack of cigarettes he held and a smoke appeared from out the top like a gopher from out its hole. In one fluid motion it was on his lips, then lit, then smoking. When he exhaled it looked like a waterfall defying gravity.

"Wellity, wellity, wellity well," returned Johnny, affecting a Clockwerk accent. "He's lived in my neighborhood pretty much all my life. He was the guy whose house you avoided like the plague on Halloween, you know. Always a car out the front on cinder blocks, half a toilet still covered in shit stains on the lawn. Believe me, we'll be doing the world a favor; no one's going to miss him, no wet tissues at this guy's funeral. And, no great fuss from the cops. They'll probably assume his extra-curricular activities finally caught up to him and he took a drunken header off a cliff somewhere."

"What about his family?"

Johnny eyed Jack for a second, then shrugged. "As far as I know he doesn't have any. Not that I've ever seen anyways. If he does then chances are they hate him, as much as everyone else I know hates him. Like I said, he's a real piece of shit. Type of guy who couldn't even be loyal to his own villainy." He spat on the ground once, then rubbed the phlegm into the dirt with the toe of his shoe. "He needs to suffer perfectly."

Jack watched Johnny closely, evaluating. But it was already a done deal; if Johnny said that was who he wanted done, then that was who they would do. He turned to Jillian.

"You in?"

"Nothing but death could keep me from it. Or maybe a Duran Duran concert."

Jack flashed her his pearly whites. "Judging by their last two albums, wouldn't those be the same thing?"

"Funny guy. Funny guy." She turned to Johnny. "So how we gonna do this? In his house?"

Johnny shook his head. "No can do. He's got security lights all over the place. Cameras too I think, too risky."

"So what then, we invite him to tea, and throw a bag over his head?"

"Nothing so refined as that. I've been thinking about it these last couple days, and I've got a couple ideas."

"Sounds choice. You wanna lay it on us?"

Johnny looked first from Jackie Boy to Jilly Jill and back to Jack. Then he reached out and placed an arm around each of them, pulling them into a huddle.

"You two wanna go see a porno flick?"

--

It was seven-twenty-one p.m. on December 31st, 1989, when Jack 'Jackie Boy' Barber walked into a porn theatre and asked for a single ticket.

It was a first for him, going to a porn theatre, but he approached the ticket counter so coolly he could have been Larry Flynt flipping through the latest *Hustler*. The man behind the counter looked old and grey, and faded as chalk on the sidewalk; the only real color Jack could see was on his fingers which were dry and cracking, stained the color of weak chicken soup.

His eyes saw without seeing, and his lips pulled back to reveal teeth like burnt kernels of corn and gums that seemed stretched, ready to tear. His hair was a greasy mess, so oily that Jack thought that if he were to rub his head on a wall he would effectively turn it into a window. The man eyed Jack with some suspicion but Jack didn't take it personal; he had a feeling that was how the guy viewed everybody.

"Just one," Jack told him, pulling out a tenner, sliding it through the little window of the box office. The guy glanced first at the bill, then up at Jack. He shrugged.

"You know this place closes in half an hour, right?" Jack stared back at the man. He had an accent, not too thick, but still there, and Jack tried to place it. Czech, possibly. Eastern European, most likely.

Jack nodded, pushed the bill closer to the man. "I'm aware."

The man eyed the bill once more, then back to Jack. "You got ID? You gotta be eighteen to get in this place."

Jack had had a feeling that it might come to this, the old troll on the bridge routine, but luckily Jack had it on good authority – namely Johnny's – as to what the password was.

"How's this for I.D.?" he asked, reaching into his jacket and pulling out a mickey of *Smirnoff Triple Distilled*. He placed it on the wicket counter beside the ten-dollar bill.

The man grunted, his eyes flashing to the bottle and then back to Jack, but Jack also saw the man's tongue, grotesque and wholly biological, come darting out of his mouth to swipe a line of white spittle across his lip. It occurred to Jack that he shouldn't have bothered with the tenner; Johnny had been right: Vodka was this man's poison, and he was looking to get *ill*.

Oh, you're gonna get a lot more than that tonight you grotesque old bastard, Jackie thought, *oh so much more than you bargained for.*

The man continued to stare, but Jack could see his lower lip begin to tremble, the fingers on his right hand to twitch, clearly wanting to pick up the bottle. His eyes narrowed.

"You wouldn't be trying to dupe me, would you boy? Maybe hand me an old bottle you found on the street filled with nothing but tap."

Jack shook his head. "Pure as the cold driven snow, sir," he said, and then immediately rebuked himself; 'Sir' was out of order for this guy. 'Sir' would set off alarm bells. But if it did, the bells weren't loud enough to drown out that whisper in the man's head, the incessant droll that called to him over and over: *drink me. Drink me. Drink meeeeeeeeeee.* Finally, his eyes broke from Jack's and fell to the bottle lying on the counter. The man picked it up, turned it over, examined it closely.

"It's not even been opened," Jack told him. "The seal is still intact."

The old man took one look at Jack, and laughed right in his face. "Ha. Still intact. What's a little boy like you know about 'still intact?' Five'll get you ten that *you're* still intact, boy." He leaned in, right to the glass, and eyed Jack up and down, top to toe. He laughed again, though it was more like a cough than anything resembling pleasure, and allowed his eyes to return to the bottle. With a broken thumbnail scored with grease and God knew what else, he felt along the seal of the bottle. The kid hadn't been lying; it was a brand new bottle. Jack smiled inside, his face never moving a muscle. It was true what he'd said, the seal was intact, but the part about the bottle never being opened, that was a straight up lie. There's more than one way to get into a bottle if you get creative about it, and last night in Johnny's basement, the three of them had done just that. Meticulously peeling away the label ever so slowly so as to not rip it. Then drilling the tiniest of holes into the side. Draining the bottle drop by drop, and then mixing it with whatever magic pill Johnny had managed to pilfer from the local pharmacy. *"Three hours,"* Johnny had promised, *"Assuming he manages to drink the whole thing before he passes out, it will give us three hours. He'll be dead to the world unconscious."* Jack smiled at that, laughed. *"And once he wakes up, he'll just be plain old* dead." And Jack's hand had been shaking so much with excitement that Jillian had had to take over, refilling the bottle with a syringe. Then a tiny piece of tape over the offending hole, a dab of glue to hold the label back in place, and *voila!* One brand new looking bottle of Vodka with the mother of all surprises inside. He wouldn't know what hit him, no way no how.

"Why you wanna get in there so bad?"

Jack was about to answer, to say something lame like how he was simply horny, or how the man was right, he'd never gotten laid and he figured that this was the next best thing, but he didn't want to give the old cocksucker the satisfaction. So instead, he stared the man down, his mind and his body made solid by the fact that at some point in the next couple hours, Jack would place his seventeen year-old hands around this man's neck and squeeeeeeeeze. Eyes locked, Jack refused to back down; backing down was not an option, like getting caught. Backing down, Jack reckoned, was like guns: for pussies. Without thinking of what he was doing, Jack leaned into the glass that separated him from the man – glad for it because he had a feeling that the man's breath would smell about as pleasant as a urinal puck – and exhaled once, long and slow, right onto the glass; it fogged, making it impossible to see the man's face clearly anymore, and vice versa. Then he reached up and pushed the bill toward the man once again.

"You can keep the change."

Jack stood there, hands in pockets, waiting for his ticket. He had no doubt that he would get it simply because he wanted it. He thought about what Jillian had said the other day – *nothing but death could keep me from it* – and he reveled in the knowledge, a knowledge that only *he* possessed, that death was everywhere. It was waiting around every corner, it was stitched into every word and action ever encountered. And as it was the only thing that every human – *every fucking human who ever took a breath and rolled an eyeball* – had in common, it was to Jack the purpose of all things. If life was the greatest gift ever bestowed, then death was the currency with which you paid. It truly was the meaning of life: to die. And Jack and his friends were going to help this old bastard achieve the single greatest purpose that he would ever aspire to. To die. To rot. To release all the collected nutrients held in his putrid skin, his innards, his shit stained bowels, all of it, back to the earth. To finally break that habit that every human has been guilty of since breath one: to give back after a lifetime of *take, take, take.*

Jack continued to stare. From somewhere off in the theatre, behind some wall and around some corner, through some door, the sounds of fuck and suck pumped, low moans and high screeches; the poetry of *uh-uh-uhhhhhhhh* permeated the air like a meaty smell. Forget Spector's wall of sound, this was a wall of *sex.*

Finally the man shrugged – his shoulders rose like two shapeless mounds of Play-Doh – and slapped a hand down on the bill. It disappeared and though Jack didn't see where it went, he had a pretty good feeling that the cash register was the last place it would end up. Then he picked up the bottle, twisted the cap – the seal made a satisfying little *snap!* as it was broken-and took a rather generous swig. The Play-Doh shoulders melted, his eyes glossed ever so slightly, and the tightness of his face relaxed a little. He motioned with a jerk of his head for Jack to go in.

"My ticket," Jack asked, not because he really wanted or felt he needed a ticket, but because he liked to be in the presence of this guy, alone with him. It was fascinating for him to know that in a few short hours Jack and his friends were going to change this guys life in ways he could not possibly imagine; here this guy was, thinking he'd just sold a ticket to some horny teenager bent on nothing more complicated than rubbing one out, when really, what he was doing was signing his own death warrant.

The old guy blew a puff of air over a scarred lip – whether from a fist busting or a latent case of herpes, Jack couldn't tell – and shook his head.

"This ain't Mann's Chinese Theatre bub, just walk right in. No funny business in the washroom. And if I catch you pedaling your ass in the theatre, you'll be outta here faster than a..." His voice trailed off as his eyes were pulled back to the bottle. "Well, fast," he said finally as he glanced at a clock on the wall that instead of numbers, depicted twelve open mouthed girls, their gaping orifices all aimed at the center of the clock; the small hand was a set of droopy, and badly drawn, testicles, the big hand was a large and exceptionally veiny penis.

"You've got thirty-six minutes," he added as he picked at a crust of snot on the edge of his nostril.

"What kind of porn theatre closes at eight p.m.?"

The old man rolled his eyes. "It's New Years. I got a life too yah know."

Jack thought about what Johnny had told him, prostitutes and animal carcasses. "I don't doubt it," was all he said.

"Well, get outta here then." A dirty grin spread across his face. "And have fun."

Jack bit his lip; it was all he could do to keep himself from bursting out laughing. He felt like a kid on Halloween examining his haul.

"Oh don't worry about me," he told the man with the tip of a non-existent hat, "I certainly will."

--

Jack stepped into the theatre, surprised at its enormity. Johnny had said it was a big place but Jack had underestimated it; there had to be three hundred seats in here at least. The scene on the screen was almost dizzying; a penis the size of a full-grown adult was rocking back and forth into the folds of a vagina that looked big enough to stuff a twin bed.

"Well, *that's* sexy," Jack muttered under his breath, and quietly took a seat in the back row. He gave himself a full two minutes to allow his eyes to adjust to the dark, then he looked around.

From what he could tell there were five guys in the entire place, which was more than he'd expected at this hour. He cursed porn, and its magnetic pull; then he rethought and cursed the guy at the counter. Why couldn't he work at the local art house cinema? The theatre would be empty and chances are he would have been asleep at the counter. Jack shook his head and surveyed each of the men.

Two of them, one bald and the other bearded, were watching the film on the screen with about as much interest as one would reserve for drying paint. The third was fiercely concentrating on something in his lap – his belt buckle jiggled constantly making Jack think of street-corner Santas soliciting for the Salvation Army – and the fourth's head was repeatedly shooting around, obviously looking for somebody to love. The last guy, up near the front, had his head lulled back in what Jack could only assume was ecstasy; either that or he was dead to the world asleep.

Jack smiled, relaxed, crossed his legs. The hardest part of the night was over; all he had to do now was wait.

--

For the most part, Jack avoided looking at the screen; he found it dizzying as well as somewhat repulsive - too biological and not remotely sexy - he questioned how anyone could be turned on by it; he likened it to masturbating to photographs from an anatomy textbook. Only when the scene changed to a male-male-female threesome did Jack throw it another glance, but only for a second; it was getting late, and he had work to do.

The body count had stepped down to four by now. Old jingle bells - or jingle *balls* might be more accurate -had left three or four minutes ago after a long and drawn-out moan of pleasure, followed by the quick buckling of a belt and a hasty exit. Guy number one had changed seats at least three times, guy number two remained sitting quietly, bearded, bored and uninterested. Guy number four's head was still darting around, birdlike, looking for a worm of another kind, Jack guessed. And guy five still had his head back, lolling from side to side. A glance at his watch told Jack that it was ten to eight; he balked. He couldn't believe he'd already been here more than twenty minutes. *Oh well,* he thought, *you know what they say: time flies when you're watching gigantic genitalia* . He stood up: like these guys around him it seemed it was time to take things into his own hands.

The first thing he did was go back into the lobby; he moved quickly and with purpose, making a beeline for the bathroom. Halfway there he threw a glance at the box office where the old guy sat and immediately a smile came to Jackie's lips. Johnny had been right; the old guy sure loved his sauce. The mickey sat on the counter in front of him, already half empty. As Jack walked past, the guy picked it up and took another long pull; Jack increased the speed of his strides and once in the bathroom he stopped, thought. True that they *wanted* him to drink the whole bottle, but not *that* fast. If he got to the bottom before eight then there was a good chance he would pass out, and that might not go over to well with the exiting customers. Police may be brought in, or an ambulance at least, and that wouldn't be good for anyone.

Jack did some quick math. Johnny had said the pill would take a solid thirty minutes to kick in and render the old guy comatose. Given that he'd started drinking as soon as Jack gave it to him, that gave him maybe another ten minutes to clear the place out, fifteen on the outside. He'd have to work fast.

Back into the theatre he went, not bothering with another glance at the old alky behind the glass. His eyes shot around in the dark, settled on the bald guy closest and strode directly over to him, sitting down in the same aisle a few seats away. Acting purely on instinct, Jack shoved his hand inside his jean pocket and pretended to play with himself; the guy was over to him like a flash, Jack had only a second or two to be amazed with how easy the whole thing was before he went on with the play.

"Get your hands off me you fucking queer faggot!" Jack suddenly shouted, and in the hazy bluish dark of the theatre Jack saw the guy wince and his face color. A second later the guy was fumbling to stand – his seat rebounded, smacked him in the ass, and he jumped a foot in the air – then he was off, hurrying out of the theatre like a rat scurrying from a fire. For a second, Jack felt remorseful – he didn't give a flying fuck where the guy stuck his dick – but time was of the essence. Next, he set his sights on the twitchy guy off to the side and as he moved toward him the guy's jerky bird-like movements gave Jack an idea. Birds didn't just eat worms after all, they ate bugs too. As he approached him he realized that Birdy had made a friend: the bearded guy who had appeared so indifferent to the whole scene had now taken a very deep interest in

Birdy's crotch. Deep indeed. Jack stood there behind the two of them, raising his eyebrows, impressed. From what Jack could see, the guy working on Birdy could swallow a banana without taking a bite, and, judging by the soundtrack to their little tryst, suck the peel right off without using his hands. It was so impressive that he almost felt bad cutting it short but, he shrugged, murder calls, and thus…

"You son of a bitch," he yelled at Birdy. The guy leaning over into Birdy's lap raised his head and jumped up, eyes open wide and mouth gaping wider. Terror was on his face, and Jack liked that; it gave him a taste of what was in store for the old man later that night. Jack twisted an accusing finger into Birdy's astonished face, drawing it up inches from his open mouth.

"You gave me crabs you bastard!" Jack shouted, and the bearded man balked. If he'd had no gag reflex before it seemed he'd found it now because he suddenly retched.

"Aw fuck!" he shouted, slapping and scratching at his beard. "It took me months to grow this thing. He made to leave, when he stopped, glanced down at Birdy with a countenance of pure contempt. His hand swung out in an arc and slapped not Birdy's face but his still erect penis; the sound produced was as sharp as a switch but still the penis refused to stay down: it bounded back up immediately. Jack couldn't help but think of one of those punching clowns he'd had as a kid, always ready to take another lick, so to speak. It all looked so comical and unexpected that Jack almost broke character, and burst out laughing and only by biting his lower lip was he able to stifle it. The man, meanwhile, turned and quickly made his way to the aisle, the exit, throwing an accusation of *"Asshole!"* over his shoulder as he went. A second later, Birdy himself was up, trying desperately to stuff his shrinking dick into his pants. Jack stood there amused, watching him fumble and flip around; he seemed in such a hurry to get away from Jack that he tried to zip up before he was fully tucked in which led to such a yowl of pain, that the guy in the front row, his head still lulled back, suddenly started; apparently he *had* been asleep and this was just the thing to wake him up. The sleepy bastard threw a glance at his watch then *he* was up too, clamoring toward the exit and shaking his head all the while.

Jack beamed, looked around the theatre one more time to be sure, then threw back his head and let out a full belly laugh.

"Well, three birds with one stone, so to speak," he announced to the now completely empty theatre. He made his way down to the screen toward the fire EXIT sign that glowed dimly in the dark – it made him think of a very sad and very old Jack-O-Lantern – his eyes roamed up to the screen one final time. He stopped. On the screen the girl, brown haired and plain, was getting filled out from both ends. *Like a pig on a spit*, Jack thought, and frowned. It seemed to him that somebody in the throes of "passion", ought to have a more contented look on her face, and not look like somebody who had been sitting in heavy traffic for the last forty-five minutes with a broken radio.

He shook it off, remembered his purpose, and continued down to the fire exit at the front of the theatre where he paused for a second, reading the warning sign on the door: *'Opening door will trigger alarm'* Jack shrugged. *So the guys a pervert* and *illiterate*, he thought, *all the more reason to put him out of his misery.* He knocked loudly on the door three times and waited. A few seconds later, the knock was returned from the other side. Jack scratched playfully at the door as his hand reached for the knob. He hoped Johnny was right about the sign being a fake. Then he took a deep breath and turned the handle.

--

Jillian practically knocked Jack over she burst into the theatre so fast; her shoulders had two inches of snow on them, her hair looked like the most exaggerated dandruff commercial ever.

"Sweet *Jesus* it's cold out there," she said, shaking off the snow and blowing hot breath on her hands. "What took you so long?"

Jack grinned at her. In the red glow of the EXIT sign, coupled with her rosy cheeks wet with melted snow, she looked like a babe just slid out the birth canal.

"Oh I'm sorry your highness, it's just that this movie was sooooo engrossing, that I simply got lost in the plot."

Jillian's gaze turned upward to the screen. Her eyes widened and she jumped back.

"Wow," she managed. Then she pursed her lips: "I bet the dentist never has to ask *her* to open wider."

Johnny also looked up, and nodded approvingly. "I don't know, she seems like a nice girl. Not the kind of girl you'd like to bring home to mom and pops maybe, but…personable."

"Oh yeah, that's the kind of girl you want to date: one who's got a punch card at the free clinic."

Johnny poked Jillian on the arm. "Who said anything about dating her?"

"Are you seriously telling me that you would be interested in a girl like that? I mean-" but Jack cut them both off with a wave of his hands.

"Hey, hey, Ward and June. As much as I'd love to allow you to continue your little discussion about the Beaver here-" he threw a swift pointed finger in the general direction of the movie screen "-time is a little bit of the essence yah know, considering…"

Johnny nodded. "Right, right." He shot a wink at Jillian. "It's just that Jillian Jealousy here seemed a little upset about that fact that-"

"Jealous!" She gave a throaty laugh. "Jealous, that I'm not on a first name basis with the doctor at the local abortion clinic. Jealous, that I don't have to use a calculator to figure out how many wangs I've had stuffed dow-"

"Guys, guys, seriously." Jack held up his hands, a little exasperated but still enjoying himself. This was after all foreplay to the big act that would be coming soon and as much as he would have liked to draw it out a little, the possibility of getting caught lit a real fire under his ass. "I'm going to go check on the box office boozer up there, see if he's still in the land of the living or fully fermented by now." He glanced at his watch, then turned to Johnny. "It's been nearly thirty minutes. He should be out by now."

He walked up the aisle, cautiously opened the door leading into the lobby, and stuck his head out. His eyes widened in surprise.

"Fuck!" he whispered loudly. He pulled himself back into the theatre, turned and yelled to his friends.

"We got a problem here guys. He's gone. *He's fucking gone!*"

--

The three of them crept out of the theatre into the lobby. There was a pretty good chance that the front door was still unlocked so who knew who might come in at any time. Jack's heart felt like it was trying to escape his chest, Jillian's was wedged somewhere in her gullet, and Johnny's was beating hummingbird style, so much so that he started to feel dizzy. If this old fucker had managed to get away… He held onto the wall to steady himself and followed his friends.

The lobby was empty. The ticket booth too. The low sounds of celluloid sex still emanated from the theatre, but other than that the place was quiet. Jack shot a look first at the front door, then at his friends.

"If he's already gone outside its game over. There's no way we can go after him, bring him back in. Someone outside might see us."

Johnny felt sick; he would not allow this to happen. The desire to kill this man was on him like a sexual requirement, and he felt at that moment if the desire weren't allowed to be realized, he would never sleep again. It was a want that would never let him go and this, he was certain, was their only chance. He pointed to Jack, then to a door off to the right.

"You go check the projection booth, upstairs and to the left. Jillian, the washroom. There's a basement where they keep supplies and old films that-"

He stopped talking, his eyes drawn to something down the hallway and out the front door. When he realized what he was seeing his body deflated, his facial features drooped like melted wax, his arms sagged, and he lost three inches of height with one drawn out sigh.

"There he is," he said, raising one weak arm. All air had gone out of him, all energy. He had wanted this so badly and now it wasn't going to happen. Now it was all going to end because… He sighed. It was his own fault. He'd underestimated the old fucker: should have gone with a double dose just to be sure.

Jack saw the man through the front door window, stumbling around, leaning into the wind-driven snow. "How the hell can he even be walking? I thought you said that pill would-"

"Fuck," Johnny spat. "It's all my fault. I once saw the guy drink an entire liquor store and he didn't even belch. I should have known that a single pill wouldn't be enough to knock him-"

"Ah, ah, ah, don't be so sure," Jack shouted, pointing to the glass door ahead of them. "Guy's stumblin' like a Mexican on Cinco de Mayo. I'd say he's got about ten more staggers in him before he passes out completely."

Johnny was practically near tears. "What does it matter? No one can go out there to get him. Might be seen."

"What if we lured him back in here somehow?" That was Jillian.

"With what? If we'd brought a second bottle of booze maybe, but… fuck!"

Jack shook his head. "As fucked up as he looks, you really think he'd go after more booze?"

Johnny nodded, depressed. "Like a moth to a flame dude. I once saw him passed out on his lawn, face down in a pile of his own puke. Fucker came to, crawled down to the recycling bin at the end of his driveway, started rooting through it till he found an old bottle with half a shot of whatever left in it. Guy downed it and then went right back to sleep."

Jillian sighed, then shook her head. "Never send a boy to do a woman's job," she told them, then quickly pushed them both aside and made her way down the hallway that lead to the front entrance. "Alcohol isn't his only vice, remember Johnny," she called over her shoulder as she went.

"Yeah but…?" Johnny began, but stopped when he saw Jillian shed her jacket on the floor behind her. A few more steps and she was working on the buttons of her blouse.

At the door she stopped, still fully clothed, and placed her hands to the glass, shielding her eyes so she could see outside. When she was convinced that the only one around was Mr. Stumblebum himself, she rapped solidly on the glass. The man, about ten feet away and about to take a step off the sidewalk into the street, stopped but didn't turn around, his head cocked to one side like a dog's listening for the repetition of a whistle. She rapped loudly again, and this time he turned, peered, shook his head, stumbled forward a little. His eyes widened, which, considering his drunken/stoned state, meant that they opened almost halfway. That was when Jillian opened her blouse and slipped it clean off.

The man stood there for ten seconds, no more than three meters away, trying to make sense of what he was seeing. There was a girl in the theatre, *his theatre,* and she appeared to be naked, or in the very least, topless. And even more intriguing, she appeared to have three or four breasts. He'd never fucked a girl with three or four breasts, and vaguely wondered if it would classify as a threesome if he did. Either way, he wanted to find out, so he took another step toward her. Then another. Suddenly his knee gave out and he half-fell, half-flew forward. If he'd been one step further away from the door he would have fallen flat on his face but luckily for him – or quite *unluckily* depending on which side of the door one was on – he managed to grab the handle and hold himself up. He didn't question who the girl was, or how he had managed to get so damned drunk off a single mickey of vodka; all he cared about was getting inside where she was, then getting inside *her.*

Somehow he managed to hang on to the door handle; he could see the girl much more clearly now that he was closer and *damn* was she young. This gave him more energy. This allowed him to get himself erect, in all senses of the word. He flung the door open, the heat from the theatre – now he remembered why he had gone outside in the first place; he'd felt hot, unnaturally hot, and wanted to cool down – immediately smacked him in the face and he took one lurching step inside, swayed, and then crashed to the floor.

Jack and Johnny were over beside him in a second, throwing the lock on the door, flicking off the light switch, effectively rendering them all but invisible if anyone happened to pass by and take a peek inside. When everything was in order they stopped, stared down at this mess of a man sprawled on the floor like a bag of garbage whose bottom had suddenly given out. The old man, dead to the world unconscious, let out a tiny but effective mouse fart. A second later the three of them were waving their hands in front of their noses.

"You sure can pick 'em Johnny," Jack said, and there was no sarcasm in his voice; he meant it. This guy was a real piece of human trash. Finally, Jack turned to Jillian.

"What would we do without you?" he asked, beaming. Jillian rolled her eyes at him but she was smiling.

"What else am I here for?" She shrugged. "Just call me *Rent-a-Tits,*" she added, jiggling her breasts in front of her. "Great entertainment for weddings and bar mitzvahs." Johnny's face reddened slightly. He was so happy his mind couldn't conceive of how to thank Jillian so he did the only thing that made sense: he walked over and grabbed her discarded blouse from beside the door, returned to her, and wrapped it around her as though the blouse were giving her a hug.

Jack prodded the old guy in the back with his toe; he didn't move, just lay there, as lively as a bag of wet sand.

"Well, I think we've already killed enough of this guy's brain cells with the drugs and the booze. What say we eliminate the middleman and get right to the body itself?"

--

The amusement park looked as welcoming as the asshole of an AIDS patient, and twice as dark. The wind was whipping around their car something fierce – it rattled the window hard enough to cause Jillian to swear – and it was passing over something on Johnny's car, a crack in the body or a bend in the fender, that drew forth a wail that rose and fell in a sharp cry.

"Are you sure this is the best place for this?" Jillian asked, trying to pierce the night wind with her eyes. It was no use. It was like trying to see to the bottom of a bucket filled with black ink.

"Hey, you guys said you wanted to have some fun with this guy, right?"

Jack was rubbing his hands together, either to keep warm or in anticipation of the festivities ahead.

"Do we ever!"

"Well then, what better place that in a funhouse?"

Jillian still looked skeptical. "Won't it be cold in there? I mean, the place is closed up for the season right. Won't everything be shut down?"

Johnny nodded. "That's the whole point. No one to bother us. No security. Trust me, I've been here every winter for the last three years. Got some great night shots. Covered in snow the rides look like picked over bones bleached white with time and greed. And don't worry, we won't freeze. Leaving a building unheated for an entire winter is like *asking* the thing to fall apart. For the pipes to freeze. The concrete to crack. So they pump in a little heat for a couple hours a day to keep things nice and kosher; we can totally adjust it to our liking. And this funhouse man, wait till you see it, it's perfect. Ab-so-lutely fucking perfect. It's creepy. It's quiet. And best of all there's a workroom right in back, underground, where they do all kinds of repairs to machinery in the park."

"What's so great about that?"

It was dark in the car and Johnny was facing forward in the driver's seat, so no one saw his face change, his eye sockets deepen, his lips peel back to reveal his readied teeth the way burning flesh melts to reveal secret bone.

"Because they have tools," Johnny said, and then the wind picked up to a great howl, hiding anything he might have said after that.

Jillian shivered. "We weren't planning for snow. What if someone sees our tracks?" She didn't know why, but she kept thinking back to that porno that had been playing in the theatre not too long ago. Two guys and a girl, and there had been nothing sexy about it, nothing desirous. Only flesh on flesh with the girl repeatedly mugging for the camera, playing it up as if to create some kind of connection between her and her audience. It creeped Jillian out a little because it made her feel like she was being watched. Like the actors on screen could see *her* instead of vice versa. Then she remembered what was in the trunk of Johnny's car. That hulking bastard who had… she tried to remember some things Johnny had said: something about fucking neighborhood animals, being: perma-drunk, a regular John to the streetwalking Jane's, a petri dish of S.T.D.s and a free-range farm for parasites. In other words, a regular human biohazard. And here he was, lying stoned and unconscious less than a foot from where she now sat.

She slowly turned around, glared at the upholstery of her seat as though Supergirl with X-ray eyes trying to peer into the trunk, daring him to make a sound. To make his presence known. But nothing doing, it struck her as both funny and frustrating how easily a burning interior rage could be quelled by physical cold. She turned to Jack.

"What do you think about it Jackie Boy?"

"What do I think about what?"

"Well, you're the one who's always saying 'Leave no trail.' Don't you think a series of footprints in the snow, and a single line that could only be the parting made by a dragged body, is pretty much the definition of *leaving a trail*'?

Jack frowned, thought about it for a second. He already had an answer for Jillian: this wasn't like last time after all. Since Jillian had no personal investment in the victim, she was getting cold feet, literally and figuratively, but he didn't want her to think that he was placating her like parent to child. The truth was, there was no turning back now. They already had kidnapping under their belt; any cop worth his cuffs would manage to throw in breaking and entering, assault, drugging, and God knows what else too, so in truth, *murder* was actually the easiest option. At least things would be cleaned up a little. And speaking of cleaning up…

"That's why we've been sitting here waiting," he told Jillian. "We've been here exactly nine minutes now. I'm gonna go take a look and see how things are going."

Without another word Jack threw his shoulder into the passenger door and stepped out of the car. Took a few steps toward the back. Surveyed the ground. When he got back in the car a few seconds later, his face was red from the wind and wet from the melting snow, but he was satisfied. He turned and looked at Jillian.

"See. Less than ten minutes and our tire tracks are already erased. One hundred percent. There's even a half-inch of snow on the roof. In twenty minutes this car will look like it's been here a week and any tracks we make dragging this degenerate fucker into the park will be long gone before any stranger comes happening by."

Jillian nodded, smiled mildly, but still didn't seem entirely convinced. "What if someone sees us going in?"

Jack turned and looked at her and when he spoke his voice was calm and warm. "Aside from the first car that drove by right when we got here, we haven't seen a single car, right? It's nearly ten. There's only one restaurant around here and it closed at nine – I checked- so any stragglers should be long gone by now. It's New Years Eve, which means everyone is already in for the night or gone to where they want to be until those bells start chiming and that glowing globe drops."

Jillian nodded. "Something seems off..." She shook her head, wishing she had thought to bring some tapes with her; she could really go for some Cure right now. Some Duran Duran. Hell, even Tiffany would do.

"Guys, if we're gonna do this, I think it should be now. Jack?"

"Agreed. Jillian?"

She nodded. "Agreed."

Johnny shrugged. "Satan is waitin'" he said, and then made to open the driver's side door. His hand was trembling so much with excitement it took him three swipes before he was able to get a firm grip on the handle and open it up.

Stepping outside into the cold night air, a great calm fell over him and his hands stopped their shake. His breath came out white, mingled and hung in the air, and for a second, in all that cloud and mist, in his very breath, he thought he saw an angel suspended, not moving, just watching him, and he knew that what he was doing was right. A moment later and he was over to the gate of the service entrance and his tool slid into the lock as smooth as a fish into a downstream river. A minute tops and the gate parted like seaweed in the path of that same singular fish.

They opened up the trunk and hauled the body out. Johnny grabbed his knapsack too, Jack his own large duffle bag, which they each flung over their shoulders, then they began dragging the man across the road, through the gates and over the asphalt of the park; they only stopped once so that Johnny could go back and re-close the gate, adjust the lock – leaving it unlocked, of course, as he had at Mendoza's Meats - so that it looked like it hadn't been tampered with. In less than thirty seconds he was back to his friends, and once again the body of the old man began to move.

If the man felt any pain, he did not make it known. Johnny had been right, that pill had really done the trick and if it wasn't for the warmth of his body, they might have thought him already dead.

Three sets of footprints they created and though they tried their best to carry their load, it was thick and cumbersome and at times, heavy as rocks, so if they let it drag, who was going to complain?

Six feet, with one line between that stood out on the earth like a fresh scar oozing black blood.

Almost immediately, the snow began the quick and natural process of erasing those prints, rubbing out that line, but it took time, and the evidence was still there some minutes later when another set of prints followed. The feet that pressed this time were large and deep, and the distance between each was almost too great to be believed, so that at times the prints stepped on the original, previously forged marks, and at others, created a new void in the snow. But always, always, there was the suggestion that the lone set followed the others. The lone set was just a little behind.

But the snow kept coming. The wind kept blowing until eventually it was all but impossible to distinguish the first group of prints from those that followed. And soon after that, they vanished altogether. Soon after, it were as though the snow had been there since the beginning of time.

All was erased, and clean.

2010

The three of them sat on the bench, the giant statue of Paul Bunyan still large but looking like a child's stupid plaything from where they now sat, and thought about what Jack had just said.

"Someone was in the room with us the entire time."

It made them sick, all of them, not only because of what it meant for them now, caught and pinned, but because of what it meant for their younger selves back in 1989. It robbed them somehow, like a child reevaluating all their past Christmas joys upon finding out that Santa Claus was and never had been a true thing. In short, they felt duped, and they all hated the feeling, but it was Jack who was the most affected by it.

"How the holy *FUCK* could this have happened? How could anyone have…" But he stopped, physically incapable of going on, the rage inside him so strong it was bubbling up and clogging the tract of his throat the way dirt and oil clog the pores of one's skin. And Jack knew that if it were allowed to do so much longer, then

– like the skin – he was going to explode in a fit of red rage and poisonous pus.

"I need to see it NOW," he exclaimed, rising up from the bench. His toes were curled and his fists were tight, he was madder than he could remember being in a decade or more.

"Jack what are you-" but Jack waved Jillian away. *Leave no trace,* he had always said, *leave no trace.* But they had left a big trace, a grand-fucking-canyon of a trace, and Jack wanted to know how.

"I'm going in," he said, and before either John or Jillian could stop him, he was off.

--

Laff in the Dark was created to be a funhouse, but the cheapness of the props and the inevitable disrepair it had fallen into after years of existing in an amusement park that made no money, had turned it more into a house of horrors than anything resembling mirth. The ride comfortably sat two so long as you were no more than five feet tall; if you were your knees would constantly bang into a metal bar that was about as effective a safety device as a length of frayed dental floss. It was comprised of a mini-car that rode along a single track, whisking and weaving its way from one hilarious/horrific tableaux to the next. It was dark, nearly pitch black for most of the ride and as the track was unpredictable it was not recommended for pregnant women or anyone who was turned off by the idea of a slipped disc or chronic back pain later in life. Every thirty seconds or so a scene would appear: a mechanical ghoulie rising out of a toilet, for instance, or a series of mirrors that made the viewer look as though they'd had a vat of acid thrown in their face. At one point the car would hurtle forward at breakneck speed toward a red-bricked wall, only to turn sharply at the last second, disaster averted. It was a ride that, in its heyday, had appealed to young kids who felt no shame in screaming or giggling at each new scene, but to any child who had moved on to double digits, it was a bore-fest through and through. Not so anymore.

They entered with no resistance other than a sharp push on the side entrance, and a bird-like squawk from the one rusted hinge that remained. Darkness fell over them like a dropped curtain.

The first thing they noticed was a deep heavy smell that clogged their noses and compressed their chests. It was the smell of rot, mold, and rat carcass converted into insect shit: the circle of life, and death for the dead.

When the smell came to them Jack was arrested in his step and covered his mouth. Jillian gagged. Only Johnny appeared not to mind. He paused briefly and swallowed once to force his gourd back down, a skill he had learned after years of changing diapers hung heavy with the weight of his daughter's excrement, and perfected through the two years it had taken his wife to succumb to her cancer. Once one had routinely dealt with pillow cases and pajamas caked in vomit, feces, and in the later months, a black blood that reminded him of tar and brain embolisms, there was no way a whiff of mold and rat crap was going to upend his lunch.

They stepped out of the light and into the past.

Time had not been compassionate to the old place. Floorboards creaked as they made their way through the labyrinthine structure with its many twists and turns, dead-ends and confusing corners, no matter that there were three of them walking single file with only the glow of Jack's cellphone to tell them where they were going; to each of them they felt as though they were walking alone, into, perhaps, the very hall of their memories. And the memories they had of this place were not kind; they were wet, slippery, and each step they took was like pushing their faces into an overripe bucket of squirming leeches ready for the suck. How different it had been when they were younger, the three of them carrying the drugged body of the old man to the basement workroom like a giant bag of cats readied for the chilling reality of the river. There had been no great struggle, in fact it had almost been a pleasure with their wiry frames so full of youth, their heads stocked full of hate, and the feeling of acidic injustice spurring them on with every step.

God, they had been alive.

Now they felt tired and unnerved, almost terrorized, as though whatever ghost that had been watching them all those years ago might still be haunting this carcass of a building, waiting for them in the cracks and corners for the right moment to splash out of the dark like one of the tableaux of the ride itself.

Eventually they came to a fork, but they had twisted and turned so many times in the dark that Jack had no idea which way to go. He turned to John.

"Any ideas?" With the glow of Jack's cellphone touching his skin, John's face floated in the darkness like a lone candle flame; there was even a waxiness to it brought on by sweat and must.

John swallowed, and for a second his face seemed to flicker as though threatening to go out. He nodded.

"Left," he said. "Left."

"You sure?"

John's voice was suddenly so dry he had to cough to bring it back. "I'm sure," he said.

They moved as one, a train of flesh on track to the only destination possible: the terminus, the target, the end. Jack, leading the way, slowed his step. The anger he'd felt upon realizing that they'd been had, had abated, given way to a low, stolid fear and now that fear too was dissipating, being pushed out of his core to make room for a much more final and useless emotion: dread.

When they finally found the door – a thing so black it negated space – Jack stopped.

"You guys don't have to come with me you know," he told them, his free hand on the doorknob. "But I have to know."

"I think we *all* have to know Jack," Johnny answered, placing a hand on Jack's shoulder. "I'm right behind you. Jillian. You in?"

Jillian gave a half-laugh, half-snort. "Just because I'm the only one here with a pussy doesn't mean I *am* one," she said, and sighed. She had forgotten how base her sense of humor used to be; it wasn't something she entirely missed, or entirely minded returning.

Jack nodded once in the dark, squeezed the handle, and turned; the sound that arose off it as it moved reminded Jack of a Formula One mashup, all twisted metal and angry reverb. Then with one dull shove he pushed the door open.

The smell that wafted up the stairs was a cross between dead skin, dried oil, and old farts. It was the smell of things forgotten and it was so thick Jack believed that if the light on his cellphone were any more powerful, they'd actually be able to see it wavering in the air like heat on a distant highway.

"Shall we?" he asked, holding the light out in front of him as though a crucifix intent on warding off the undead.

"Satan is waitin'" Johnny said and immediately wished he could take the words back. He had used the phrase a thousand times before but now there was something sinister sounding in it, as though it were the kick off of some domino effect that would lead to each their downfall. The words stung of prophecy.

Together they descended into the bowels of the funhouse.

1989

Johnny hadn't been yankin' their crank when he said the drugs would knock the guy out for a good couple hours. It was currently ten p.m. and he was still dead to the world, rippin' out snores like a stubborn starting chainsaw and drooling all over himself like a dog in heat.

The first thing they'd done upon arriving, aside from tying the unfortunate bastard to a chair with a whole mess of cable ties, and placing a very large and ultra heavy-duty tarp underneath him, was to fiddle with the thermostat until they got the room nice and toasty. After that it was a waiting game.

Every once in a while one of them would get up and check on the old guy, make sure he was still breathing and that the blindfold they'd tied round his head was still in place. Johnny in particular had trouble sitting still and every fifteen minutes or so he would stand up, stretch a little, and flutter around the room picking up the various tools and appliances that littered the work room, hold them, raise them to his eye to get a better view. More than once Jillian saw him caress one of the instruments, his hammer, an electric knife, whatever happened to by lying around, in a manner that seemed almost sexual, and always there was such an intensity in his eyes-a concentration she associated with masturbation-that she felt compelled to turn away, as though watching him was somehow wrong, perverted, voyeuristic.

"What are we going to do to him?" she finally asked, after watching Johnny approach the man for at least the seventh time, place a hand on his forehead, and squeeze.

Johnny turned to her, apparently surprised. "What do you mean 'what are we going to do to him?' We're going to kill him of course." His hand on the forehead continued to contract and expand, contract and expand, it made Jillian think of a cat pawing at a dead mouse that, now robbed of life, had become merely a plaything, a lump of flesh that existed only for fun, for the amusement of the captor. This, and the blank look on Johnny's face, made her glad that he was on her side.

"Well, I know, but…well, I mean, what *specifically* are we going to do to him? Are we just going to cut his throat? Bleed him out like the pig he is? Or…?" She shrugged. "What did you guys have in mind?"

Johnny's voice came out low and solid as a headstone. "We're going to do everything we can. Everything we can think of. Nothing's too base for this subhuman piece of trash. I want to redefine *pain* for this fucker. I want to…to…" Johnny's breathing became fierce and his nostrils flared; for a second Jillian half expected him to reach over with his free hand and twist the guy's head clean off but instead he turned to the man, placed his mouth directly to the man's right ear and screamed.

"WAKE UP YOU SICK FUCK WAKE UP!"

The man didn't flinch, and this infuriated Johnny even more. In a flash he was over to the workbench, grabbing the hammer, and then back at the man with the weapon brandished high; for a second it quivered in mid-air – it looked like Johnny was holding it so tight Jillian was surprised the wooden handle didn't splinter under his grasp – and then he was bringing it down as hard and fast as he could. Only he didn't hit the man. Instead, he dropped to his knees, straight to the floor, and pounded it on the concrete hard enough to throw sparks off its rounded end, sending chunks of concrete shrapnel streaking across the ground. When he finally calmed down enough to stop, there was a fist-sized divot in the floor and a puff of concrete dust that hung around the spot like a dry mist.

For a minute no one spoke and then Jack, who had been the least vocal of the three since arriving in this dark place, turned to Jillian. "You heard what Johnny said about the guy. Torturing animals. Fucking anything that moves. The drugs, the drink, disease."

Johnny looked up from where he half-sat, half-lay on the ground. "Not to mention the incest."

Jillian and Jack both turned to Johnny.

"Incest?" Now Jillian looked angry. "You didn't say anything about that before."

Johnny shrugged, pulling himself up from the floor; his face slightly red. "Must have slipped my mind. Anyway, it was never really proven, just neighborhood talk."

"Go on."

Now Johnny looked uncomfortable; it was clear that he hadn't meant to bring it up but there was no turning back now. He spat once on the ground and continued. "Everyone on the block knew about it but couldn't really do anything about it. After his son died, well, what's there to prove?"

Jack was eyeing Johnny with frank curiosity. "You think he killed his son?"

Johnny shrugged and when he answered he stared down at his feet. "Maybe not directly but I knew the kid. He was a friend of mine." He pursed his lips, swept at the dirt on the floor with his shoe. "I think over time the old man got to him. Whatever it was he did behind closed doors I'll never know, but like I said, we could guess. All you had to do was look the kid in the eye for fifteen seconds to know that *something* wasn't right. I mean, with a dad like that..." He trailed off, his voice fading to insignificance. He was shaking his head.

"How'd he die?" Jillian was watching Johnny carefully; for a second she'd almost stopped herself from asking but she needed to know. This old guy had never done anything to her personally and if she was going to stand up in the next few minutes and put a weapon to him, she'd need a real reason. She'd need *fuel*.

For a long time Johnny didn't answer, only stood silent, staring down at the drooling mass before him. When he finally answered his voice was barely a whisper

"Drank a quart of Drano."

"Jesus." Jillian thought she was going to be sick herself. Jack only stared.

"Yeah, tell me about it." His lower lip was trembling, and he looked like he was on the verge of tears. "Waited till his father left the house and then made himself a toxic cocktail, a real nail biter. Drank it down without so much as a word to the rest of the world."

"And it killed him?"

Johnny's eyes never moved as he answered; he was staring at the wall opposite, a plain wall with peeling paint and cracked concrete.

"Ate him from the inside out."

For a long time no one said anything; in each their mind's eyes they could see the kid, lying on the floor of his kitchen, rolling around, clutching his belly, too old to forget the horrors he'd experienced, too young to understand that things might have gotten better. In the end it didn't matter one way or the other; he'd died, and this man in the room was responsible.

No one knew what to say. Sometimes there are no words. It seemed the man in the chair, bound and blindfolded knew this too, for this was the moment he chose to open his mouth and let loose a gruff, throaty moan. It rolled across the room like a foghorn and it sent cold chills down each of their spines.

The man was awake, and the time had come. *His* time had come.

Jack stood up. Jillian too. Johnny was already turned in his direction, the hammer still tight in his grip.

"Suffer," was all Johnny said, but that was enough. They all knew what he meant, and they all agreed.

2010

Stepping into the killing room was like stepping into a cave, all of them drawn into the darkness as though sucked, as if they had no choice.

It was cold, and comprised of a darkness so full it were as though the dark were *eating* at the surrounding space, gnawing on it like a dog to fresh bone, wet tendrils of flesh on its lips, viscous saliva bungeeing off the hairs of its chinny chin chin. Yes, the place was dark and cold, but there was also something organic about it, something breathing. *Ah yes,* Jack thought, *someone died here once. In this room someone hiccoughed their last puff. And I was there. And I was the cause. Or one of three anyway, one of three...* He blew a shot of air out his nose, his head shaking slightly. He felt disgusted, sickened, as though that old bastard's death had coated the room in the rank stench of slaughter and extinction. As though his death were somehow still alive.

It was an elimination, Jack thought to himself, *like a bowel movement or the emptying of the garbage disposal receptacle. We were getting rid of some trash; ridding the world of some of its undesirable waste.* And on the heels of that last thought: *in the end we were doing him a favor. In the end we sent him away from this place because life was the worst thing we could do to him. His death was a welcome one, and he greeted it with a bloody chest and arms stretched wide.*

Jillian was also deep in thought. *We were the monsters,* she mused, and a set of tears, hot to the point of being painful, sprung up from her eyes and burned tracks down her face. *We were the monsters, and we reveled in it. Pride was our plaything, and we laughed at it. We made jokes. But there is no laughter now. And chances are, there never will be again. How can I smile knowing that...remembering...oh Jesus how did I ever forget? How could I ever have allowed myself to forget? How is it possible that –*

"We're gonna need a better light. I can't see the bend of my elbow with this fucking thing." Jack shrugged. "You guys see anything round here we can use?"

Slowly, cautiously, the three of them shifted around the room, always sticking together, always huddled as one. Johnny found an old rag and a quarter bottle of paint thinner, Jillian a mop, and together they fashioned a makeshift torch. Within a minute the thing was ablaze and the smell of must and mold was replaced with the equally unpleasant stench of chemical burn and scorched oil. Mad shadows stained a Bacchanalian dance on the outer walls, flickering, leaping, clashing with other shadows, dripping into one another. Strangely, the presence of fire didn't make them feel any warmer, in fact it brought a chill to each of them; now they could really *see* the room, and what they saw was not pleasant.

Twenty-one years had passed and though the room had changed, there was no doubt that it was *their room*, as it is, was, and forever shall be. There were still the upturned milk crates that they had sat on all those years ago, now scattered pell-mell in one corner of the room. Most of the tools had vanished, pilfered by looters or simply sold off when the park shut down, but the desk vise still remained – Johnny felt his stomach lurch when he remembered what they had put in there – and the base of the Shop Vac – cracked in several places it looked as though it would be more suited as a garbage can now – sat overturned to the far left. Nuts and bolts littered the floor, looking solid and old beside the rat turds and spider carcasses scattered around like sprinkles on the most macabre cake ever baked. Dust covered everything like a shroud, and time didn't seem to exist as they slowly stepped their way around.

"Let's figure this shit out quick and be done with it. I don't want to spend any more time in here than I have to." Jack held the torch up in front of Johnny's face. "John, you're the camera expert. Based on the photos you showed us, and what I saw of the video, any cameras used would have had to have been set up…" He drew a line in the flickering light straight to his right, looked over his shoulder to check, and then adjusted it several inches back to the left. "There," he finished. He frowned. He was pointing directly at a wall about fifteen feet away. He shook his head. "Impossible. There's no way someone could have been standing right there, and we didn't see them. Do you guys remember if that wall was really there? Maybe they've done some renovations since…" He walked toward the wall in question, a frown on his face and his eyebrows knitted tight.

Johnny was nodding. "That wall was definitely there, I just want to see if… There," he said, pointing.

That would have been the spot, right there, where that calendar's hanging. He ripped it off the wall – a *Sports Illustrated* swimsuit edition from 1993 – and tossed it aside. Then he frowned, sighed. The wall was solid. Just a normal fucking wall.

"I don't get it." He turned, pressed his back to the wall and thought about the photos. He shook his head. "This is perfect. This is exactly where they must have been taken. The height matches, the angle." With his right hand he reached up and caressed the wall. "It doesn't make sense. There should be a big hole right-" With absolutely zero expectations Johnny formed his hand into a fist and made to rap once on the wall, but instead of the sound of flesh and bone hitting drywall, there came a rough tearing sound, the sound of falling dust and debris, they watched as his fist disappeared completely. In the guttering shadows of their crude torch it looked as though the wall were actually *eating* his hand, consuming it, and Jillian shot out her own arm to brace Johnny in case the wall decided his hand was not enough and began munching on his arm as well. His elbow. Torso. Eating him up, churning him to bits of raw meat and flecked white bone, cutting his nerves to ribbons. *Consuming* him.

But no. Johnny's hand stopped at the forearm and the hole sucked him in no further; he turned to his old friends, and the erratically jumping torch threw deep shadows around his eyes, pulling them down, making them appear stretched and tired, like a melting figure of wax. His looked twice his thirty-eight years.

"There's something on the other side," he said, "another room." He took the torch from Jack, held it up to the hole and tried to peer in but all he succeeded in doing was singeing his eyebrows and lighting a piece of cobweb on fire.

"Christ on a cross," was all Jillian managed. She wanted this to be over, to be out of there and done with all this shit. Her stomach churned as though there were something alive within it, slithering around and feasting on the half-digested contents of her belly.

"How can there be another room? We came straight down the stairs and there were no other hallways, no other rooms, no other doors."

"Jackie Boy, Jackie Boy," Johnny began, and if it bothered Jack to hear his old name he gave no sign. "You forget that we're in a funhouse. And what better place to hide a trap-door or a secret passageway or two?" Still holding the torch out in front of him – it was already beginning to sputter, to smoke and die – he brought the two back out into the hallway where he immediately began rap, rap rapping on different points of the wall. Within ten seconds the echo that returned to his ears was different, more hollow, and he knew that he'd found his mark. A few more seconds banging told him where the latch was, and no more than five seconds after that, he had the secret door shifting its way open, grumbling and protesting at the pull.

The room – if it could be called that-was no more than three feet wide, though it looked to be at least a hundred long and was really no more than just the space between two walls. A great series of wires snaked all over the place, from one section of ceiling to the next, tangled as cooked spaghetti. Some were long and thick, others coiled in metal to prevent corrosion and water interference. There it was: about twenty feet down this half hallway of a room – a hallway that led absolutely nowhere – sat a lone chair, wedged in between the two walls. Directly in front of the chair was the hole Johnny had busted open and beside it a stack of milk crates that reached all the way up to said hole, the top one looking high and steady enough to place a couple cameras for a little late night voyeur action.

"Well that's not much help," said Jack.

"What did you think we would find," Jillian asked, "his phone number scrawled on the wall?"

Johnny shook his head. "There are other ways of leaving a signature," he said, thinking. He stared at the setup and scanned it from top to bottom. There was a can on the ground beside the chair in which there lived a black moldy mess. Johnny picked it up, shook it gently, and nodded slowly to himself. *Cigarette butts,* he thought, *twenty or thirty Pall Malls gone to mold over these last twenty-one years.* Then he brought the torch closer; it wasn't easy because of the confines of the space, more than once he almost set his own sleeve on fire, but eventually he maneuvered it so that he could see the chair itself more closely. Stare down the pile of garbage that lay beyond its seat. His breath gathered in his throat, his chest…and stayed there. His body refused to let go, afraid that if it let this breath out, there might never be another to take its place.

Johnny blinked twice, then a third time for good measure, but what he was seeing refused to go away. It were as though it were real, but that was impossible, Johnny knew. There was no way. Not after all this time. No way that…He reached down and picked the thing up, examined it and for a second his vision blurred.

Johnny shook his head roughly, slightly confused, slightly elated, and one hundred percent scared shitless. Piece fell around him, slammed into his chest, his mind, his heart, melded with other pieces until they slowly, very slowly began to come together. Finally he turned to his friends wedged into the frame directly behind him.

"I know who it is," he told them, "I know who's been doing it all." then without warning all wind fell out of him, all bones left his body, and he was falling back: deflating. If the chair hadn't been there he would have fallen right down, cracked his skull a good one on the concrete floor and bled his mind out right then and there.

Considering what was to come, and soon, that might have been a blessing.

1989

The first thing Johnny did when it became clear that the man was recovering consciousness, was to check the plastic ties that bound his wrists to the arms of the chair, his ankles to the legs. He whistled as he did so, smiling when he saw that they were tight enough to cut lines into the man's bloated flesh with no room for any give whatsoever. That was fine with Johnny; he didn't want this man to have the slightest chance. Then he stood up, removed a small white plastic bag from his back pocket and placed it over the man's head. An elastic around the neck completed the act; he now looked like a stupid makeshift scarecrow.

The man's reaction was immediate, surprising all three of them; if he'd seemed groggy before he was now fully awake, and his head thrashed back and forth as though on fire.

"Fuck is this?" he yelled, "Fuck is this?" More thrashing, and the chair beneath him began to buck; the man's feet slapped at the concrete and his whole body swelled. All a sudden, the yelling stopped and the man gasped for breath, his head rocking back and forth with each inhale and exhale, the bag over his head expanding and contracting like a bleached lung. Within thirty seconds the gasping began to slow, to calm; the man was already on the verge of passing out. That was when Johnny, standing directly behind him, reached around and gripped his neck in a choke hold. The man thrashed again, tried to resist, but Johnny's grip tightened and the man was stilled. From where Jillian stood she could see the guys neck, a band of flesh between the collar of his shirt and the plastic bag, the tendons that stood out looked thick enough to hoist a piano; *we'd better be careful here, this guy was one strong mother.*

With his free hand Johnny reached up and hooked his index finger into the gaping hole that represented this guys mouth, which was opening and closing like some great stupid fish thrown onto land. He was trying to bite a hole in the bag – Jillian could see the man's lolling tongue pressing at the plastic, trying to lick it forward, to gain some suck – but it was pointless. His head continued to nod up and down as though he couldn't agree more, but the movements were desperate, quickly exhausting. And just when Jillian thought the guy was once again going to pass out, Johnny gave a quick sharp poke through the bag, and the man's air supply was returned.

The suck that came through that hole was so intense, so powerful, that Jillian imagined she could actually feel it pulling her in, moving her towards him, in a way she wasn't far off. She *was* drawn to him, not because of his breath but rather because of what Johnny was doing, of how Johnny looked to her. Standing there with one arm wrapped around this old pervert, this pig, this piece of shit pedophile who had no business, no *right* to continue to live. No right to have thoughts. To sleep in a bed, to eat apples. To gain erections, and to use those erections on the helpless, the destitute, those lacking the power to stop it or say no.

She didn't go to him directly, no. Instead, she went to the tool bench at the back of the room. She examined the wares available, then she made her choice. A second later, Jack was beside her, his own tool in his hand. Together they turned to look at Johnny who remained standing, statue still, behind the man. There was a deep look in Johnny's eyes, razor sharp focus, and Jack reflected that if ever there was a look that could kill, that would be it.

"You ready?" Jack asked, and Johnny answered the question with a slow nod. He was staring so intently at the wrapped head in front of him that the rest of him appeared shut off, dead; his mouth hung open, zombie-like, and a thin line of drool slid out, extended silently all the way to the floor.

"You okay?" That was Jillian, her voice heavy with concern.

Hearing Jillian's voice woke him up a little and he blinked twice, shook his head and closed his mouth. He looked at Johnny and Jillian and nodded firmly. Then he motioned to them and the tools they held in their hands. He seemed not to want to talk, scared his voice would crack or warble.

Jack shook his head and returned the *go-ahead* gesture to Johnny. "He's your guy. You got first dibs."

Jillian smiled. "Make us proud," she told him, and at these words the guy in the chair once again came fully awake. It was dawning on him what was happening. He had no idea why he was here, or had come to be so, or even where *here* was, but it was clear that *here* was not a good thing. The tendons in his neck tightened, the muscles in his arms flexed, laboring against the confines of the electrical ties that bound him.

Johnny took Jillian's cue and slowly, fascinatedly, raised his hands, fingers splayed and palms open, and placed them around the skull of the man in the chair. The man bucked under Johnny's touch but it was no use; Johnny was getting into it now, the moment was upon him, and the adrenaline had begun its pump. He pressed his hands tighter into the skull, squeezing them together like a vise with the man's head in between, and a sound rose from the man's throat, first a moan then a full on scream, though whether it was from fear or pain, none of them could guess. Probably a healthy does of both.

The man's cry rose, the wail escalating into a kettle-call boil until Johnny too joined in the fun and began screaming himself, a howl of rage and want, until he could press no further and he relaxed his grip, let his hands fall to his side. Slowly, he lowered his face until it was directly in front of the man's. Through the hole torn in the bag Jack and Jillian could see the man's mouth working up and down, his teeth gnashing, trying to bite his captor, but to no avail. After a minute of this his snarl faded, turning into a whimper, a pathetic squeak that sounded to Johnny more like a sad fart trying to escape than the dramatic begging it should have been, and for some reason this brought him a dark joy that cooled his insides and readied him for the coming kill. He was so excited he felt ready to burst and he was shaking as he leaned in toward the man, so close to his face it appeared as though he were about to plant a kiss on his quivering lips. There was a smile on Johnny's face that seemed carved out of glass and the teeth that gleamed from under those lips looked large enough to devour the man whole, body and soul, if the man had a soul that is. He certainly had a body, and perhaps that was what Johnny was smiling about. The man had a body but right now, that body was Johnny's. Johnny owned it, and could do whatever he wanted with it. And so he would…now.

He turned his eyes to the floor, searching for the hammer. He liked the hammer for its simplicity; it was simultaneously both a dull and sharp weapon and to him this made it ideal. It could be used to smash and bash, for heavy hitting and powerful lumps, but turn it around and it could be used to scrape, to cut, and best of all, to dig. Johnny definitely planned on doing some digging tonight. Oh yes, flesh would come undone and the insides, the true nature of this man, would be revealed. In fact, his first order of business would be to turn that hammer around, claw end facing forward, and literally tear this guy a new one. To wedge it in far enough up this guys asshole to get a good purchase and then *yank* it, twisting and gouging, ripping him apart the way this bastard had ripped apart that little boy all those years ago. And he was about to, had moved behind the man and was readying himself for the excavation when something made him stop.

He turned and there were Jack and Jillian, standing side by side with the workbench pressed into their backs, and with their arms around each other they looked like a happy couple. A blissfully beautiful couple, and out of nowhere he thought: *I wish they were my parents. I wish I was their only son.* They smiled at him in unison, and Johnny knew that he was ready. He tightened his grip on the hammer. He turned down to look at his captive who, perhaps sensing that something was coming, had bolted his hands to the arms of the chair, his fingers as white as shards of chipped teeth.

"Now Johnny, now," Jillian told him, but instead of having the intended effect, Johnny froze, glared down at the back of the head in front of him and dropped the hammer.

They all heard it fall, the dull metallic thud as it met the concrete, the light hollow *rat-a-tat* as the wooden handle came to rest. And then the man exploded.

"Sin! Sin! Sin!" he cried, over and over again, his voice throbbing, his words so large and loud that they pressed at the room, threatening to overflow it with noise. *"Sin! Sin! Sin!"* he bellowed, his head twisting and jerking, threshing around like a shark on a hook, and all at once three things happened very quickly:

Jillian took a step back, shocked, and when she bumped into the table behind her she let out a small but sharp cry of surprise.

Jack's brow furrowed, wondering why the man had erupted so suddenly, so extravagantly, and why his word repeated sounded more like a question than an accusation.

And Johnny, Kid Johnny, took no time for conscious comprehension. Instead he acted, and he acted fast. Over to the workbench he flew, dashed aside anything in his way with a messy sweep, and seized on the exact tool he was looking for. A second later and he was standing on the tarp in front of the man, his free hand wrestling with the mans face, pinching the nose under the plastic bag to get purchase, and when the man opened his mouth yet again to let loose another cry of *"Sin! Sin! Sin!"* Johnny jammed the tool – a pair of wire cutters that looked like they might have been around when Edison lit up Pearl Street Station for the first time – directly into his mouth. The man gagged, tried to toss his head to the side, but Johnny had him good by the nose and the wire cutters were in deep, forcing the man's head back further and further. A moment later, Johnny's hand came down on the wire cutters; there was a squeal as rust scraped rust, contrasting sharply with the organic sound of tearing wet meat, then the man's mouth – barely visible through the torn hole in the white plastic bag-erupted in a geyser of hot blood and fresh pain. Within seconds the hole around the bag was coated red and they could see, as he finally managed to jerk away from Johnny's grip, the bag itself, still pinched at the neck by the elastic, begin to fill up with blood. Back and forth the man reeled, his head and upper body writhing in panic and pain, his screams only half realized as he drowned on his own blood, choked on his own tongue. But this old bastard was a survivor, and after fifteen seconds or so, he managed to steady his head enough to lean forward and allow some blood to flow out of the hole. Gagging sounds arose now, there was so much liquid coming out that Jack and Jillian thought Johnny had somehow cut the man's head clean off; there couldn't possibly be that much blood coming just from his mouth. It took them a few seconds to realize that it wasn't only blood spewing forth but vomit too, in a moment so surreal they both had to grip the table behind them for fear of dizzyingly passing out, they watched as a single blood soaked maggot, as big as a baby's fist, came slowly writhing out of the hole, pressing at the confines of the plastic, stretching it bigger, teasing it, until the bag could hold it no more and it shot out several feet in front of the man, landing on the floor beyond the borders of the tarp with a single sopping *plop!*

"Oh Christ," Jillian said, her eyes huge and unable to blink.

"What the fuck?" came Jack's response, his jaw hanging somewhere around his knees.

Johnny took a step back. The man was shaking now, convulsing, his screams replaced by a low gurgling sound in his throat. His body twitched several times more and then his head slumped forward, gave one momentous shudder, and fell silent.

"That's for what you did to your son," he told the man, and then he spit on the white plastic bag, which was thin enough to reveal that the inside was now totally coated in a red so dark it looked black. From the hole in the bag blood continued to flow; it drooled out of his mouth and pooled in his lap below.

Staring at all that blood, something occurred to Jack. "Shit, what if he's got the AIDS?"

Johnny shrugged. "I doubt it, but anything's possible with this pig fucker."

Jack moved, walked over to his jacket flung over the shop-vac against the wall, and fished through the pockets. When he turned around a moment later he had a pack of rubber gloves in his hand. "I brought these for the clean up. For wiping down the tools and stuff afterwards. Leave no trail, right? But maybe we should wear them now. Just in case."

Jillian nodded. "Good thinking." She paused for a second, then looked back at Jack. "Dustbuster." She was smiling.

"What?"

"That's what we should call you: 'The Dustbuster.' Cause you're always so good at cleaning things up."

Jack shook his head. "I've got a nickname already, thank you very much."

"Whatever you say," she told him, then mimed flicking a switch with her thumb. "Vroom vroom. Dustbuster."

"Just take the gloves," Jack told her.

She did, but as she was sliding them on the old guy started to move again. He wasn't awake yet but he looked like he was coming back to consciousness. Doubled over, his head lolled slowly from side to side, the thin line of blood drizzling fine lines on his knees like the scratchings of a polygraph test. Finally he stopped, slumped and absolutely motionless.

"Is he dead?" she asked, her voice a blend of awe and horror.

Jack shook his head. "I don't think so. I think he's still passed out from the pain."

"Why don't we ask him?" Johnny said, and took a firm step forward. His hands were covered in blood, splattered all the way up to the elbows, and he felt great. He felt ready to take on the world; his face was aglow as he moved right into the man.

"Hey you there you old wet-head," Johnny screamed. The man didn't move. "You still with us? You still hanging in there you worthless piece of human *filth?* Say something! We're all waiting! You've got the floor!"

When the man didn't move, Johnny gave a simple shrug and turned to his friends. With a wave of his hands he indicated the thing on the ground that the man had spat out. "Well, I guess *he* doesn't have the floor, but his tongue certainly does."

Jack and Jillian's gaze followed Johnny's and understanding dawned on them. That thing the guy had spit out was not a maggot. It was not an insect at all. It was the man's tongue. Johnny had cut it clean off and there it lay, a small puddle of blood spreading round it with a stripe of dust and dirt streaked on one side from where it had hit the ground, slid, and come to rest.

Jillian stared at it, for some reason thinking about that first day when they all visited the slaughterhouse of *Mendoza's Meats*. A second later a stench arose around them that clawed at their eyes, clogged their throats.

"Aww *Jesus,*" Jillian barked. "I think he shit himself."

Jack was nodding. He had smelt it already but remained silent; no use drawing attention to the obvious. He thought of something, walked over to Johnny, and lifted Johnny's wrist; if the blood splattered all over it bothered him, he gave no indication; it was such a familiar gesture that Johnny's heart broke a little.

"It's nearly eleven o'clock," he said, glancing at the numbers. "Just over an hour until we ring in the new year. I'd prefer it if this fucker didn't live to see it."

Jillian smiled at Jack, but there was sadness in her face. Saying goodbye to the eighties was like giving a final kiss to a cancer ridden loved one; even though you knew it was for the better, you hated to see them go. This pathetic fucker in the chair, however…as far as she was concerned they couldn't tear him apart fast enough. She watched as Jack turned to Johnny, held out his hand.

"Kid Johnny, it's your call. You guys are my two favorite people in this world, and this guy here is…well, you know what he is as well as any of us. What say we act like a J.C. Penny temp at Christmas and *wrap this shit up?"*

Johnny felt so happy he could burst. The four eyes on his were the warmest he'd ever experienced, and it occurred to him that from where they stood now, they were exactly equidistant from each other: they formed a perfect triangle, with the man slumped in the chair – his head still hung on his chest but the flow of blood from out his mouth had retarded to a slow and obscene drool - directly in the middle.

Johnny breathed: this was looking to be the best New Years ever. He winked at his friends.

"Let's get this done quickly then."

They each went for their respective tools.

The triangle tightened.

--

The man in the chair suffered. His screams were proof of that. And his screams, to the three involved, were like a symphony composed by Gore, Hook and Sumner, Marr and Morrissey.

Even after Johnny removed a sock from off his foot and stuffed it into the mouth to silence the shrieks, to stay the flow of blood, somehow the man managed to let his pain be known, and that was fine with them. It told them that they were working well. Doing their duty. The howls only served to egg them on.

And his writhing. His blubbering through the clog of a severed and bloated half-tongue. The steady stream of tears that – they all thought – would have been tears of blood, were it humanly possible.

They did too many things to his flesh to name, but there were some of note, though not all of them left their mark in the physical sense. Some were done and then forgotten by even the victim; one has little time to think of the thumb so recently pressed and rubbed into an open eyeball when only seconds later the sensation is replaced by the cold slow tightening of a desktop vise around one's own testicles. The knowledge of their *pop!* is both relief and a regret; how does one put into pronounceable words what it is like to lose a part of oneself?

It was beauty and hate.

It was beautiful hate as his body was transformed into an orgy of pain.

In life he'd had a burning desire to impose his sexual proclivities on others, and for that they doused his hair in crude oil, and set it to burn.

He'd taken advantage of prostitutes, street-walkers, and for that they made sure that he himself would never walk again. One by one they tore out his toenails, curled yellow things that looked cancerous and dry, and when they were finished, they removed from his mouth the sopping sock soaked with his own vile blood, and stuffed them in, ground them into the open flesh of an amputated tongue that would never speak again.

In his past life he'd worked in a porno theatre, and during that time he saw things that no man should ever see, depraved scenes not just on the screen but in the flesh in front of him, and for that they took an Xacto-knife to his eyelids and cut them clean off, so that he never be able to turn away. So that *they* became his master of sight.

His son had committed suicide by drinking Drano, effectively burning holes right through his stomach from the inside out, and for that they took a drill and bored holes through his cheeks, his ears, the head of his penis, and the web of flesh between thumb and forefinger.

And through all this they made sure he was conscious, that he was aware. If ever he passed out from the pain, they threw water in his face, pinched his earlobes, slapped his head or dug old nails through his bloated scaly man-nipples.

By the time they were done with him he'd bitten clean through his lower lip till it hung by a quarter inch skein of flesh, dangling like an obscene and abused remnant of genitalia. A sharp twist of his head would have separated it completely, but no, it stayed there still. It hung there limp and unused.

For all this and more, he suffered. If anyone desired more proof they need only look to the remnants of his face.

It was no longer human.

It was no longer there.

In the end it was no specific wound that killed him, no great bloodletting that drained him dry, and who was to say what the final straw was that broke the camel's back? Tiny tears make up an ocean and by the end of it all, this man cried himself dry. In the end there was nothing left. Eventually they realized that he was no longer responding, that fresh cuts failed to produce any more of the ruby-red, and like that their fun was over.

It was all so anticlimactic, and Johnny, the one who'd started it all, decided that he had to be the one to finish it. In one final act of half-anger/half-despair that the ritual was over, Johnny stepped forward and stuck a six-inch paring knife into the man's belly, twisted it, and ripped it once straight across from left to right: the wound opened up in a hideous smile and his bowels fell to the floor in a great tumble of guts and stink.

Johnny took a step back, dropped the paring knife, and silently began to cry.

It was the eve of a Sunday, December 31st, 1989, eleven twenty-one p.m., and the man they had been torturing for the last hour or so, was dead.

They stood around the corpse and for a long time no one said a thing. Johnny wiped at the tears on his face, leaving a small streak of blood and viscera. Finally, Jillian broke the silence.

"I guess he got…*bored with life.*"

"Thank the Lord," Johnny returned.

"For small mercies," Jack finished. He wasn't smiling. His face was blank. But he couldn't take his eyes off of what they had done. Something – he had no idea what it was, but *something* – felt to have died along with the old bastard.

Whatever it was, Jillian felt it too. And Johnny. With each drop of blood drained from this man it seemed that their anger had drained too. Justice had been served and for the first time in as long as any of them could remember, the world seemed right. *Balanced.* Now that the old guy was finally dead, the euphoria of murder ebbed away. Their hearts calmed and their blood slowed. Their minds came back to their bodies, which, no longer hot and fired by the act itself, were growing cold.

Jillian stood in front of the defeated corpse and stared down at the mess, the gore painted on its flesh and on the floor like some orgiastic output of a schizophrenic artist gone ten types of crazy.

The colors were all there, and the colors were glorious. The rustic wet reds caught the light and set the blood to glow. The pounded purples, on the flesh in the form of heavy bruises and on the floor in the curled lumps of intestines, stomach, and liver: cold offal waiting to decay. Swirls of yellow too, streaking the entrails like weak sunny veins, looking oddly stuck, caught like color in the middle of a cat's eye marble. The gray matter of a once thinking brain, oozing out of what was left of the right ear, like old toothpaste desperately squeezed too hard. And mixed within it all, and fittingly so, the earthy black/brown of shit, intertwined, coating, sticking to everything. *The real measure of this man*, Jillian thought; *a piece of shit in life, and a piece of shit in death.* Her lips curled back in a snarl and she shivered as she walked over, picked up another tarp sitting on the workbench, and threw it over the dead man and his spilled guts. Now that he was dead, she didn't want those lidless eyes staring out at her, watching her, accusing her. With the second tarp thrown over him, and the first tarp they'd placed under him before all the madness began, he was like a dead man sandwich waiting to be devoured. Or in this case, disposed of.

Jillian took several steps away from the mound, her gaze never leaving the tarp, and slowly wrapped her arms around her body. Her teeth were chattering she was shivering so badly now but it had nothing to do with the temperature; the room was actually quite warm. It were as though her teeth were trying to bite themselves, to gnash themselves out of existence. The last time she'd felt this alone she'd taken a blade to her wrists and *pressed*.

It didn't take long for them to come to her. Even if they mistook her shivering for a sign of coldness, they could see that she was upset and needed them near her. Hands and arms wrapped around to warm her from behind, first Jack's and then Johnny's, and soon their hands pressed with more intensity, not just to caress but to grip, to hold tightly enough to let it be known that it wasn't simply their bodies they were holding onto but the instant itself, afraid to let go, as though aware on some base molecular level that once they did the moment would pass forever, and they would be left as three separate entities, three strangers who had once shared something cathartic that had been lost in death and the bare passage of time.

They drew each other in until all their bodies were entwined, a windmill of limbs, legs pressing against legs, thighs to thighs, chest to chest to chest. When they finally looked each other in the eyes directly something passed between them, something more alive than life, and without conscious thought they one by one began to remove their various bits of soaked and gore-splashed clothing, not by use of their hands, but rather like a nest of shedding snakes, slithering and pressing, pulling themselves out of their pseudo-skin by rubbing against each other, writhing, mashing themselves together until they became one great bloodied thing, a three-headed monster intent on eating itself up. One moment it was a single person's mouth leeched onto another's thigh, the next it was an orifice devouring the member of someone else. It wasn't long before their bodies descended to the floor and that was when the moaning really began, deep and low and unending as a horizon. Fingers probed holes, tongues, penises, and soon they were rocking in unison, all three of them connected, joined in the oldest of unions until the climax – inevitable as cold death – came to all of them and they relaxed, still in each other's arms.

It was finished, and they lay still.

Eventually their breathing slowed, they closed their eyes. Exhaustion had finally come to the basement workroom of *Laff in the Dark*, exhaustion and contentment, and a curling melancholy regarding the fact that something great and unique was slowly slipping away, was coming to an end.

They had no fear of being caught, after all they were invincible and young, which to the youthful mind amounted to the same thing, and they felt safe cocooned in their hideaway basement retreat, wrapped in each other's arms. Even death seemed faraway, impossible; were Death to return to this room surely He would pass them over unseen, for their bodies reeked of Death, of spilt and spoilt blood. They were as forgotten bodies littering a battlefield, and like those bodies, they did not move. It even seemed that they did not breathe as the carnage of the scene became their blanket, the echoing of that man's screams and fresh butchery, their lullaby.

It was at 11:57 in the p.m. of December 31st, 1989, that the last of them finally succumbed to sleep, and the sleep that took them was black and soundless, and devoid of dream. It was the purest sleep any of them had or would ever know, save The Big Sleep itself.

When they awoke several hours later they were surprised to discover that they were stuck together, physically melded by the coating of blood that had dried and congealed while they slumbered, and their skin stretched, pulled painfully, as they pushed themselves apart. One by one they stood, still naked and savage in their pajamas of slaughter, and stared down at the mess they had made. By some strange trick of the passing from one decade to the next, their actions of the night before were faraway and hazy, remote somehow, as though they had been done by someone else, someone separate and much worse than they knew themselves to be.

With the new day and decade upon them, and a silence that was almost religious, they set about the long and gruesome task of cleaning up their mess. Of trying their best to erase what they had done. They scrubbed long, and they scrubbed hard, at times harder than need be, as though trying to make the bloodied floor, the gore encrusted tools, and their own stained clothes, forget what they had done.

They played no games as they worked; they smoked no cigarettes, and they sang no songs.

One by one they washed themselves, scrubbed the blood from their bodies, scraped dried flesh from under their fingernails. Wordlessly they ran wet cloths over each other's backs, dabbed at each other's faces, always avoiding each other's eyes. Like automatons they washed each other's hair, inspected themselves for missed spots, and went back to the sink again and again as though silent and nervous parishioners blessing themselves repeatedly with holy water. Jack had thought ahead and his motto shone true; *leave no trail.* He'd brought soap and shampoo, bleach and blankets. He even brought a quart of Drano to pour down the sink when they knew they were one hundred percent done, lest any of their DNA get left behind. When the room was bleached and sanitized and they were cleaned and looking fresh as store model appliances they all stood together and stared down at the bulge under the tarp that grew out of the ground like a tumor.

"Now what the hell are we going to do with this thing?" Johnny asked, and for some time no one said a thing. Staring down at it was like eyeing a drained bottle of Tequila from the night before, the one that had induced the present mind-splitting headache and chemical warfare currently taking place in one's stomach. Last night they couldn't get enough of the old guy – they practically had to fight each other for a chance at him – and now not one of them could stand the thought of bending down and picking the guy up, tarp or no tarp.

"Just like we planned," Jack said, his voice slow and dry of emotion. "You two head out to the car, make sure the coast is clear. If you see anyone, start making out; nothing makes people more uncomfortable and less suspicious than two horny teens. Johnny, you deal with the gate, Jillian, back that car right in here as close as close can be. I'm gonna gather up all our stuff, get everything ready. Wrap this poor bastard up,"- he nodded with his chin in the direction of the lump on the floor – "with duct tape. Call it a belated Christmas present to the world." He looked at his friends who looked almost as tired as he felt. "You guys up for it?"

They nodded, too exhausted to speak. They had been looking forward to this night for weeks, now they couldn't wait for it to be over. Finally, they moved and together Kid Johnny and Jilly Jill ascended the stairs. They saw no one outside, and that Jack had been right; the car was sitting under a good six inches of snow. It looked like it had been there for a week or more. It was so cold outside that by the time Jillian got to the driver's side door her hair – still wet from their makeshift shower – had become a black helmet, as hard and shiny as obsidian.

Johnny had no problem with the gate and Jillian backed the car into the park with ease, right up to the entrance of the funhouse. It was less than a ten-foot walk from the trunk of the car to the door but she had a feeling that it would be the longest walk any of them would ever make. If somebody were to see them now, or worse, to see them coming out carrying what looked like a rolled up carpet exactly six feet long, there would be trouble, and plenty of it. She had felt so safe in the basement; now all she could think of was how exposed they were, and her heart began beating so fast she barely heard Johnny tell her to stop as they stepped back into the warm darkness of the funhouse.

"What is it?" she asked, and then she heard it too. Noises from downstairs, coming from directly below them. Johnny's flashlight caught her face, hers got his, and for a second they were two mirror images of each other: confusion. *Utter confusion.* It was a sound they couldn't place for it was a sound neither of them had ever heard, or expected to hear. They stood there for a full ten seconds, listening, wondering, and then…

Even as their minds grasped what it was, conscious thought was working equally hard to reject it, to affirm that such a sound was not possible, that such a sound did not exist. Their countenances of confusion melted into masks of horror.

It was screaming, raw and unfiltered, it came up through the floorboards the way shark fins might rise from the seascape of the ocean during a feeding frenzy, seemingly everywhere at the same time.

"Jack?" Jillian asked, her voice cracking with impossibility.

"Jack," Johnny said, and then he was running as fast as the darkness would allow, with Jillian trailing, doing her best not to fall too far behind lest she get lost, trapped, and find herself wedged in the all-encompassing darkness, with only the sounds of Jack's inhuman cries to keep her company.

--

Their first reaction upon entering the workroom was that Jack had disappeared but somehow his screams had remained, had left an impression on this room so heavy that they lingered behind like a haunt, or a stain, or the smell of burning hair. It took a few seconds for them to realize that it was a trick of the light; he was hiding in the shadows. So help them God, Jack Barber was hiding. If they couldn't see it with their own eyes they never would have believed it.

"What the..?" Johnny began, but then he followed the line of Jack's terrified gaze, and saw what Jack was seeing through eyes so bugged they looked ready to burst, and he understood, or at least he *kind of* understood.

It was the body. The tarp had been thrown off it and it now lay there open and exposed. What had been so captivating hours ago was now obvious and biological, about as exhilarating as the gynecological exam of an eighty-year-old woman. And it appeared to be moving.

Jillian squinted in the half-darkness. "What the...?" Jillian said, unintentionally repeating Johnny's own sentiment. But really, what else was there to say? *'What the...?'* indeed.

Dark shadows moved over the guts like liquid smoke. Black blobs morphed and rolled over his flesh, moving spots that defied logistics and empirical experience. If the thing upon which the shadows moved hadn't been so downright grotesque, Johnny and Jillian might have thought it a cartoon; they literally didn't believe their eyes. And then Johnny gave a flick of his flashlight and all was revealed, all became clear.

Cockroaches. Hundreds of them, maybe thousands, scuttled over the dead man's corpse, sometimes wiggling out of the cavity that was once his stomach, their mandibles thick and heavy with black blood, and other times pressing themselves in, forcing their way between the various lips of flesh that Jack and Jillian and Johnny had opened all over the dead man's body.

"Ugh," Jillian wailed, "how can they stand that? I mean, it's..." But it was unnecessary to finish the thought; it was completely obvious what it was, namely, unfiltered repulsion. She turned away before she had the chance to be sick.

Johnny shrugged. It was disgusting, yes, but not all that surprising – he had once heard about a species of cockroach that had a special penchant for eyelashes, particularly those of young children while they were sleeping – and he was sure that at some point in his life he had witnessed something more disgusting than what he saw now, though he couldn't place what it was exactly. Actually, considering what he thought of this man and his relationship to him, he thought it kind of fitting that he was being devoured by the most repulsive and reviled creatures on the planet; the idea that cockroaches would soon be shitting him out almost made him smile.

But there was someone in the room who did not find it amusing, not in the slightest, and he was still screaming at the top of his lungs. It was his friend, and he needed Johnny's help.

"Jillian," Johnny called sharply, and she turned. "Get him out of here, now, as quick as you can." He threw another glance at the infested corpse. "I'll take care of that."

Jillian did as she was told. She moved to Jack, placing her arm around him, leading him out of the room. He was shaking so badly she lost her grip several times and once, when one renegade cockroach ran right across their path Jack jumped – he actually *jumped* – backward to avoid it. It wasn't until they got to the top of the stairs and she'd rubbed his back for several minutes, rubbed his back and whispered soothing things softly into his ear, that he finally began to calm down. His breathing stopped its hitch, his heart its gallop, and he looked Jillian directly in the face; in the blinding glare of her flashlight his eyes looked like Ping-Pong balls scorched with two tiny black dots.

"I don't like cockroaches," was all he said, and then he had his arms around her and his head tucked into her neck. She felt a wetness on her shoulder that she knew was his tears and she thought, quietly and comfortably, that if she hadn't been in love with Jack Barber before, she certainly was now.

--

The cockroach corpse was the last surprise for any of them that day. In fact, it was the last surprise they ever experienced collectively until twenty-one years later when John, Jack, and Jillian each received an unexplained piece of post delivered to their front door mailbox, their own office desk, and the passenger seat of their ten-year-old Civic, respectively.

Both were surprises that they all could have done without.

Eventually, Johnny emerged from the depths of the basement looking sweaty and double tired.

"It's done," he said, nodding slowly. "Fucker's tied up tighter than an S and M whore."

Jillian nodded. "And the…bugs?" She felt Jack tense against her but he stayed silent.

"Signed, *sealed,* and delivered. And those that didn't make the cut…well let's just say that any stragglers left behind learned to respect the almighty power of my boot." He reached up and placed a hand on Jack's shoulder. "You won't see any more down there Jack, I promise."

Jack nodded at his friend in the half darkness.

"It's all cleaned up. All we need to do is haul up our stuff. And *it."*

A collective sigh escaped them all. It wasn't going to be easy. It had been hard enough getting him *down* the stairs, and that was with the excitement of the slaughter on their minds. Now they were tired, bone-wearied, and all they wanted to do was escape, get away, put a fork in the day and be done. But one last thing. Jack nodded. Jillian too.

"Leave no trail," Jack said, he reached out and took Jillian's hand, who in turn, took Johnny's, and it was like that, hand in hand in hand, that they descended the stairs of *Laff in the Dark* for what would be the last time for the next twenty-one years.

--

They didn't discuss it, in fact none of them even mentioned it, but it was fitting to them all that the night ended exactly where this whole adventure began.

Mendoza's Meats was dark and deserted as they approached – the place was unionized and it was four o'clock in the morning of New Years day; there wouldn't be a living soul around here for at least another twenty-eight hours – and once again they slipped through the gates with ease. Up and into the great building they carried their cargo and this time when Johnny snuck away to turn on the lights he made sure not to leave his flashlight behind.

It took the same one hundred and twenty-one seconds for the lights to kick in and when they did, they lit up the same drab and sterile interior. Even the security office looked the same, though the *Playboy* with the cover depicting a girl resembling Jessica Rabbit had been replaced with a slightly newer issue, this one with a girl in glasses, titled *'Women of Wall Street,'* but the corners of the pages were still *Cheeto* stained and the bowling ball bag still contained that same old pair of binoculars.

From room to room they passed, hauling their load – wrapped in the green tarp the way it was it looked like a giant overstuffed letter en route to an army base – which seemed to grow heavier and heavier with each step. Jillian's arms felt ready to snap off they were so tired, either that or start stretching like heated taffy, but she kept quiet to show that she was as tough as either of these boys; having a dick didn't give one a monopoly on perseverance. Johnny stayed silent too, though his silence was more out of reverence, and a curious confusion born of the fact that he wasn't enjoying himself nearly so much as he thought he would, certainly not as much as he had on their first trip here some three months previous. But the one who had the most difficulty keeping silent was Jack, though it wasn't words he wanted to express, but whimpers. The idea of placing his hands on the polyurethane tarp gave him a severe case of the willies, each time it moved or rustled he half expected a great sea of cockroaches to come pouring out like water from a broken damn. For what had to be the hundredth time since they'd left the basement of *Laff in the Dark,* he thanked Christ that he'd gone with the thickest tarp that the hardware store sold.

When they finally reached the kill room – it briefly occurred to all of them to wonder why they hadn't brought the guy here in the first place and saved themselves a helluva trip and inconvenience – they dropped the package with an unceremonious thud that was both squishy and dull. On the right of the room were the holding pens – there were twelve in all – and they were currently packed to the brim with sleeping pigs.

Not for long, thought Johnny, and just as a weary grin was surfacing on his face he registered their snores, realized how much they sounded like this fucker on the floor sitting there drugged and bound a few hours previous, and any trace of a smile disappeared.

"How are we going to…?" Jillian began, but Jack was already on the move. He had spotted the sledge-hammers off to the left, seven of them looking very old and very used, the stain from their wooden handles worn right off so that the grip section was yellow-white and plain. For some reason they reminded Jack of an old whore he had once seen in his childhood while exiting the movies with his mother, in a time before he even knew what a whore was.

"You'd think they'd have switched to electricity by now," Jillian said as she watched Jack pick up a hammer, bounce it up and down a few times to assess the weight. "More humane, no?" she asked.

Johnny shrugged. "Welcome to corporate America, where the bottom line is the bottom line, and it must always, *always,* be written in black."

Jack nodded. "Electricity costs money. So do the tools it takes to deliver it." He held the hammer out in front of him the way a king might hang on to his scepter. "This thing cost probably twenty bucks ten years ago and I bet it's put an end to more lives than Caligula."

Johnny walked over and picked up his own sledge-hammer. For a second Jillian felt like she was being left out, like the guys were insinuating that she couldn't handle one because she was a girl, but then Johnny stepped forward and handed her the one he was currently caressing. A second later and they each had their own.

They all stared down at the tarp. They had discussed the details before, days ago when they had put the whole plan together. It should have come as no surprise but they couldn't help it: once the tools were in their hands it was hard to believe how heavy they were; gravity pulled at them like physical guilt. Finally, Jack moved; it was the idea of the roaches that he knew to be cavorting around inside the folds of tarp that got him going, he had just enough time to reflect how easily a petty and pathetic fear could motivate one's hand and one's mind before twirling the hammer like a baton so that the business end hung low.

"Try not to split the tarp," he said, and then he raised the hammer high.

"Wait," Johnny said, and the urgency in his voice caused Jack to do just that. He looked over at his friend, the sledge-hammer poised and ready.

"I need to be first," he said, and in a moment he was beside Jack, his hammer also at the ready.

He held it over the end bulge – what could only be the skull – and paused, inhaled once, held it, then brought the hammer down as hard as he could. From inside the wrapping of the tarp there came a sickening crunch, like fortune-cookies crushed into a thick soup, but Kid Johnny allowed no time for it to sink in. He raised the sledge-hammer again: brought it down.

Again.

And again.

And again.

Eventually Jack joined in, Jillian too, and together their three hammers pumped up and down like oil derricks on the move, only stopping when exhaustion overtook them and their arms could lift no more.

By then it was okay. Skull was no longer skull. Femur no longer femur. Were they to open the package, they would find something that looked like a cross between a Spanish *Tomatina* festival and the doorstep of a newly opened Greek restaurant. Primordial soup. It didn't matter. They had done what they set out to do, and when their hammers finally came to a standstill, they relaxed.

Together they lifted the giant tarp, carried it over to the great trough beside the sleeping pigs, slit it open and poured the mess in.

It sludged its way out of the tarp like old raw sewage. Then Johnny walked over and hoisted up his own still warm sledge-hammer.

"Dinner's served," he screamed, so loudly that his throat actually split, brought blood to his mouth. A few of the animals stirred. Several of them rolled over in their sleep, but it wasn't until Johnny swung the thing full arc into the thick metal bars that made up the perimeter of their pen that the animals really started to move and once they did, there was no stopping them.

Dozens of bulging pink bodies, their skin leathery and sprouting sporadic tufts of coarse hair, rose, braying, snorting, crying afoul at having their beauty rest disturbed. But then they caught a whiff of what was in the trough they came running, ramming into their bedmates over and over, head butting, beating and biting their way to the trough to get a taste of whatever mess it was their masters had seen fit to deliver into their awaiting bellies.

The remnants were gone in a matter of minutes, and when they were, Johnny tossed the tarp into the pen as well and watched as the swine went to town on it, licking at the wet parts, chewing at the goop that clung there, devouring anything remotely biological. By the time Johnny managed to wrestle the tarp away from them it was clean as a newborn's conscience. It would have looked brand new save for the fact that the pigs had managed to tear several bite holes into its surface; now it looked like a giant piece of green Swiss cheese.

"Bon appétit," he said, then he remembered what it was they had just eaten, and a tight grin wholly absent of mirth hardened on his face.

"Once a pig, always a pig," he mused, then he was folding up the tarp, tucking it securely under his arm, motioning for the others to follow him to the door. They did so silently, almost reverently, as though a funeral procession in mourning. But what was it they were lamenting? Certainly not the death of the old bastard now being broken down by the stomach acid of three-dozen contented swine.

They moved languidly, their steps heavy, their faces blank. They did not walk three abreast but to step single file with Johnny in the lead, Jillian a close second, and Jack bringing up the rear.

All of them felt confused. The death of this man had brought about the death of something in each of them but none of them could put their finger on what it was exactly, though each had the feeling that they would be able to figure it out once they were alone. Solitude suddenly seemed paramount.

Halfway back to the entrance of the building, Jillian had an idea; if they really were to go full circle, then they would have to go back to the exact spot where this whole adventure started. Namely, to that stupendous beast they'd found suspended in that lone room, the sterile white box that had reminded them of an inverted sugar cube.

"Wait a second," she said, and the others stopped, stared at her. "I want to go back to that room," she continued. "That square one with – " for a second she almost said "that monster" but revised and ended with "that thing with the empty eye sockets." She stared back at them, waiting for a response, certain that they were about to challenge her, to deny her request. She didn't know why – they had *literally* committed murder for her in the past – but she felt that she now annoyed them. That they saw her as something to escape rather than embrace. Perhaps she was projecting.

Jack nodded. Johnny shrugged.

"Okay. Okay. Which way was it?" Jack turned to Johnny and Johnny pointed with his free hand.

"Through that door and to the right."

Jack nodded. They trudged on, unspeaking, and when they finally made it to the door that led to the room they paused, stared at it. Finally, Jack reached forward and pushed it open.

It was like stepping into their past…only it wasn't.

The room had changed: it was larger somehow. It was still that perfect cube, and the walls remained virginal white, but the carcass of the unidentifiable beast was gone, as was the pancake of blood that had lain congealed beneath it. The pile of bones that had rested in the corner had been taken away as well so that the only thing that remained from their first visit was the great looping chain – it looked long and thick enough to serve as a 'dog' collar for a Tyrannosaurus Rex – hanging directly down into the middle of the room.

Jack frowned, Johnny shook his head, and Jillian shivered, each of them glad that the spot where the carcass had hung was empty. They had had enough of beasts for awhile.

"It looks like a giant noose," Johnny finally said, and one by one they looked at the chain in this new light, then back to each other. Jack shifted his weight from his left foot to his right. Jillian rubbed her neck. Johnny felt like he was going to throw up.

"Let's get the hell out of here already," Jack said, and the others quickly agreed. When they left the room, and eventually the slaughterhouse itself, they didn't look back.

--

They drove for a long, long time, and during that time not one word was spoken, their minds too crowded with thought to form coherent sentences. Eventually they stopped; they had one more piece of business to attend to, and it had to be done before this night was allowed to pass. They dealt with it slowly, languidly, still no words spoken until:

"We can't do this anymore." It was Jillian who said it, her words broke a seven-minute scene in which the only sound that existed was the fuzzy sizzling of the tarp as it set to burn.

The smell of melting plastic was around them, a chemical smell that was almost thick enough to be physical, it rose not in plumes but in frantic stabs from the half-rusted barrel they'd found beside an abandoned gas station about forty clicks from *Mendoza's Meats*. Together they stood around it, forming a perfect triangle for the second time in the last twenty-four hours, the shadows on their faces dancing and twisting their features as they watched the last piece of evidence slowly melt into a gelatinous goo. Their breath came out in cumulus little bursts, punching into the shapeless wisps of smoke and together the whole mess mingled and climbed into the air, disappearing into the pure black of the sky the way a wave is swallowed by the ocean, and oceans have no memory.

"What do you mean?" Johnny asked, though he knew perfectly well. He didn't want to believe it.

"We're tempting fate," replied Jillian. "Not to mention the gods."

"She's right," added Jack. "Not so sure about the *gods*, but…"

When Johnny replied he knew he wasn't just arguing against his friends and logic, but against himself as well.

"But we've done so much. And we haven't gotten caught. Not even close, right?"

Jack shook his head. "On a long enough timeline…"

"Every crime will have to be accounted for," Jillian finished. "It doesn't matter if it's two hours later or two decades. We'll pay for what we've done, whether through guilt or the gallows, but if we keep this up, eventually all our luck will run out and someone's gonna come knocking Johnny, be it detective, or Death."

Johnny's voice was low, almost a whisper: the voice of a man who knows the argument is already lost. "But we made such a good team."

"That we did Kid Johnny. But can you honestly say you still feel the need?" Jack moved his head from side to side. "Something died last night. It wasn't just that old pedo, and it wasn't the eighties either. I don't know what exactly, but maybe it's like Sheedy said in *TBC:* 'When you grow old, your heart *dies.*'"

Jillian, who was staring down into the smoldering mess of the melted tarp, slowly raised her head. "No Jack. I'm sorry but you're wrong." She shook her head back and forth, her eyes unfocused and it struck her that sometimes letting go the control of your eyes was the best way to see something clearly.

Both men stared at her, expectant. She went on.

"I think in our case it was the opposite. Before we met each other we were lonely and out of place, and cared only about ourselves. What we did, what we did *together,* somehow…woke us up. I mean, I know I can't speak for you two, but for me…I feel like I'm alive now. My heart, for the first time is pink, beating and pumping life through each crisscrossed tunnel of my nerve system. And you're wrong too about the eighties Jack: that it was a conspirator in these so-called deaths. That was our decade, right? Of all the major life events that could possibly happen to a person – their birth, their first loves – "

"Their first kills," Johnny interjected.

"First fucks," Jack said, and grinned.

Jillian was nodding. "All those firsts, all those billboard big events, all of them happened to us in the eighties. And the eighties *were* our decade. We own them – and always will – in a way that no one who came before or after us ever can. But it's January 1st, 1990. A new decade. A new time." She looked around and realized that the sun was coming up. The sky was turning from a spilled-ink blotch to a bluish-gray canvas. The stars were fading and there was a slight sprinkling of snow coming down around them. "A new day," she added, then repeated her original sentiment. "We can't do this anymore. We can't."

She glanced down quickly, her head heavy with want and emotion, and then looked up at the two men in front of her. *Her boys.* Something inside her broke, wept, renewed. *Is now and forever shall be: Her Boys.*

She looked around. The wrecked smoke drifting off the smoldering tarp had thinned till it was debatable as to whether it was there at all. The remnants in the can looked like something a cat might have puked up under the stairs six-months ago. They had no need to fear it. All evidence was gone. And so was the need for more words.

One by one they got back into Johnny's car. They relaxed in their seats, smoking cigarette after cigarette. They were holding onto the moment as long as they could, until daylight could no longer be denied. The darkness was retreating step by cautious step.

The snow stopped.

A warmth was born into the air.

It was a new day, finally.

Jillian sat up, stretched her arms wide across the length of the back seat. There was an air about her that suggested that this was the end, that it was coming to a close.

"You guys want to get heading back?" Johnny asked, his hand already on the ignition key, but Jillian shook her head.

"It's such a beautiful day," she said. "The sun is out and it's starting to melt the snow." She placed her face to the glass of the window, cupped her fingers around her eyes so she could see better but her breath fogged up the glass. "I always loved to hear the sound of the snow melting, see it dribbling by in the gutters. It always looks so clean. So pure. Like…like a baptism." She leaned forward in her seat so that her head was directly between Jack and Johnny who were sitting side by side in the front. "I think I'm going to walk."

Johnny started. Jack said nothing. He'd been thinking the same thing.

"Are you crazy? It's gotta be like three hours walk back to town: you'll freeze."

Jillian only pursed her lips; it was impossible to tell if she was creating a smile or a frown.

"No, I'll be alright," she breathed, and then the smile became certain because she knew that she was speaking the truth. "Now give us a kiss, both of youse."

One by one they kissed her on the lips. There was nothing sexual about it; for some reason they both likened it to kissing a corpse, though her lips were warm and soft and had that slight give the way only living flesh did.

She sat back in her seat, fumbled with the door, then she was out of the car. She stopped for a second, staring at the road ahead, and with a slow wave that looked like one brushing away dust from a mirror, she moved away from them.

"Just one question before you go," Jack called to her back. He was leaning out the window, his arm hanging low at the side of the car.

"What's that?" asked Jillian, turning around but not coming any closer to the car. She was smiling, and in the goldenrod glow of the rising sun, she looked radiant, a dark haired angel if ever there was one.

Jack shrugged. "Where's your fucking math? *Your* birth *was in the eighties?!* What does that make you, ten years old?" If his grin were any wider the top half of his head would have lopped right off like a split coconut.

Jillian laughed with such a carefree lightness that both men felt prickly hairs stand at attention from crown of head right down to their toes. "Hey, my birth certificate may say 1973, but I'm an eighties child through and through." She paused for a moment, glanced up at the now blazing sky, and looked back at them both. She threw them a single wink, thrust her hands in her pockets, turned, and began walking.

They watched her go until she was nothing but a spot, where the 'V' of the road met the horizon and disappeared.

The two men remained, sitting in the car, not talking, not looking at each other. Finally, Jack reached up to the dashboard and scooped up his pack of smokes, flicked it open with his index finger.

"Uh oh," he said, looking into the pack. "Only one left."

Johnny shrugged. There were butterflies in his stomach, an uneasy acid in his veins. His emotions felt balanced on a razor's edge; the slightest thing might set him off. "I've got some," he said, offering his pack to Jack.

But Jack shook his head. "I'll be alright." He stared at his friend. "I'm leaving now."

Johnny stared back. He knew that Jack wasn't just referring to the car.

"Ok," he said.

"Ok."

Jack opened the door, made to leave, then paused. They didn't hug. They didn't shake hands. But Jack lowered his head in a nod and Johnny did the same, their eyes never breaking.

"Kid Johnny," was all Jack said.

"Jackie Boy."

"But a kid no more," said Jack.

"Nor a boy."

"Time to put the ways of childhood behind us."

Johnny said nothing, not even when Jack slid out of the car, stood and stretched. The closing of the car door made Johnny start, jump a little, and a gaseous burp escaped his lips. If he'd had any food in his belly it probably would have been vomit. He watched as Jack circled the car, stepped onto the road, began striding down it with calm and confident steps – not the self-aware confidence of a model or actor, but the low, concrete confidence of a writer or a painter who knows he has done a good days work: nothing can touch him – until he came to the fork in the road.

Jillian had chosen the right fork; Jack chose the left. For a second Johnny considered calling out to him, blaring his horn to call attention to Jack's mistake, but then he remembered that Jack Barber never made mistakes. He chose to go left because he didn't want to be following Jillian. Didn't want the possibility of running into her an hour down the road. Taking the left fork would mean doubling his walk home, but Johnny was certain that Jack didn't give a flying fuck about that; no matter which way he took, Jack would end up exactly where he wanted to go.

Johnny sat behind the wheel of his father's car – now his – for some time. A long time actually so that the coldness began to seep into his bones and he had to start the engine to warm up. The windows began to fog, but he stayed there still, not bothering to wipe them off, liking the way they cocooned him in, creating a bubble around him, the product of his own breath and in essence, his own life. He wished he could go to sleep for a long, long time.

He didn't know how long he stayed there but at some point he cocked his head to the side – for no reason that he could think of. His gaze fell on the back seat window on the passenger's side, and his breath caught in his throat. There was a slight circling mist there brought back by the heater and his own breath, a haze that could have only been created by the throaty exhalation of a woman of circumstance. Jillian Jarblonsky.

It was obvious that the window had once been more fully fogged, for there were streaking crystals around the edge of the bloom jutting out at strange and impossible to replicate angles. Johnny thought briefly of Superman's fortress of solitude but pushed it out of his mind. There was something more pressing, something more peculiar to arrest his attention, he leaned forward to see exactly what it was. When it came to him he nodded, feeling dizzy, sick and unstoppable all at the same time. He didn't know it but he was biting his lip so hard that it was bleeding.

What he saw there was this: in that ever tightening bloom there were some letters, some symbols, and as time and sun-heat pressed on, those letters and symbols were pressed ever tighter, and tighter still. But he was glad he saw them while he had the chance. If he had turned around just a minute or two later, they might have been gone, lost forever somewhere between darkness and the light.

Three letters. Two symbols. And though they were gone before the cigarette smoldering in his ashtray had let out its last lick of smoke, it was long enough for them to be branded on his mind, then and forever after.

"*J + J + J,*" was what the girl had inscribed, and a minute later – *seconds, really!* – all traces of it were gone.

And a moment later, so was he.

2010

The three adults sat on a bench outside *Laff in the Dark* feeling so exhausted it were as though they had just committed that murder *now*. They had relived it so intensely, in such detail, that each of them was almost scared to look down at their hands for fear of seeing the blood on their palms, scraped flesh under their now white-collar fingernails. It was terrifying to remember what animals they had once been, what vicious creatures had lurked beneath their tender seventeen-year-old skin. And the idea that said monster might still be there, sleeping, in hibernation all these years, was one too uncomfortable for them to consider.

"So are you going to tell us or do we gotta wait another twenty-one years before we get a fuckin' Christmas card from this guy?" Jack was staring at John with an intensity usually reserved for professional boxers seconds before the first *ding!*

Johnny nodded. His throat was so dry it was hard for him to speak. His head was still swimming from when he'd nearly passed out. Jack and Jillian had had to support him the entire way up the stairs and through the maze that was *Laff in the Dark* until they'd finally made their way here. He rubbed at his temple and was surprised to find a coating of sweat there; he felt cold enough to shiver.

"Mendoza's Meats," he said, finally. He shook his head. "It all started where it all started."

Jack and Jillian glanced at each other, eyebrows knitted.

"Can you elaborate on that a little?"

John nodded, took a deep breath, reached into his pocket and pulled out the bag of Cheetos he'd picked up off the floor in the stunted hallway downstairs.

"Mendoza's Meats," he said again, more sure this time. "That first day we went there, the *first day we met,* when I went to turn on the lights, I found a bag of these," – he held up the bag, covered in dust and an outdated design – "in the front office. There was a magazine too, a *Playboy,* and the corners were stained with…with cheese powder. The second time too, when we went back, the same thing. Another bag of *Cheetos.* A different *Playboy,* but also stained."

"That doesn't mean much John." Jillian shook her head. "I mean, I admit that it's a coincidence but… it was the eighties. *Cheetos* were a pretty popular brand back then." Jillian didn't want to believe it. Up till now she was hoping that somehow all this would be revealed to be some elaborate practical joke. Or something supernatural involving specters and haunts. Imagining that their tormentor was a *Cheeto* munching voyeur who had a job and paid taxes and jacked off to Playboy at work made all of it too real, too quantifiable.

"Was there anything else in the office?"

"Yeah. There was...*oh Jesus.*" He shook his head. "Binoculars. A single pair. They were there both times: binoculars."

"A surveillance man then." Jack's face was withdrawn, thinking.

"A surveillance man," Johnny agreed. It all made sense, at least the *who* part. As to the *why* or the *how,* he had no clue.

"We were doomed from the start." Jillian was staring down at the ground, shaking her head with a look that suggested she was fantasizing about pile-driving her face directly into the concrete. Jack reached over and placed an arm around her shoulder, rubbed her back absently.

"It would appear that way." His face hardened, turned bold. Jack Barber was not a man easily beat; he was too much in the habit of winning. "But that's all in the past. It's done with, and there's nothing we can do about it. We need to focus on the present. The here and now." He nodded quickly to himself, his mind racing furiously. "They'll have records. Not sure if their computer files will date back that far but if they do I'll get the info. I'll find out who he is. Was. If it's the last goddamn thing I do, I'll find out who he was."

"And then what?" Jillian's voice was clammy and thick, dreading Jack's response, but knowing that she would have to go along with whatever he proposed; like it or not they were all in this together again, for the first time in twenty-one years.

"And then we'll do what we have to."

Jillian's head was suddenly weaving back and forth as though it had forgotten how to stay on straight. Johnny's face was bloodless, his eyes unseeing. Like Jillian, he didn't know if he could go back. To that life. To that person. Didn't know if he could, or if he wanted to. There was of course another alternative, but he had Arabelle to think about. No. *No.* He gritted his teeth. Jack was right. He would do what he had to. *They* would do what they had to.

"Whatever we do, we can't rush into this. We have to be smart."

"Smart like we were back then?" That was Jillian, and her words stung Jack, as though they were aimed at him directly. After all, hadn't he always been the cleaner. The *'leave no trail'* guy who had indeed left one mother-fucking transport-truck sized highway for them to be followed on. But Jack Barber dug in his heels, put a stop to the negativity. Jack Barber wasn't going to regret anything. Regrets were for the dying, for those who had no hope of remedying their past mistakes. While he still had red blood in his veins, Jack Barber would regret nothing.

"We've got age with us this time. And wisdom. At least now we have some idea what we're up against, and we do know this: whoever he is: they're dangerous. *Very* dangerous."

"What makes you say that?" Jillian had been thinking that their ghost was quite the opposite; a coward who stayed back in the shadows, who hid behind mail and anonymity and stealthily recorded audio tracks. Who never showed his face, never let his presence be known. There was a hope in her that once confronted, the guy would disappear like other less tangible problems from one's past.

Jack pointed off in the distance to *Laff in the Dark*. "For the simple fact that he *watched* us do what we did. He didn't try to stop us, he kept himself hidden. He followed us there then he snuck in behind us, hid in his little alcove and he sat there and watched, and not only that, he took pictures. He *videotaped* it. He didn't do it to blackmail us, or to collect evidence against us. He had no interest in upholding the law. If that were the case we would have been arrested twenty-one years ago." Jack's words were hot with anger and decisiveness and his heart was pounding in his chest so loudly that he could barely hear his own words. "No," he went on, "he did it because he wanted to. He did it because he *liked* it." He looked at his two friends and his eyes were wide and dark and alive: a wolf's eyes as it delivers the killing bite. "He's crazier than all three of us put together," he said, and then he bit his lip.

"And he's methodical." John was staring into the horizon, his eyes unfocused; all he could see was Arabelle. "He's been watching us all these years. Keeping tabs on us. I mean, how else would he know where we lived? Jack: your office. I mean, if he is a surveillance guy, that would explain how he was able to get all the way up to your office without being detected. He knew how to bypass security. To avoid the cameras. Jillian, didn't you say he broke into your car? Left the tape on the seat. And Christ, he walked right up to my front door and delivered the package by hand. For all we know he could be watching us right now. Those binoculars… and the audio tape. He could be list – "

John's head darted around chicken-like, snapping mental pictures from all angles. "He could be anywhere," he said, his words coming quick as a finger snap. "He could be everywhere."

Jack reached out and gripped John's shoulder, steadied him. "Keep thinking like that and you'll drive yourself crazy."

"I've been crazy," John said without a hint of humor. "You were both there, and it was one of the best times of my life. It was the first time I think I truly felt alive."

"Funny how death can bring that out."

Johnny blinked. "Not really. Funny I mean. Seems to me the most natural thing in the world."

"Death yes," replied Jack, "but not murder. Murder may be a necessity at times, but it is not natural. It disrupts things, throws off the flow. Murder is a blip in the scheme of things. That moment when the needle slips out of its groove and the record skips a little. It's a mistake."

Jillian took a deep breath. "You can say that again."

Jack nodded, and then his eyelids slowly closed. He kept them that way as he went on. "Did any of you ever wonder why things went bad at the end? Why it felt so good those first two times, and then went to shit the last? Why it all went...sour?"

Jillian shrugged. "I think we'd all just had enough. I mean, there's only so many times you can...you know, before it starts to lose its excitement."

For some time Jack didn't move. His eyes remained closed, his body looking relaxed yet solid. When he finally opened his eyes he turned to John.

"And you John? What do you think?"

A shiver zigzagged over John's flesh; he had the impression that this was Jack's real question and it flashed in him – guilt and shame – the idea that: *Jack knows.*

"I...I don't know if I understand the question."

Jack looked sad. There was no anger, but a fogs breath of disappointment wafted over his features.

"We were always honest with each other, right from the get-go, remember? Nothing between us. No bullshit. Hearts on our sleeves and nothing but truth."

The sadness drifted over to Johnny now, seeped into his chest. *He knows.*

Jack's eyes now met Johnny's. "Why did you lie to us Johnny?"

"I…" began John, but he didn't know how to complete the thought. How do you form words you never intended to speak?

Jillian was confused. "What are you guys talking about? Jack, what are you getting at? What did Johnny-?" but Jack only answered with a shake of his head.

"I'm not mad Johnny. I never was, not even when I realized what you'd done. I loved you. I loved both of you."

Things were welling up in Johnny that he hadn't thought about in years, things that he thought he had put to rest with fire and blade. When he spoke again, his words came out choked and moist.

"But don't you guys see. I loved you too. I loved you both. *That* was the reason I didn't tell you. That was the reason I *couldn't* tell you."

For the first time Jack's face broke a little and his lips parted ever so slightly. He shook his head. "But that was the exact reason that you *should* have told us."

Jillian, her head moving back and forth between them as though watching a tennis ball in slow motion, raised her hands in protest. "Will you guys *please* tell me what the hell you're going on about? I mean I'm sitt—"

"It was my father." John didn't blink as he spoke, not once. "That last time. It wasn't just some old pervert from my block. Not just some old man. It was my father." He turned to Jack. "How did you know?"

"He looked just like you."

"Oh. Oh." John's head dropped a little and his shoulders drooped like the boughs of an under-watered aloe plant . He'd never felt so ashamed in all his life.

"Still, I wasn't sure. Wasn't positive. But, I know you mentioned once that you were part Hungarian. And it was when he first heard your voice that he started screaming, really going off the handle. "Sin, sin, sin!" he kept screaming. Afterwards I got curious. Went and looked it up. He sighed. 'Sin' is Hungarian for 'son'." Jack's face was steel. "He was calling out to you."

John and Jack's eyes were locked and Jillian felt that were she to extend her hand between the gaze she would receive a sharp electric shock.

"You must have thought I was an asshole."

Jack shook his head, never breaking the stare. "The opposite. I thought you one of the strongest people I'd ever met. I knew you must have had a reason."

"That I did."

"Good," said Jack, and then he didn't say any more.

For a long time none of them spoke. Jack had said his peace and Jillian was wordless; she couldn't have said anything if she'd wanted to. And finally, as it should be, John spoke.

"I remember very little from my childhood. From ages zero to eight, a big blank space. Whited out, as though covered in snow. My first clear memory is drinking that Drano."

Jack continued to watch John but said nothing. Jillian's face rippled with recall. There was something familiar about this story…

John looked like he was going to be sick, or cry, or both, but he went on. "It wasn't my friend I told you about. I *said* it was my friend, but it was me. And the fucked up thing was that it was *like* it was someone else, someone outside of me, because I don't actually remember doing it. Don't remember why. All I remember was the after. The pain in my stomach – like a wet fire – and my father finding me and the yelling, the screams. The hospital and the nurses who I think, were the first encounter with kindness I ever had. I fell in love with the smell of formaldehyde and that sterile odor of convalescing. I started learning about pills and potions, various drugs. I became fascinated with the idea of healing under fluorescent lights – like a plant – my insides magically knitting back together, creating scar tissue that I would never see. Like in my brain." John paused, scratched at his temple.

"I never told anyone why I drank that stuff because, and I swear to God on this – no wait, even more, *I swear to you both* – because I never knew. I never remembered. At least not until I was sixteen when I – "

A graceless croak exploded from his lips – a gaseous thing like when one is trying to throw up but finds their stomach to be completely voided – and his body leaped forward. For a second he teetered on the edge of the bench but he caught himself. When they saw that he was crying they didn't look away.

"It was a regular afternoon and I was a regular sixteen-year-old kid doing what sixteen-year-old kids did; looking through my old man's dresser for a forgotten pack of smokes. There were usually a half-dozen of them laying around the house, but for some reason that afternoon I couldn't find any and I was jonesing. He would have beat me senseless if he'd known that I smoked, and had since I was twelve, even though the old hypocrite smoked two packs a day and then some, but he probably would have *murdered* me if he'd known what I'd actually found that day. Drinking that Drano fucked up my stomach and smoking those cigarettes blackened my lungs to a degree I'll never know, but that day I got to see into my old man's head. And more unsettling, into his *heart.* And what I saw was blacker than any lung. More scarred than any chemically burned stomach lining. I may not have told you the truth about who that guy was all those years ago, but I wasn't lying when I said the guy was evil. That he was a living breathing piece of shit." John's face suddenly mashed, blossomed red, his lips, eyebrows and lines around his nose twisting in a mien of simple and perfect pain. It became the face of a child that has been utterly hurt beyond repair. Whose world-view has been shredded to ribbons by someone possessing large shears and a larger smile.

It was the face of one hopelessly lost, and knowing that they were damned for it.

"Photographs. That was what I found. A whole shitload of them. Hundreds." His lips were clenched tight into a straight line, thin as a blade, his eyes looked like they were peeking out of paper cuts in flesh.

"What was in the photos John?" Jillian's voice was less than a whisper; if it had been any softer, there would have existed only the movement of her mouth.

John's eyes moved to her, took her in, then over to Jack, who nodded silently. *Go on,* that nod said, *now while you still have the nerve, go on.*

"Me," he said, and then the floodgates opened and his bones turned liquid and he would have spilled right out onto the dull concrete of the amusement park plaza if his two old friends hadn't reached out together and grabbed him, held him up, and prevented him from falling.

--

"Well, that explains why you were so fucked up."

It was Jack who finally broke the silence, and there was a hint of amusement in his voice that was wholly absent of mock; it was the voice of a comrade who knows how to comfort, and it did the trick just right.

John laughed, loud and free, and wiped at the tears on his face. Jillian handed him a tissue, which he used to clean his nose; it made him think of Arabelle again and he laughed even harder.

"That it does," he said, and shook his head. You know for a long time afterward I went on a kick, trying to find things more fucked up than those my old man had photographed, as a way of – I don't know – *negating* them. It became an obsession, believing that if I *could* find something worse, it would render what he had done to me forgotten. Denied somehow."

Jillian shook her head. "But you never did, did you? How could you?"

John shrugged. "I guess after awhile I realized that, and decided that if I wanted to see something even more fucked up I would have to go out and make it myself."

Jack nodded. "And that was where we came in."

"Yeah, I guess so." John wiped absently at the last remnants of tears on his face. "Man, I'd thought I'd gotten over that. I mean, I had quite the catharsis with my wife, but she never really *knew.* I mean, I told her about the pictures. The abuse. But never about…what *we* did."

"You know what they say: we might be through with the past but the past isn't through with us."

"You can say that again," Jillian said, and for a moment her eyes glossed over as though she were not just *looking* at the past, but actually *in* the past; she looked like a woman possessed. She still couldn't fully believe it. *That last time, it was his father. Kid Johnny's* father. *I mean, the old bastard deserved it, obviously but…* Images machine-gunned through her head like in a child's flip book, and she thought of all the things they had done to the man. Things with nails. Fire. Burst testicles. *That's why he cut off his tongue,* she thought, *so that he couldn't call out his name. So that he couldn't call out his own son's name as the three of us tortured him to death.*

A sensation of spinning hit Jillian straight out of the blue, a feeling not unlike a partier who has had too much to drink. In her case however, it was more a matter of too much to *think*, and like the drunk, she knew the solution: a change of scene. A change of mood. A change of, well, *anything*.

"There's something else," began Jillian, "something important." She was choosing her words carefully, the way said drunk chooses each step: one at a time. There were landmines everywhere, and she had exactly zero desire to set one off.

"What's that?" Jack asked. He was looking at Jillian with a keen interest, also apparently done with the topic.

"Well, *did* you guys finish with the past? I mean, did either of you ever…again? What I mean is, well, have either of you given this guy any reason to keep following us?"

"You mean, did we quit?" Jack took no insult in the insinuation; he thought it was a great question.

"Yeah. Did you?"

"Well I can't speak for John here…but do you remember that last time we saw each other?"

Jillian thought about it. John too. They both nodded slowly but only Jillian spoke. "In the car. By that abandoned gas station. We sat there in the winter sun and smoked about a gazillion cigarettes. Then I left."

"Yeah. That was it." Jack was smiling, so deep in the recall that he could actually feel the sun baking him through the windshield of Johnny's car. "You left, but I stayed a little longer and we smoked more cigarettes. And then I realized I was down to my last one and John here, like the great friend he was, offered me some of his, which I declined. A minute later and I was on my way, walking down that service road and into a new life." He took a deep breath and his chest expanded a good six inches. It was good to remember good things.

"It was January first, remember that?" Now he could feel not only the sun on his face but the bone chill frost in his toes. "I must have walked for four, maybe five hours, and you know, I had that last cigarette in my mouth the entire time. Didn't realize it till I got home. Walked up my front porch, tried to take it out and you know what happened? That son of a bitch was frozen to my goddamn mouth. Took half my lip with it when I pulled it off." A satisfied puff escaped his lips now, as one reveling in a great triumph. He went on.

"I walked into my house and I stomped the snow from my shoes. My feet were so frozen I wasn't even sure they were still there, and then I went up to my room, slid the cigarette back into the empty pack, and threw it on my dresser. Never gave it another thought. Then I lay down and slept the sleep of the contented dead.

"When I woke up I realized that I'd slept the clock around. It was January second, and it struck me that I'd gone a full twenty-four hours without having a cigarette. That was the first time I'd done that since I picked up the habit at thirteen. I made a move to remedy that as soon as I could, but when I picked up my pack and saw the blood there, that little chunk of flesh that was *literally* a part of me, I stopped. Stared at it. All desire left me and I felt a great calm come over me. I no longer wanted it. I no longer *needed* it. But I kept it. For a long time I kept it, and every time I felt the urge I pulled that ciggie out – over time it started to rot, to stink, and eventually the chunk of flesh fell off – and looked at the stain. That stain, a rusty red blotch that always reminded me of a used tampon – sorry Jillian – never failed to kill my desire and after staring at it for a minute or two, back in the pack the ciggie would go. Eventually it became so hand worn that it started to crumble and fall apart, and at some point I either lost it or threw it away…" Jack pursed his lips as it struck him that his life had been a long one. All pretension aside, he knew his life had been longer than most.

"I dropped out of high school. Didn't see the point. I mean, what could I learn from a school that wasn't smart enough to put a firewall on their own personal academic records?" He puttered his lips. "In totally unrelated news I graduated with flying colors." He winked at them both, then shook his head.

"The point is, I never smoked that last cigarette, and I never killed anyone in my life again. At least not in real life." He smiled a Jack Barber grin. "In my video games however…" He fired off some hand-blaster guns. *"Pew, pew, pew,"* he said, and finished with a mime of an exploding head. "Could probably go for one now though. A cigarette that is, not a murder." He fell silent for a minute. A lived life was not an easy thing to contemplate, especially when there were two: the before and after. When he realized he had nothing more to say, he shrugged and turned to Jillian.

"What about you Jilly Jill? Any jilting lovers out there missing both heads? A bag of bones in your vegetable garden perhaps?"

Jillian almost smiled but didn't. Why smile when your face could remain exactly as it was: smooth, cold, considering. There were too many thoughts in her head, too many goddamn emotions rolling into each other so erratically that she didn't know where the good ones ended, and the others began.

"No," she answered, and it took all her willpower to suppress a shudder. It was the second time in less than twenty-four hours that she'd lied to these guys. She quickly changed the subject.

"What about you Johnny? Was that last time – " *with your father,* she almost said, but edited herself in time " – actually *the last* time?"

For a brief moment John considered telling them the whole story: twenty-one years flashed through his mind. The police report of his missing father. Selling the house and getting the fuck out of dodge. Living alone and slowly drinking away his savings, eventually taking on an apprenticeship as a builder more out of boredom than need – he always had been good with his hands – and years later meeting Karen at a bus stop at three o'clock in the morning of a Tuesday in March. He'd been in the roughly balanced state between drinking and drunk and she'd had a black eye and mismatched socks and when they started talking about cigarettes and flame, their conversation was natural and easy, full of a sadness more tangible than their life situations. He asked about her black eye and she asked him why he'd drank so much. They made a vow then and there that the past was the past and on this wakening morning so close to spring there was no need to discuss either matter further.

They began seeing each other. Hesitantly at first, cautiously, like children peeking around corners to see what horrors lay in wait, and when they soon discovered that there were none to be found, more openly, even happily, and it wasn't long before they were sharing each other's beds, and bodies.

They moved in together and the only thing Johnny ever hid from her was the contents of a locked box which he kept in his closet – a collection of every photo he'd ever taken – and the only thing she ever hid from him were the contents of a certain corner of her heart where all the ruinous memories from her past resided, and eventually they agreed to let the two go together.

She took him to an abandoned farmhouse – her childhood home that now smelled of sulfur, stale piss and rat turds – and together they went from room to room thumb-tacking his photos to the moldy, crumbling walls one at a time. He told her that it was his father that got him into photography and she told him that her father had, at various times in her childhood, raped her in every room of this house and together they sat in the corner, talking about what a let down fathers could be. They cried in each other's arms and felt the rare and spacious joy of what it was like to be one-hundred percent honest with another human being, and to know that they were being honest with you. When they were done they picked themselves up, and Karen went to the trunk of their car and came back with a great drum of gasoline and together they wet the world that was their childhood and holding hands, dropped the match that sent their past to a blazing hell where they hoped both their fathers were burning too.

For some time they stood back from the house, watching it burn, watching it melt. He never knew exactly what she saw in those flames, but what *he* saw was as clear as any of those burning photographs that would never exist again. He saw images of slaughterhouses and boudoir photo shoots, abandoned automobiles filled with headless kittens and funhouse rides in a place that was neither fun nor a house. He saw a million cigarette butts and scenes of snow and sleet through Christmas coffee shop windows. He saw pilfered pills, dogs named Jesus, and a beast so monstrous it had no name, hanging from a silver chain thick enough to lasso God Himself. These scenes flashed through his brain like so many photographs he had once produced by standing behind a camera, aiming it at a victim and going *click!* And as the house crumbled, as the framework began to fall, a great peace fell over him and his girl and in the dying flickering flames of baptismal perfection. She asked him if he thought *he* could be a better father and when she smiled and wrapped her arms around him he understood, nodding he understood. This time when they cried in each other's arms they were tears of joy, and they turned from the blaze and together they never looked back.

A daughter came and a new town, a new job. A house. A good life. A really *good* life. Honest and simple and totally void of anger and vindication. He slept well. He smiled without realizing his lips had moved. And the past lay behind him, forgotten like a bad dream someone once told you about but wasn't yours, until…

A dark thing called Cancer came, came to his wife and to his house, and even when she was dead and covered over with cold impersonal dirt, he kept his eyes forward, for his daughter Arabelle and for his own sanity; it was the least he could do for his dead wife. The least he could do for someone he loved, dead *and* alive. He kept his eyes forward and he never looked back, until one day a package arrived in his mailbox and his entire world came crashing down around him, like that house he and his wife had set to burn so many years ago.

John sat there now, on a bench beside his two oldest friends in the world, and thought about telling them all this and then some, but in the end he was simply too exhausted – blood wearied – and so he said in a voice as plain as pavement: "I met someone. I met someone and I was saved."

Jack couldn't believe it. "Don't tell me Johnny Megolni found religion?"

"No," Johnny said, a tired smile on his lips, "but I did find my savior, and in her I found peace."

"Good for you Johnny," Jillian said, overcome by the desire to hug this man. She didn't though, and it made her sad to think that there had been a point in her life when she would have wrapped her arms around him and squeezed for all she was worth without thinking twice. Hell, on more than one occasion she had stripped down naked in front of him without so much as a moment's hesitation. It was sad how age and time constructed these invisible walls, these barriers of face and mores, when what they should be doing is knocking them down. After all, if her skin didn't fit after all these years, would it ever?

The three of them sat there on the bench, each of them silently reliving their own private horrors and victories from their lives. Either that or thinking nothing at all. If they sat there forever it couldn't feel this long.

Finally Johnny, puffing his cheeks and blowing a thin steady stream of air from out his lips, asked: "Does anyone know what time it is? Jack?" He looked over at him and was surprised to see Jack sitting up rigid, his back as straight as a pine tree.

"Well, I don't know the o'clock exactly, but I'd say it's definitely time we get a' moseying." Jack's words came out low, swift, tight.

Johnny nodded. His head felt like it was ready to fall off. "You've had enough too, huh?"

"I feel like I've gone ten solid rounds," Jack said, "but I do believe we're about to take this game into overtime."

"What makes you say that?" Johnny asked, feeling himself deflate a little. He'd really hoped they were almost done with what was surely the world's most fucked up childhood reunion to ever take place.

"Him," Jack said, indicating with a slow point of his chin the security guard striding toward them, a hand on his walkie-talkie and a squinted set of eyes on his face.

--

The guard was tall, as tall as any man any of them had ever seen, and if he'd been a cartoon character, he would have been drawn with the sharpest pencil possible. His joints were all angles and cuts, his face a cubist wet dream; a serpentine tongue slithered across his bloodless lips as he spoke into the walkie-talkie before he replaced it on his hip.

"Play it cool," Jack breathed, his lips unmoving. "We're just three old heels revisiting the glory days of our youth; stepping out for a little fandango with our past."

"Sure," John returned out the corner of his mouth. "But don't forget you've got a sniper rifle in that case of yours; might have a hard time explaining that one to the cops." He twitched his head to the side. "If the shit goes down, I'm ready to make a run for it if you are."

Jillian spoke through a fake smile and gritted teeth. "Don't even think about it gents. That guy may be moving slow but he's got legs like stilts; he'd be on us like white on rice. So, let's all take a chill pill please. We can talk our way out of this. Or hell, Jack you're rich; you can buy our way out."

"Believe me, if that's what it comes down to, I got no problem whatsoever."

The man continued his approach, his eyes never focusing on anyone specific in the trio, but seeming to take all in as a whole. When he was no more than ten feet away, he stopped, stared down at them, and began twisting his fingers at the side of his mouth as though pulling on an invisible moustache.

"You folks realize this is private property, don't you?" the man asked, his head cocked to one side. Now his gaze moved from one to the next: Jillian first, then John, then Jack.

Jack eyed him up and down, a process that took longer than usual due to the man's impressive stature, then spoke. "Didn't mean any harm. We were just leaving."

"Ah, ah," the man said, raising a splayed hand. "Got a few questions I'd like answered first." He smiled at them pleasantly. *A little* too *pleasantly,* Jack considered, and it wasn't that Jack thought the man was being false that worried him, but the feeling that he was being wholly genuine. *It's almost like he's* happy *to see us.*

"Such as?"

The man's smile vanished. "Like what you three are doing here?" His eyes darted to the large portfolio case at Jack's feet. "Wouldn't happen to have anything to do with *Janus Properties Incorporated* would you?" Jack turned to John and Jillian. Shrugged.

"That's the guys who were trying to develop this place into a bunch of condos before they started experiencing…problems," Jack told John.

The man's eyes narrowed onto Jack now. "So you do know about this place." He pointed to the case at Jack's feet. "Full of schematics and plans I'd wager. Blueprints, diagrams, and doodads On a little scouting session to see what else might be done with all this wasted land, are you?"

Jack said nothing: *play it cool – just three old heels revisiting the glory days of our youth.* He shook his head.

"No such a thing. The only thing I know about this place is what I've read in the paper the last couple years." He motioned to his friends beside him on the bench. "We used to come here a lot when we were kids. When I heard they might be tearing the place down…"

For a few seconds the guy didn't move, just continued to stare at John and then, ever so slowly, his head began to nod, his sharp chin slicing at the air like a sickle. A warm smile broke out on his lips, and his body relaxed a little.

"You guys decided to stop by for a little two-step into the past, huh?"

John nodded back, an image of his own father bound to a chair with electrical ties and half his guts spilled out on the floor superimposed over his sight. "Something like that," he managed, then coughed.

"Really, we didn't mean any trouble," Jillian chimed in. "It's just that – " it took all her willpower to suppress a shudder at this point " – we had such good times here when we were kids." She shrugged. "You know how it is."

"Sure do," the man said, "sure do. Unfortunately, most people that make their way in here have a little more in mind than taking a trip down memory lane. Mostly they come to take something else. Usually its builders looking for some free copper wiring. Scrap metal hunters. More often than not, it's a couple of teenagers looking for a private place to *copulate*." That last word he spit out the way one would a large piece of gristle: disgusted to even say it, as though it had no place on his tongue. "But that's not why you're here this time," he said. He stared at the three of them as he reached up and licked at the middle finger of his right hand.

"No, it's not," said Jack, eyeing the man. "And like I said, we really are sorry to have caused you any trouble, but – " he motioned in the general direction of the fading sky " – it is getting dark and we really ought to be getting off now." He turned to John and Jillian. "Don't you guys think?"

"Absolutely," Jillian said, and she reached up to wrap her arms around herself, to warm herself from a sudden chill that had nothing to do with the weather.

The man appeared unfazed, as though Jack hadn't spoken at all; he stood there staring at them pleasantly. Then his gaze passed through them, and he motioned with an arm that seemed as long and thin as a golf club, to the funhouse off in the distance. A smile spread across his face.

"I bet that place brings back a lot of memories, huh?" His eyes returned to them, moved from one to the other, the smile never faltering. "Yeah that sure was a popular attraction back in the day." He chuckled quietly to himself. "You know, they call it a funhouse, but I always thought of it more as a *house of horrors* myself. On some nights you didn't even have to be inside to hear the screams, sometimes they got so loud that they actually seemed to *cut* the night air, you know what I mean? That high-pitched howl, almost like an animal put to torture." His eyes twinkled; in the near dark they could see them glow an outer-worldly yellow. "Children," he finished, shaking his head, "how they love to be terrified," and he once again reached up and licked at the tips of his fingers. This he did slowly, relishing the motion, the taste, and it was because of this unhurried gesture that Jillian really got a look at the man's hands, his skin, his flesh. Her eyes widened, her body stiffened, and a barely audible squeak escaped her lips.

It was the man's nails that she was looking at, uncut, unkempt, and long enough to be considered feminine, and of an inhuman color that reminded her of –

They all noticed it at the same time.

"It's him," she heard John whisper in her ear and at the same time, in her other ear, from Jack: *"Bastard."*

The man's fingers were yellow, stained a watery urine-color by nicotine and time – but the nails themselves, the little concaves into which the man's tongue kept scraping, were dusted a bright, almost neon orange. The color of Kool-Aid. Or Lik-M-Aid. *Or Cheetos.*

This time when the man removed his wetted fingertips from his mouth, a low chuckle tumbled out with them.

"I never *could* eat just one," he told them, and then he laughed, a great bellow that exploded out of his gut like a smattering of vomit. Indeed it seemed to coat the three of them sitting there on their bench as they collectively experienced a grand army of gooseflesh marching over their skin. Their stomachs churned and their minds grew pale: here was their phantom before them, not made of wisps of smoke and conjured memory, but of blood and bone, hair and meat.

They were wholly unprepared.

Jack's instinct – ingrained after countless hours of designing video games in which garroting, decapitation and the occasional spine-wrench was the norm – was to simply attack. There was a gun at his feet but it was a sniper rifle, and would do him no good at such close range. He didn't care; for this job he was certain his hands would suffice.

John – ever the photographer – remembered what this guy was capable of, and immediately began searching for surveillance equipment potentially hidden around; find it, take it out, and *then* go for the source. Whatever it took to save Arabelle from this man's madness, John would do it; he was suddenly seventeen again with a porn-cinema sized chip on his shoulder.

Jillian – it flashed in her mind how similar her reaction was to both love and loathe – instinctively thought of going for the man's balls, of simply reaching out, grabbing tight, and yanking down for all she was worth. At least that would wipe the smile off his face.

But no.

They were adults now and years of experience had taught them that sometimes there was a better way. Sometimes wrath had to be put aside for words. Or maybe it was simply that they knew when they'd been bested and that at such times it was better to keep their mouths shut.

For nearly an entire minute the man said nothing. Instead, he stood there beaming down at them, looking warm and blissful; he could have been witnessing his only daughter pledge her wedding vows to a man he greatly approved of, or watching the ribbon cutting ceremony to the new hospital cancer ward he had personally funded. His gaze didn't find any one of them in particular, didn't linger, but moved from one to the next, bouncily so: jaunty.

"You," Jack finally managed, but for the first time in a long time, he found himself at a loss for how to continue. The word came out a statement as much as a question.

"Me," the man said and though all three of those once kids sitting on the bench before him would have bet it impossible, the man's smile stretched even wider across his face; a sharp set of silver hooks couldn't have pulled it any further were they digging into the cheeks, opening flesh, drawing his mouth open like red velvet curtains. He was nodding sporadically, and as he did, a large dollop of drool spilled along the cusp of his lip, overcame it, and secreted onto the concrete below. Jillian watched it fall, watched as the thin gossamer-like spittle dropped, stretched, and broke, and when it finally did she came very close to screaming; it terrified her, as though that string of spit was the last bridge in her mind between sanity and mania, and once it snapped, so too would she.

Finally the man spoke.

"Forgive my sentimentality, but you three cannot possibly imagine how long I've waited for this day."

"I've got a pretty good guess," Jack said, "bout twenty-one years by my watch."

The man nodded, pumping a tight first in Jack's direction. "Jack Barber," he said. "Right you are. Right you are. But only by the *world's* concept of time. In my heart…in my heart it's been so much longer. At times it almost seems a lifetime." He reached up and hugged himself, actually wrapped his arms around his own body, then let his hands drop. "To see the three of you together again. Truly, it warms me to the core."

"Why wait so long? Why twenty-one years?" That was Jillian. John was impressed; his mind was so jumbled right now that coming up with a coherent thought was like trying to write sentences in a pot of boiling alphabet soup.

The man paused, pretending to think, but Jillian knew it was false. He was acting. Playing with them as a cat with a dead thing, and why not? He knew he had them. He knew he had them wholly, completely: body, soul, and anything in between.

"I could tell you, but I don't think you'd believe me."

"Try us," Jack said, and Jillian felt her teeth clench. She'd never heard Jack speak so tightly; she saw his words punching rivets in steel.

"Jack." The man raised his hands in supplication, shaking his head. "Jack Barber, calm down. And whatever you do, don't do anything rash. I assure you one-hundred percent, I mean none of you any harm." The man shook a pointed index finger at the three of them. "But, I'm sure I can't say the same about you three when it comes to my own safety, can I?"

None of them said anything. Jillian could barely hear Jack's breathing over the beating of her own heart. John was tapping his foot nervously on the ground beside her, looking pale enough to pass out.

"So before we go any further, I need a little reassurance. And by that, I mean a little *insurance*." He folded his hands together and the sight of his fingers curling into one another made Jillian think of a pair of grotesque arachnids in the spindly throes of horror show copulation.

"Now John, I sent you photos." He glanced down to the manila envelope tucked under John's leg. "I assume those are them? I wonder, how did you like them? I know they're probably not up to your artistic standards – I was *ever* so disappointed when you gave the hobby up – but I hope you didn't find them *too* abysmal. Anyway, as I'm sure you noticed, I sent only the photos themselves. And where do photos come from initially?"

John was staring at the ground feeling zapped; he no longer had the energy to lift his head. "From negatives," he said, dutifully. He knew where this was going and understood that there was nothing he or Jack or Jillian could do about it; this was the end of the movie, and this guy had already written the script.

"From *negatives,* that's *riiiiight.* And the tape I left for you Jillian, surely you understand that that was a copy, transferred from a video recording?" Jillian nodded slowly, a flood of shame washing over her as she considered the fact that this guy had watched her – and not just watched but *recorded* her – getting fucked by her two friends. The idea that he had seen her naked, seen her *sex,* made her both furious and sick; it was Mr. Wolfe's hand on her tit all over again.

"And speaking of recordings Jack, now the DVD I sent you obviously wasn't *recorded* on DVD initially, but a transfer. You got that, didn't you? I mean, you probably noticed those wiggly lines that zigzagged their way down the screen – you don't get that from digital recording now, do you? No-sir-e-bob. You can trust me; I know my technology. You might even say I'm a bit of a techno-buff, oh yes, you could definitely say that. Guilty as charged. Anything to do with technology really, cameras, computers, ones and zeros, ones and zeros. Now Jack, I'm sure you're a man who can appreciate that, the fact that all those things you see on screen, you and your friends John and Jillian here, doing all those things, those horrible, horrible things, and all they are is a series of ones and zeros arranged in such a way, turning what would be nonsense into…well, into evidence. That's what they are when you really think about it, all those ones and zeroes: *evidence.* Amazing isn't; a bunch of ones and zeroes could put the three of you in prison for a long, *looong* time. And for a long, long time those same ones and zeroes have kept me occupied, kept me watching, given me a reason to go on."

"You're not going to turn us in." That was Jack, and though Jillian was glad that he had broken the one way silence, she found herself wishing that Jack sounded a little bit more sure of himself; she knew him well enough to know that he was guessing, bluffing, taking a stab in order to see what stuck. The man snapped his fingers once at Jack, and the sound was so sharp his fingers clicked like a clapboard striking home.

"Correction Jack Barber, I don't *want* to turn you in. No, that's the last thing in the world I want, truly it is."

"And why might that be?" Jack's eyes were ice, his words: steel.

The tall man laughed, his body shaking like sticks on a string. Then he shrugged. "Everybody needs a hobby," he said finally, "and for twenty-one years plus, you three have been mine. But to go back to your original question – and pose it as a statement all you might like Jack Barber, it was a *question* – given the right circumstances, I *will* turn you in. Won't hesitate to do so no more than I would hesitate to scratch my own ass should it get to itching, but like I said, I don't *want* to turn you in. So whether I do or don't: well the way I see it, that depends entirely on you three."

"How so?" Jillian had found her voice again and though it came out small, quiet, it was still there. She could feel it growing with each second that passed.

"Well let's get the obvious out of the way first, shall we. Anything happens to me, and I mean *anything* – be it head on collision or heart-attack – all this stuff gets sent to the police. I have three separate safe deposit boxes at three separate banks, and all staff at said banks know my stipulations; if ever there's a week that goes by that I don't come in to check on the wherewithal of my boxes, they get opened up and all contents are turned over to the police. Everything. I'm talkin' an envelope as thick as a phonebook, all of it filled with evidence against you three. All of it gruesome. All of it *damning*. By the time they let you three out of prison you'll be so old you won't know whether to shit or go senile. Imagine it: thirty or forty years in the slammer, rotting away, decaying. Death for the living....

"Jack: your company will disappear, swallowed up by a thousand other gaming companies just like yours, and all that you worked for...*poof.*" He blew at his hand like a magician proving the disappearance of an overly large coin.

"Jillian: your students will have grown, become adults, parents, grandparents even, and they'll always remember, maybe enthrall their grandkids with stories of their old teacher Ms. Jillian Jarblonski who though nice on the surface – she used to stick little rainbow stickers on any exceptional piece of homework produced – was actually ten types of crazy, loonier than a toon, but boy did she have them all fooled, until... Well, until the boys in blue came a knocking and took her to the place where the windows are barred and the doors only open from the outside.

"And John. *Kid Johnny.* Well, I don't have to tell you twice, do I? You know what's in store. You know what you'll be missing all those years locked away, don't you." The man stared down at John, their eyes locked.

"So. Now that we've got *that* out of the way, let's move on, shall we?" He turned to Jillian. "Ms. Jarblonski. I believe you asked me a question, and oh, where are my manners, I have yet to answer it."

"What do you want from us?" Jillian interjected, and for a second the thin man's smile faltered; it was obvious that *he* liked to be in control and having his subjects blurt things out like that didn't gel with him at all. No, not one bit. But it only took a second for him to regain his composure and that great sliced-skin smile once more grew out of his face.

"In order now Ms. Jarblonski, in order. All will be revealed in good time, all questions laid to rest. And as a sign of good faith Jilly Jill – " he smiled warmly at Jack and John, addressing them directly " – remember when you two called her that? It was sweet, wasn't it?" He sighed, a happy sigh of memory long passed, then returned to Jillian. "As a sign of good faith, I *will* answer your first question: *why wait so looooong.* Wellity tell, you know I've been watching you, right?" He shrugged, raising his hands. "Sorry, sorry, stupid question I know. *Obviously,* you know I've been watching. How else would I have gotten the photos, and the videos, and the tapes that are audio? How else would I know that John, in your daughter's bedroom, Arabelle – " he turned to Jack and Jillian " – you two haven't met her yet, but I assure you she's a lovely little girl. Pretty as a peach. Looks more and more like her mother every day, doesn't she John? Don't answer that; I'll show you guys pictures later should you wish. Anyway, in your daughter's bedroom there is an embroidered hoop on the wall that reads *'Hair today, gone tomorrow'*, and would you believe it Jack, Jill, there's a little snippet of Arabelle's hair woven into it from when she got her first haircut at age two. It took Karen three tries to get the script of it just right but in the end she did it. Oh yes, she certainly did. She did it."

"Now *Jack,*" he went on, ignoring the red rage that was threatening to erupt from all orifices of John's head, "about seven years ago you started on a project that you called, tentatively, *Trio of Terror.* Your first foray into adventure gaming. I personally thought it was brilliant, and was proud as a papa when I saw some of the screen grabs. The amount of time you spent on that thing…it was almost as though you were trying to recode your very *past.*" He shrugged, and a forlorn sigh brushed his lips. "Now, of course, knowing you like I do, I can imagine why you abandoned it – too many memories being dredged up that I'm sure you were more than happy to have drowned long ago – but I have to say I was thoroughly disappointed that you did. The mindless stuff that you'd been churning out – riding the Egyptian craze with *Mummy Dearest,* and the anthrax scares with *Mail Carrier Massacre,* seemed so beneath you. But *Trio of Terror: that* was an idea with legs. That game had *style.* That game had *panache.* And so original! I mean, who *wouldn't* want to play an adventure game about three serial killers on the run while simultaneously trying to rack up more and more kills? It was *gold* Mr. Barber, *gold!*"

"Is that true? Did you really make a game like that?" Jillian looked so hateful at the moment that Jack half expected her to spit in his face. He shrugged.

"I toyed with the idea. Wrote a bit of it. Put together a few screenshots." Suddenly Jack became angry. "But I never showed it to a goddamn person, not a soul, so how the hell did you – "

The tall man raised his hands in supplication. "Jack my boy, Jack..." Something occurred to him and the man nodded to himself with satisfaction. *"Jackie Boy,"* he said with fond remembrance, "that was what they used to call you. Ahh, I'd almost forgotten. Jilly Jill and Jackie Boy and Kid Johnny." He held his arms aloft as though about to embrace them all. "And here you all are, together again. It's so..." And they all watched, horrified, as this man's face teared up with emotion; he was enjoying this, he really was. Finally, he went on.

"How do I know all this? Is that what you're asking? Well I've already told you; I'm a surveillance man, through and through. Anything to do with a camera or a microphone, that's my bread and butter. And speaking of which, did you know that they make microphones smaller than the head of a pin that can send a transmission up to five miles? Isn't technology great! I mean, *the head of a pin!* You could stick one of those things anywhere – hell, you could stick one *everywhere* – and a person could carry one around for years and not have any idea. Not even realize that they were bugged. And once you get one bug in, well, they're kind of like cockroaches aren't they? Jack, you know all about cockroaches don't you?"

Jack shifted visibly in his seat, thinking of the envelope from just three weeks previous, and the size of those damned things that had spilled out. Fuck the plan, if this guy pulls out one of them now Jack was hightailing it right the fuck out of dodge, consequences of the police be damned.

"Of course you do, of course you do," the man said in a tone that might have been confirming the desire for a piece of cake or a second cup of tea. "Well, as I was saying, like cockroaches, *bugs* – the electronic kind that is – have a way of multiplying once one gets into the cracks. See, if I know when you're out, and for exactly how long you're going to be gone, it's more than easy to sidle my way into your house, your apartment, your vehicle – by the way, you got a nice one Jack; not too sure about the color but the model, an *Audi A8,* very choice, very choice indeed – and drop a few more bugs – or a mini-camera – and *voila!* You got access to every word, every action and reaction that a person can make. *Hell,* drop enough of them, say beside their bed, in their bathroom…in the bottom dresser drawer where they keep their vibrator" – he shot a quick wink at Jillian from which she visibly recoiled – and you can practically read the person's mind."

"Now, why am I telling you all this? *Why?* It all comes back to Jillian's initial question: *why have I waited twenty-one years to get in touch with you guys? Why?!?* I know, I know, people say they're going to write and they never do. *Let's get together over the holidays! Yes, yes, we really have to do this again soon! We'll set it up a.s.a.p. and make it happen!* But the truth of it is, life is busy. And I'm a busy man. As I'm sure you've figured out: surveillance is not only my job, but my way of life. You might even say it *is* my life. And so your answer dear Jilly Jill, is two-fold. The first one is simple, and I apologize in advance if this sounds harsh, but the truth of it is: you're not my only project. *Aaaaaand,* with any project worth spending time on, the period of gestation is oh so important. I mean, think about it: what would you guys have done if I'd contacted you just a week or two after your last little – " he motioned to the funhouse with a backward thrust of his thumb " – shall we say: *soiree?* I'll tell you what would have happened. You would have had your knives in my throat quicker than a Chinaman can say *chop-suey.* Either that, or you would have each taken to the wind and disappeared like a fart in the breeze." He shook his head slowly, happily, knowingly. "No, no, no. Better to wait it out. Let you get comfortable. Let you all *settle.* If one of you moved away, I could follow. Not too hard to keep tabs on one man. Or one woman. But if all three split?" He shrugged his shoulder and raised his hands. "Well, I'm only one man and my microphones and hidden cameras can only reach so far. So therein lies the second reason. And in truth, it's the one that *really* counts. It's the exact one why we're here today. Would any of you care to know what it is?"

None of them said a word. They were caught, totally and completely; what was there to say? The best any of them could manage was a half-croak from Jack. The tall man licked his lips.

"I'll take that as a yes. Well, the plain truth of it is simple." He shrugged, the bones rising up under his shirt making his body seem disproportionate and fake, like a child dressed in his father's suit. "The truth of it is... *I missed you.* I mean, not just *you*, all, one by one; I've had access to any one of you at any given moment, twenty-four hours a day for the last twenty-one years. But I missed you all *together. Collectively.* And I wanted to see you all joined once more, working as one: *meshed* as it were." The man flashed a smile that was all teeth and no warmth while above, his eyes took on a perverse twinkle. "I struck gold with you three, I really did. I mean, dropping that first bug was something I did on a whim. There I was, working the graveyard shift at the slaughterhouse when up show these three misplaced looking teens, all jaunty and jovial. I could tell from the start that you guys didn't mean any harm, that you were just a bunch of tiny rebels out to buck the system a little – I remember what it was like to be your age myself – so I let you be. Thought it would add a little excitement to the job, which up to that point had been just another boring night in an infinitely long string of boring nights. I watched as you guys picked the lock, and I remember being impressed. Few professionals could pick a lock with such ease, never mind a wet-behind-the-ears *kid.* That got my attention. I watched you guys approach the building – which by the way reminds me: just because you can't *see* a camera, doesn't mean there isn't one there, and at *Mendoza's Meats,* there is *always* a camera on you whether you know it or not.

"And while you three did your little dime store tour, I –"

"You snuck out and bugged my car." John was staring at the man with such a blank look he could have been watching paint dry. Actually he was thinking back, lost in the past of that first night when they'd left the factory, and he'd found that lone cigarette butt beside the door of his car. He'd passed it off an irrelevant at the time, but now he knew better. Now he knew a lot of things.

"Indeed." The man nodded, his head bobbing up and down like a candy apple on a stick. "That was the first, but others quickly followed. Your camera for example; now that was a stroke of genius. The only thing I think you were more attached to was your penis! Ha! You took that thing *everywhere,* and as such, you took *me* everywhere." He laughed, licked his lips, and rubbed his stick fingers together in some grotesque parody of glee. "You cannot imagine my surprise – and joy – when less than an hour after leaving the factory it became apparent that you three were the perpetrators of manslaughter. Manslaughter! *Jackpot!*" The man looked up to the sky, his eyes twinkling in recall. "Yep, when I dropped that first bug I had no *idea* how fertile the ground would be, and believe me, there ain't no ground more fertile than a disgruntled teen: and with you guys, it was three for the price of one! But still, I had no idea it would grow into…well, into a beanstalk *Jack.* And I'm not just talking about the murders either, though they were the icing on the cake no doubt. It was you three, together. What fun you had! What moments you made! It was like my own private soap-opera made solely for me. And I could record it, and watch it, and re-watch it, and edit it whatever way I liked. And I did… oh I certainly did. Some people build train sets or miniature models of entire cities. Others collect baseball cards for half a century or more. I wanted something more priceless, something more real. Information about you, that's what I wanted. And I didn't just collect recordings, snippets of voice and vision. No, what I did was so much more unique. So much more *grand.* Comic books and polished rocks: *pfft!* What a waste!" His eyes widened and the three each, simultaneously, understood with repulsive certainty, what a live butterfly must feel like as pins are pressed into their body, readying them for the display case. "I collected your lives. I gathered your ideas on life, love, art and the great cosmic *why* of it all. And let's not forget the music! Ha! *The music!* My *gawd,* how I loved to hear the three of you wax philosophical about the so-called gods of the eighties. Duran Duran. The Cure. The Smiths. And of course, who could ever forget *Depeche Mode?* I actually went out and bought a copy of *Black Celebration* on your recommendation Jillian. I liked it. A little too synth for my taste – give me Petula Clark or Gerry and the Pacemakers any day – but a solid effort on their part. Definitely better than when Clark was part of the mix; that *Devo* reject didn't know when to tone it *down.* "

"But once again I *digress. Why wait twenty-one years?* That was the question. And the answer: I'm getting old. I'm falling apart; that's the bald truth. I don't have the stealth that I used to, I don't have the drive. When you guys first went your separate ways I thought you'd all be back together within a week. A month maybe, on the outside, but I underestimated you, all of you. I watched you all make changes, conscious changes, and I watched as your lives slowly turned into something better. At first I didn't think that was possible – I was especially skeptical in my younger years – but now that I've seen it, I'm not sure how I ever doubted it. I mean, the three of you were strong. Strong as anyone I've ever come across. The things you did were testament to that. I mean, the amount of willpower it takes to press your thumbs to someone's eyeballs and *press* until the pupils go *pop!* To place someone's balls in a vice and *squeeze.* That takes determination. That takes *resolve.* And Johnny! To do those things to your *father!* Wow. Really, wow. Hats off to you good sir, hats off. You must have testicles of titanium, unlike your father, obviously, ha-ha, and nerves of hardened steel.

"So now we come to this." The man leaned back, placed his hands in the divots of his spine, and stretched. Then he raised his hands and indicated everything around him. "We've come full circle." He stabbed a taut finger in the direction of the funhouse. "That's the last place you ever did your business, your *eliminations* as you used to call them, am I right Jillian?" He stared down at her pleasantly, expectantly. She felt so tired, so sick, that she could barely give a nod. Her whole body felt like old soup: thin and weak and shapeless.

"So what now?" Jack stared coldly at the man before him, hating the fact that he was still sitting, was being forced to look *up* at this man. To Jack Barber, the idea of looking up to any man was something disgusting and foreign, but he was too tired to stand. *Correction,* he thought: *too weak.*

"Yeah," joined in John, whose own voice vacillated with emotion; it sounded like he was a blink or two away from full-blown tears. "What do you want from us now?"

The man stared down at the three of them, these three thirty-somethings who had once ruled the world, and now sat hunched and broken at his feet. He wasn't a vindictive man, nor prone to sadism, but at that moment it felt really good to be the master. To be the master and *know* it, and know that *they* knew it too. To know that he had youth in his hands, and the power to crush it at a given whim.

He nodded. Smiled. He was taking his time. He had waited twenty-one years for this moment and he wasn't about to be rushed. Time was his to control, as were their lives; he felt like a man who had already paid the prostitute and was now sidling up to get inside her. *To breach her.* A blade of a tongue extended from out his mouth and drew itself once across the pale set of thin lips. He was so excited his hands were shaking slightly, and there was an ethereal jumpiness in his stomach that he hadn't felt since the last time he'd done something like this.

"I remember those first few months with the utmost fondness, watching you three, and more than once feeling a great urge to approach you, to let you in on my little secret, which was the fact that I knew all about your *big* secret, but I never did. Do you know why?"

"Because we would have recognized you for the psycho you are and laid the boots to you?"

The man's smile widened. He knew exactly what Jack was trying to do; he had intimate knowledge of how Jack Barber's brain worked.

"Goading me will get you nowhere Jackie Boy. I'll reveal nothing more than exactly what I want to. And let's not forget, if we're pointing fingers at psychopaths, it was never me that took a rusty box cutter to a man's eyelids and went *swoosh, swoosh.*"

"No, you just shot it in 35mm black and white." John was staring down at his hands; if it wasn't for Arabelle he'd use them to kill this fucker right now.

For a moment the man's face clouded, his smile faltered, and his right eye tightened ever so slightly but he recovered quickly.

"Well, I didn't think you should be the one to have all the fun now, did I Ansell Adams? I mean, man does not get a chance like this everyday to photograph such, such…*honesty.* Beauty comes in many forms, but the best, the purest, the *truest* is when it depicts things that aren't, by conventional standards, *beautiful.* No, no. Some people go for newborns wearing watermelon rinds as hats. A stark ray of sun perfectly lighting up Machu Picchu at five in the morning. Not me, so sir-e-bob, not me. Give me a half-crushed worm, too stupid to know it's dying, still trying to inch its way along the rain-splattered sidewalk. Give me a shot of an AIDS infested prostitute, still proffering her wares, framed by old neon signs advertising even older brands of beer, husks of abandoned factories and tenement houses fading into the background like the forgotten dinosaurs they are. Give me a photograph of a ripped dress that hasn't seen a washi–"

"Oh shut up will you! Shut the fuck up right fucking now!" Jillian was staring up at the man with bug eyes and flared nostrils, her teeth bared as her throat clicked again and again as though trying to consume itself. "No more bullshit," she told the man, "no more of your crap. We've been sitting here for the better part of an hour listening to you spout this shit without you giving us a straight answer one time, not one Christing time, and I'm fucking sick of it!" Her hands shot up to the hair at her temples and gripped – even in the ever-encroaching darkness Jack and John could see her fingernails fade to white from the pressure – and pull at the hair, hard. It strung taut and a corrugation of flesh immediately grew out of the sides of her head, threatening to rip a great patch right off. Her head thrashed back and forth several times as a high scream exploded from her throat, and when she finally stopped a minute later there was a small clump of hair in her hands and a single streak of blood running down her left temple; it looked so dark in the fading light of day that it might have been dripping tar.

For a second, Jillian stared down at the clump of hair in her hand, then she simply opened her fingers and let the thing blow away like a miniature tumbleweed. When she looked up this time her eyes were puffed, rimmed red, and there was a white smattering of saliva in the right corner of her mouth.

"Tell us now or I walk. Now. No bullshit. No beating around the bush. What the fuck do you want from us?" She raised both her hands in supplication and the way they hung there, loose and unsteady, it was obvious that she was exhausted. This would be her last stand, no doubt; she had nothing left to give. She had nothing left at all. A moment later, she felt an arm around her: John's. And then another: Jack's. They were holding her up, supporting her. If not for them she might have fallen clean off the bench.

If Jillian's little outburst affected the tall man in the slightest, he gave no sign. She might as well have told him that she preferred *Skittles* to *Starburst*, *Smarties* to *M and M's* or that her favorite show as a child was *Jem and the Holograms* but her weakness, her near collapse, did make the man seem even taller than he was, and more unbeatable. But then he opened his mouth and did something that surprised them all, Jillian especially. He opened his mouth and told them the truth.

"Isn't it obvious," he asked, his hands spread and a chuckle on his lip. He clapped his hands together once, sharply, and at the exact moment of the clap, his face opened up, eyes, mouth, nostrils: everything widened as though readying itself for what was about to come out.

He stared at them all, looking down, with an expression of revelry and school-boy excitement.

"I want you to start killing again," he told them matter-of-factly, and then, for the first time since addressing them, he cursed his own stupidity; he'd forgotten his camera. And what a nice addition to his collection their reactions would have made, their mouths hollow, their eyes slowly deadening in defeat. If he timed it just right he might have been able to press click at the exact moment that their souls hit rock bottom. That they truly were *beaten.* He sighed. *What a nice addition indeed.*

--

Jack, Jillian and John were surrounded by a darkness so thick it felt gelatinous.

It had been nearly an hour since the tall man left, and none of them had yet got off the bench; it seemed like they had been sitting there forever, what was a few more millennia in the grand scheme of things?

One by one they went over their options. The first, and most optimistic, was *research.* That was Jack's idea. Find out who this guy was. Anything and everything that could be used against him. Find out if his threats had any merit. Jack thought that while it would be pretty much impossible for him to gain access to the man's security deposit boxes at a bank, he could probably find out whether the boxes existed or not. That would at least let them know if the man really had them by the balls or was bluffing.

"And when we find out that he isn't, that he told us nothing but the truth, what then?" The voice coming out of Jillian's mouth was so soft, so quiet, that it might have been a voice in her head but for the fact that John answered it.

"Then we're no worse off than we are now." He shrugged.

"But at least we'll know," said Jack.

"And then what?"

"Well," began Jack, trying his best to weigh things out – his brain was so muddled that picking out coherent thoughts was like trying to pinch a watermelon seed in a vat of oil – "if it turns out that he's full of shit, then I guess our next step would be retaliation. We turn his video fantasies into reality, only with him the star this time instead of the cameraman. Am I correct in assuming that this is something you two wouldn't be against?"

John thought of his daughter, his new life, his dead wife. Jillian thought of her apartment. Her students. A bottle of pear brandy, and a little black boy named Arnold who always called her 'Double J.'

"You're correct," they both said in unison.

"Good," said Jack, liking that they were all on the same page.

John's eyes were half closed when he asked. "And what if he's not bullshitting? What if it's all true?"

"Yeah," chimed in Jillian. "Let's be honest, it seems much more likely that he *is* telling the truth rather than not. He has all the evidence after all. He's had the time. He has no reason to lie to us."

Jack shrugged. "We could kill him anyway. I mean, if we're gonna go to prison, then we might as well go out with a bang. And take him with us to boot."

John shook his head. "I don't know if I have the stomach for that sort of thing anymore Jack. I really don't. The truth of it is...I think I've seen enough death in my life to last *three* lifetimes. I don't want another on my hands."

Jillian was silent, staring down at the ground.

"And you Jillian? Was three murders enough for you, or do you think you could add one more to the lot?"

Jillian shook her head. For a second it looked like she was going to say something; her mouth opened and her tongue moved, but nothing came out. Finally she shrugged. "Maybe," she said, "but probably not."

Jack's shoulders drooped a little: disappointed. He didn't want to get back into old habits either, but this guy was giving them no choice. Kill or be killed was what it came down to, and for Jack there was only one course of action: *give me a knife and let's get to work.*

"Well that doesn't leave us many options then," he said, "but if that's the way you want it, that's the way it'll be." He nodded once as though affirming his own thoughts. "It's gotta be unanimous. I won't do anything without you guys, I promise, but I think you should at least consider the possi –"

"We could run." The shame was evident in the tone of John's voice, which was barely a whisper.

"He'd follow us," returned Jillian. "He's already made it obvious that he's got us tracked. He knows where we are at all times, knows where we're going. No, running is not an option that I can see. The guy would be on us like a shadow."

John nodded, slowly at first, then quicker, an energy returning to him. "But he said it himself, he couldn't follow all three of us at the same time; that's impossible. So we clean ourselves off, trade in our cars for ones that surely aren't bugged. Empty our bank accounts. Take nothing with us that could possibly be traced, and head off in three different directions, down to Honduras or Panama or…wherever. Meet up again in a year and laugh about how the three of us came face to face with the devil and somehow managed to leave him behind in the dirt. What do you guys think?" He turned to Jillian, pleading. Then Jack. But both their faces were impassive. Finally, Jack reached out and placed a tired hand on John's shoulder.

"Not this time Johnny. I've spent the last twenty-one years looking over my shoulder. I don't want to be doing that for another twenty-one."

"Me neither," said Jillian sadly, because she felt like she was not just letting down, but actually betraying one of the best friends she'd ever known.

"Do you?" Jack asked, and Johnny's head dropped a little at the question. His face crumpled.

"No," he said finally, "no. But what else can we do? Really, *what else can we do?*"

"Well there is one other option," said Jillian, "but I don't think either of you are going to like it."

"What's that?" asked Jack, already knowing full well exactly what Jillian was going to propose.

Jillian reached up and rubbed at the spot on her temple where she'd ripped out the chunk of hair an hour or so earlier. She winced as her fingers made contact, then drew them away and examined them for traces of fresh blood. When she saw there was nothing there, she answered him.

"We could do what he asked us to do."

"Yeah, and become his personal pawns in the process." Johnny shook his head quickly. "No fucking way. He said we'd only have to do it once, only this one time right, but who's to say he wouldn't go back on his word right after? That we go out and kill whoever it is that he wants us to kill, and then – and it wouldn't have to be *right* after, maybe he waits a few months, or a few years – sometime down the road we get another mysterious package in the mail, this time showing the more *recent* murder, and the whole fucking cycle starts all over again. We'd be his tools. His puppets. His fucking *slaves*."

"But, we don't even know what he wants yet. It could be something easy. Cut the brake lines on the car of some neighbor that's been blasting *Motorhead* too loud for his liking. Slip some rat-poison into his ex-wife's apple pie. It doesn't have to be like last time, all knives and flesh under fingernails. It might be just..." but she gave up when she realized she didn't know how to finished the sentiment.

"Just *murder?*" Jack interjected. *"Murder,"* he repeated, more solidly this time. "No, no thanks. I'm with John on this one; anything we do for this guy only digs us in deeper. Only allows him to tighten the noose a little bit more."

Jillian's head lilted; she was too tired to argue. "Yeah I guess you're right." Her thoughts drifted back to what the man had said after he told them he wanted them to start killing again.

At first they'd been shocked, too taken off guard to speak. It was the last thing any of them had expected, but once the request had lingered in the air for a full minute or more, Jillian tested the waters by asking the man directly.

"And let me guess, you want to come along this time. Do a little vicarious *living* through three people creating death?"

The man had shaken his head. "No, no, no, my dear Jilly Jill. Two is company, and three turns a crowd...but to add a fourth is simply not allowed." He smiled, reached up and twisted the ends of that invisible moustache. "But don't worry my dear, I'll be watching. I can assure you of that. I'll *always* be watching."

Jillian, *present Jillian,* shivered in recall and not for the first time her eyes roamed around the abandoned amusement park, trying to pierce the darkness and coming up with naught. *He left, but he's still here. I can feel him, sure as I could feel Rudy Wolfe's clammy hand on my tit that day in detention. Sure as I can close my eyes, and still hear the* click *of Johnny's 35mm Pentax, feel the swish of that pleated kilt as it scraped across my knees. See the blood on our faces, our hands, our bodies. Close my eyes and feel both John and Jack's bodies grinding against my own, pressing into my flesh, fingers exploring tracts of skin that were both infinitely hot and cold at the same time, a live membrane brought to exquisite life by the death of –*

"I want to go home," Jillian said, and the two men stopped – she hadn't even realized that they were speaking – and looked at her directly.

"Jillian, I know you're tired but we really need to – " but she was having none of it. She cut Jack off with an extended palm that wavered precariously in the air. It flashed in her mind that she couldn't remember when she'd last put food in her mouth, or taken a drop to drink. She didn't care. All she wanted now was to get the hell out of dodge, go home and sleep for a spell that would put Rip Van Winkle to shame. If there was a God, maybe she wouldn't wake up at all.

"No Jack. No. I'm done. I can't do this anymore, not now, not tonight. Right now I don't care, I really don't. Sleep is what we need, and sleep is where I'm going. Now." She nodded once at the men, then wondered where she was going to get the strength to stand up. *I'll manage,* she thought, *somehow, I'll manage.*

Johnny took up the cause. "I think she's right Jack. We're not going to get anywhere tonight. Why don't we all go home, sleep on it. We can get in touch tomorrow.

Hash it out when our brains aren't so scrambled. Maybe we'll see things differently…yah know, in the light of day."

Jack thought about it for a second, then nodded. "And once again it's two against one." He smiled. "I think it's a good idea. Now." He stood up, his back cracking, the muscles in his legs crying out. He swayed for a couple seconds until John and Jillian both reached out to steady him. Even after he'd regained his balance he didn't let go of their hands; instead he used his own arms to hoist them up.

When they were all standing they slowly moved away from the bench, away from the house that was not fun, the park that was not the least bit amusing. When they reached the gate Jillian made to shimmy her way through the gap afforded by the half-rusted chain looped around it, but stopped. She stood there for a minute staring through the diamond holes in the fence, knowing that if she stepped out of this space, *this place*, without telling these other two what she'd almost told them before, she never would. She shook her head, made to move, then paused again. Swore under her breath. Did her damndest to fight back the tears she could feel rising within her like mercury in heat. She placed one hand on the fence, curled her fingers round it. It felt real, *there,* and it occurred to her that this was probably the *exact same piece of metal* that she had touched all those years ago when they had entered this park for the first time. They had opened the gate wide that day, wide enough to let an entire Buick in, and now it was time to close it. Once and for all.

"Before we go, there's one more thing." Jillian looked every day her thirty-eight years, if not older, though perhaps it was just the unforgiving shadows pulling at her eyes, her nose, the divot below her lips;

from the exact angle they saw her, it appeared as though the shadows were sucking at her face, tugging life out of it as though an appetizer for the darkness and it occurred to Jack to wonder what the main course would be. John was so tired, he just wanted to ask for the check.

"What Jillian? What is it?"

Jack's voice was low, soft, quiet. She could hear exhaustion in his voice but not impatience, it occurred to her that if she asked him to, Jack Barber would probably wait till the end of time for her. Kid Johnny too.

Jillian took a deep breath. *Like a Band-Aid,* she told herself, *quick like a Band-Aid. Do it now or you'll lose your nerve, and if you lose it now, it'll be gone forever.*

"You asked me before if – " and without warning her voice cracked and emotion spilled forward in buckets. *"Oh Jesus,"* she blubbered, her words turning to mush, but she pushed it away, straightened, strengthened. *Do it, and do it now Jillian,* she told herself, and for once, thank God almighty, her mouth and her mind listened.

"I lied to you guys. I'm sorry. I'm so sorry." Tears were streaming down her face but she didn't notice. She focused on the words the words the words. *Get the words out,* she told herself, *and deal with the emotions in the aftermath.* "I lied and for that I'm sorry, truly I am."

"About wh – " but Jillian cut off John directly. She shook her head quickly.

"No interruptions this time. I have to – I have to – " Her mind searched for the right words, decided there were none, and just went for it, full throttle, balls to the walls.

"The kills. Jack, you mentioned three kills and asked if I was up for a forth. I said no. No, I said no, and I meant it. But the truth of it is, I'm already there. Four I mean, I'm already there. After we split, after that last day – " she turned her head and glanced in the direction of the funhouse " – over there, there was one more. But understand that I had to. I mean I fucking had no choice, really I didn't. How could I be expected to…?" Her head was swimming and all of the sudden she wasn't just holding onto the fence to feel something, for the tactility of it, but for support; if she let go of that fence she was going to fall right on her thirty-eight year old ass.

John watched her with a countenance of pure curiosity; he had no idea what she was going to say next, let alone guess who it was she had killed all by her lonesome. Jack, however, froze. His eyes narrowed in on her as powerfully as the scope attached to the rifle in his bag; his face was a mask, hard as plaster, and behind that mask, his teeth ground into one another. If she said what he thought she was going to say…

"It was four months later," Jillian went on. "Almost. Maybe a little less. Time kind of drifted during the year or so after, things passed over me, like water in a river, while others, seemingly random, stayed like silt. At some point, I realized that I couldn't remember the last time I'd gotten my period but it didn't concern me much. I'd…oh I know how fucked up this sounds, but I'd *forgotten* what we'd done." She couldn't look either of them in the eyes; she stared through that diamond hole in the fence as though a magnifying glass focused on her past. "I figured my cycle had gotten fucked up. It happens sometimes when I'm stressed, or upset, or…whatever. When I started getting morning sickness I finally went to the doctor and I…well you can't imagine my confusion. Really, you can't. I was…I don't know the right word to use. *Lost* I guess. Totally and completely lost. *Immaculate conception*, that's what I thought. I mean, I *actually* thought that, believed it. I had done such a good job of blocking it out, that it wasn't until the doctor examined me that I remembered. I was lying on the table, uncomfortable and scared shitless, and he turned around and I saw the gloves on his hands – those sterile latex gloves – and like a goddamn slap in the face it all came back to me. I screamed – I actually screamed I was so surprised – because I remembered not just the sex, but the killing itself. The torture. How we placed our gloved hands on a living man and tore flesh. Brought out the blood. Opened him up.

"I went into hysterics. I mean, I totally lost my shit. Started thrashing around, knocking things over, clawing at the wall. Finally, had to be sedated. They told me later that it took five people to hold me down while they gave me a shot." Now she looked up at both of them, her face full of dread; in the darkness it looked like a Halloween mask melting while still worn.

"Eventually, they let me leave the hospital. I felt sick, dazed, lost. I don't remember how I got home that day, or anything else about the matter, only that I had to get rid of it. The idea that this thing was growing inside me... You have to understand that it was not something I associated with you two, not exactly, but rather something I associated with *him*." She glanced at John quickly, then returned her gaze to the ground. "To your father. As if somehow it was *his* seed that had been planted. Through death comes life, that kind of shit. I don't believe in reincarnation, but at that moment, I was *certain* that somehow the baby inside me was the reimagining of that man."

"What did you do?" Jack's face was still frozen, cold, impassive. John's lower lip was trembling.

"The only thing I could. I took care of it."

"It was four months," Jack said. "Too late to have anything legally done about it. So what did you do?"

Jillian's eyes met Jack's and this time they didn't falter. "Like I said, I took care of it."

"By yourself?"

She nodded. A single tear cut a glowing line down her face. "By myself," she responded, and then she looked at them both, pleading. "Of course you understand, I *had* to do it. I *had to*. How could I have raised a child that was…that was…" She searched for the word but came up with nothing.

"Evidence." The word floated out of John's mouth and hung in the air like a bad smell. It was true. That's what the child would have been: evidence. And it had to be got rid of.

Don't worry," John – who had a child of his own,- went on, "I don't blame you Jillian. You did what you had to do."

Jack – who was thirty-eight years old and had no children that he knew of – said nothing, only continued to stare. The child could have been either of theirs – his or John's – but there was no doubt in his mind – call it what you will: machismo ego, delusion, or plain old *desire* – that the child was his. A child that *he* had fathered, and had never been allowed to be born. It made his stomach churn to consider it. Finally, he opened his mouth and allowed words to fall out, words he didn't realize were there until they had passed over his tongue.

'Was it a boy?"

Jillian shrugged. "Does it matter?"

Not a muscle moved on Jack's face, then he repeated the question. "Was it a boy?"

Jillian's eyelids dropped a little; the corners of her mouth drooped. "Yes," she said, finally, and Jack nodded. He had never hit a woman in his entire life but he was suddenly overcome by a colossal desire to do so now, of taking his fist and not just laying into her face but actually *breaking* it, of knocking her teeth so far into her head that a great clattering of molars and incisors came shooting out the back of her skull. *My only chance at ever having a son,* he thought, and on its heels, *he would be twenty-one years old now.* For a second his insides burned, the integral parts of his biology fused together, threatening spontaneous combustion, and then all of a sudden he relaxed, accepted, understood. He placed a hand on Jillian's shoulder. Without thinking, John mirrored the gesture.

"It's okay," Jack said, finally. "You did what you had to do." He couldn't believe how quickly that rage had come…and just as quickly disappeared.

"We all did," added John, and Jillian was so thankful – ever since finding the tape she had dreaded this moment more than anything – for their understanding that she too reached up and gripped her hands on their shoulders, their necks, and once again, for the first time in twenty-one years, they formed a perfect triangle.

"And we'll continue to do so," Jillian finished, and they each in turn nodded. This time when their arms dropped and the triangle was broken, it remained broken, never again to be rebuilt.

"I think that's enough emotional roller-coastering for one day. Time we mosey," Jack said, and Jillian and John both nodded in agreement, but for another half a minute the three of them stood there staring at each other, each of them swaying slightly from exhaustion. Food entered some of their minds. A bed. A hot shower. But mostly they thought of escape; the simple desire to get away. Enough was enough.

"Lets sleep on it for a few days," Jack said, "and then we can meet again. Somewhere safe. Somewhere secure. Sound good?"

John and Jillian nodded; speaking required too much effort, words: too much thought.

"I'll call you both in three days," Jack said, not knowing that he was completing another kind of triangle: a trio of lies.

John had lied about the identity of his father. Jillian, the murder of their son. And now Jack was taking his turn, by stating something untrue. He would not call them in three days. He would not even *consider* calling them in three days, not with all that was to happen in the next twenty-four hours.

They each went their separate ways, deep in thought, and even deeper into the past.

--

One by one they returned to their homes. They parked their cars and killed the engines. Unlocked their front doors and stepped inside. Each of their houses were dark, and silent, and wholly absent of life, and they moved around these once familiar spaces as though encountering them for the first time.

None of them were surprised to discover that someone had been there in their absence, someone, most certainly, who pulled at an invisible moustache and had to duck when stepping through each of their doorways. Someone who would have left a stain of *Cheeto* dust on their door knobs were it not for the latex gloves covering his bony hands like some grotesque second skin.

Jack found his envelope propped up on the keyboard of the computer in his den. Written on the front was simply:

JACKIE BOY

in large block letters.

Jillian found hers next to her stereo. The same type of envelope, the same block letters:

JILLY JILL

And finally John, who found his in, of all places, his daughter's bedroom. He had dropped her off for the night at a sitters but she had left her favorite teddy bear behind and tucked under one of its floppy arms was the same plain envelope bearing two simple words:

KID JOHNNY

None of them opened their letters for the longest time. They knew what was in them of course – their assignments – but none of them could bear to give in and see what kind of madness the tall man had cooked up for them. At one time or another they each considered not opening the letters at all, of burning them, or tearing them to shreds and flushing their remains down the shitter where they belonged, but no. It wasn't fear that got them each to finally open them up, nor was it morbid curiosity. In the end, it was simply the knowledge that *he* was probably watching them and they didn't want to know what he would do if they didn't act as they'd been told. The threat was still clear in each of their minds, even after Jack had downed a half bottle of *Johnny Walker Black* and Jillian nearly an entire bottle of *Gato Negro* red. Johnny, still the teetotaler, simply sat on his couch and wept into his own hands, his daughter's name continually blubbering over his lips. And just as a clock's hands seem drawn to the midnight hour, that great looming *twelve* that signifies both a beginning and an end, so too were all of them drawn back to those envelopes, as the witching hour drew nigh. For three souls who had once chummed together, loved together, hated together, actually *thought* together, is it any surprise that it was *together* that they each, in their own separate homes in their own separate cities, sat down and finally tore open the flaps off said envelopes to reveal the words that would have a greater impact on their lives than all other words they had up to that point ever encountered?

In Jack's envelope there was a single sheet of foolscap, nearly blank save for several tiny words printed directly in the center.

KILL YOURSELF OR I WILL EXPOSE JILLIAN AND JOHNNY

was all it said.

Jillian's letter was the same, only

KILL YOURSELF OR I WILL EXPOSE JOHNNY AND JACK

is what hers read.

John's letter, unbeknownst to him, completed the triangle:

KILL YOURSELF OR I WILL EXPOSE JACK AND JILLIAN

Each of them stared at their letters for a long, long time, till the moon began to fade, and a golden light to creep in around the corners of their shades, their curtains, the things that hid them and their deeds from the judging eyes of the world. As tired as they all were, sleep would not find them that night. They were each too scared, each too worried, each too concerned as to how exactly they would go about – *if* they would go about – this business of killing.

It was in a waking daze that they each stood, moved, their minds a rubbed blur.

Jack thought about Jillian and the first time he'd seen her. In his fingers, he'd held a tiny blade wrested from a discarded pencil sharpener, and he toyed with it as he watched from across the room as this lovely pale girl with hair as black as space clamped a lone spider between her fingers…and squeezed.

In Jillian's mind she saw Johnny, thin and lanky, a blossom of rose on his cheeks as she stood before him in his basement and he photographed her, naked from the waist up; if she closed her eyes she could actually hear the *click* of his camera, see the strap digging into his neck as he strained to capture her at just the right angle.

For Johnny, it was the image of Jack with that electric drill in his hand, pumping it again and again: *whir, whir, pump! Whir, whir, pump!* 'Guns are for pussies,' he had professed back in the day, but standing there in that funhouse basement brandishing a drill made him look like the world's youngest gunslinger, and Johnny had thought that a gun suited Jack just fine.

And one by one their thoughts drifted back to that first night in the slaughterhouse, the night that started it all. The night that led them to this. And finally: The Beast.

In a white room, square and pure, they had found that great thing looming over them as big as God and twice as scary. An animal of unknown origin, unknown species, it could have been a deity or a devil, and they moved toward it as bat to blood, drawn to the emptiness of its eyes pitted into that massive skull, a skull so large it seemed as though it were the world itself and they simple ants crawling upon its crust. Below was a congealed puddle of blood, so dark it could have been a gateway to another dimension, or a negation of the floor itself. Perhaps, had they looked close enough into that puddle they might have seen a path before them, leading to this their future, now: their present.

It looks like a sacrifice, one of them had said, and though none of them could remember who had actually voiced the words, the truth of it came back to them all now.

A sacrifice, they each thought in their own way, their own words: *that's what this is. That's what needs be done.*

And one by one they moved, searching out their weapons of choice, planning it in their heads, knowing that it must be so.

A sacrifice, they thought, *a murder born of necessity.*

It was the least they could do for those they had once loved.

--

It was ten days later and the man was humming a happy tune to himself as he ducked his head and stepped out of the elevator. He moved down the hallway with long confident strides, some electrical cable tucked under his arm, a half-smile on his wafer thin lips.

Inside the apartment he placed the cable on his kitchen counter – directly next to a half-eaten bag of Cheetos-and put the kettle on the stove. He stretched, raising his wire-frame arms high above his head and reached up, up, up, and when he felt his fingers rake across the ceiling he knew that he had reached high enough. His gaze dropped to a duffle bag sitting on his kitchen table and a toothy smile cut wrinkles across his face.

He moved over to it now, unzipped it, and removed its contents onto the table already scattered with little bits of electronics, transistors and minute microphones, tiny bulbous glass eyes that seemed more insectile than anything mechanically engineered. Now that the three were out of the picture – he chuckled silently to himself over the bad pun – the safe deposit boxes at the banks were unnecessary, and so had cleared them out yesterday. Their contents he had no use for anymore-the photographs, the DVDs and audio recordings, copies of everything he had sent to his three amigos – so placed them to the side. He would deal with it all later, with flame and with hammer.

It was the electronic stuff that held his attention now, and he sorted through it the way a trick-or-treater might examine his booty after a long night of ringing doorbells. When he found what he was looking for – the three hard drives that had recorded all data from the CCTV feeds found all over Jack Barber, Jillian Jarblonski, and John Megolni's homes - he carried them into another room and plugged them into several of the computers already whirring away. His hands worked without thought – he had done this so many times it was all instinctual – and while they did his eyes roamed across the sixteen monitors he had set up all along the far wall. Each monitor displayed a different scene – some were black and white, others the alien green of night vision - while some were static shots that never changed, several of the displays flicked every few seconds, scrolling through up to half a dozen feeds from similar sources. Some depicted the insides of houses, others: businesses. Offices. Two were of classrooms, one university and one elementary. One was a bathroom and this he had set up not for any perverse sexual proclivity, but simply because that was where the subject always did their cutting. All of them were from local sources no more than a kilometer away, some of them from the very building he was in now: his neighbor's. He heard the kettle whistling so off he went to pour himself a cup of tea, leaving it beside the stove to steep. Back he strode to his workroom, once again his eyes moved from one monitor to the next; seeing them all in a row like that, all of them working, recording, relaxed him completely. Some men went fishing, others did puzzles. Give this man a hidden camera and a live feed, and he was in heaven.

When all data was downloaded from all three hard drives the man sat down and began working his way through the videos. It didn't take him long – in this digital age one could scroll through hours of video in mere seconds and after only a few minutes he found what he was looking for. A few clicks of his mouse and the videos were trimmed, copied, spliced together. There were three shots in total and he stared transfixed at each of them, frozen like a painting on three separate monitors, for a long, long time.

The final shots were static, unmoving. The first showed a man – or what *used* to be a man: he was now nothing more than a lump of flesh – lying on the carpeted floor of an ornately decorated living room. At first glance, it was hard to tell if he was lying face down or up due to the fact that most of the upper part of his head was missing, shorn off from the jaw upwards; a dark liquid spread out from the neck and from the angle the camera had recorded it, it looked like toothpaste from a smashed tube.

The second shot was a woman lying in a bathtub, naked and pale. One leg hung over the side of the tub, but the other three extremities were hidden below the water, which was a reddish pink just dark enough to turn the surface to glass, to hide everything below. The water was as still as a broken clock, as was the woman's face, which hung limp over the back of the tub as though awaiting a professional shampoo. Her forearm had been slit all the way from her wrist right to the crook of her elbow.

The final shot depicted a man hanging from some kind of strap attached to a support beam in the basement of his house. The body had long since stopped its pendulum swing, its spasmodic twitching; it hung there now like some dead fruit not yet ready to drop. Below it, there lay a puddle of urine, perfect and round.

For a few seconds the man lamented the fact that he had not been able to enter the apartments and inspect the bodies personally - he would have to settle for the pixelated versions before him – but it had been too risky. It was one thing to enter the buildings, or in the last case, the garage, to collect the remote hard drives, but going inside the actual homes was out of the question. Who knows who might be watching - just ask *him*, ha-ha! - who might see him enter or leave, and what if he were to be discovered while still inside? It would be one thing to be caught entering someone's home to plant a camera or two, but a whole different set of felonies awaited the man who did so knowing there was a dead body on the premises. Thanks, but no thanks. When things settled down and the police tape disappeared from off the front doors he would pay the houses a little visit, collect all remaining traces of his equipment, but for now the videos would have to do. And speaking of which…

"Done," he announced to the empty room, and nodded once to himself, contented. He couldn't have felt better if he had just completed the construction of a brilliant symphony, or a great tome of literature. And when he reached over and clicked the *BURN* button, heard the soft *whirring* as the DVD burner began to spin and scribe, he actually felt a slight erection pushing at the crotch of his pants.

He stood, sighed, then moved to the kitchen to get his tea. He added no milk or sugar – *'My life is sweet enough without sugar in my tea,'* he would joke whenever someone asked how he took his – and then returned to the computer to look over the daily news.

He didn't have to search for it; booting up *Explorer* it was the top article in his news feed and his heart leaped at the headline, which he read a good half dozen times before proceeding to the article itself. By the time he got to the end his heart was beating so fast he almost didn't hear the *bing!* of the computer announcing that the DVD was done.

Deus Ex Machina President Jack Barber Found Dead in East Side Apartment

In surely what must be considered one of the most baffling criminal cases in recent history, police are now investigating an apparent connection between what, up to this point, was being treated as three separate suicides.

This strange series of events, which has caught the public attention due to its unprecedented nature, began four days ago when the body of *Deus Ex Machina*, a video games software company famous for titles such as *Holocaust Heroes* and *Mail Carrier Massacre*, founder and president Jack Barber was discovered in his East Side apartment. Barber, who had been reported missing two days earlier after failing to appear at work, was found dead of an apparent gunshot wound to the head on the afternoon of July 21st. With no signs of forced entry and no signs of physical distress to the victim other than the gunshot wound itself, initial police reports suggested it was a pretty clear-cut case of suicide by shooting. However, several recent discoveries have thrown into question the possibility that there might be a greater story at work here.

When pressed for more details, detective Andrew Bosszunk made reference to two other apparent suicides that had taken place within twenty-four hours of Barber's, one by a thirty-eight year old woman in Morrisville by the name of Jillian Jarblonski and another by one John Megolni, also thirty-eight. Although police have declined to elaborate on the connection, one source with close ties to the investigation who has requested to remain anonymous, has suggested that a series of letters found at the scenes were the most concrete link, as well as the greatest sources of confusion.

Although our source declined to comment on the specifics of the letters themselves, it was discovered by *Times Herald* reporter Robert Magasferfi, that there were in fact several other connections; in addition to all three of the victims being aged thirty-eight, Barber and Jarblonski attended the same high school, St. Nicholas High, between the ages sixteen to seventeen and although the third victim, Megolni, did not matriculate at St. Nicholas, he did grow up less than five miles from said high school at the time Barber and Jarblonski were in attendance.

Refusing to comment on the high school connection itself, Detective Bosszunk did note that police were treating the deaths as "suspicious" and that they would be investigating the matter further in the days to come. When asked to elaborate on rumors that the suicides were staged and were in fact murders, Bosszu declined comment.

"Some things have come to light after the initial discovery of Barber's body that seem to suggest there is more to this case than meets the eye but until we've run further tests and had a chance to examine all evidence, the case will remain open."

"If they only knew," the man announced to the screen, he began to laugh, a chuckle at first, then a big hearty, bone-shaking guffaw. He was still laughing as he turned away from the working monitor to glance at all

the others glowing beside him, jumping sporadically from one to the next, seeing the people moving in their vast complexities of life, like ants, or...*puppets,* he thought. *Yes, puppets, and I stand above, which makes me...*

He didn't need words to complete the thought; the answer was with him always, as a shadow, a feeling, his own name.

For a few seconds longer he continued to stare at the screens, then finally tore himself away, turning back to the working monitor.

"Just a quick test," he told himself as he cued up the DVD and began watching it. His smiled deepened as the images sprang to life on the screen in front of him.

"I'm going to miss you guys," he told the screen as he watched Jack Barber loading a single shell into his double-barreled shotgun. With a few taps of his finger the scene changed: a naked Jillian Jarblonski climbed into a steaming tub and closed her eyes. More taps, more jumps. Johnny Megolni's body twitching on the end of a strap, life exiting his body in a series of orgasmic jerks.

Satisfied that the burn was good, the tall man reached to eject the disc when something on the screen made him falter. For the first time in several minutes the smile left his lips and his eyebrows creased. He backtracked the scene several seconds, watched again. And again. And again.

There was a glitch, almost wholly imperceptible, as Johnny's body twitched on the end of that strap; one frame it was in one position, the next frame, another. But it was impossible to tell if it was a fault of the file, or the natural spasms of a body giving up its hold on life.

The tall man shook his head. "Just a video glitch," he told himself, but the smile he'd been wearing before refused to return. "Just a glitch," he told himself again, then he was standing up, ejecting the disc and leaning over to write some words on its surface in large black letters so clear they could have been a typeface and then, seeing the words printed there, he relaxed once more. *It's done,* he told himself: *done.*

As was his habit, he flipped the disc over and examined the lines, looking for any flaws, but he saw none. He relaxed further as his eyes refocused he caught his own reflection in the DVD and he stared at it, enjoying the way his face looked distorted and pulled in the purple/blue reflection; he stuck his tongue out at himself, wiggled it in some parody of a common sex act, and grinned once more. "If they only knew," he said again, and then he was walking over to a bookshelf on the far side of the room, removing a preprinted case and placing the disc inside.

There were seven shelves in total, each filled to varying degrees. One contained only three DVDs, each labeled *'Sweet Marian,' Volume One, Two, and Three*, most of them ten or more, one series labeled *'Politics, Politics, Politics!* and another: *Habits and Clergymen.* But, the shelf from which he removed the DVD case now was by far the most stocked; it had in fact only space for this last DVD and nothing more. All cases were pure white, showed no pictures, and were lined with identical impeccable handwriting on each one. With a reverence usually reserved for holy artifacts or very valuable pieces of antiquity, the man placed the DVD inside, snapped it shut, and put the case back on the shelf. He sighed: it was his life's work – or part of it at least – but it was finished now. The story was at its end.

Project Masterpiece, was what it read on the spine, and then, below it and in much smaller print, was the legend: *Volume Twenty-One.*

"One for each year I've known you three," he said to himself, "and I must admit, I'm a little sad to see you go." He breathed in then, deep and full, and felt his entire body relax. He couldn't remember feeling more contented in his entire life, couldn't imagine feeling more at peace. For almost another ten minutes he continued to stare at the shelf, fast-forwarding through, in his mind's eye, a million and one scenes that he knew to be contained within those little plastic discs. It was because of this that he failed to notice another glitch on one of his computer monitors, this one showing the hallway directly outside his apartment door. The scene flickered, black, but a split second later it was back to normal, as though nothing had changed at all.

Finally, when the man acknowledged that his muscles were beginning to ache from standing still for so long, he forced himself to pull away from the bookshelf, from the collection of so many moments in so many peoples lives that made his own life complete, gave his own life such purpose.

"Project Masterpiece indeed," he said, and the words were barely over his non-existent lips when his thoughts were interrupted by the single toll of his front doorbell.

He frowned – he wasn't expecting anybody – and shook his head once. Then he glanced up at the monitor – top right corner – that displayed the CC feed filming his hallway. It was empty, quiet; there was nobody there.

He frowned, shrugged. *Must be a bug in the system,* he thought, and relaxed once again. He knew all about electrical bugs, he did. They got into the system and if they weren't taken care of directly, they came back. Multiplied. *Like cockroaches,* he thought.

He took one last glance at the working monitor, remembered the article about his three dearly departed friends, and smiled. A moment later he was moving with long strides toward the front door to investigate, the half-smile still on his lips, his bony fingers playing at the invisible moustache he imagined to be sprouting from his upper lip.

END

About Your Author

Adam Burnett writes when he can, sleeps when he needs to, and eats only when absolutely necessary. Every morning he wakes up tired and every night he goes to bed wide awake.

His solitary goal in life is to write books that smell like *old* books and believes that if there isn't a noticeable crack in the spine of the book you are currently reading, then you are reading it incorrectly.

Although his main passion in life has always been writing, he also enjoys holding a camera and making it go 'click', and is the owner and operator of Umbrella Photography (www.umbrellaphotograhy.ca).

In addition to writing and photography, he has also whittled away the days as an English teacher, dance instructor, door to door salesman, S & M bartender, fry cook, bouncer, busboy, hardware salesman, cleaner, and sexual ninja. He promises that only one of these jobs was made up.

He's had a number of short stories and poems published in various Canadian and American literary journals including *Midnight Time, Rhapsodia, Peeks and Valleys, Chrysalis Reader,* and *Ginosko*. This is his first published novel.

He lives in Toronto, Canada with his wife and son, and is currently working on a novel dealing with his life-long obsession with the film *Jaws*.

Other HellBound Books Titles
Available at: www.hellboundbookspublishing.com

The Children of Hydesville

"A contemporary ghost story made all the more terrifying for being based upon actual events."

When the terrifying entity that Maggie and Katie Fox unleashed in Hydesville in 1848 returns in 2018, a gallery owner, his wife, a journalist and her boyfriend join forces to battle it.

Manhattanites Derek David and his wife Edith receive an invitation to visit the Keilgarden Colony. Founded in 1948 with funds from Derek's great grandfather, the Colony is a secluded community dedicated to nurturing children with psychic abilities. Located five hours north of the city in the village of Hydesville, the compound was built on land that includes the cottage where Maggie and Katie Fox first heard the ghostly rappings in 1848 which started the Spiritualist movement.

Evolution of a Monster

A terrifying insight into the deteriorating mind of a serial killer.

"I took Heather to the bathroom to mask her identity before we departed, and she became hysterical at the sight of her parents - still lying where they dropped.

It had been over 24 hours since their death, and she was still freaking out about it.

I couldn't have someone with me who was going to scream at the sight of blood; I understood some training was in order, so I sat her beside her mom and handed her a kitchen knife..."

A stunning debut novel, your unique opportunity to join the murderous spree of an escalating serial killer, who is hellbent on achieving his sick goal of killing in each and every state of the USA.

Through the killer's increasingly unhinged diary entries, gain an insight into his thoughts, imaginings and internal struggles as he fights against his primal urge to satisfy his growing bloodlust, and to justify his nefarious actions to his rapidly crumbling mind.

A wholly original novel, that will shock, amuse and appall; plus provide you, the reader, with a ringside seat inside the psyche of a brutal killer...

The Southern House

There are some places that lie where the barrier between worlds is thin and growing thinner. These corridors are as old as the Earth itself, hidden in dark and forgotten places, waiting to be found. There is a being who stalks these places and travels between those worlds. He was given the name Mr. Shift by generations of children and madmen.

Just as Hickory Grimble hits rock bottom, he inherits his grandparents' farm and believes his luck is changing. He soon finds he inherited more than money and land.

Haunted by his own inner demons, now he has new problems. He begins to see strange creatures on the dark, sprawling acreage, animals that have no business living in middle Tennessee. He also discovers a decrepit, abandoned house in the forest that never seems to be in the same place twice.

Balanced on a razor's edge between, addiction and fate, Hick is now face to face with an ancient evil that has returned once more to claim more of the town's children.

Them

Ray Sanders returns home from Florida to bury his mother.

Soon, the supernatural evidence behind his mother's demise begins to surface in the form of dreams and mysterious happenings.

During all of the madness, Sanders must face his destiny and vanquish the generations-old evil that has plagued his family since the 1800's...

In 1854, Louis Sanders, with the help of Elias Atkins, dug a well to provide water to the family farm. What they did not anticipate was the water to be infested with Odomulites - ancient sins. These malevolent beings - were trapped in our world on their way to the spirit world - formed a pact of protection with both Sanders and Atkins; the families would serve as guardians of the Odomulite nests and in return, a blind eye would be cast when the Odomulites took host bodies to inhabit and feed upon. It was this pact, which in 2016 would propel Sanders and Julie Fontaine - a young woman with a special connection to the Spirit World - into the heart of the last active nest to rid the town of its insidious Odomulite population.

Blood in The Woods

Based upon true events...

For Jody, growing up in the late eighties and early nineties in the small Louisiana town of Hammond with his best friend Jack was filled with wonderful childhood memories.

Time spent playing in the woods, shooting pellet guns, blowing up mailboxes, fighting at school and upon the dawning of interest in the fairer sex, their carefree lives typical of children with few responsibilities and no worries beyond the next pop-quiz or getting to second base. As they grow older together and experience the joys and pains of life, love, family and friendship, they uncover a grim secret that their home town has kept, and through little more than an innocent, idle curiosity, Jody and Jack stumble upon something horrific in the woods and their lives quickly take a most sinister and dangerous turn as they find themselves hunted by an unspeakable evil...

No Rest For The Wicked

From beyond the grave, a murderous wife seeks to complete her revenge on those who betrayed her in life; a powerless domestic still fears for her immortal soul while trying to scare off anyone who comes too close; and the former plantation master - a sadistic doctor who puts more faith in the teachings of de Sade than the Bible - battle amongst themselves and with the living to reveal or keep hidden the dark secrets that prevent any of them from resting in peace. When Eric and Grace McLaughlin purchase Greenbrier Plantation, their dreams are just as big as those who have tried to tame the place before them. But, the doctor has learned a thing or two over his many years in the afterlife, is putting those new skills to the test, and will go to great lengths in order to gain the upper hand. While Grace digs into the death-filled history of her new home, Eric soon becomes a pawn of the doctor's unsavory desires and rapidly growing power, and is hell-bent on stopping her.

"If you're looking for a chilling ghost story filled with mystery and escalating tension, look no further. No Rest for the Wicked is the real deal - an expansive, unfolding riddle between the living and the dead."
Hunter Shea - author of *"Tortures of the Damned"* & *"We Are Always Watching"*

Worship Me

Something is listening to the prayers of St. Paul's United Church, but it's not the god they asked for; it's something much, much older.

A quiet Sunday service turns into a living hell when this ancient entity descends upon the house of worship and claims the congregation for its own.

The terrified churchgoers must now prove their loyalty to their new god by giving it one of their children or in two days time it will return and destroy them all.

As fear rips the congregation apart, it becomes clear that if they're to survive this untold horror, the faithful must become the faithless and enter into a battle against God itself.

But as time runs out, they discover that true monsters come not from heaven or hell…
…they come from within.

Schlock! Horror!

An anthology of short stories based upon/inspired by and in loving homage to all of those great gorefest movies and books of the 1980's (not necessarily base in that era, although some do ride that wave of nostalgia!), the golden age when horror well and truly came kicking, screaming and spraying blood, gore & body parts out from the shadows...

It was the decade that brought us everything in the cinema and on VHS from the Italian 'nasties' to *Elm Street, The Lost Boys, Hellraiser, The Thing, Day of the Dead, Reanimator, Return of the Living Dead, My Bloody Valentine, Henry: Portrait of a Serial Killer, Cannibal Holocaust*....and superlative directors such as David Cronenburg, John Waters, Roger Corman and - of course - Clive Barker.

All of this was, naturally, reflected in the books we devoured - Guy N Smith, Clive Barker's*Books of Blood*, James Herbert, Jack Ketchum, Gary Brandner and Richard Laymon, to name but a mere handful.

This exemplary 80's themed/inspired tales of terror has been adjudicated and compiled by one Mr **Bret McCormick**, himself a writer, producer and director of many a schlock classic, including *Bio-Tech Warrior, Time Tracers, The Abomination, Ozone: The Attack of the Redneck Mutants* and the inimitable *Repligator*.

Shopping List 2: Another Horror Anthology

Once again, HellBound Books brings you an outstanding collection of horror, dark, slippery things, and supernatural terror - all from the very best up and coming minds in the genre.

We have given each and every one of our authors the opportunity to have their shopping lists read by you, the most wonderful reading public, and have the darkest corners of their creative psyche laid bare for all to see...

In all, 21 stories to chill the soul, tingle the spine and keep you awake in the cold, murky hours of the night from: Erin Lee, The Truth Artist, John Barackman, Serena Daniels, M.R. Wallace, Isobel Blackthorn, Alex Laybourne, Jason J. Nugent, Josh Darling, Jovan Jones, Nick Swain, Douglas Ford, Craig Bullock, Craig Bullock, Jeff C. Stevenson, PC3, David F Gray, Sergio Palumbo, Donna Maria McCarthy, David Clark & Megan E. Morales

**A HellBound Books LLC
Publication**

http://www.hellboundbookspublishing.com

Printed in the United States of America

www.ingramcontent.com/pod-product-compliance
Lightning Source LLC
Chambersburg PA
CBHW050610170726
48283CB00001B/182